Mark of The Succubus

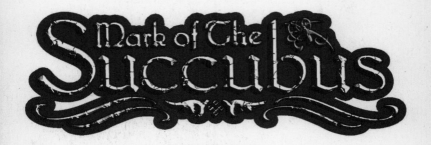

Mark of the Succubus Vol. 1
written by Ashly Raiti
illustrated by Irene Flores

Copy Editor - Hope Donovan
Retouch and Lettering - Bowen Park
Cover Design - Kyle Plummer

Editor - Lillian Diaz-Przybyl
Digital Imaging Manager - Chris Buford
Production Managers - Jennifer Miller and Mutsumi Miyazaki
Managing Editor - Lindsey Johnston
Editorial Director - Jeremy Ross
VP of Production - Ron Klamert
Publisher and E.I.C. - Mike Kiley
President and C.O.O. - John Parker
C.E.O. - Stuart Levy

A  Manga

TOKYOPOP Inc.
5900 Wilshire Blvd. Suite 2000
Los Angeles, CA 90036

E-mail: info@TOKYOPOP.com
Come visit us online at www.TOKYOPOP.com

ISBN: 1-59816-266-7

First TOKYOPOP printing: November 2005
10 9 8 7 6 5 4 3 2 1
Printed in USA

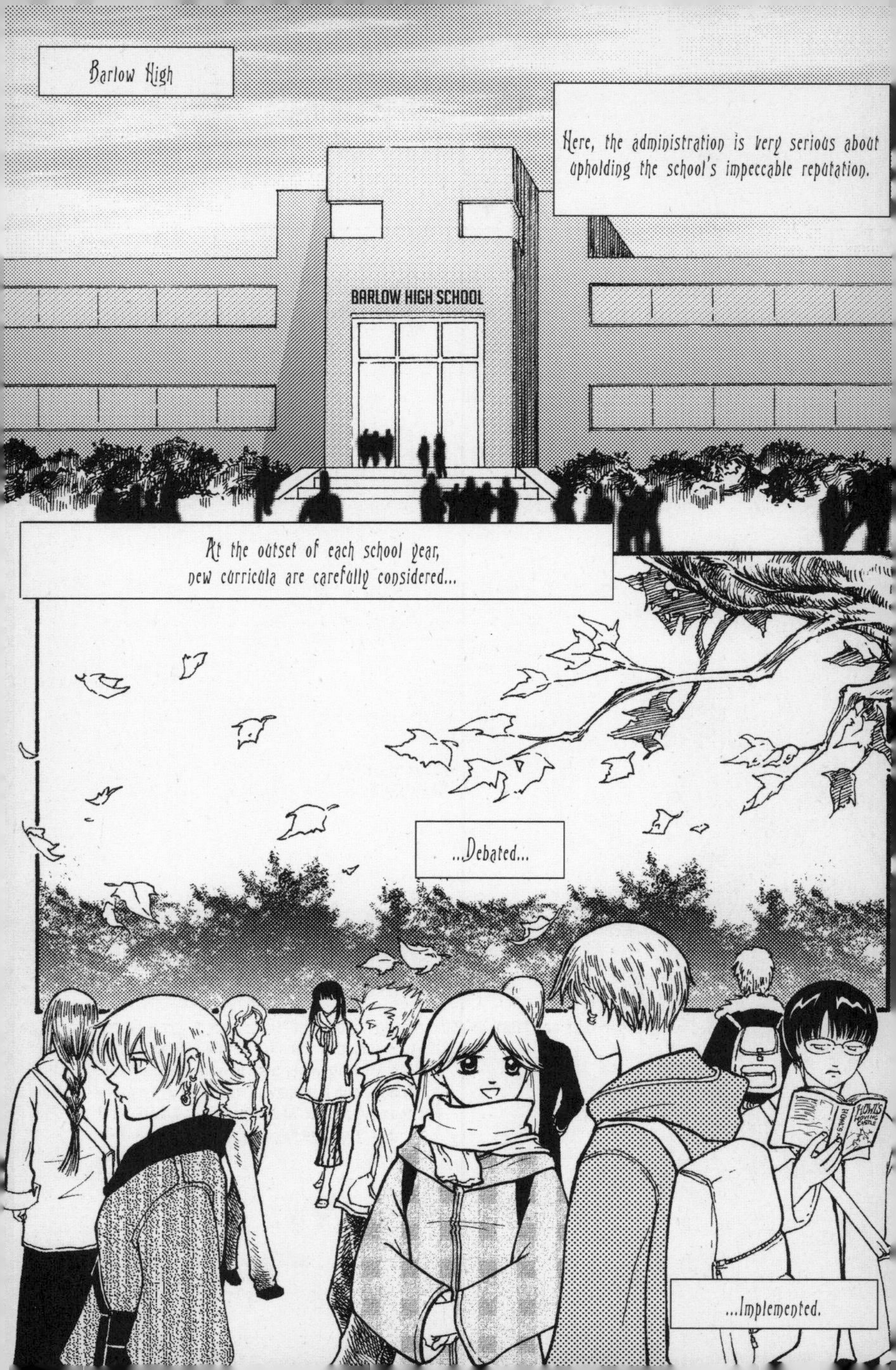
Barlow High
Here, the administration is very serious about upholding the school's impeccable reputation.
BARLOW HIGH SCHOOL
At the outset of each school year, new curricula are carefully considered...
...Debated...
HOWL'S MOVING CASTLE
...Implemented.

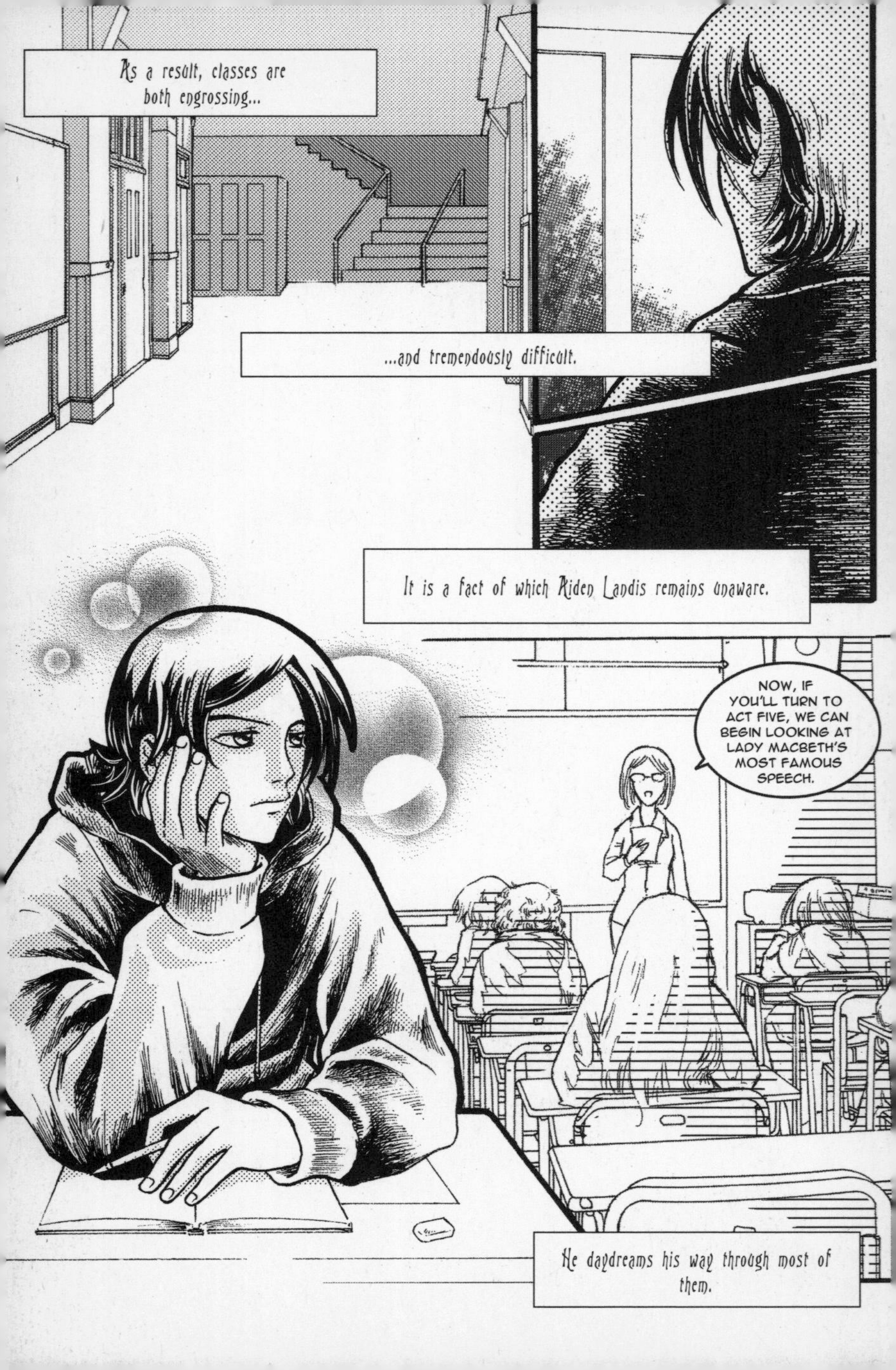
As a result, classes are both engrossing...
...and tremendously difficult.
It is a fact of which Aiden Landis remains unaware.
NOW, IF YOU'LL TURN TO ACT FIVE, WE CAN BEGIN LOOKING AT LADY MACBETH'S MOST FAMOUS SPEECH.
He daydreams his way through most of them.

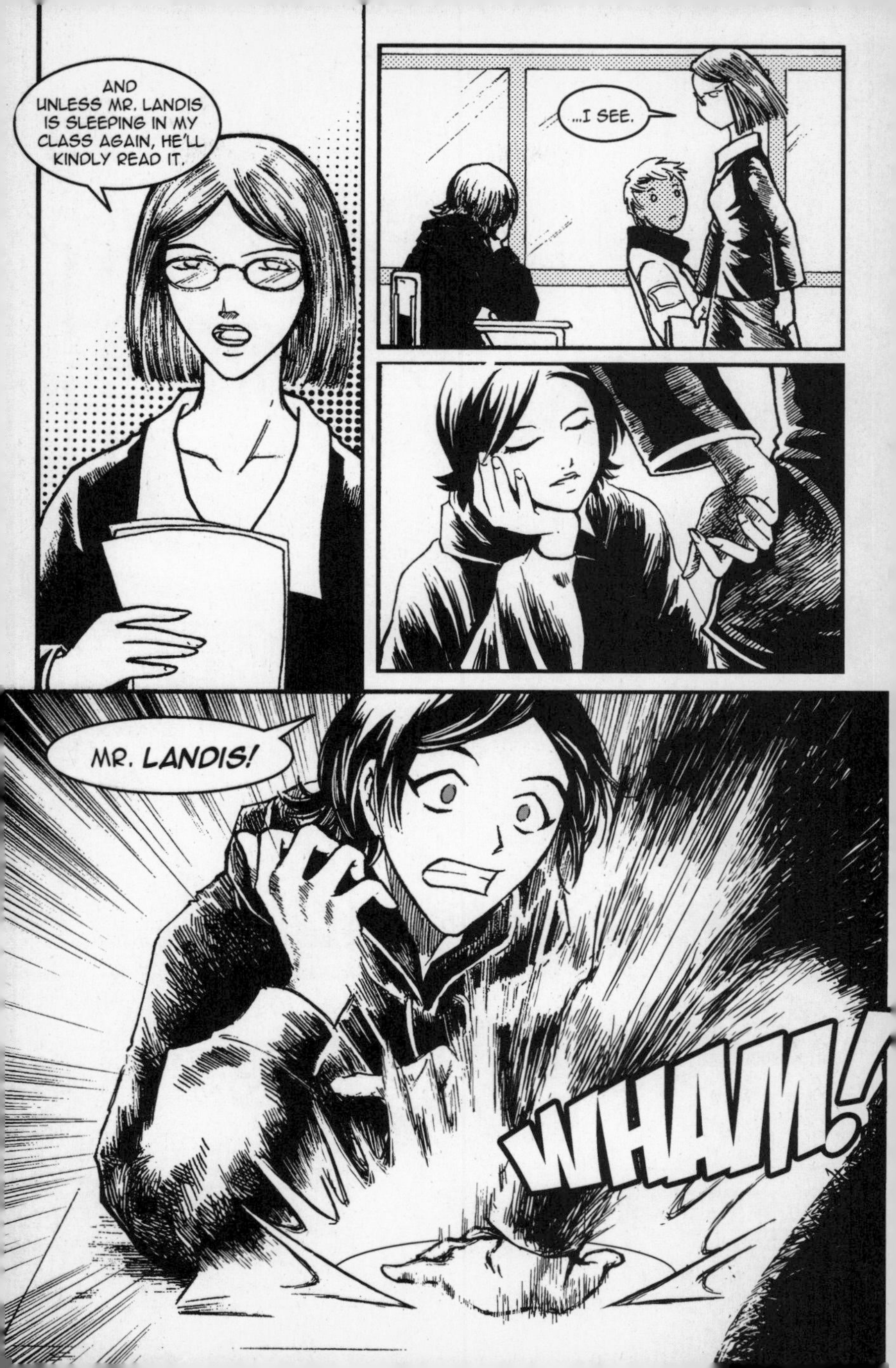
AND UNLESS MR. LANDIS IS SLEEPING IN MY CLASS AGAIN, HE'LL KINDLY READ IT.
...I SEE.
MR. LANDIS!
WHAM!

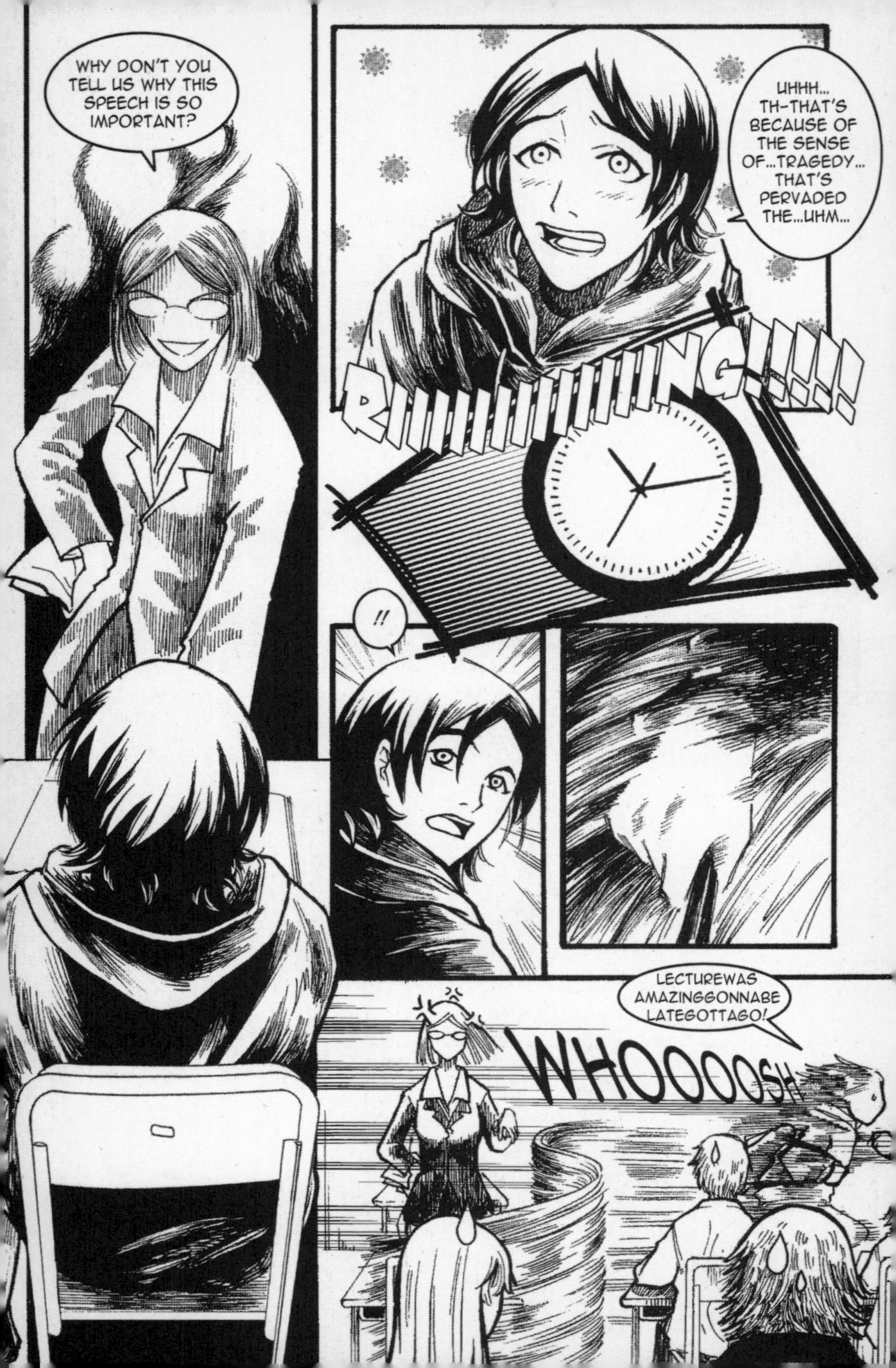
WHY DON'T YOU TELL US WHY THIS SPEECH IS SO IMPORTANT?
UHHH... TH-THAT'S BECAUSE OF THE SENSE OF...TRAGEDY... THAT'S PERVADED THE...UHM...
RIIIIIIIIIIIING!!!!!
!!
LECTUREWAS AMAZINGGONNABE LATEGOTTAGO!
WHOOOOSH

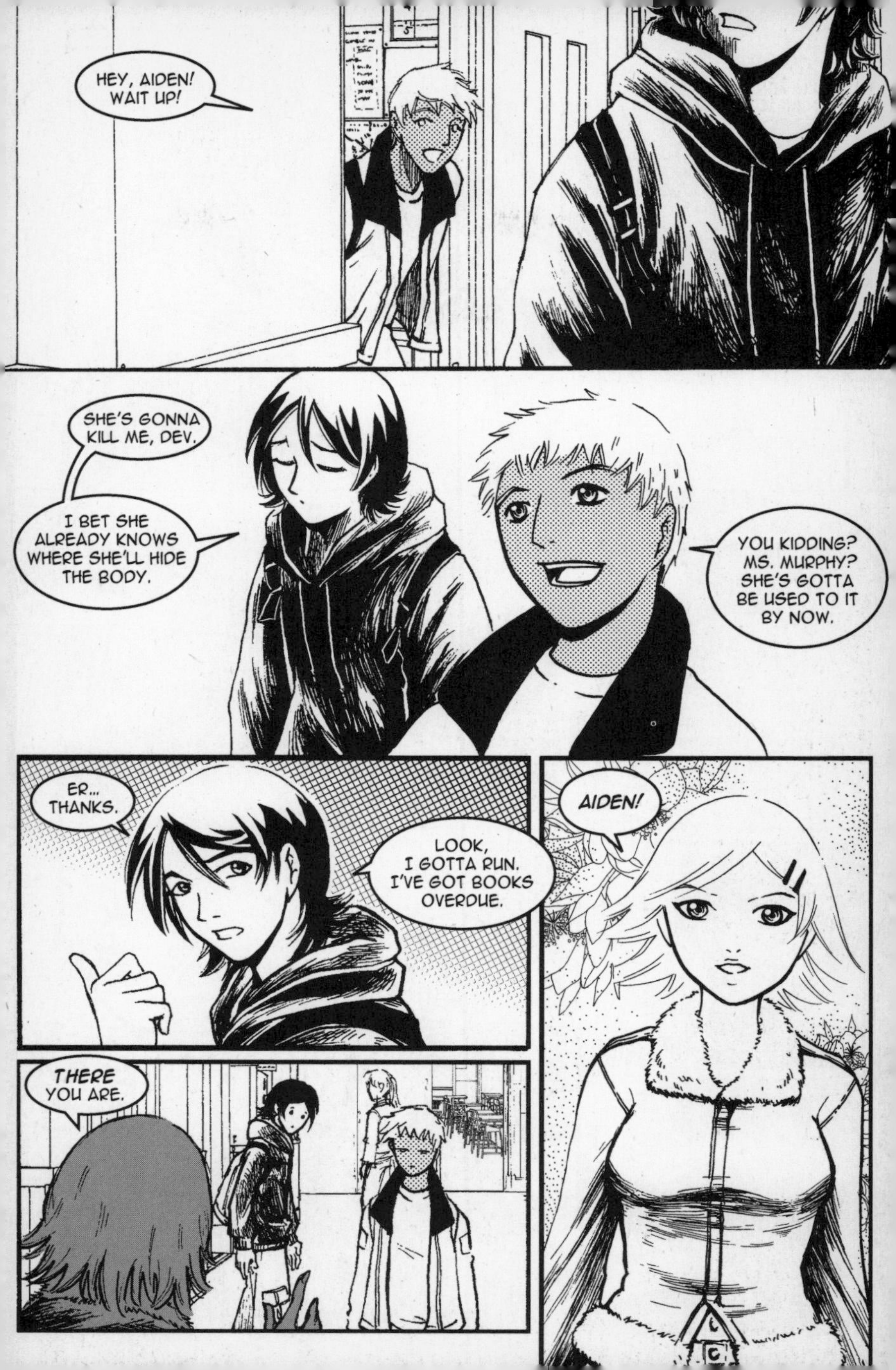
HEY, AIDEN! WAIT UP!
SHE'S GONNA KILL ME, DEV.
I BET SHE ALREADY KNOWS WHERE SHE'LL HIDE THE BODY.
YOU KIDDING? MS. MURPHY? SHE'S GOTTA BE USED TO IT BY NOW.
ER... THANKS.
LOOK, I GOTTA RUN. I'VE GOT BOOKS OVERDUE.
THERE YOU ARE.
AIDEN!

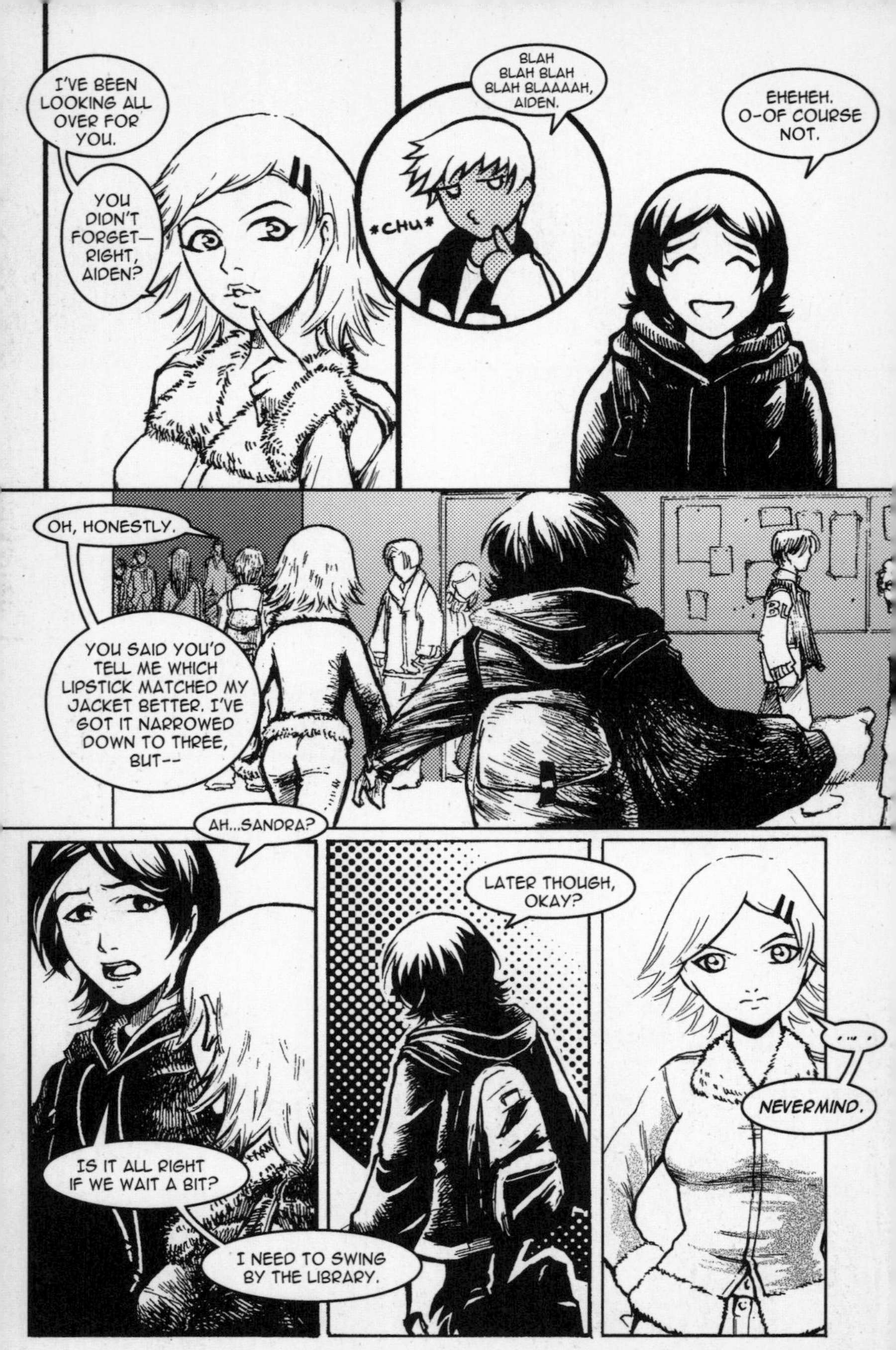
I'VE BEEN LOOKING ALL OVER FOR YOU.
YOU DIDN'T FORGET— RIGHT, AIDEN?
BLAH BLAH BLAH BLAH BLAAAAH, AIDEN.
CHU
EHEHEH. O-OF COURSE NOT.
OH, HONESTLY.
YOU SAID YOU'D TELL ME WHICH LIPSTICK MATCHED MY JACKET BETTER. I'VE GOT IT NARROWED DOWN TO THREE, BUT--
AH...SANDRA?
IS IT ALL RIGHT IF WE WAIT A BIT?
I NEED TO SWING BY THE LIBRARY.
LATER THOUGH, OKAY?
...
NEVERMIND.

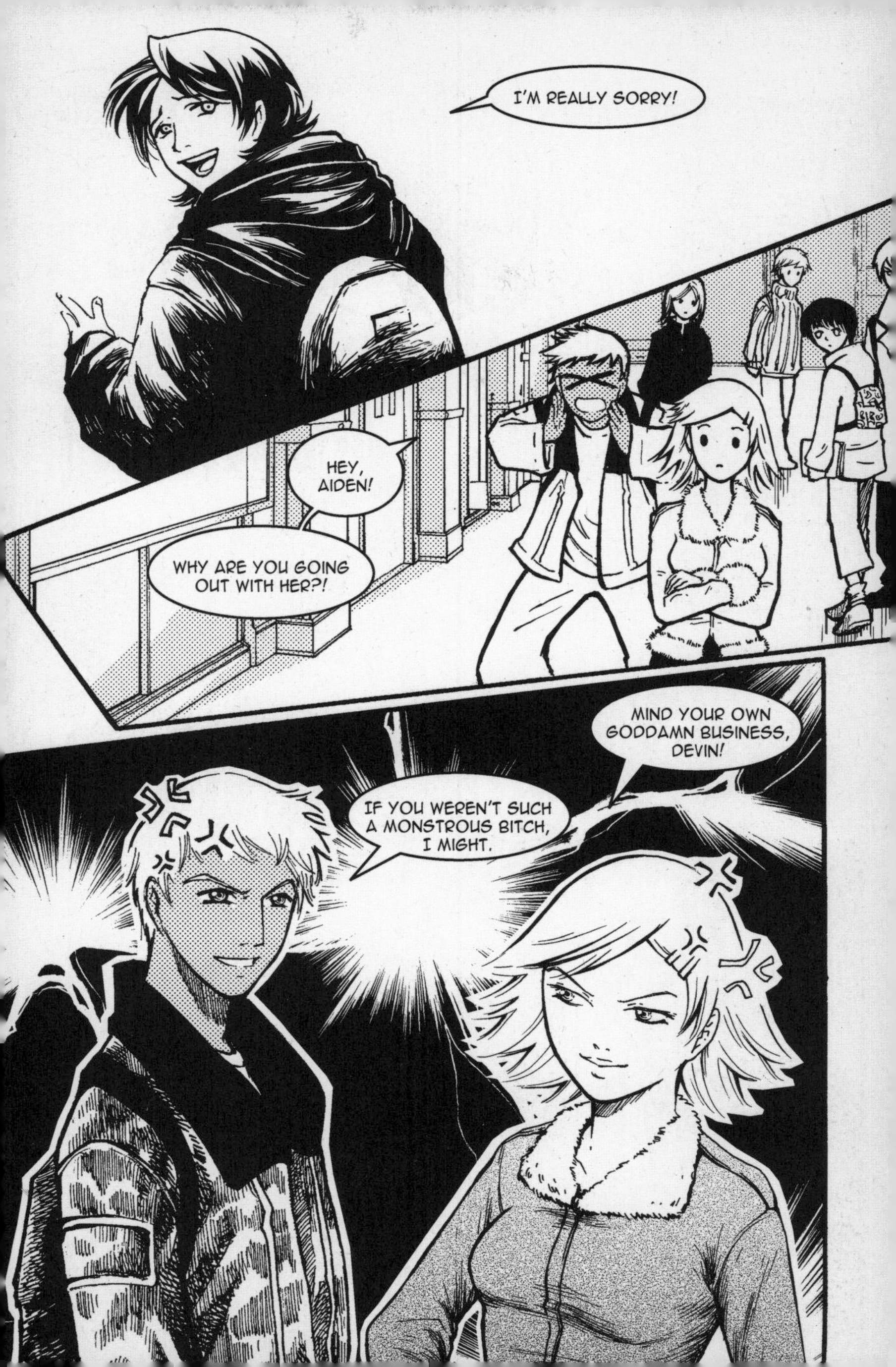
I'M REALLY SORRY!
HEY, AIDEN!
WHY ARE YOU GOING OUT WITH HER?!
MIND YOUR OWN GODDAMN BUSINESS, DEVIN!
IF YOU WEREN'T SUCH A MONSTROUS BITCH, I MIGHT.

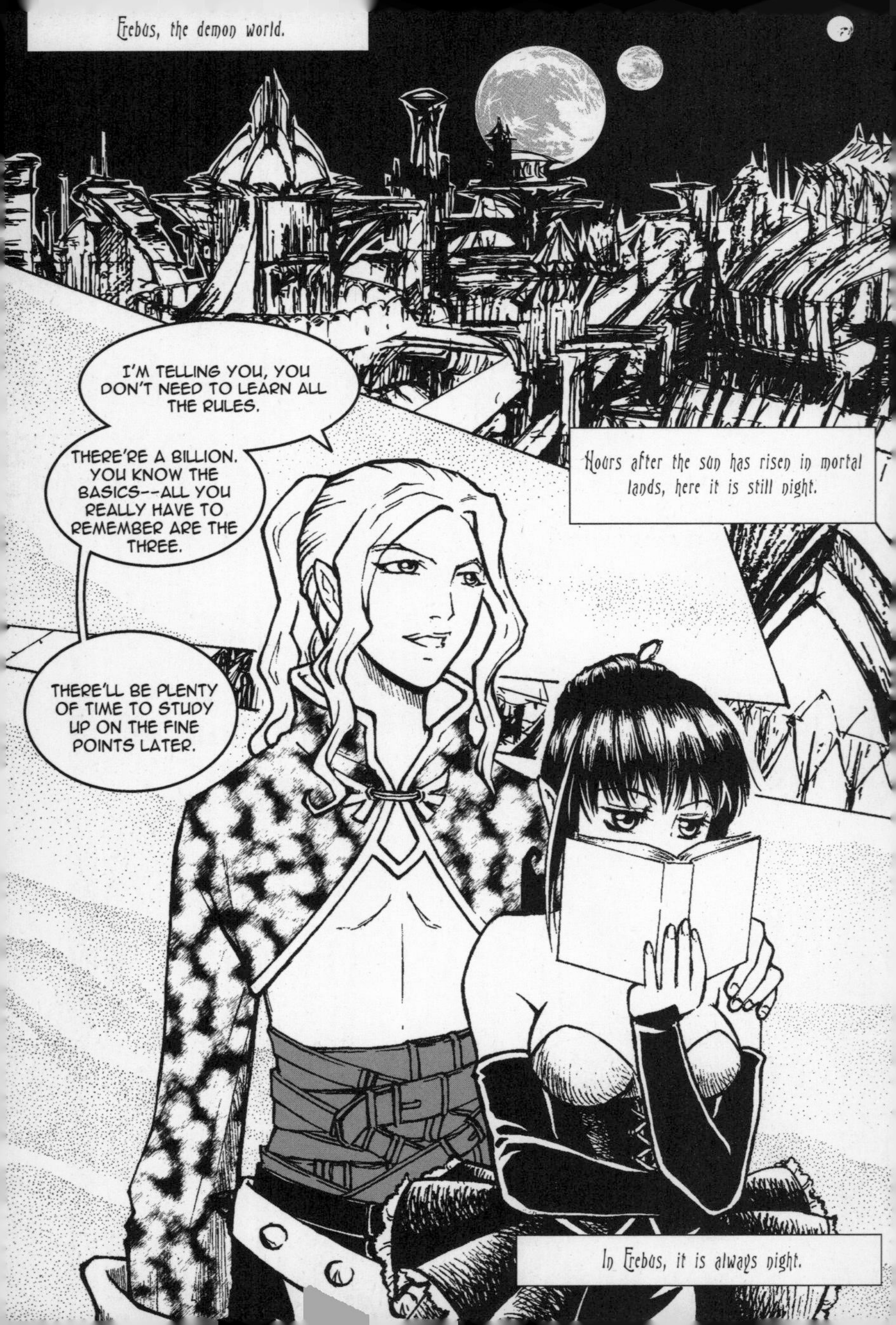
Erebus, the demon world.
I'M TELLING YOU, YOU DON'T NEED TO LEARN ALL THE RULES.
THERE'RE A BILLION. YOU KNOW THE BASICS--ALL YOU REALLY HAVE TO REMEMBER ARE THE THREE.
Hours after the sun has risen in mortal lands, here it is still night.
THERE'LL BE PLENTY OF TIME TO STUDY UP ON THE FINE POINTS LATER.
In Erebus, it is always night.

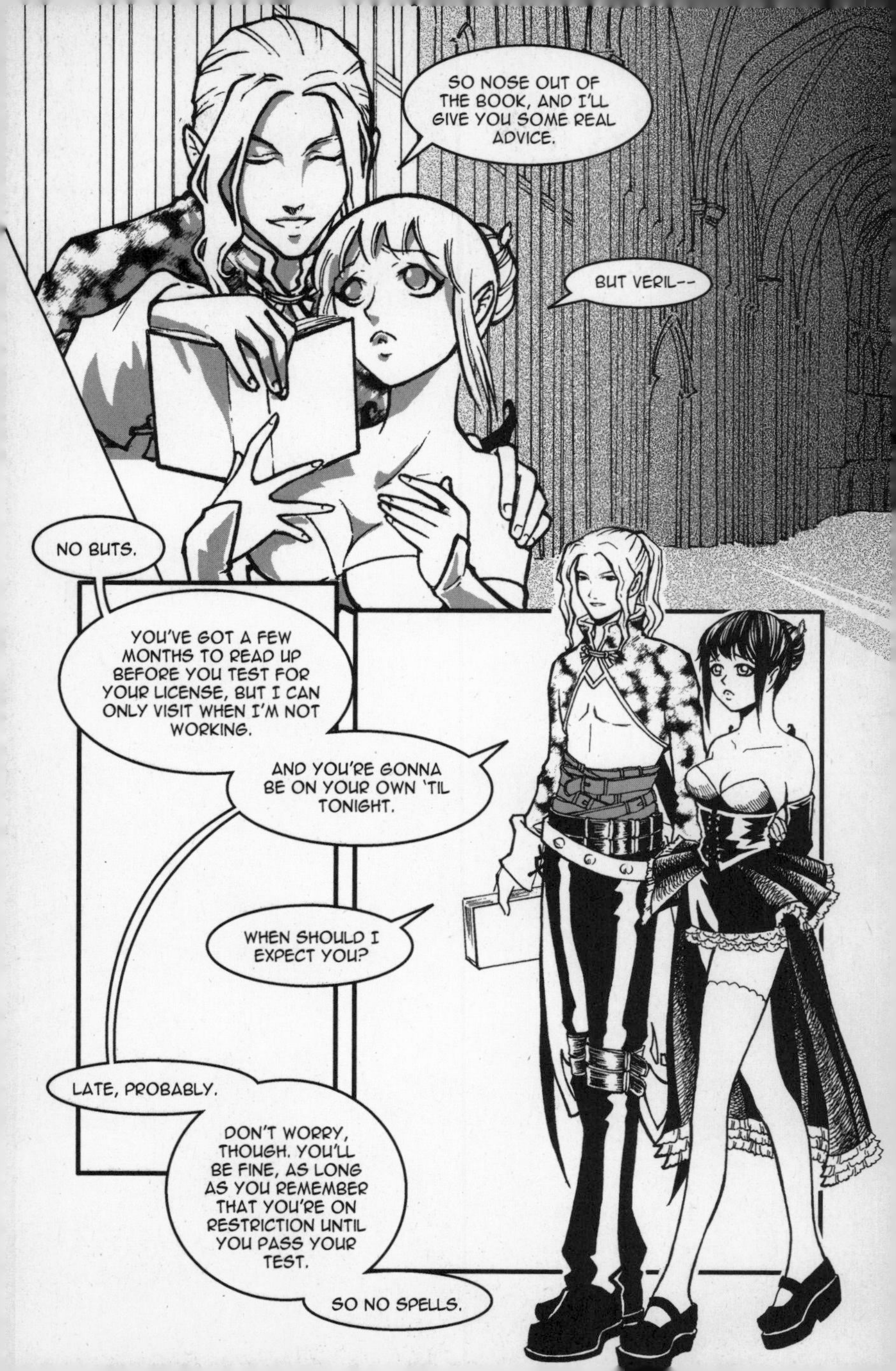
SO NOSE OUT OF THE BOOK, AND I'LL GIVE YOU SOME REAL ADVICE.
BUT VERIL--
NO BUTS.
YOU'VE GOT A FEW MONTHS TO READ UP BEFORE YOU TEST FOR YOUR LICENSE, BUT I CAN ONLY VISIT WHEN I'M NOT WORKING.
AND YOU'RE GONNA BE ON YOUR OWN 'TIL TONIGHT.
WHEN SHOULD I EXPECT YOU?
LATE, PROBABLY.
DON'T WORRY, THOUGH. YOU'LL BE FINE, AS LONG AS YOU REMEMBER THAT YOU'RE ON RESTRICTION UNTIL YOU PASS YOUR TEST.
SO NO SPELLS.

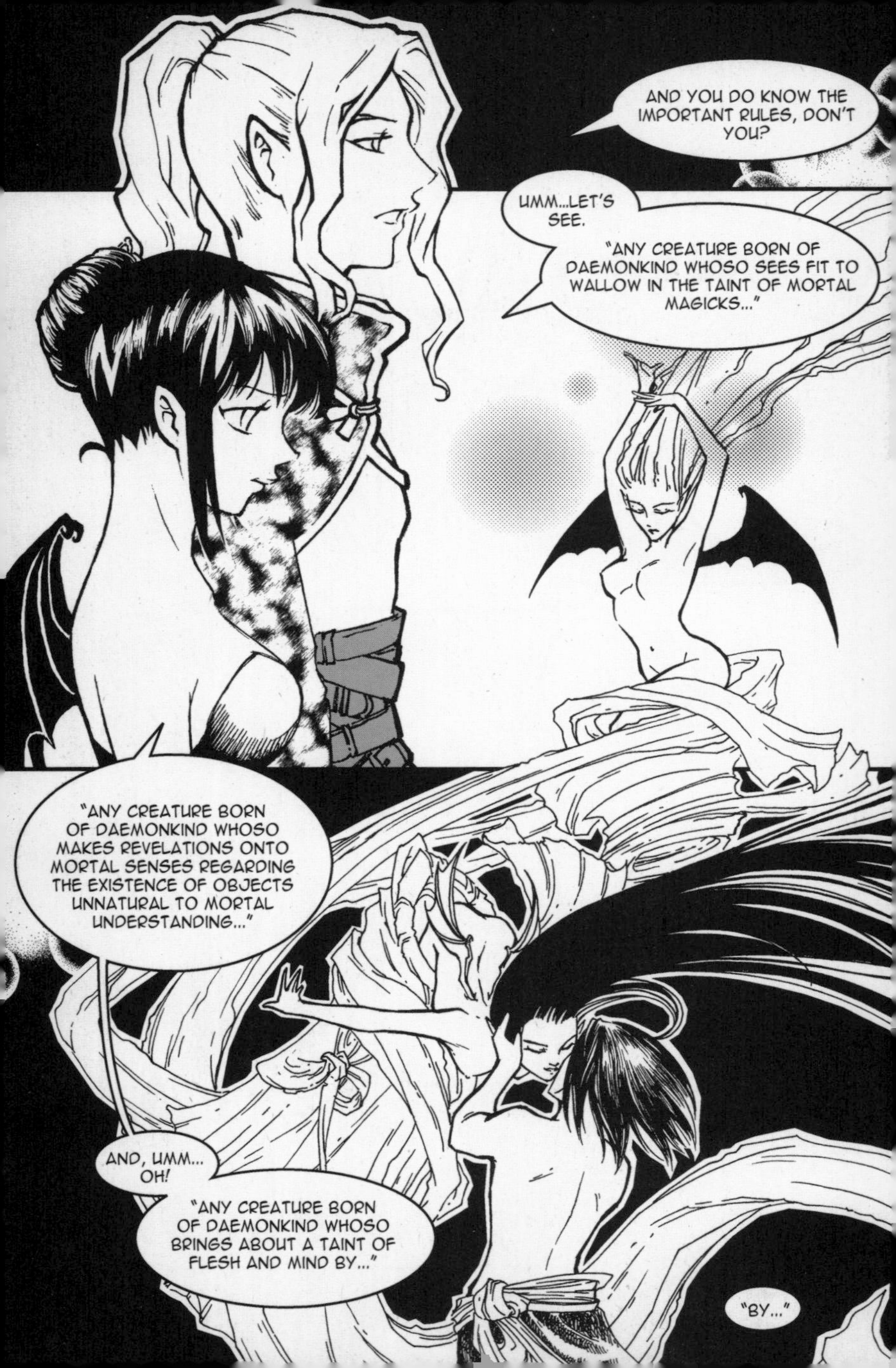
AND YOU DO KNOW THE IMPORTANT RULES, DON'T YOU?
UMM...LET'S SEE.
"ANY CREATURE BORN OF DAEMONKIND WHOSO SEES FIT TO WALLOW IN THE TAINT OF MORTAL MAGICKS..."
"ANY CREATURE BORN OF DAEMONKIND WHOSO MAKES REVELATIONS ONTO MORTAL SENSES REGARDING THE EXISTENCE OF OBJECTS UNNATURAL TO MORTAL UNDERSTANDING..."
AND, UMM... OH!
"ANY CREATURE BORN OF DAEMONKIND WHOSO BRINGS ABOUT A TAINT OF FLESH AND MIND BY..."
"BY..."

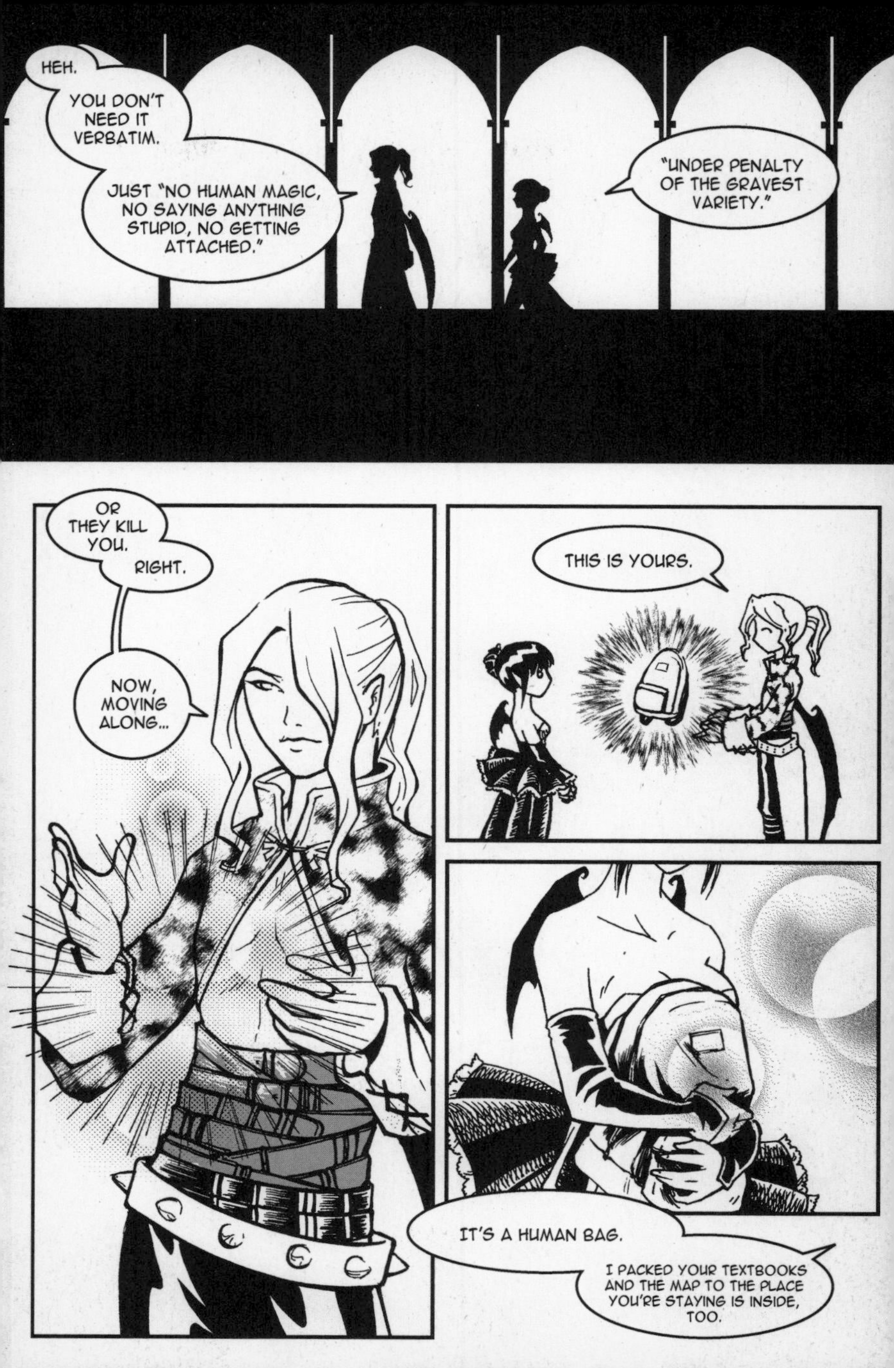
HEH.
YOU DON'T NEED IT VERBATIM.
JUST "NO HUMAN MAGIC, NO SAYING ANYTHING STUPID, NO GETTING ATTACHED."
"UNDER PENALTY OF THE GRAVEST VARIETY."
OR THEY KILL YOU.
RIGHT.
NOW, MOVING ALONG...
THIS IS YOURS.
IT'S A HUMAN BAG.
I PACKED YOUR TEXTBOOKS AND THE MAP TO THE PLACE YOU'RE STAYING IS INSIDE, TOO.

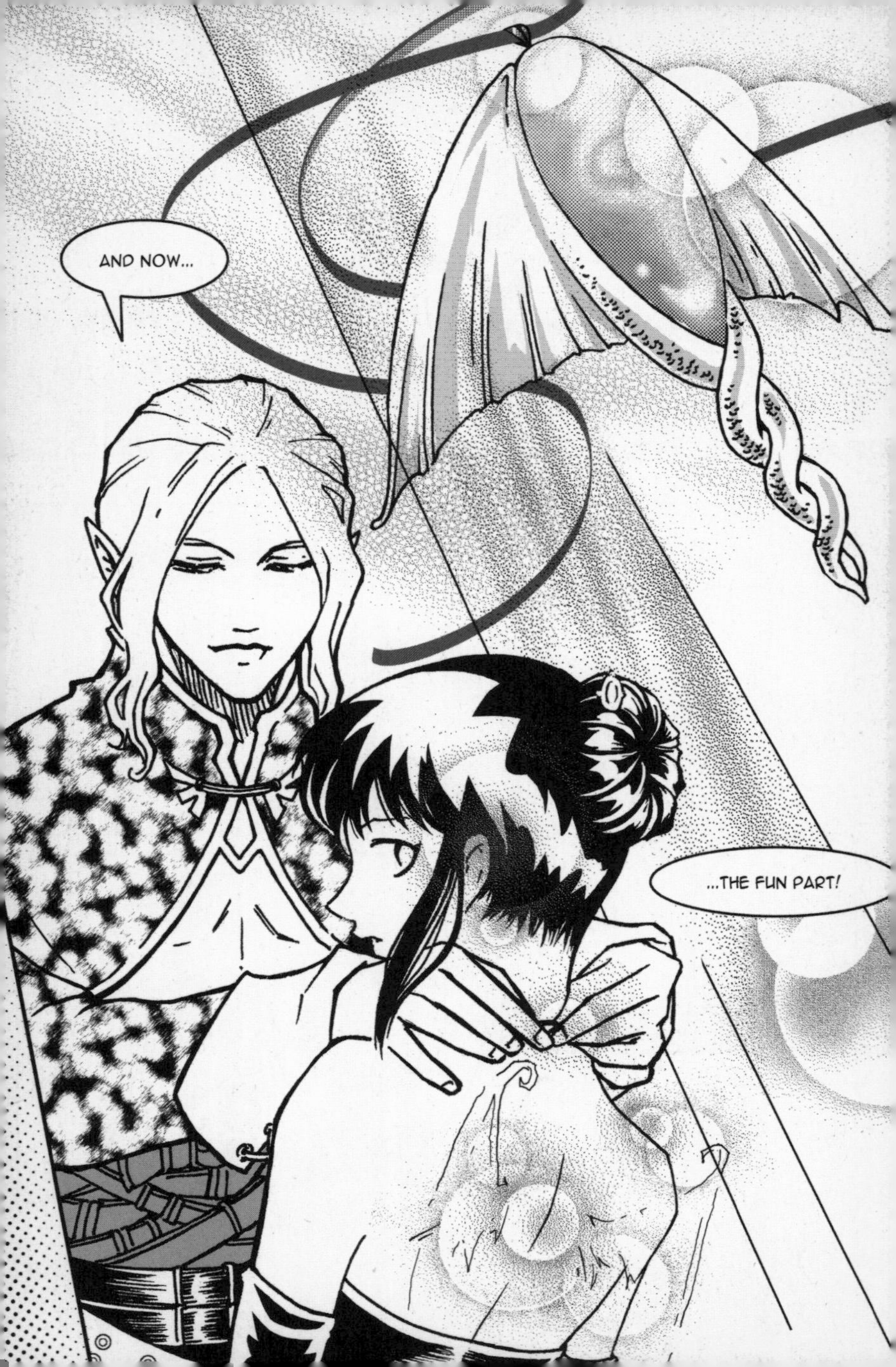
AND NOW...
...THE FUN PART!

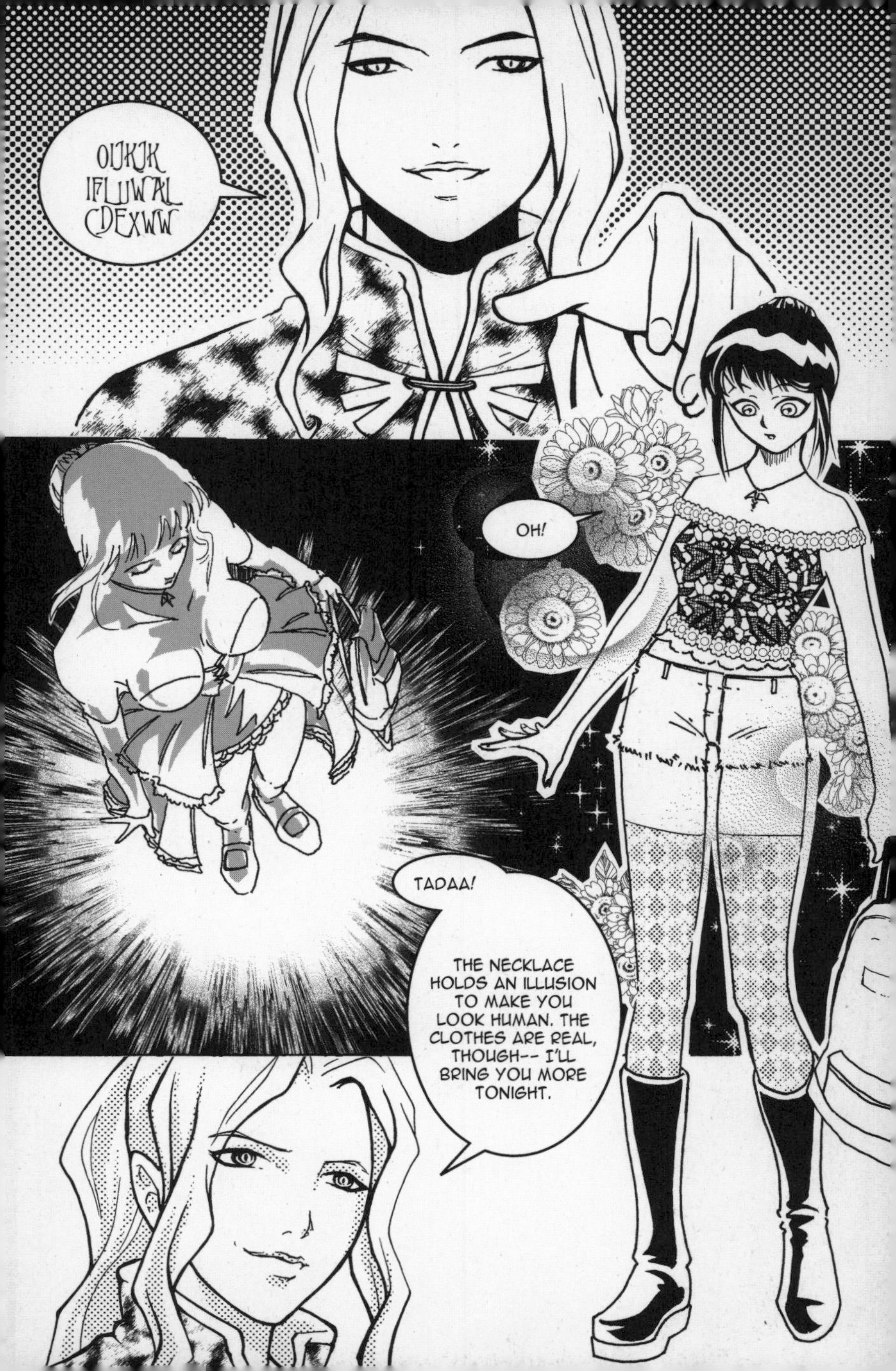
OIJKIK IFLUWAL CDEXWW
OH!
TADAA!
THE NECKLACE HOLDS AN ILLUSION TO MAKE YOU LOOK HUMAN. THE CLOTHES ARE REAL, THOUGH-- I'LL BRING YOU MORE TONIGHT.

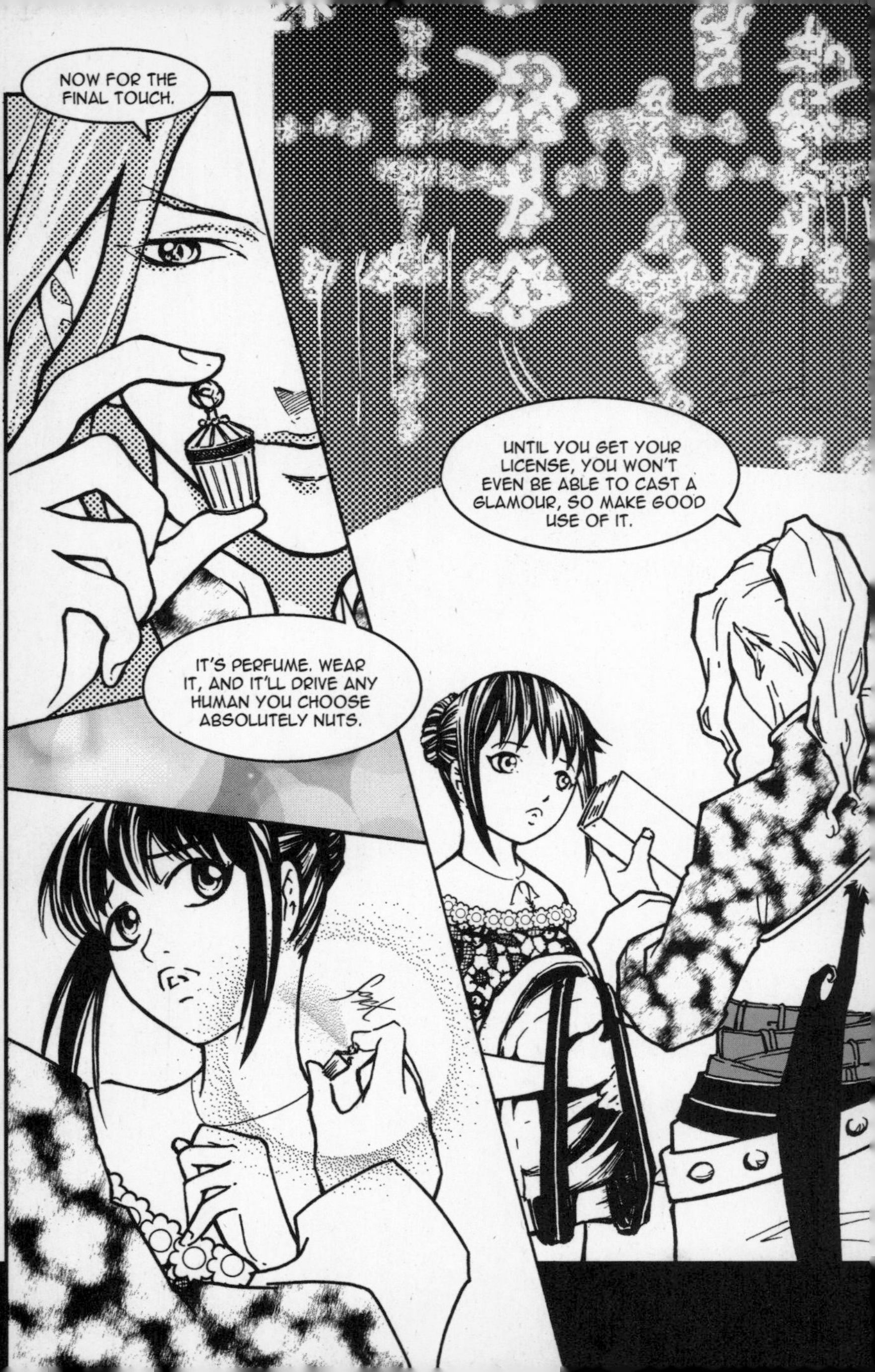
NOW FOR THE FINAL TOUCH.
UNTIL YOU GET YOUR LICENSE, YOU WON'T EVEN BE ABLE TO CAST A GLAMOUR, SO MAKE GOOD USE OF IT.
IT'S PERFUME. WEAR IT, AND IT'LL DRIVE ANY HUMAN YOU CHOOSE ABSOLUTELY NUTS.

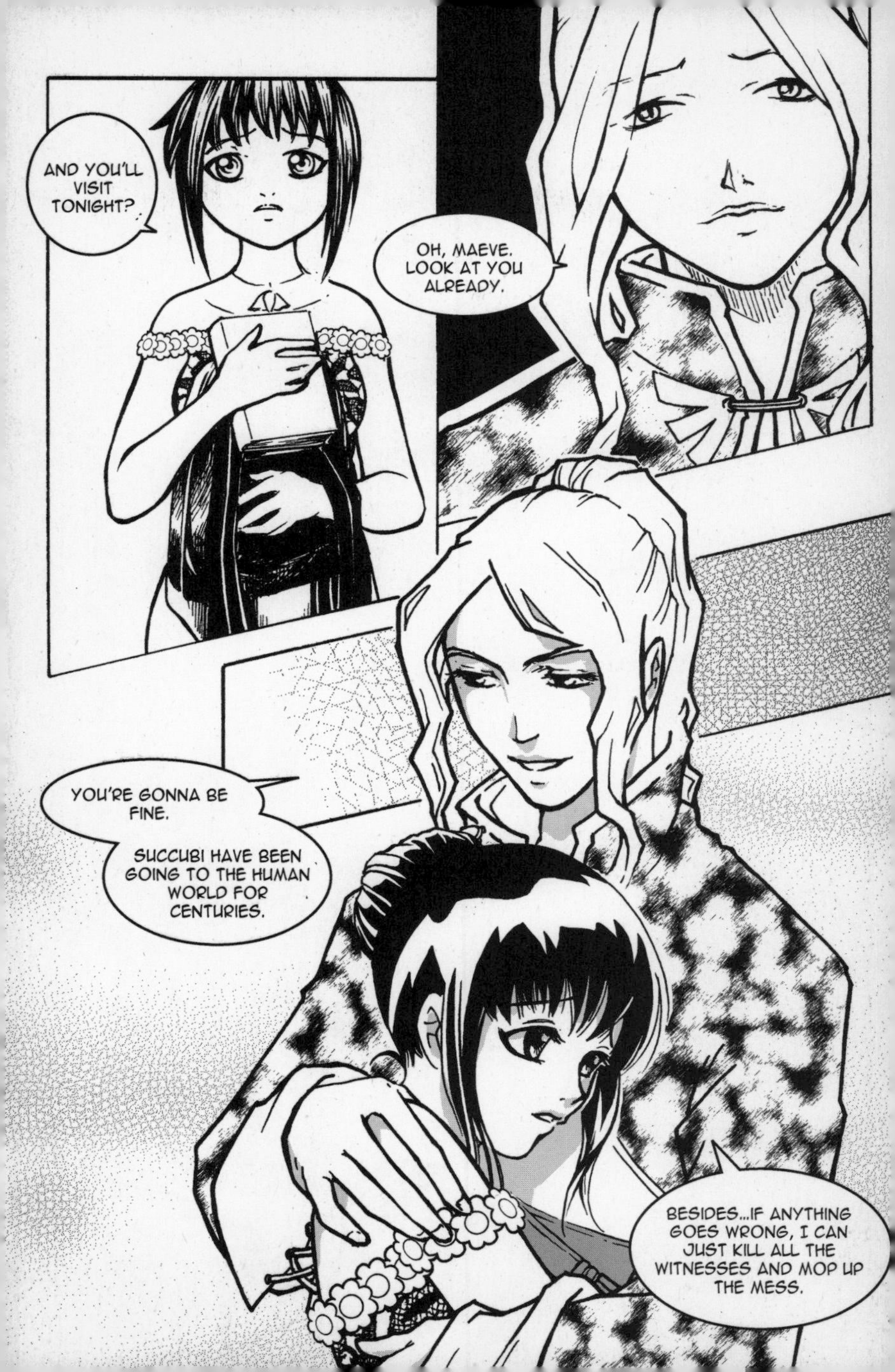
AND YOU'LL VISIT TONIGHT?
OH, MAEVE. LOOK AT YOU ALREADY.
YOU'RE GONNA BE FINE.
SUCCUBI HAVE BEEN GOING TO THE HUMAN WORLD FOR CENTURIES.
BESIDES...IF ANYTHING GOES WRONG, I CAN JUST KILL ALL THE WITNESSES AND MOP UP THE MESS.

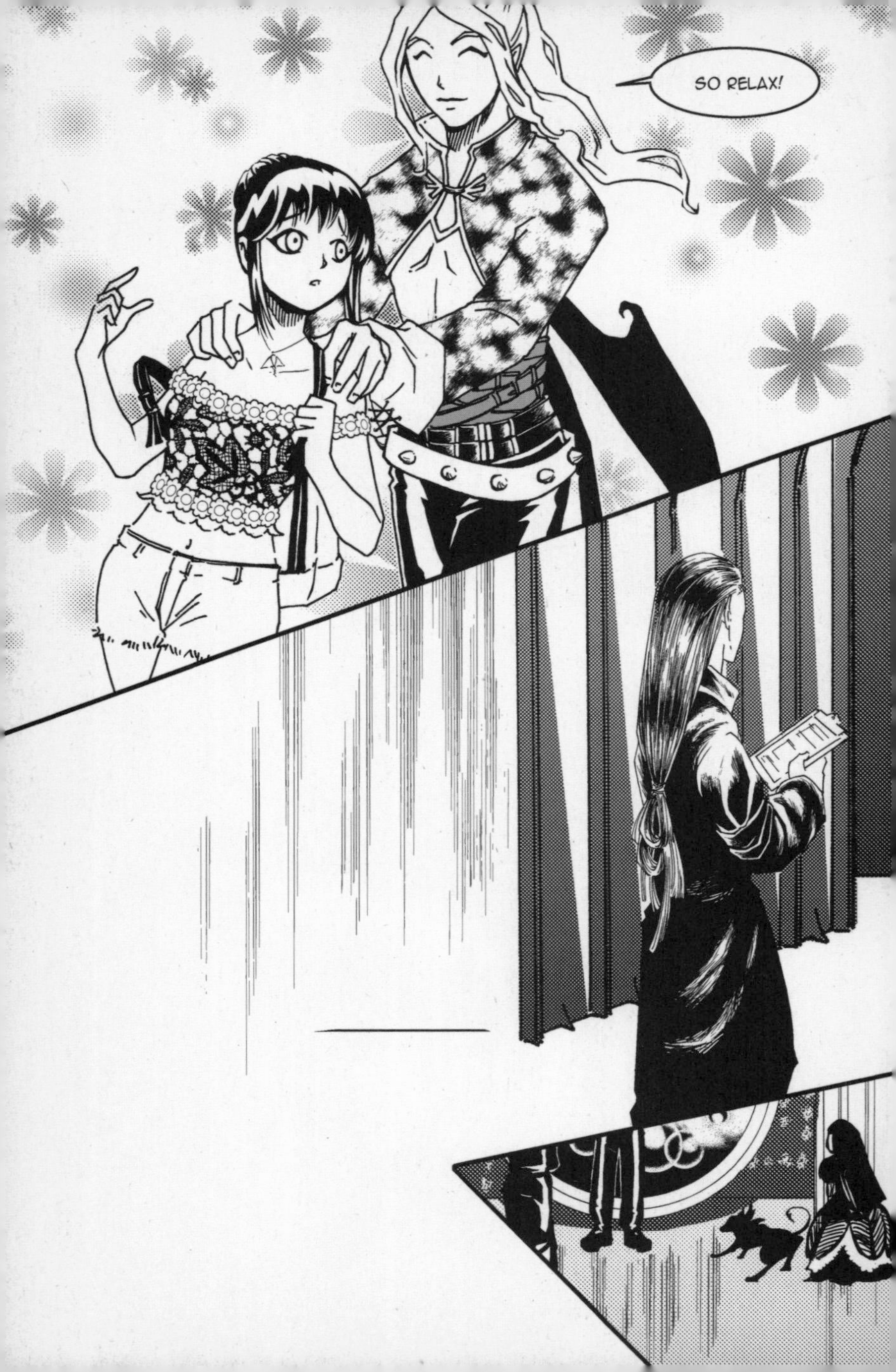
SO RELAX!

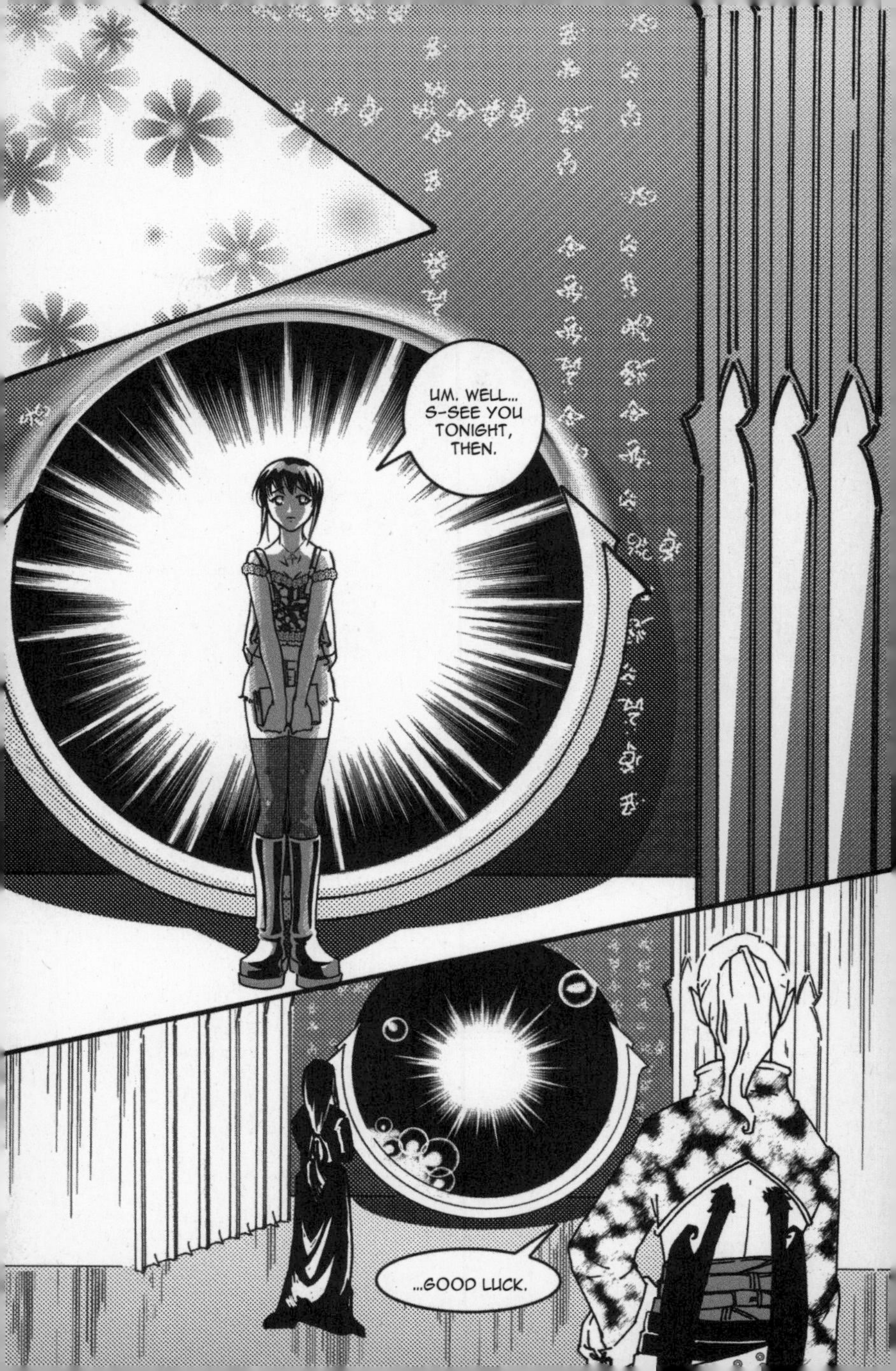
UM. WELL... S-SEE YOU TONIGHT, THEN.
...GOOD LUCK.

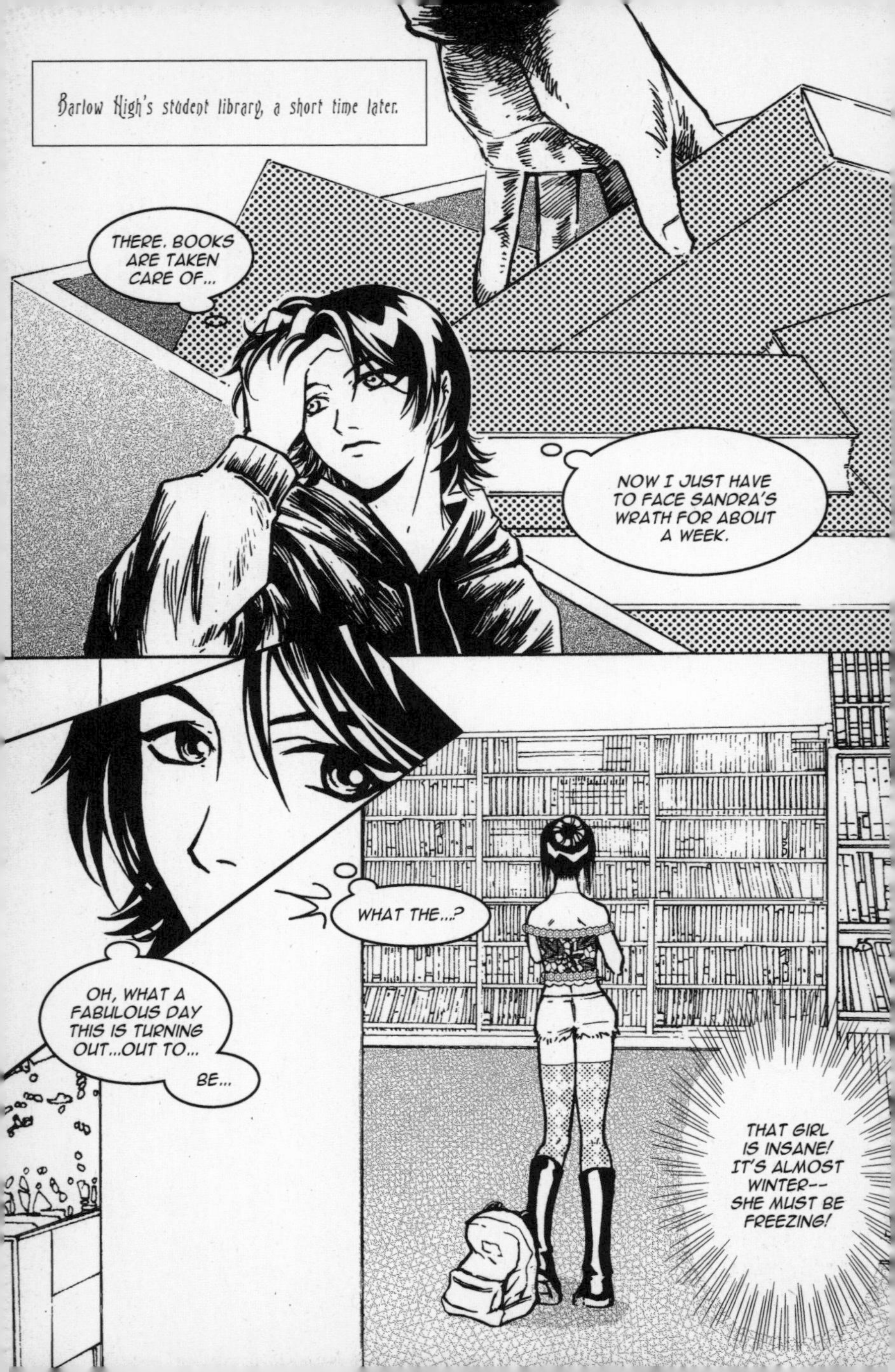
Barlow High's student library, a short time later.
THERE. BOOKS ARE TAKEN CARE OF...
NOW I JUST HAVE TO FACE SANDRA'S WRATH FOR ABOUT A WEEK.
WHAT THE...?
OH, WHAT A FABULOUS DAY THIS IS TURNING OUT...OUT TO... BE...
THAT GIRL IS INSANE! IT'S ALMOST WINTER-- SHE MUST BE FREEZING!

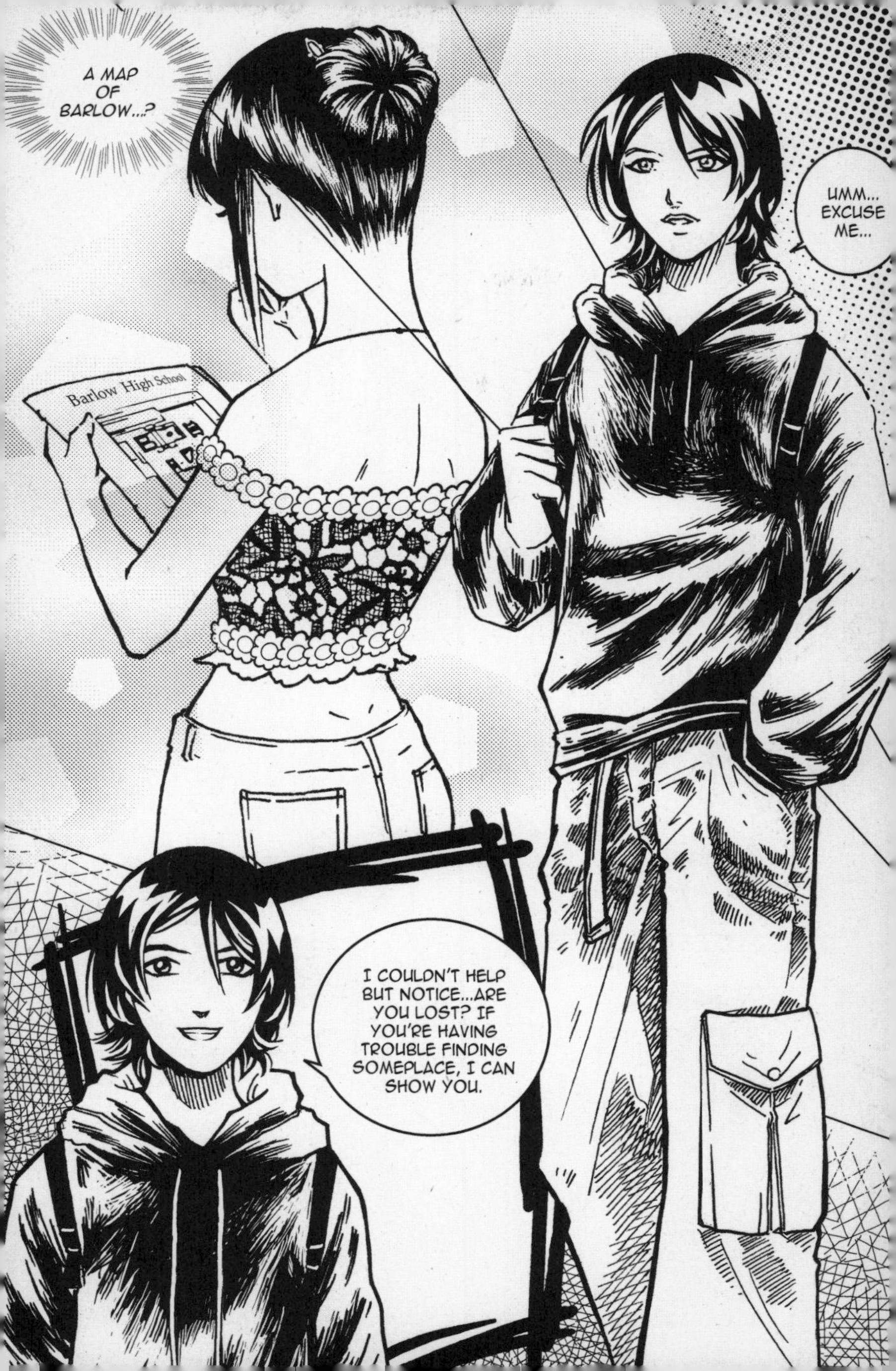
A MAP OF BARLOW...?
Barlow High School
UMM... EXCUSE ME...
I COULDN'T HELP BUT NOTICE...ARE YOU LOST? IF YOU'RE HAVING TROUBLE FINDING SOMEPLACE, I CAN SHOW YOU.

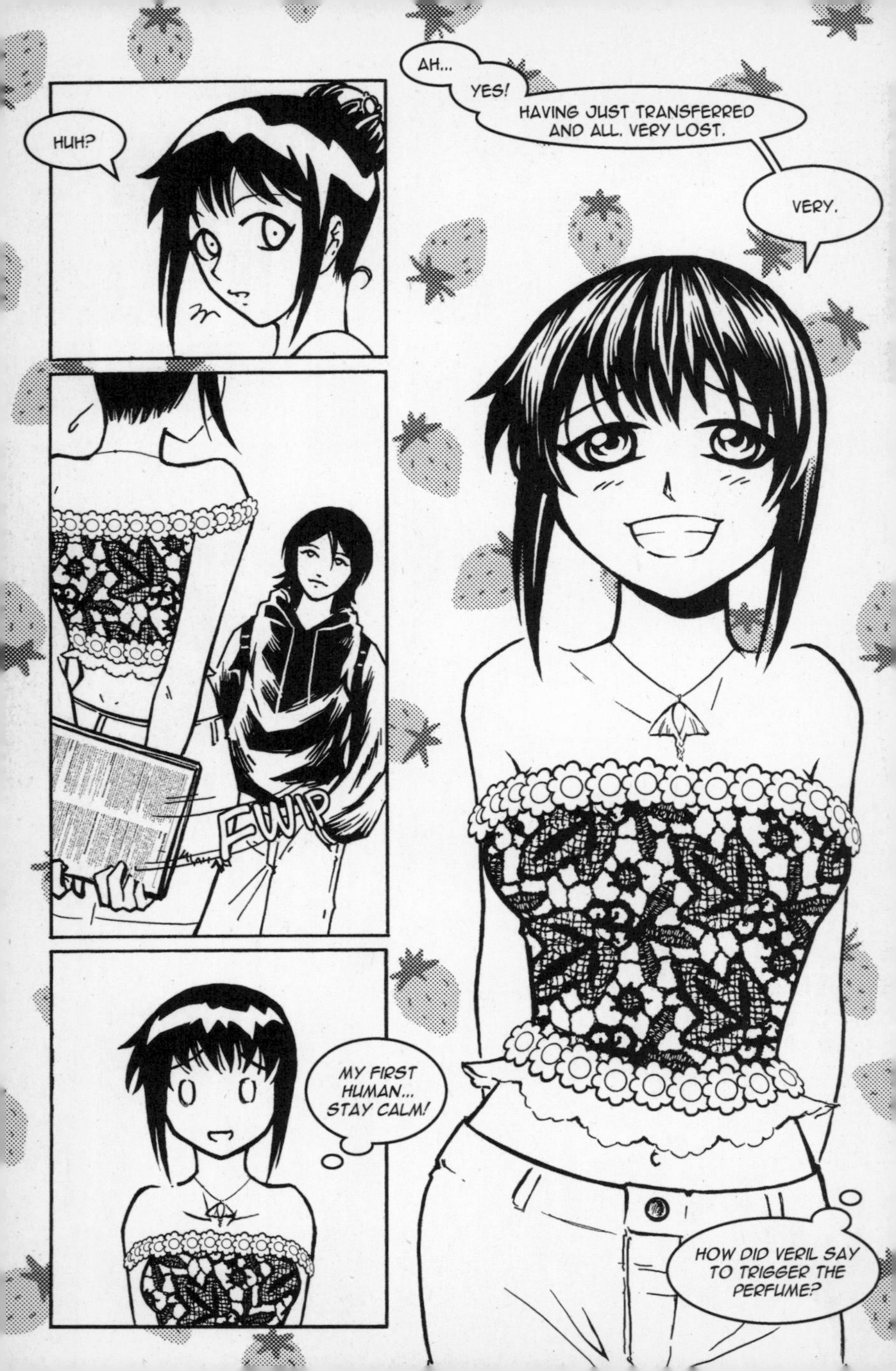
HUH?
FWIP
MY FIRST HUMAN... STAY CALM!
AH...
YES!
HAVING JUST TRANSFERRED AND ALL. VERY LOST.
VERY.
HOW DID VERIL SAY TO TRIGGER THE PERFUME?

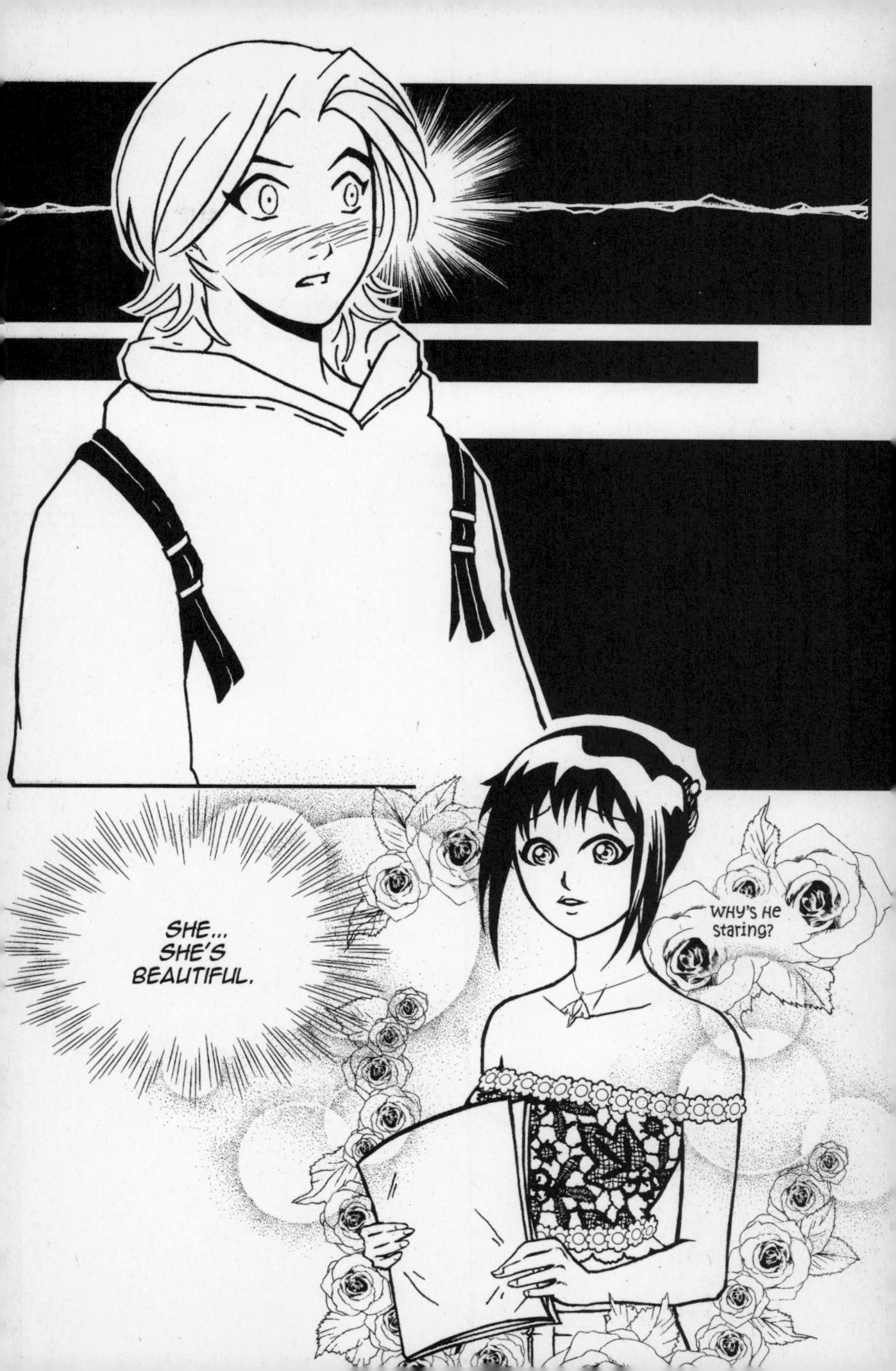
SHE... SHE'S BEAUTIFUL.
WHY'S HE staring?

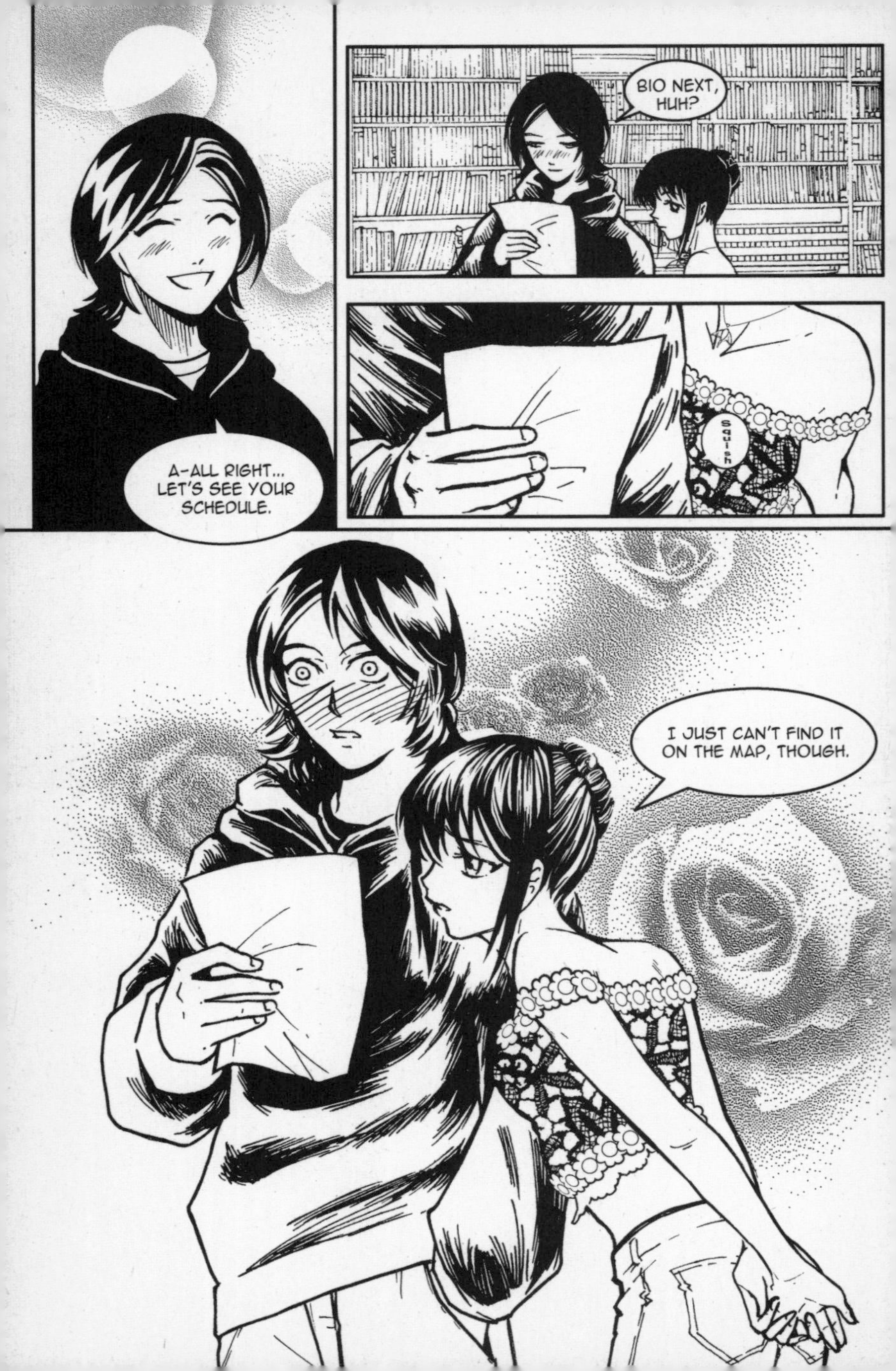
A-ALL RIGHT... LET'S SEE YOUR SCHEDULE.
BIO NEXT, HUH?
squish
I JUST CAN'T FIND IT ON THE MAP, THOUGH.

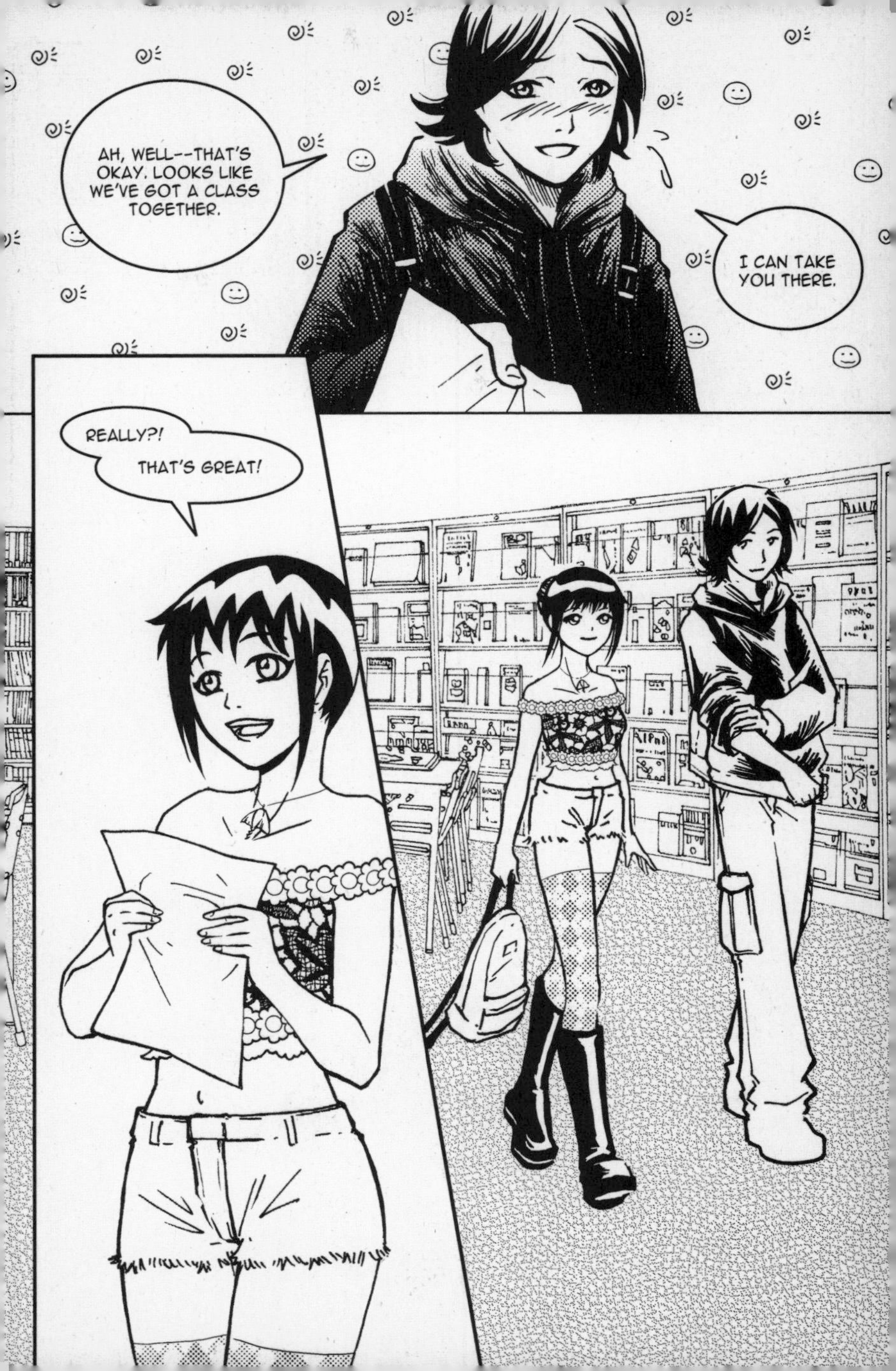
AH, WELL--THAT'S OKAY. LOOKS LIKE WE'VE GOT A CLASS TOGETHER.
I CAN TAKE YOU THERE.
REALLY?!
THAT'S GREAT!

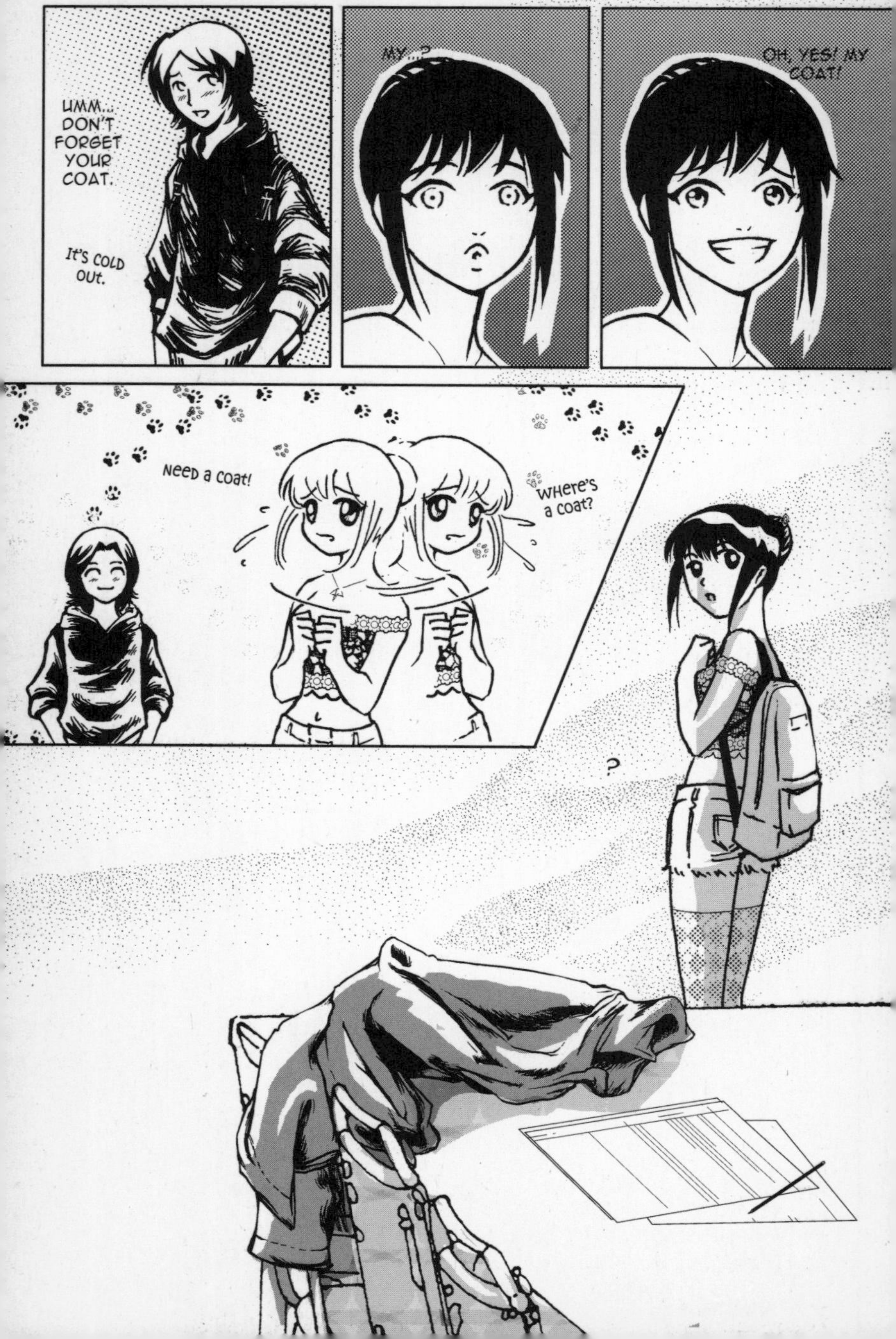
UMM... DON'T FORGET YOUR COAT.
IT'S COLD OUT.
MY...?
OH, YES! MY COAT!
NEED A COAT!
WHERE'S A COAT?
?

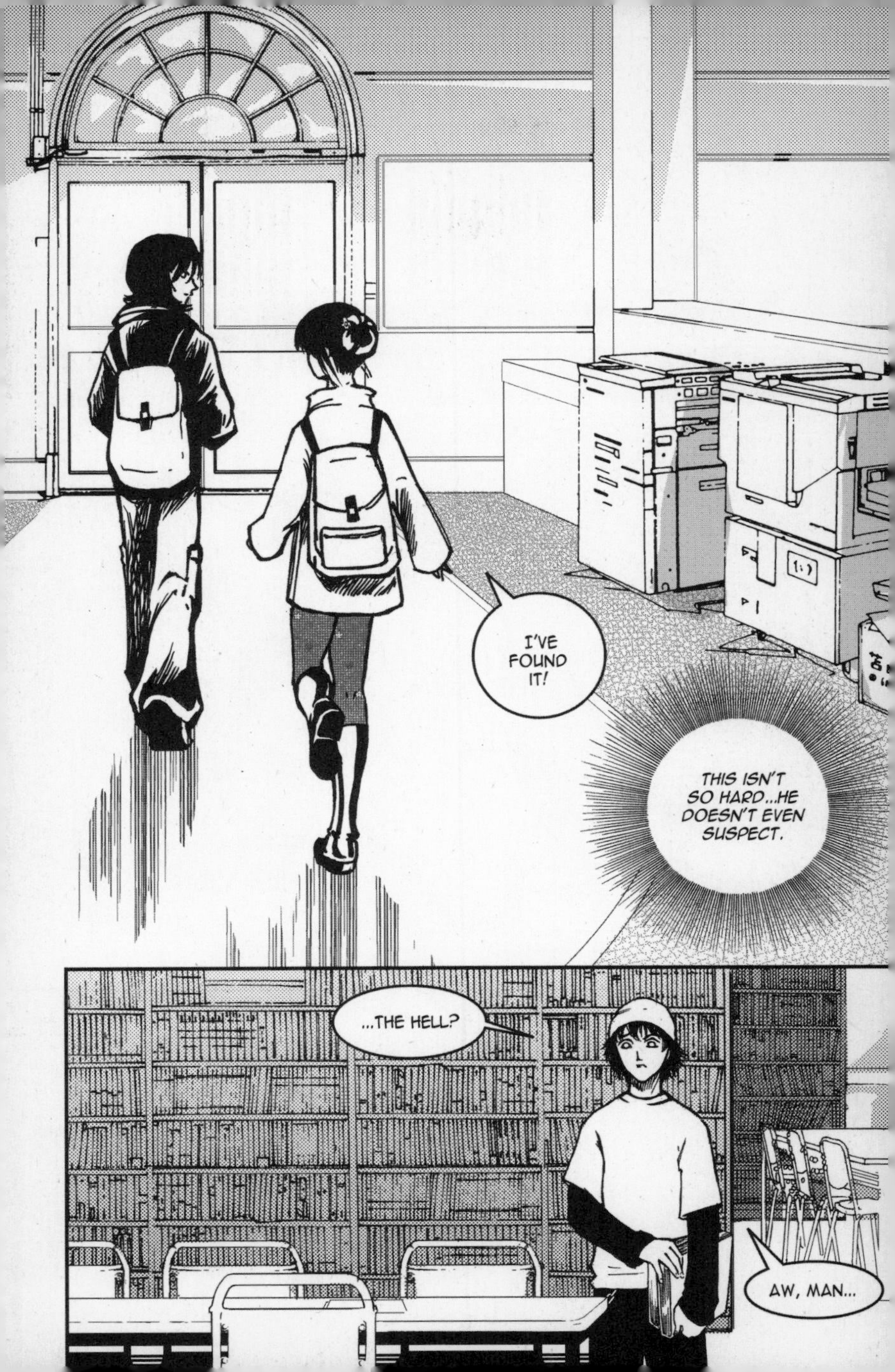
I'VE FOUND IT!
THIS ISN'T SO HARD...HE DOESN'T EVEN SUSPECT.
...THE HELL?
AW, MAN...

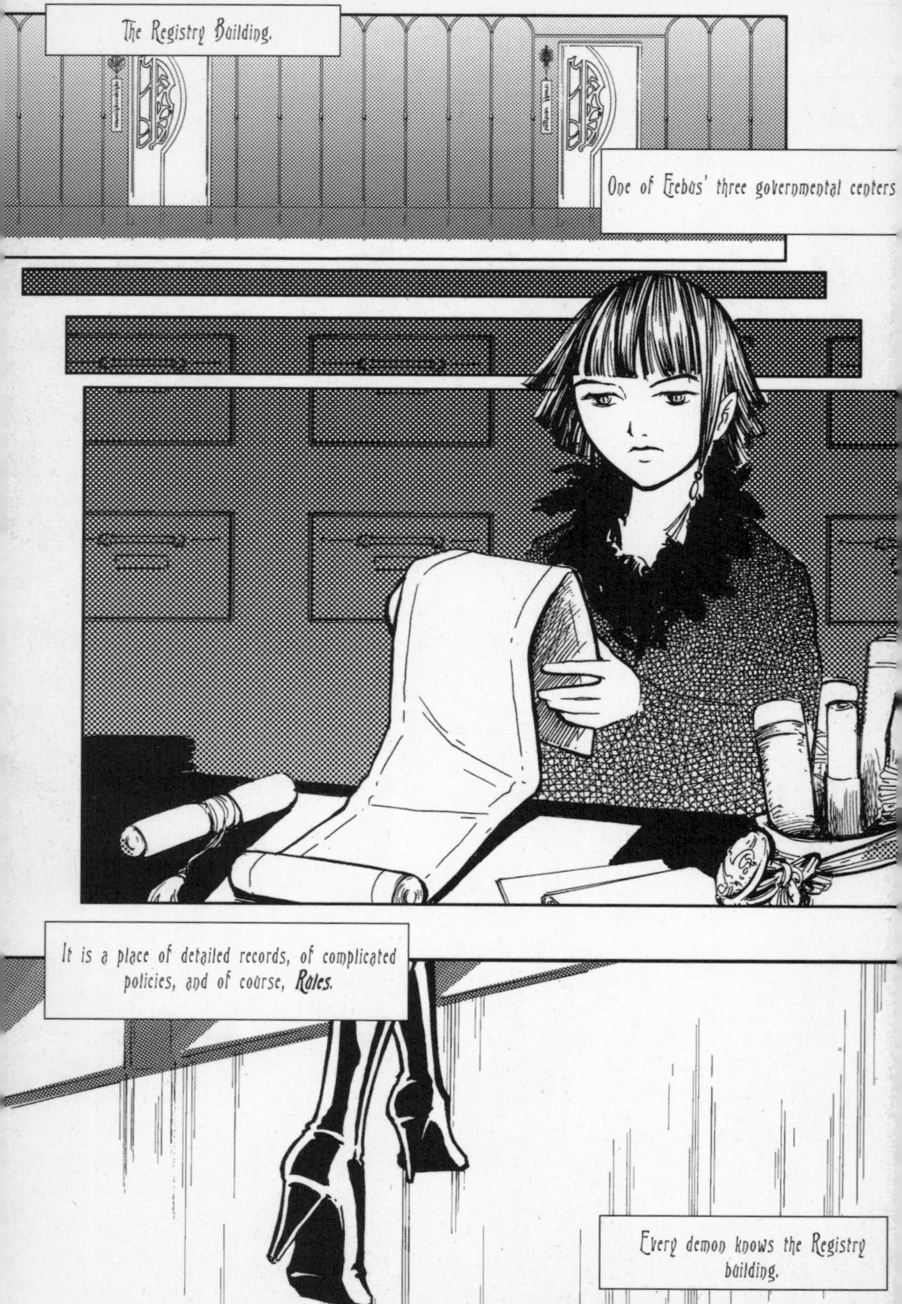
The Registry Building.
One of Erebus' three governmental centers
It is a place of detailed records, of complicated policies, and of course, Rates.
Every demon knows the Registry building.

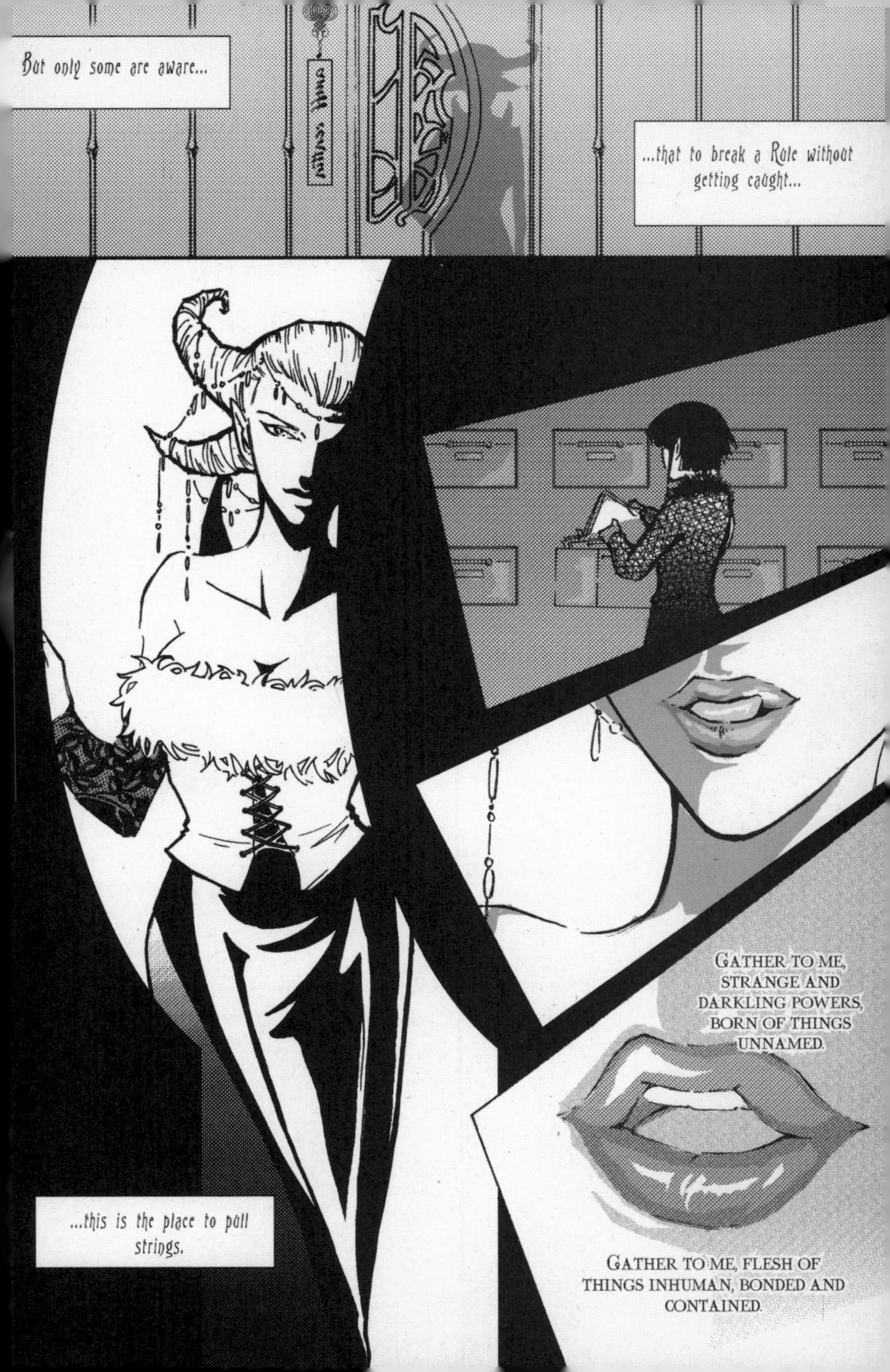
But only some are aware...
...that to break a Rule without getting caught...
...this is the place to pull strings.
GATHER TO ME, STRANGE AND DARKLING POWERS, BORN OF THINGS UNNAMED.
GATHER TO ME, FLESH OF THINGS INHUMAN, BONDED AND CONTAINED.

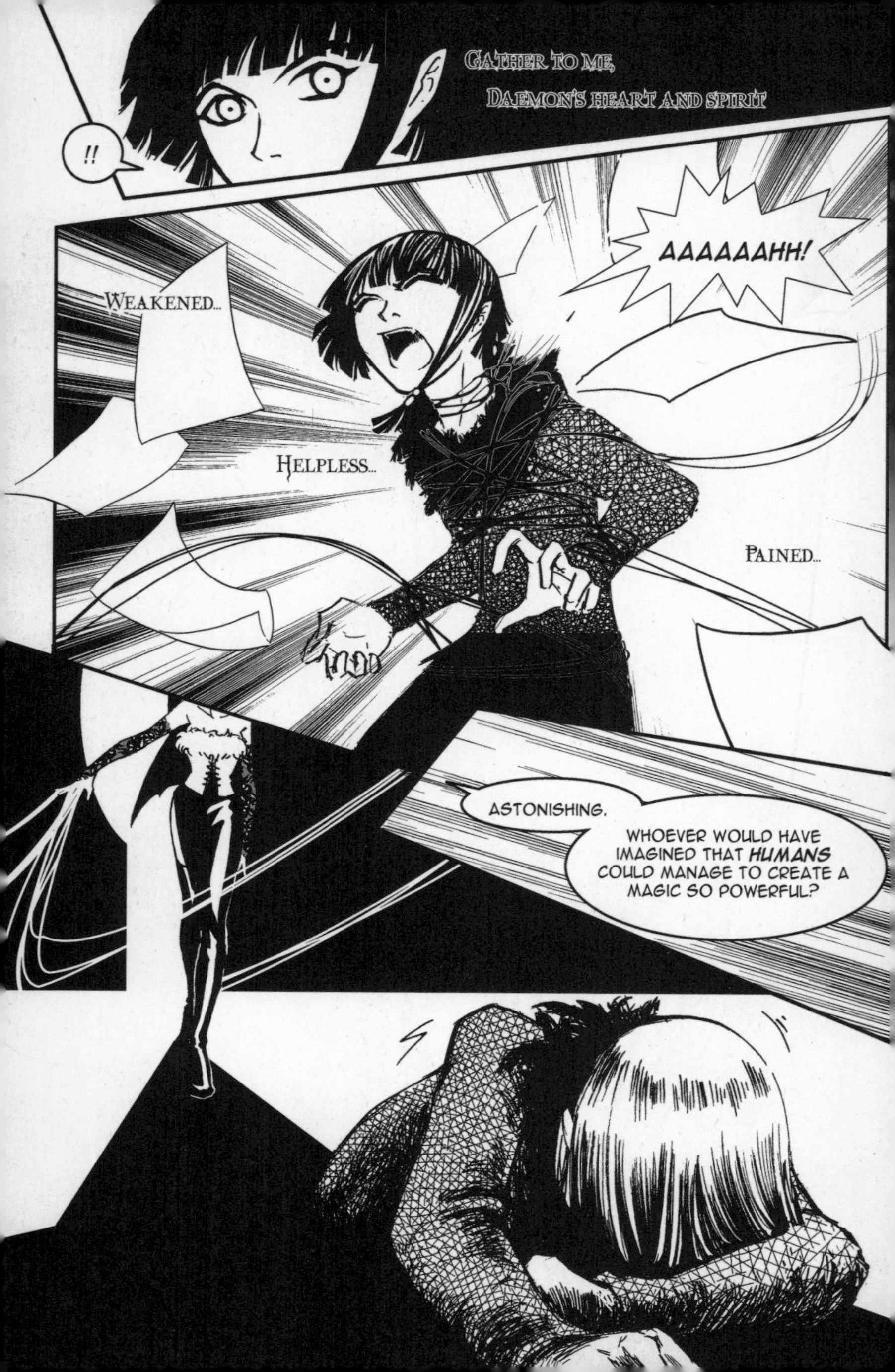
Gather to me,
Daemon's heart and spirit
!!
AAAAAAHH!
Weakened...
Helpless...
Pained...
ASTONISHING.
WHOEVER WOULD HAVE IMAGINED THAT HUMANS COULD MANAGE TO CREATE A MAGIC SO POWERFUL?

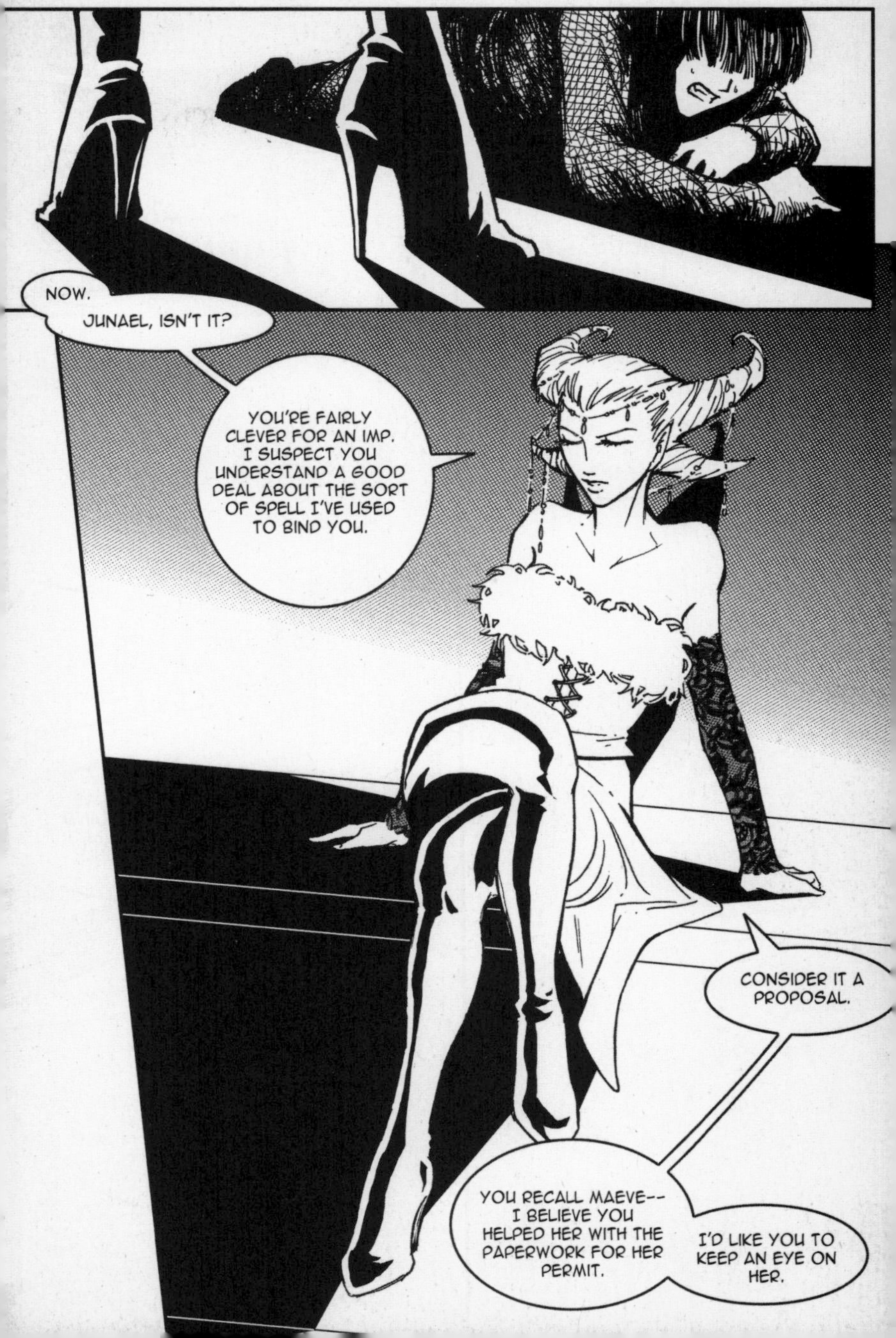
NOW.
JUNAEL, ISN'T IT?
YOU'RE FAIRLY CLEVER FOR AN IMP. I SUSPECT YOU UNDERSTAND A GOOD DEAL ABOUT THE SORT OF SPELL I'VE USED TO BIND YOU.
CONSIDER IT A PROPOSAL.
YOU RECALL MAEVE-- I BELIEVE YOU HELPED HER WITH THE PAPERWORK FOR HER PERMIT.
I'D LIKE YOU TO KEEP AN EYE ON HER.

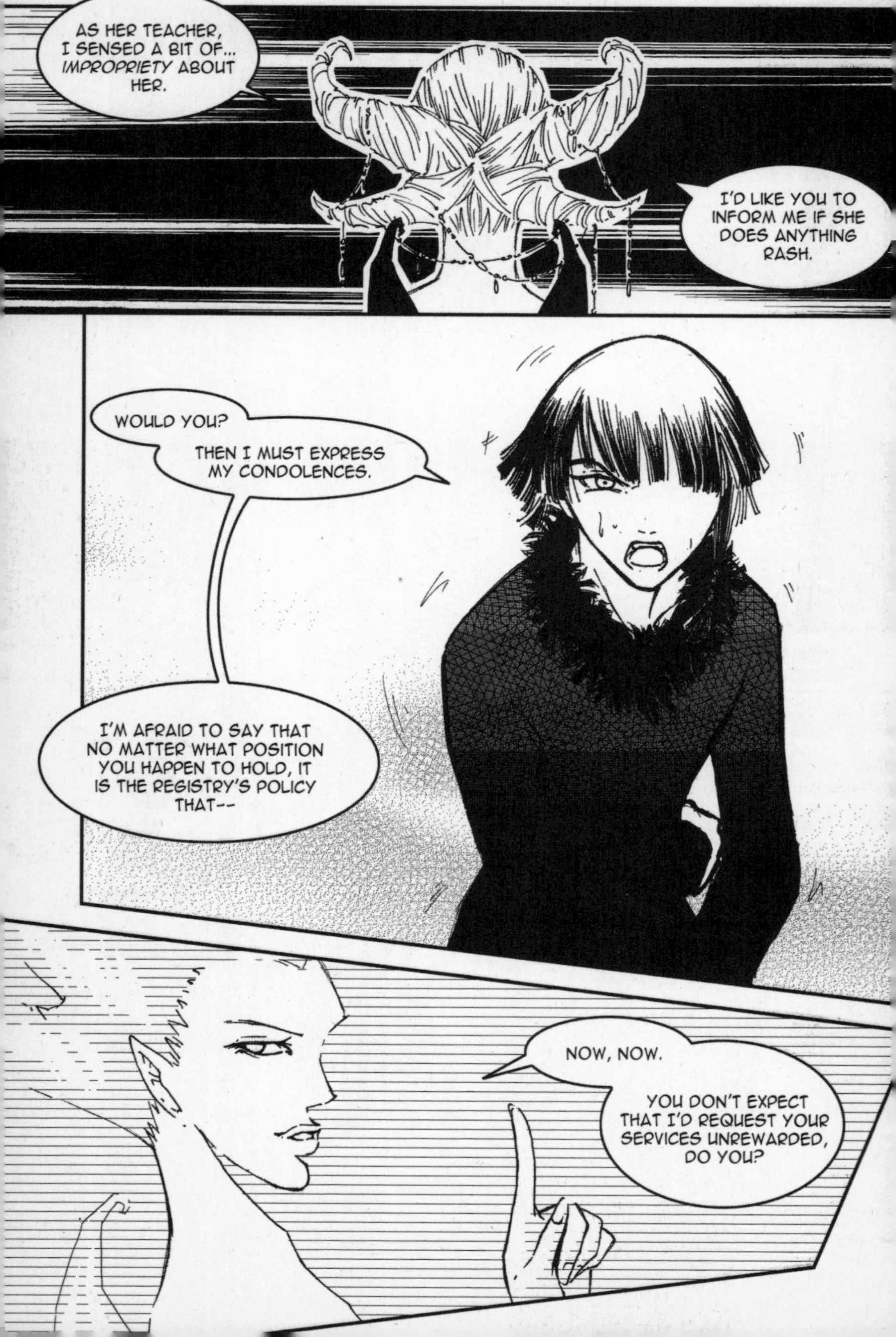
AS HER TEACHER, I SENSED A BIT OF... *IMPROPRIETY* ABOUT HER.
I'D LIKE YOU TO INFORM ME IF SHE DOES ANYTHING RASH.
WOULD YOU?
THEN I MUST EXPRESS MY CONDOLENCES.
I'M AFRAID TO SAY THAT NO MATTER WHAT POSITION YOU HAPPEN TO HOLD, IT IS THE REGISTRY'S POLICY THAT--
NOW, NOW.
YOU DON'T EXPECT THAT I'D REQUEST YOUR SERVICES UNREWARDED, DO YOU?

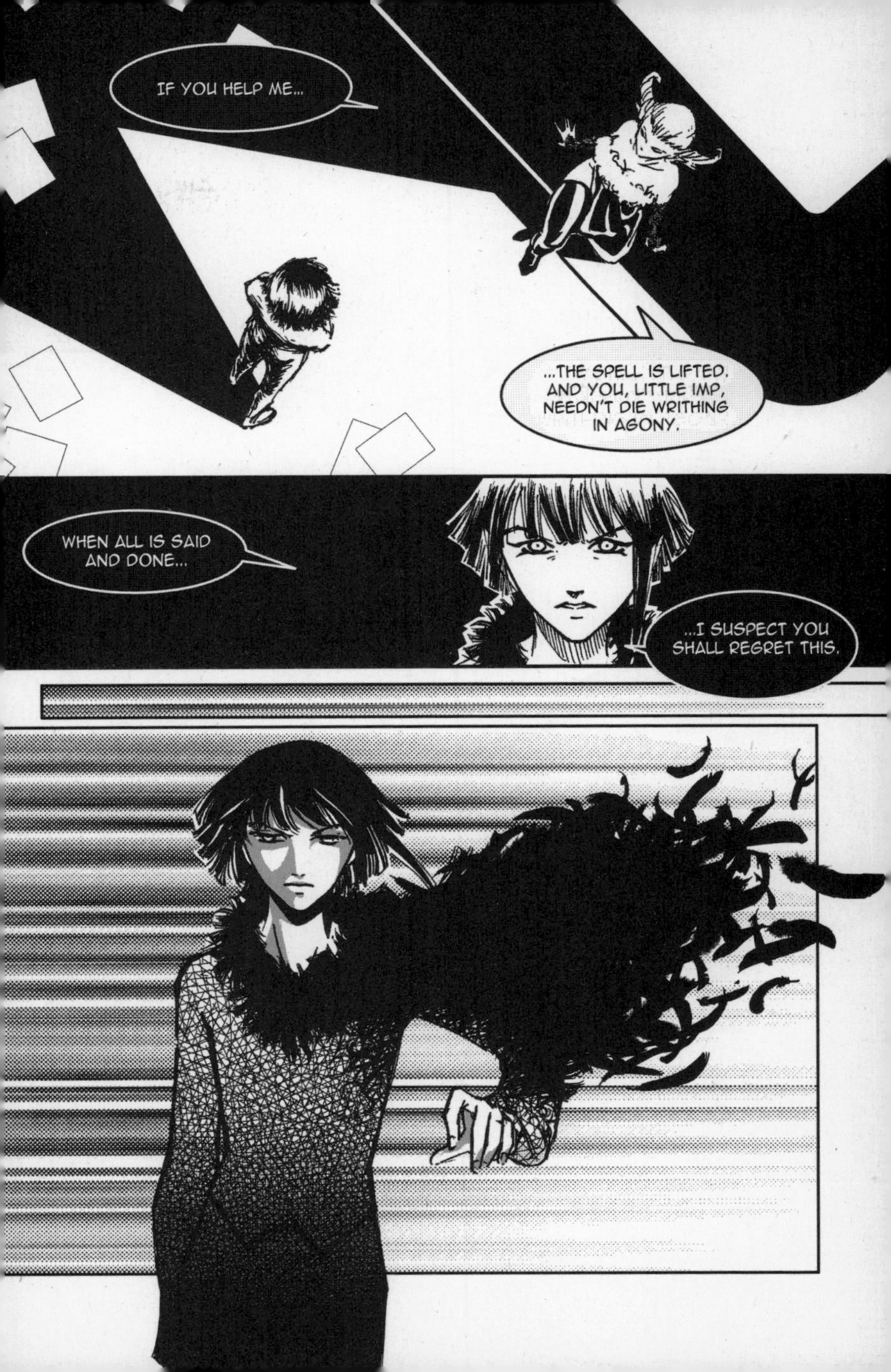
IF YOU HELP ME...
...THE SPELL IS LIFTED. AND YOU, LITTLE IMP, NEEDN'T DIE WRITHING IN AGONY.
WHEN ALL IS SAID AND DONE...
...I SUSPECT YOU SHALL REGRET THIS.

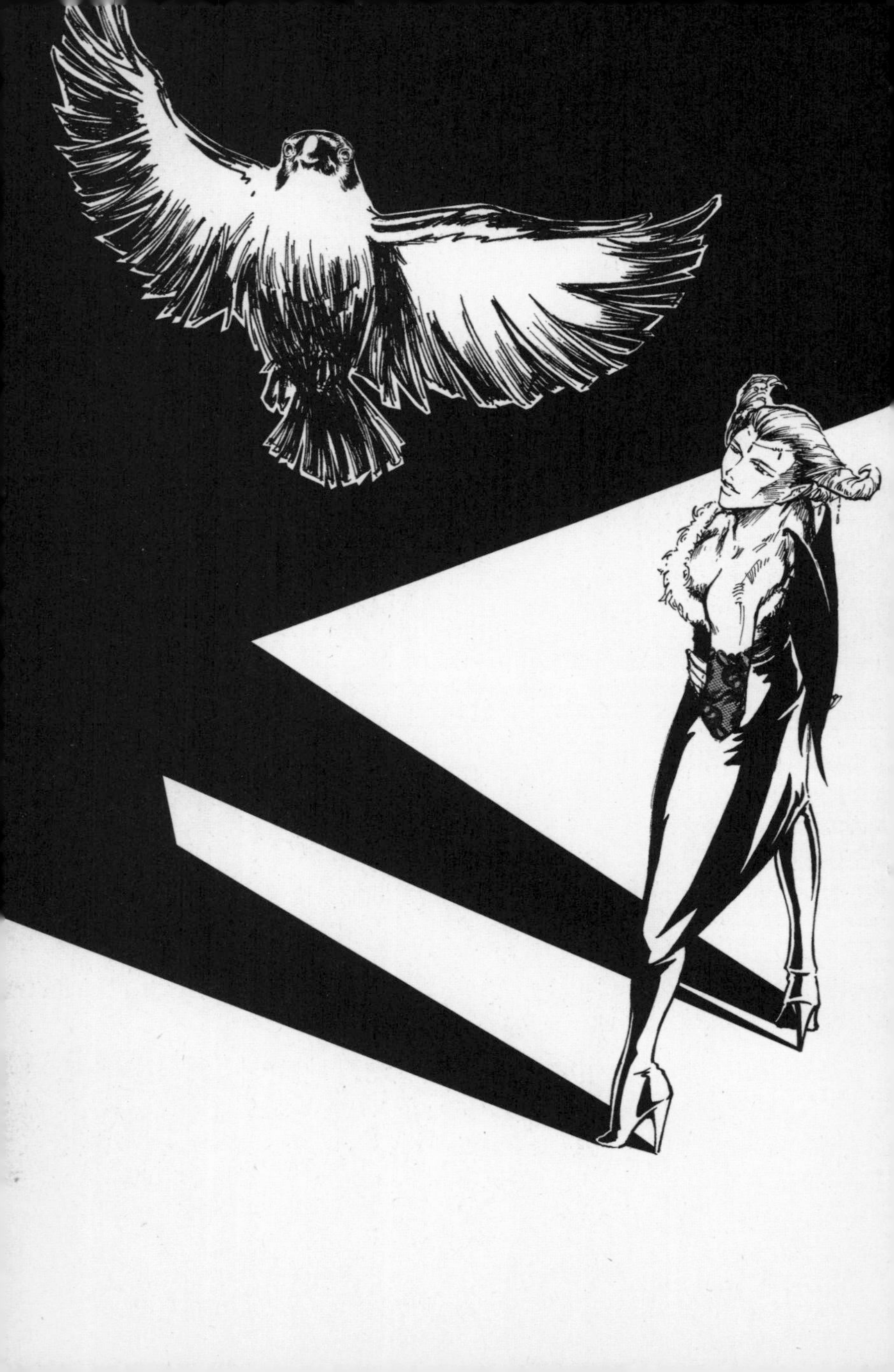

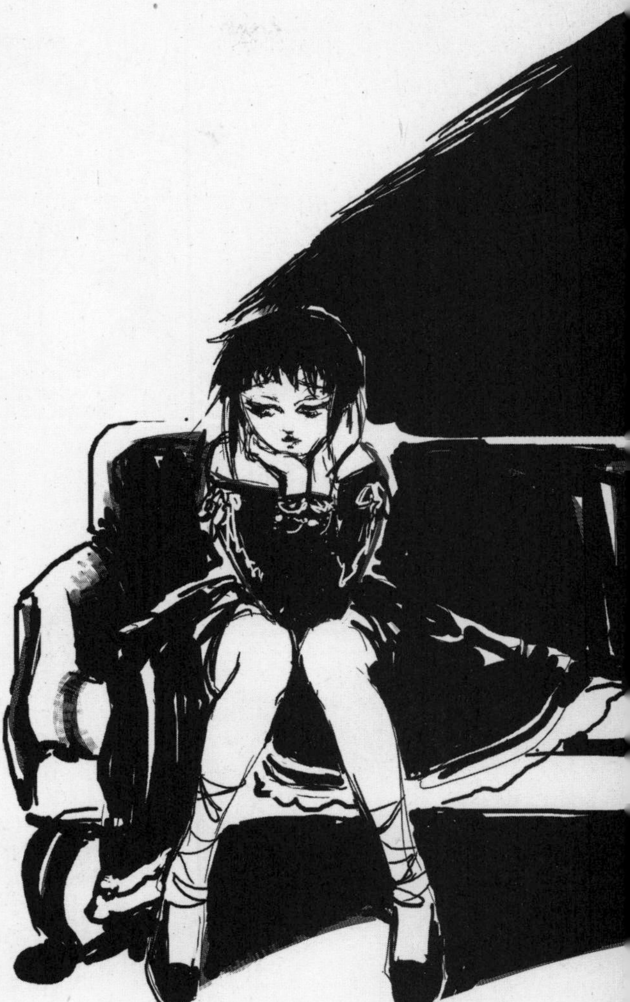

chapter 2

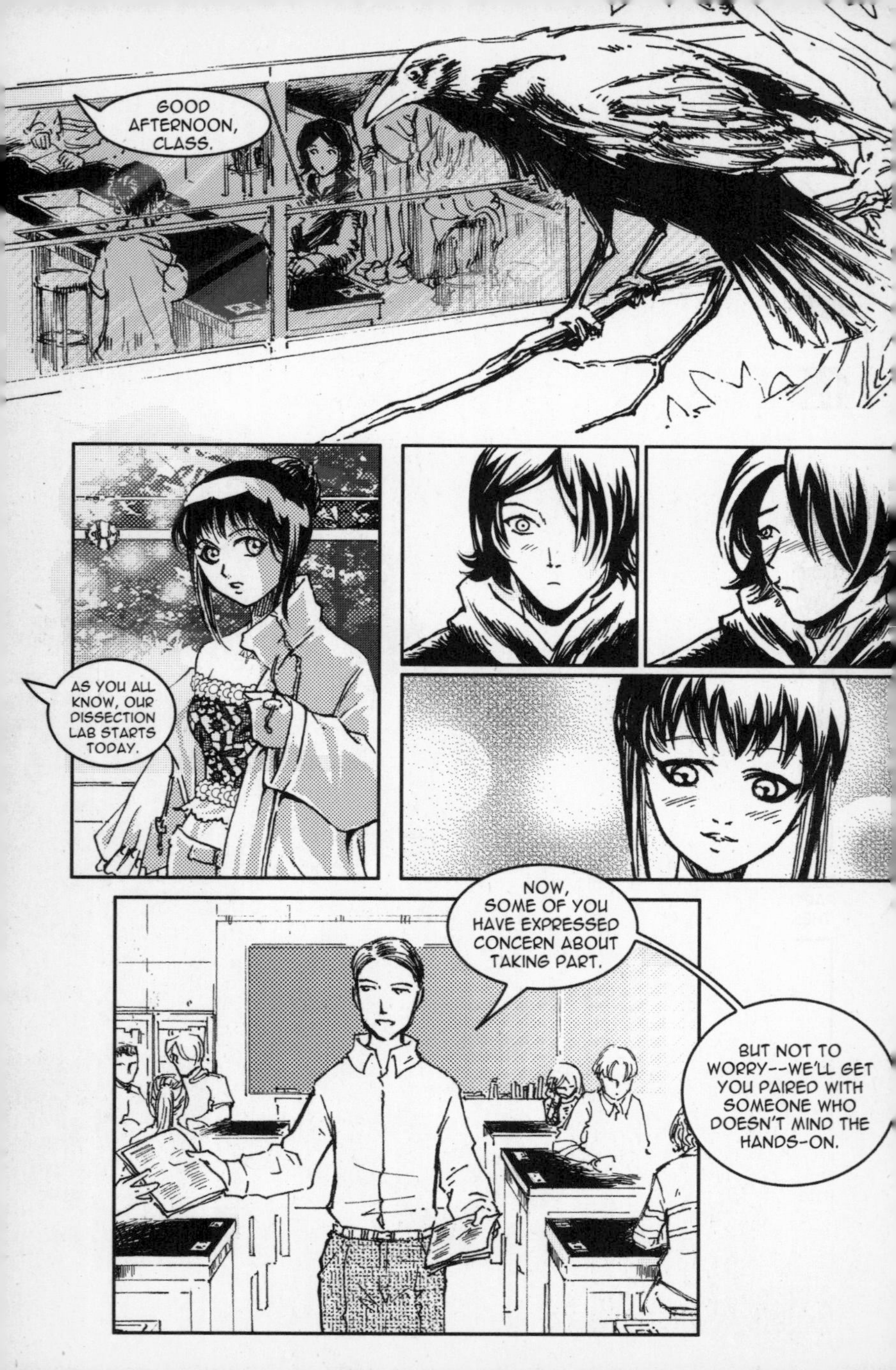
GOOD AFTERNOON, CLASS.
AS YOU ALL KNOW, OUR DISSECTION LAB STARTS TODAY.
NOW, SOME OF YOU HAVE EXPRESSED CONCERN ABOUT TAKING PART.
BUT NOT TO WORRY--WE'LL GET YOU PAIRED WITH SOMEONE WHO DOESN'T MIND THE HANDS-ON.

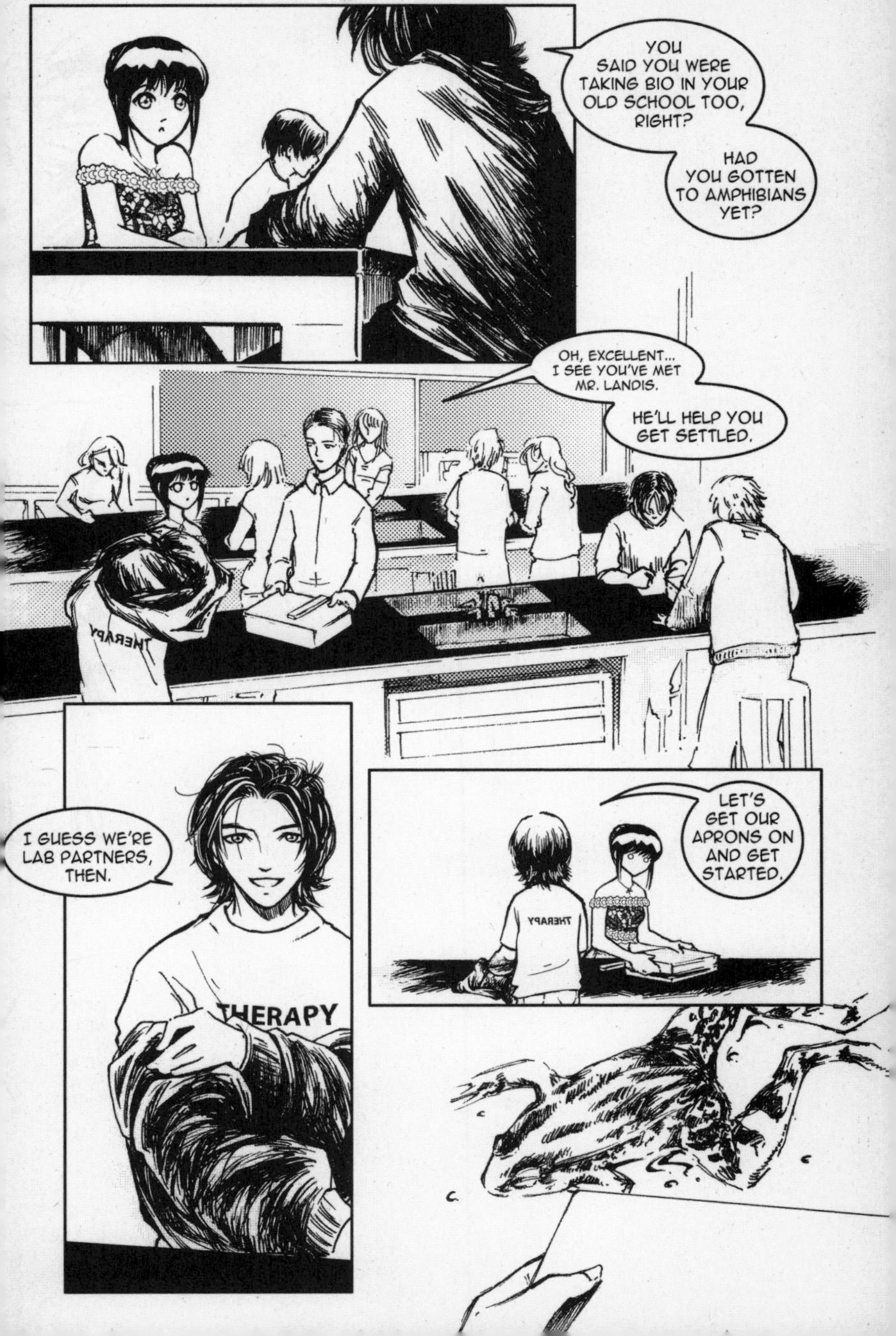
YOU SAID YOU WERE TAKING BIO IN YOUR OLD SCHOOL TOO, RIGHT?
HAD YOU GOTTEN TO AMPHIBIANS YET?
OH, EXCELLENT... I SEE YOU'VE MET MR. LANDIS.
HE'LL HELP YOU GET SETTLED.
THERAPY
I GUESS WE'RE LAB PARTNERS, THEN.
THERAPY
LET'S GET OUR APRONS ON AND GET STARTED.
THERAPY

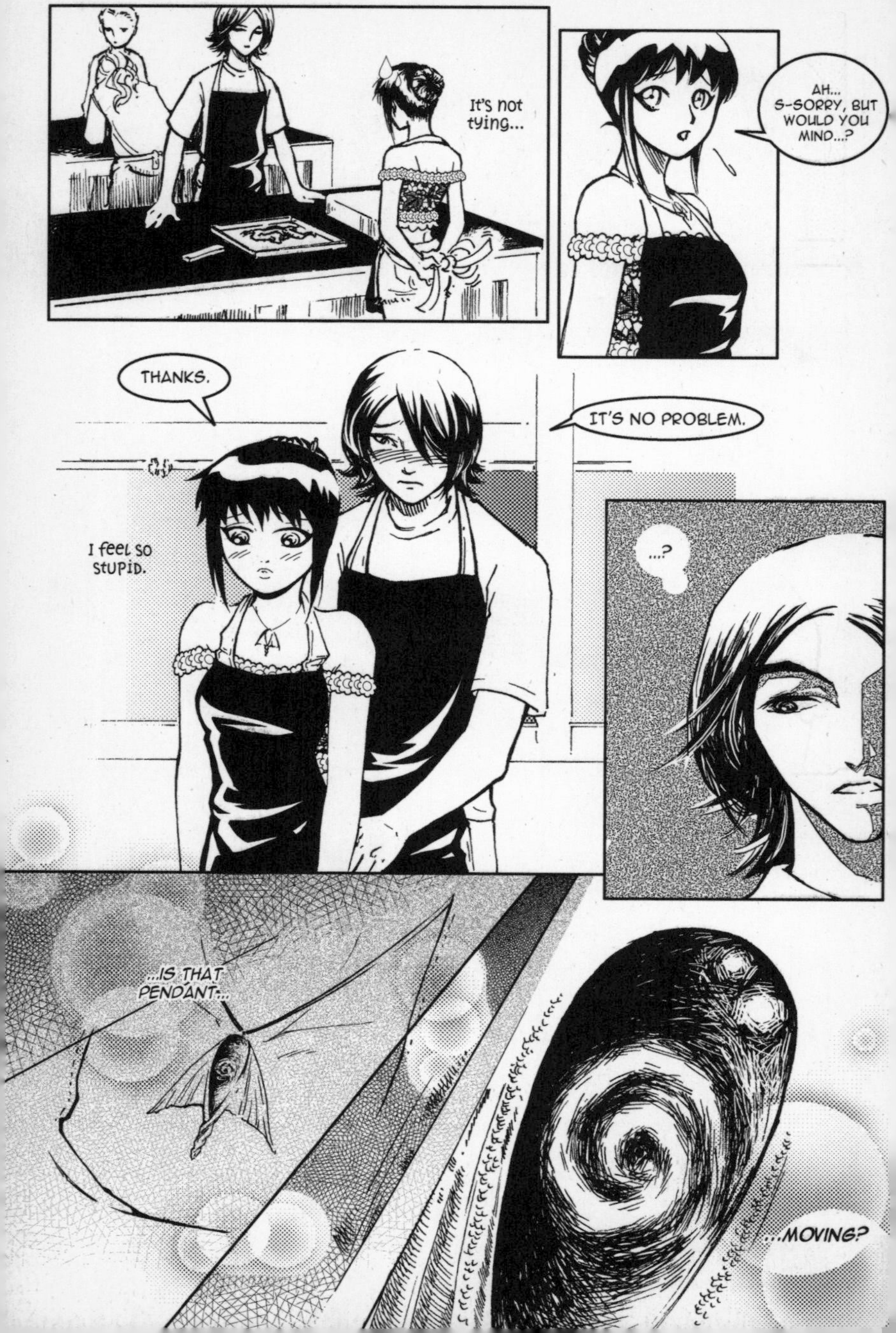
It's not tying...
AH... S-SORRY, BUT WOULD YOU MIND...?
THANKS.
IT'S NO PROBLEM.
I feel so stupid.
...?
...IS THAT PENDANT...
...MOVING?

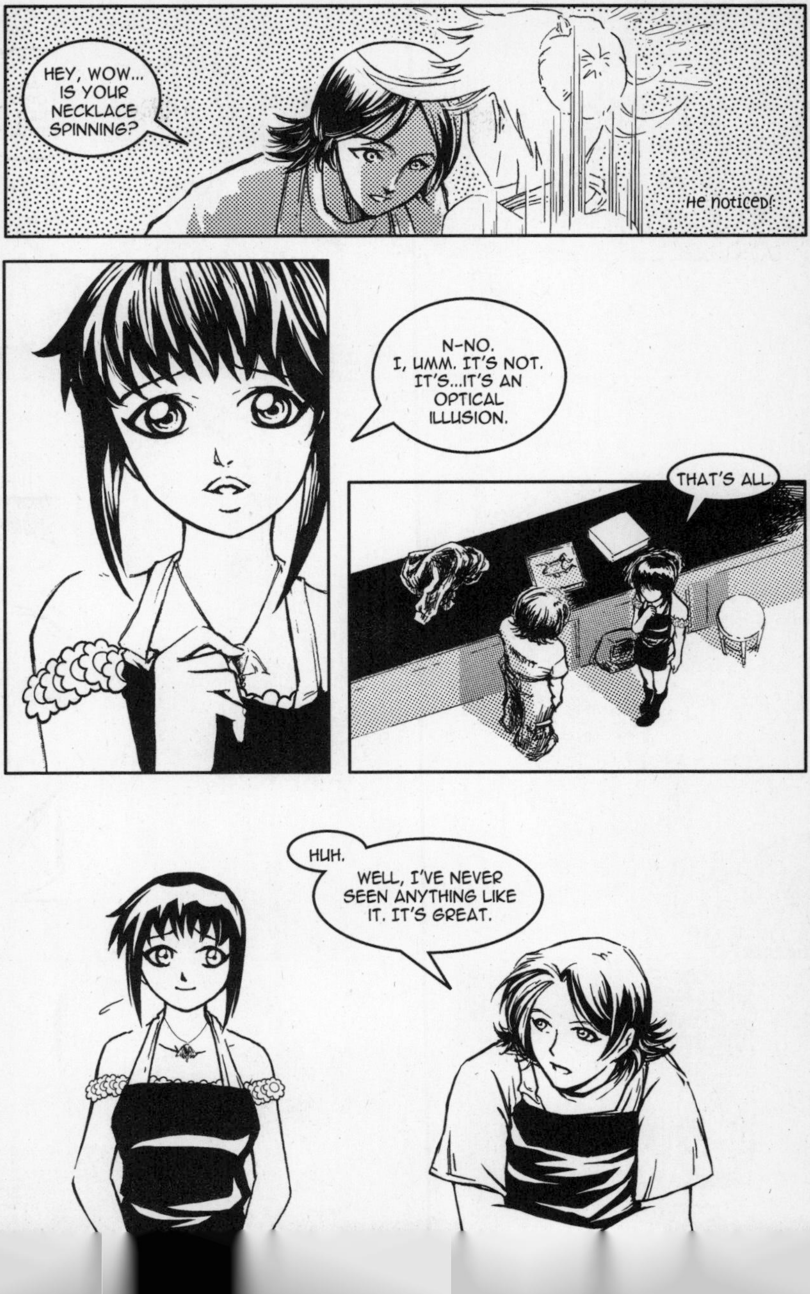
HEY, WOW...
IS YOUR NECKLACE SPINNING?
He noticed!
N-NO.
I, UMM. IT'S NOT. IT'S...IT'S AN OPTICAL ILLUSION.
THAT'S ALL.
HUH.
WELL, I'VE NEVER SEEN ANYTHING LIKE IT. IT'S GREAT.

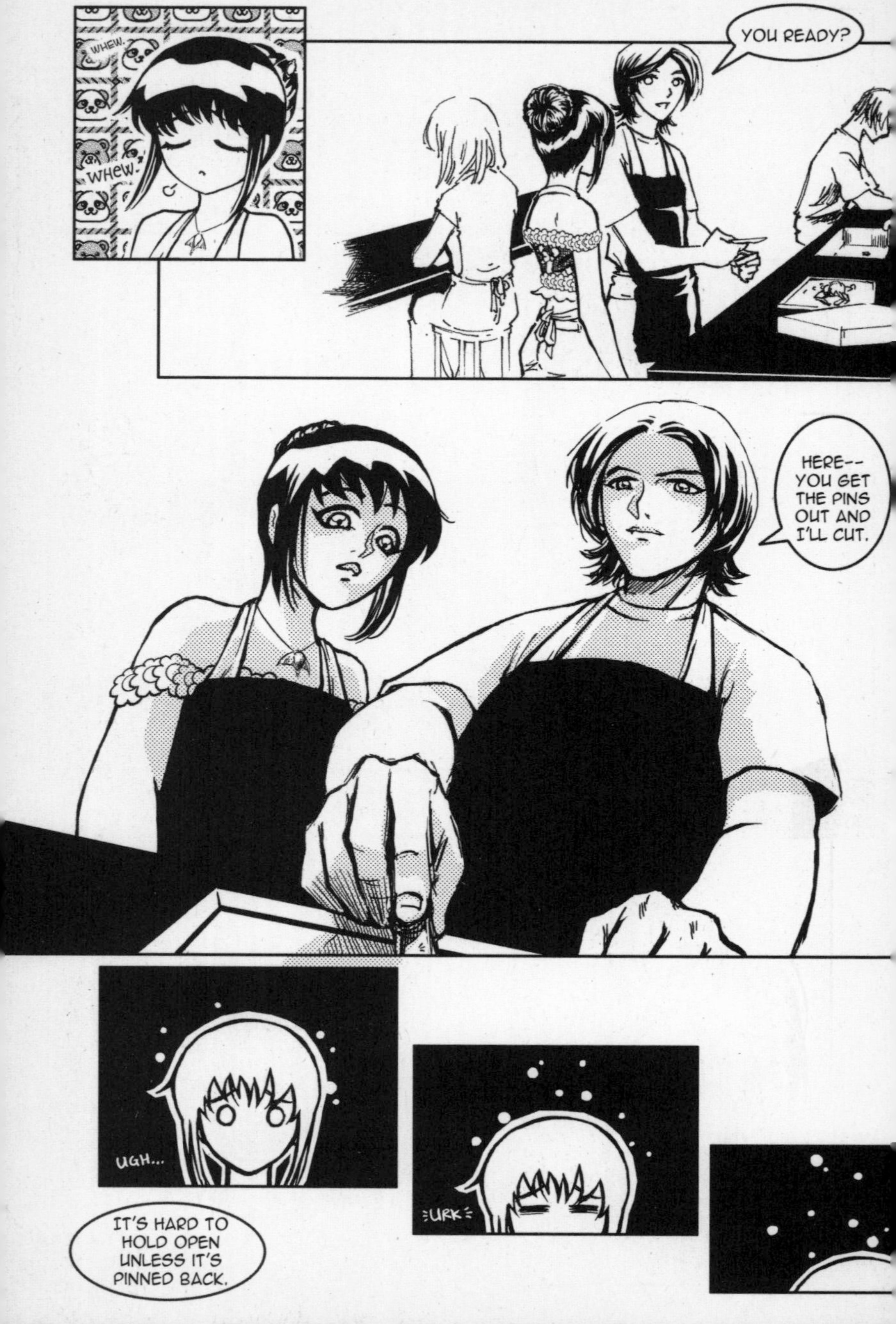
WHEW.
WHEW.
YOU READY?
HERE-- YOU GET THE PINS OUT AND I'LL CUT.
UGH...
IT'S HARD TO HOLD OPEN UNLESS IT'S PINNED BACK.
URK

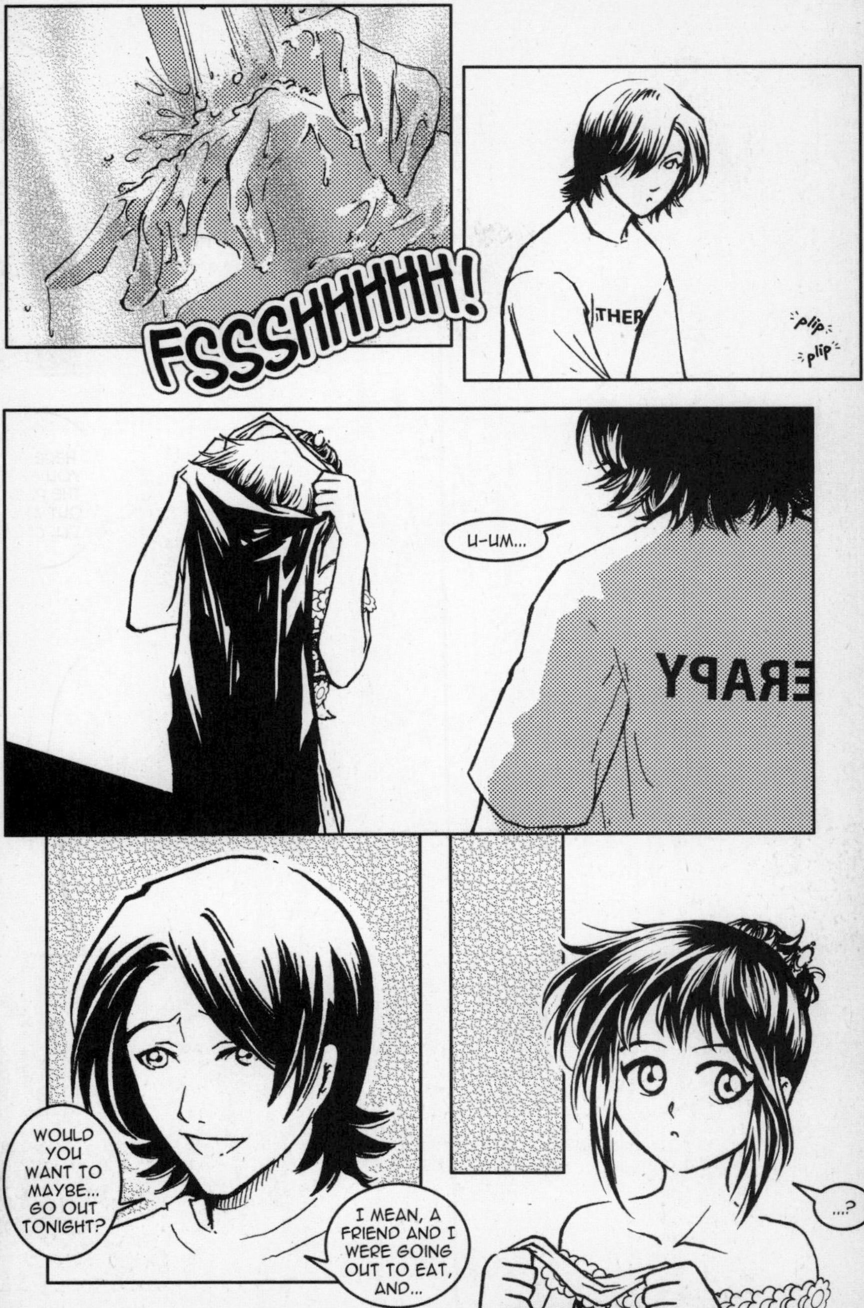
FSSSHHHHHH!
THER
plip
plip
U-UM...
WOULD YOU WANT TO MAYBE... GO OUT TONIGHT?
I MEAN, A FRIEND AND I WERE GOING OUT TO EAT, AND...
...?

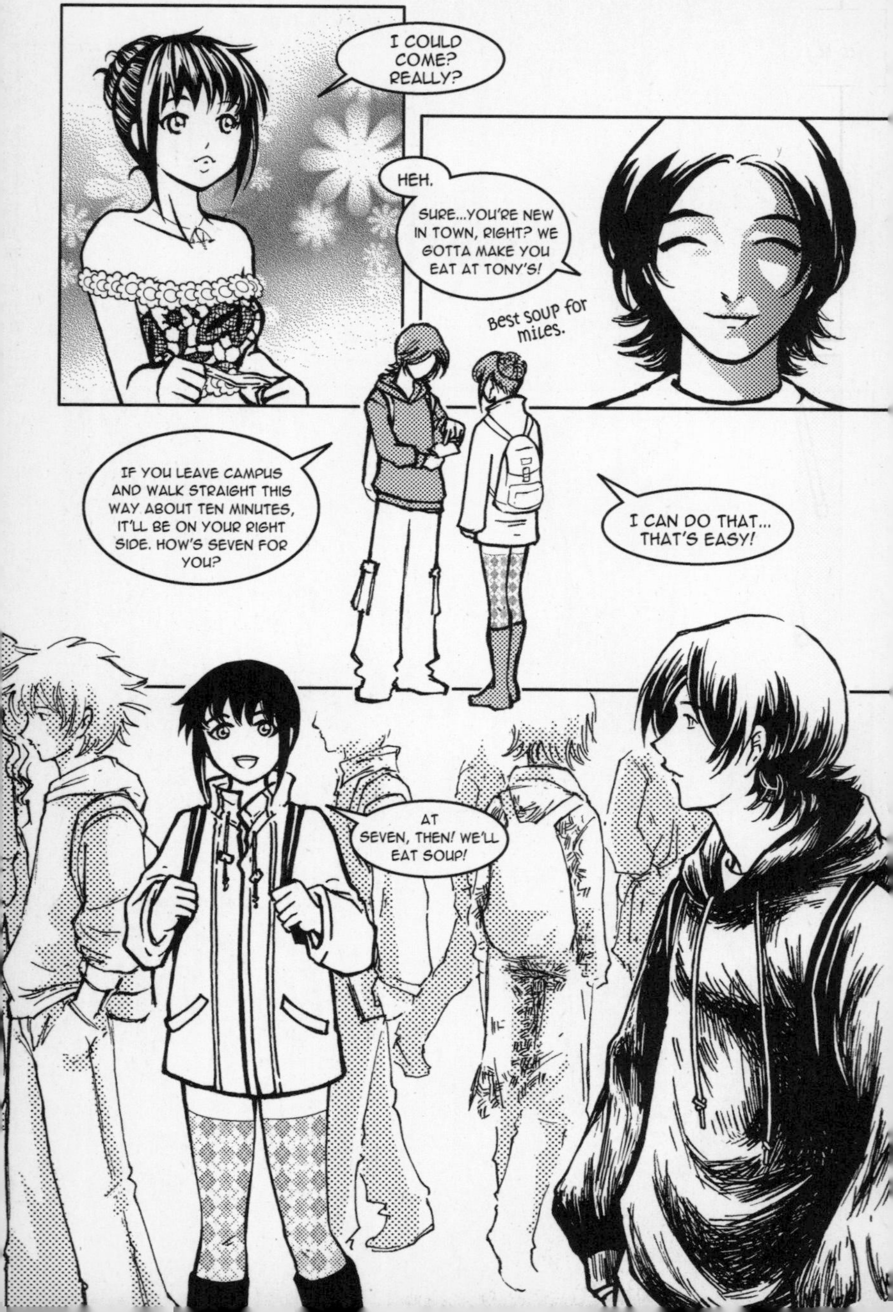
I COULD COME? REALLY?
HEH.
SURE...YOU'RE NEW IN TOWN, RIGHT? WE GOTTA MAKE YOU EAT AT TONY'S!
Best soup for miles.
IF YOU LEAVE CAMPUS AND WALK STRAIGHT THIS WAY ABOUT TEN MINUTES, IT'LL BE ON YOUR RIGHT SIDE. HOW'S SEVEN FOR YOU?
I CAN DO THAT... THAT'S EASY!
AT SEVEN, THEN! WE'LL EAT SOUP!

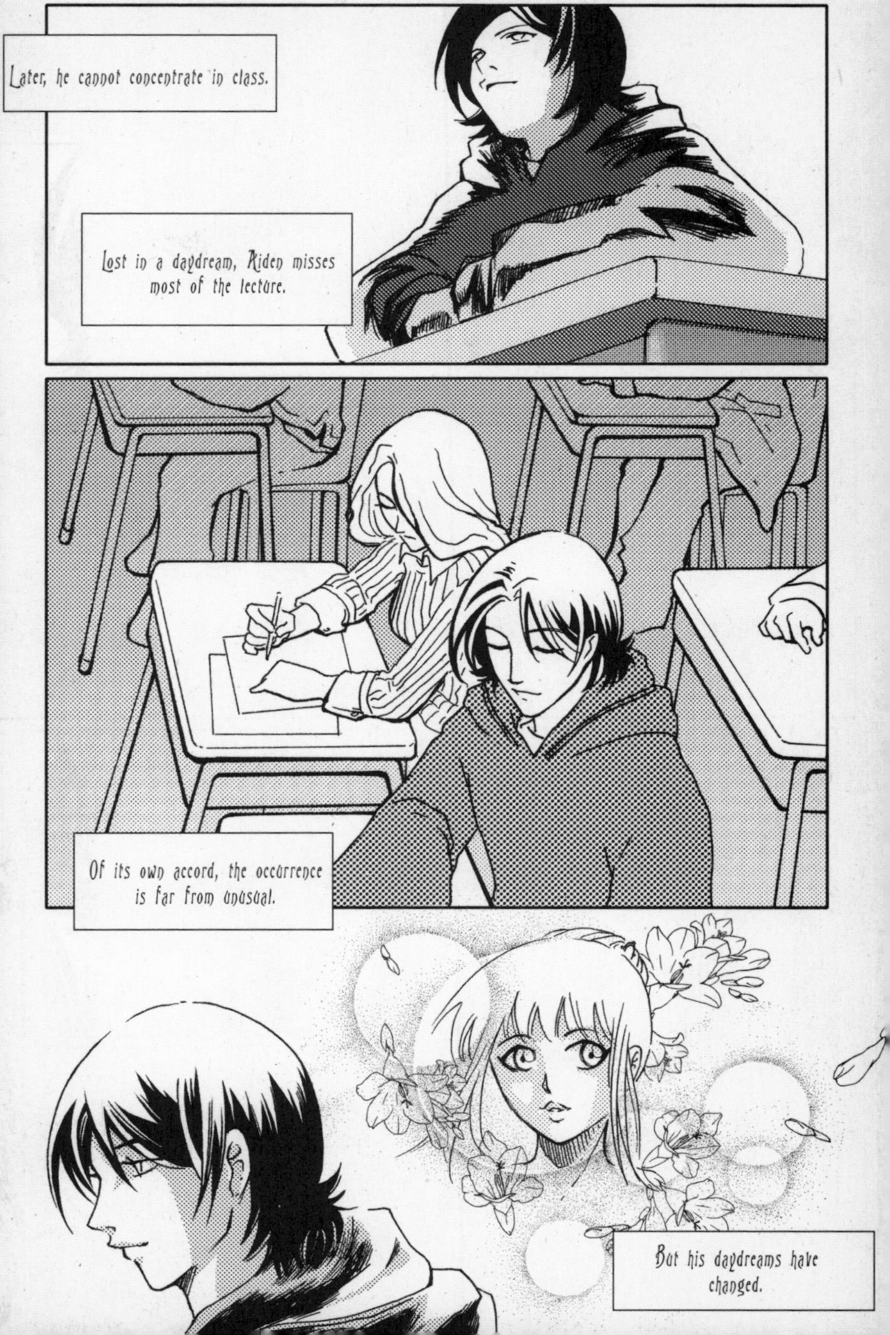
Later, he cannot concentrate in class.
Lost in a daydream, Aiden misses most of the lecture.
Of its own accord, the occurrence is far from unusual.
But his daydreams have changed.

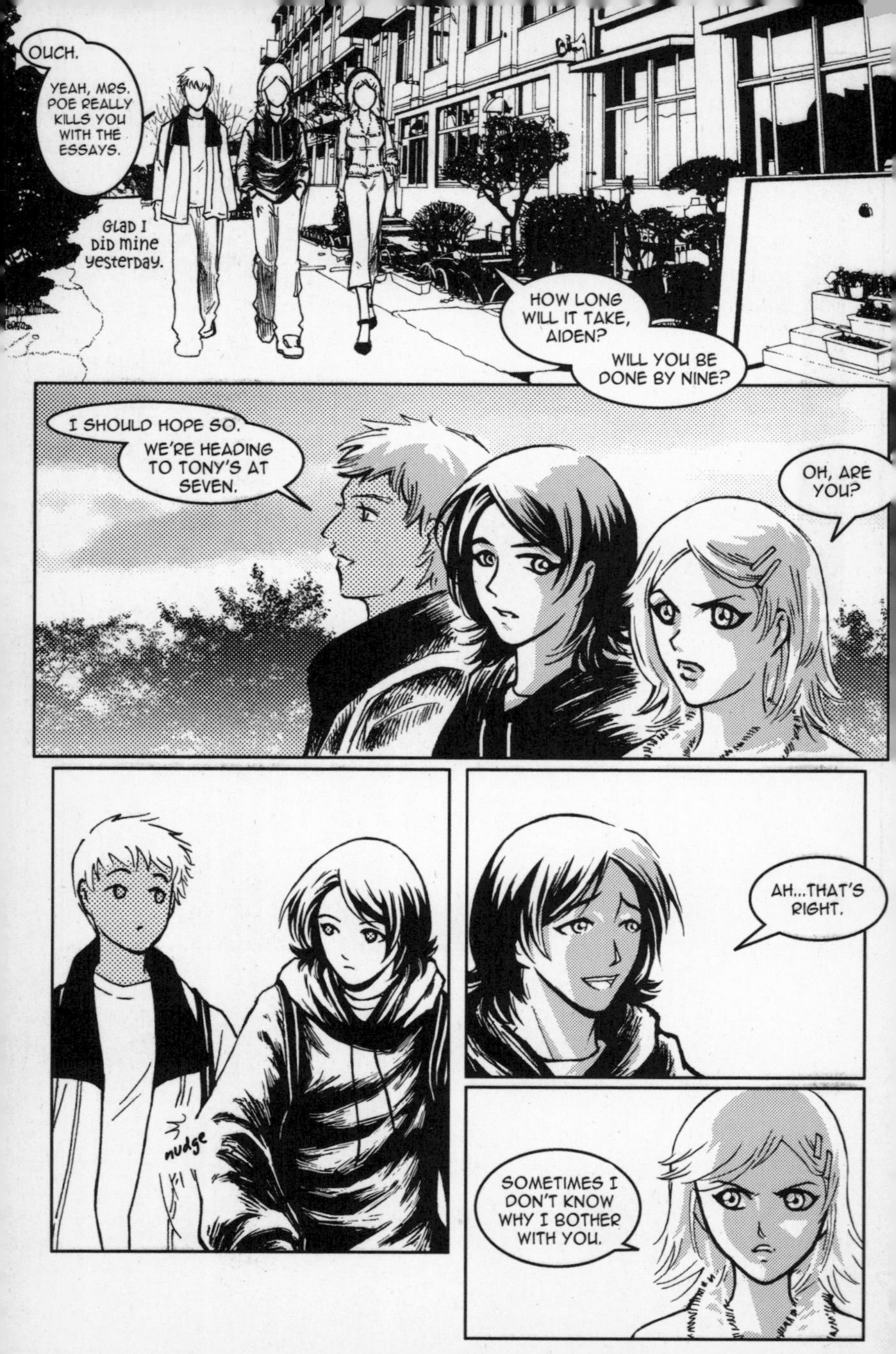
OUCH.
YEAH, MRS. POE REALLY KILLS YOU WITH THE ESSAYS.
GLAD I DID MINE YESTERDAY.
HOW LONG WILL IT TAKE, AIDEN?
WILL YOU BE DONE BY NINE?
I SHOULD HOPE SO.
WE'RE HEADING TO TONY'S AT SEVEN.
OH, ARE YOU?
nudge
AH...THAT'S RIGHT.
SOMETIMES I DON'T KNOW WHY I BOTHER WITH YOU.

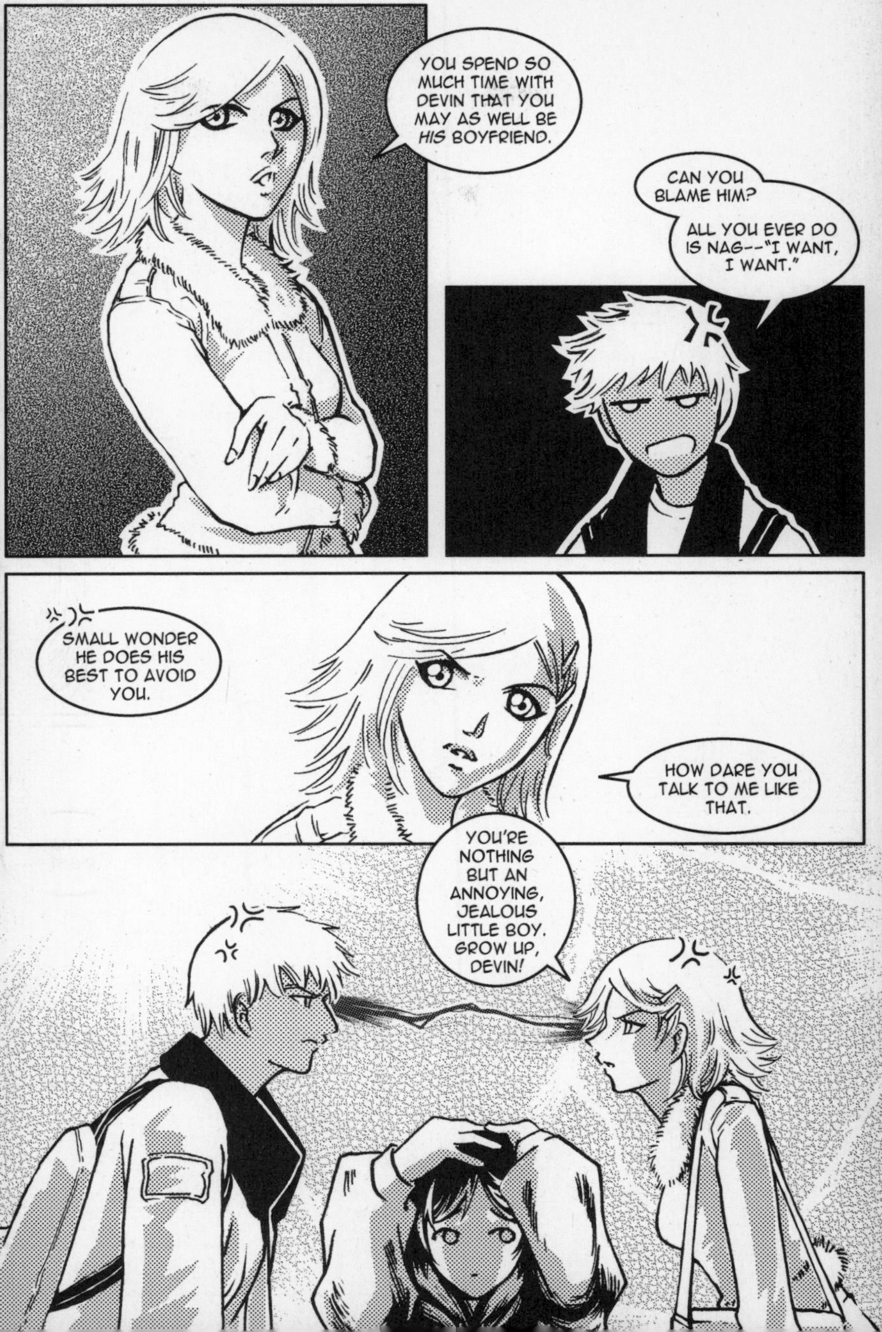
YOU SPEND SO MUCH TIME WITH DEVIN THAT YOU MAY AS WELL BE *HIS* BOYFRIEND.
CAN YOU BLAME HIM?
ALL YOU EVER DO IS NAG--"I WANT, I WANT."
SMALL WONDER HE DOES HIS BEST TO AVOID YOU.
HOW DARE YOU TALK TO ME LIKE THAT.
YOU'RE NOTHING BUT AN ANNOYING, JEALOUS LITTLE BOY. GROW UP, DEVIN!

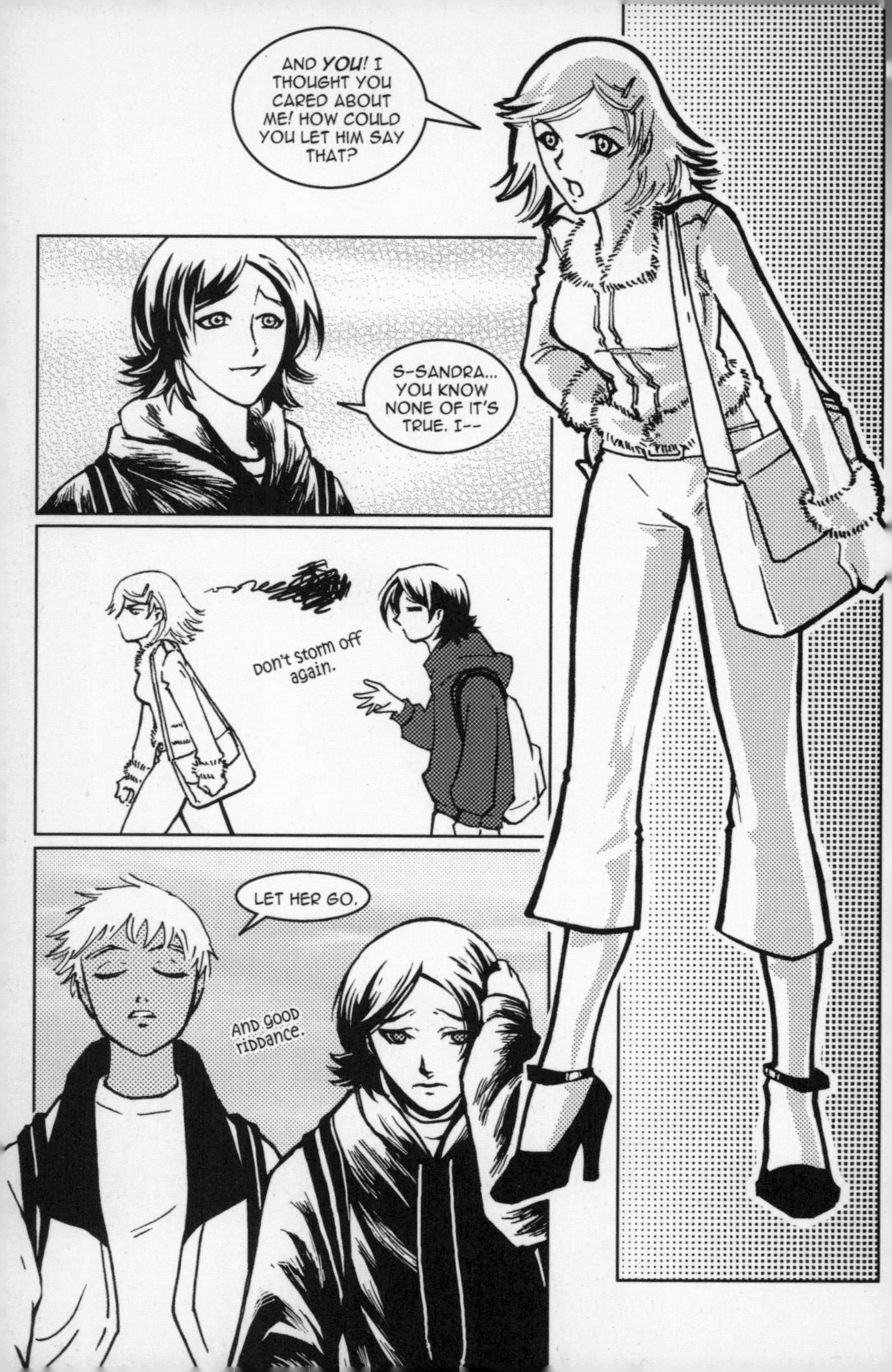
AND YOU! I THOUGHT YOU CARED ABOUT ME! HOW COULD YOU LET HIM SAY THAT?
S-SANDRA... YOU KNOW NONE OF IT'S TRUE. I--
Don't storm off again.
LET HER GO.
AND GOOD riddance.

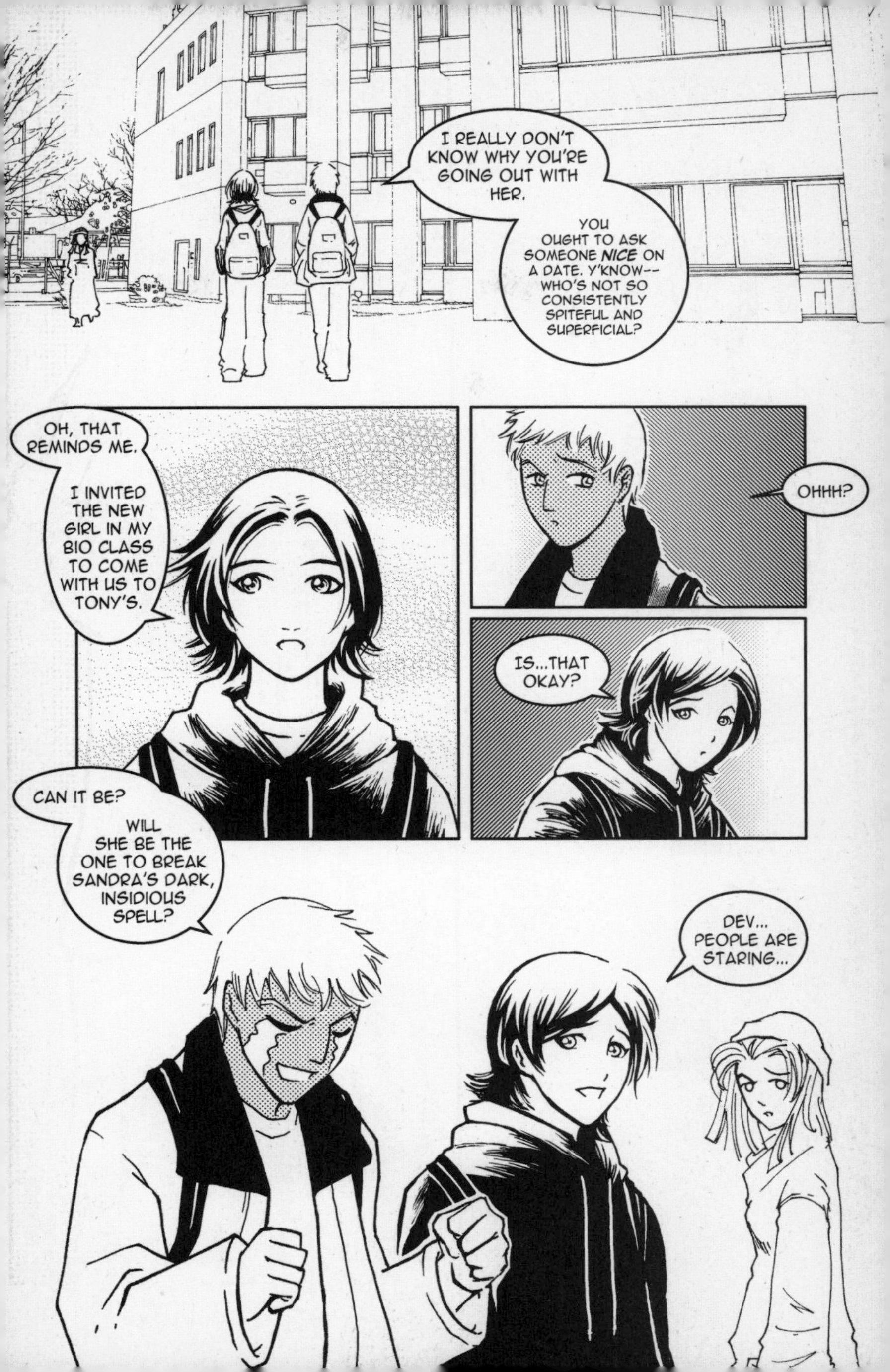
I REALLY DON'T KNOW WHY YOU'RE GOING OUT WITH HER.
YOU OUGHT TO ASK SOMEONE *NICE* ON A DATE. Y'KNOW-- WHO'S NOT SO CONSISTENTLY SPITEFUL AND SUPERFICIAL?
OH, THAT REMINDS ME.
I INVITED THE NEW GIRL IN MY BIO CLASS TO COME WITH US TO TONY'S.
OHHH?
IS...THAT OKAY?
CAN IT BE?
WILL SHE BE THE ONE TO BREAK SANDRA'S DARK, INSIDIOUS SPELL?
DEV... PEOPLE ARE STARING...

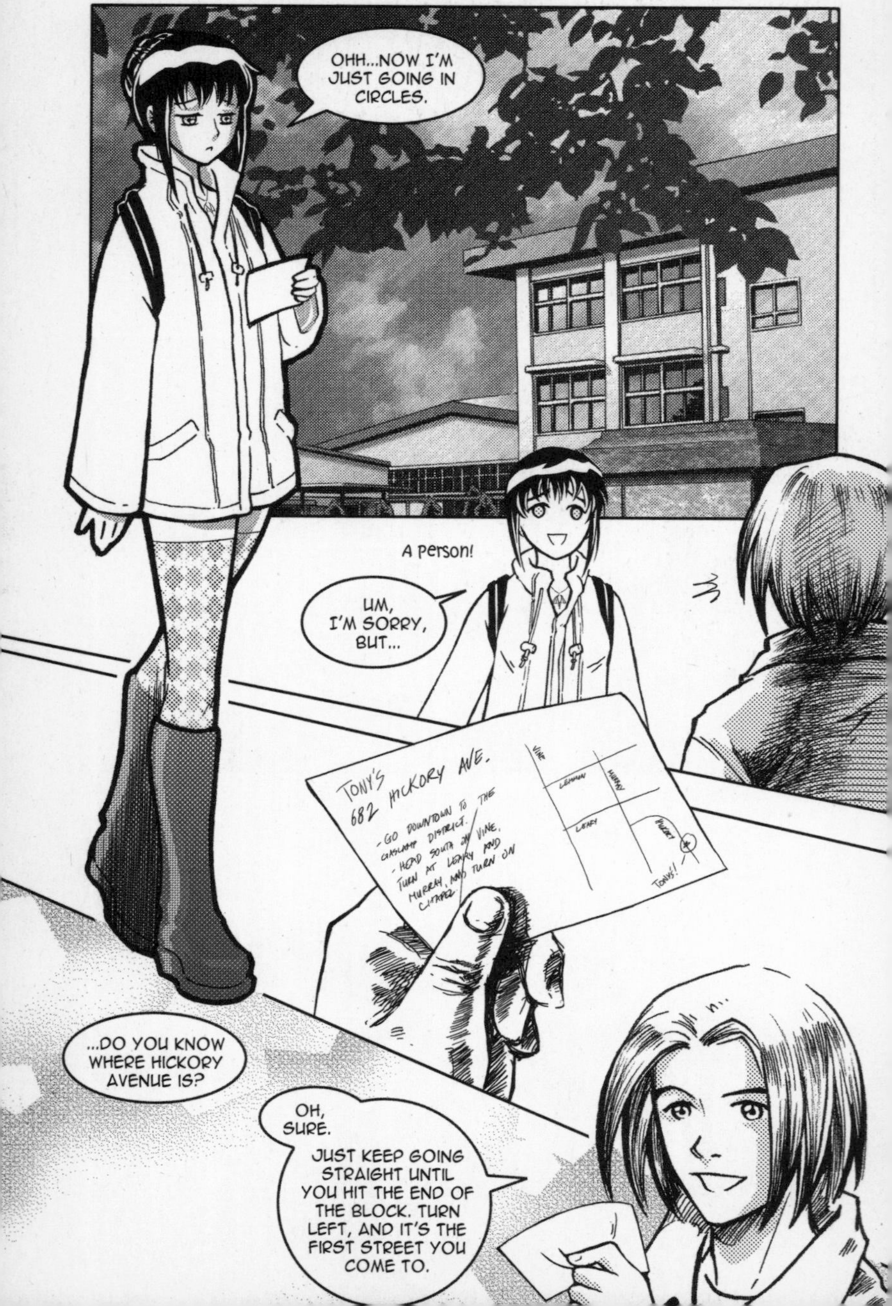
OHH...NOW I'M JUST GOING IN CIRCLES.
A person!
UM, I'M SORRY, BUT...
TONY'S
682 HICKORY AVE.
-GO DOWNTOWN TO THE GASLAMP DISTRICT.
-HEAD SOUTH ON VINE. TURN AT LEARY AND MURRAY, AND TURN ON CITADEL
VINE
LEMMON
MURRAY
LEARY
HICKORY
TONY'S!
...DO YOU KNOW WHERE HICKORY AVENUE IS?
n..
OH, SURE.
JUST KEEP GOING STRAIGHT UNTIL YOU HIT THE END OF THE BLOCK. TURN LEFT, AND IT'S THE FIRST STREET YOU COME TO.

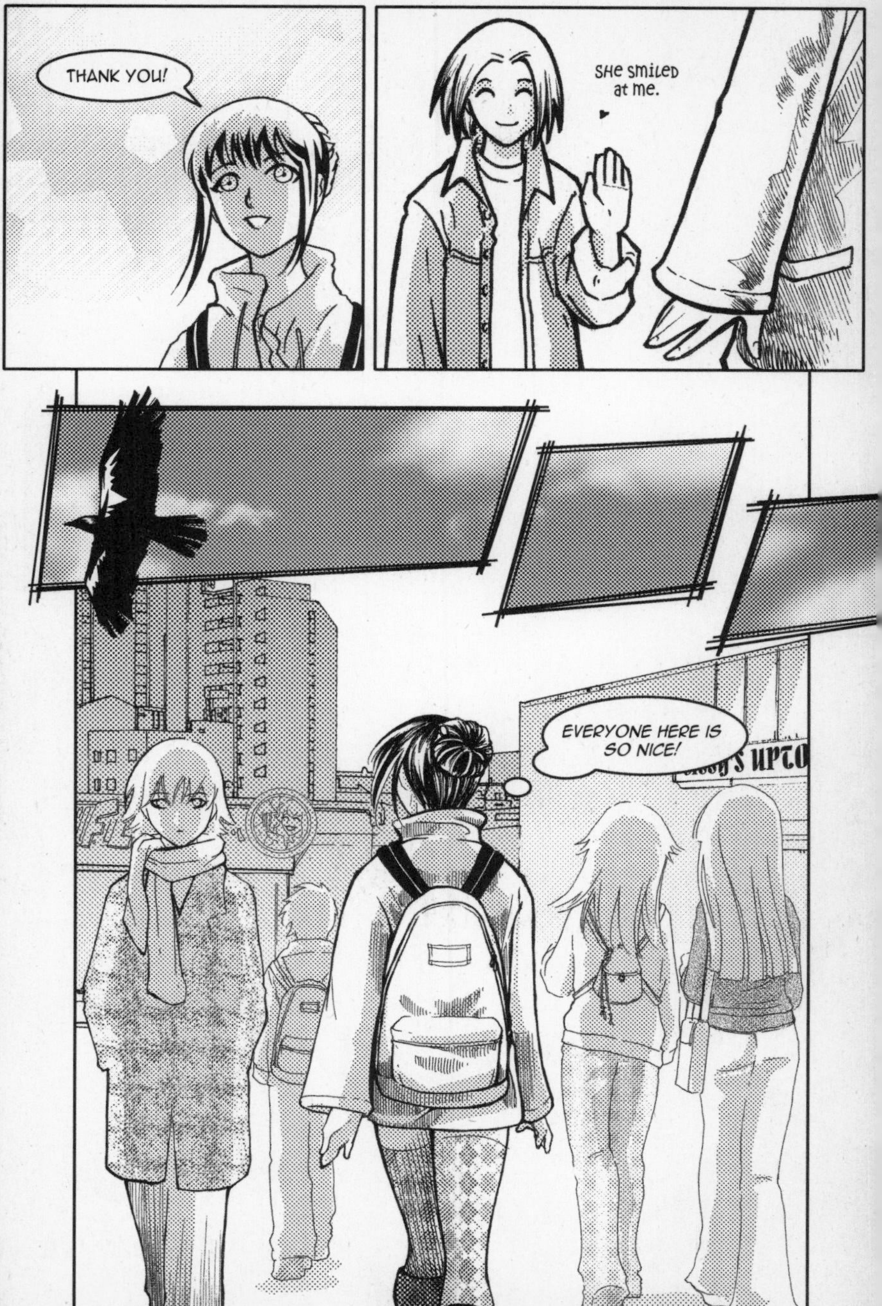
THANK YOU!
SHE SMILED at me.
EVERYONE HERE IS SO NICE!

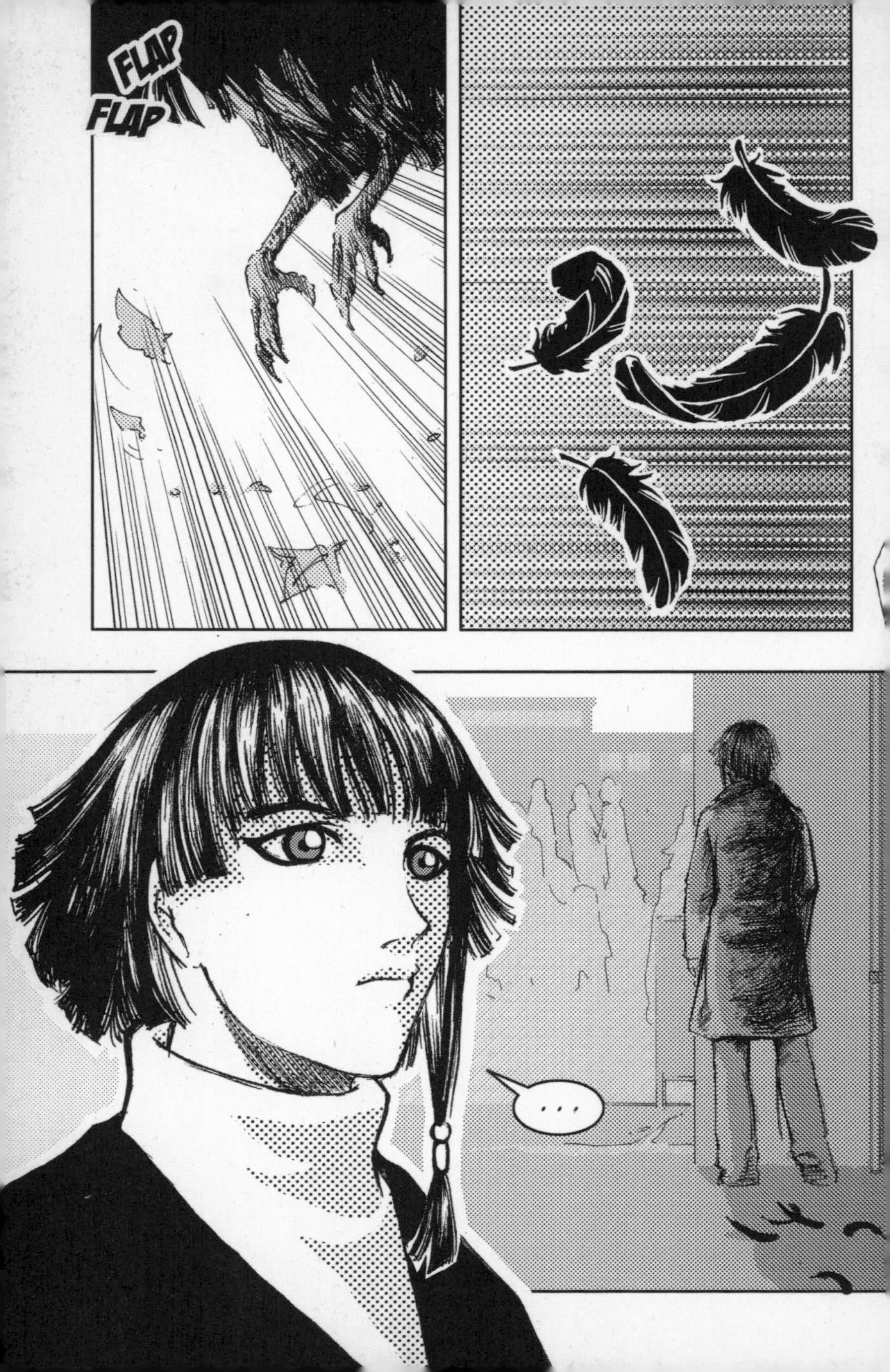
FLAP
FLAP
...

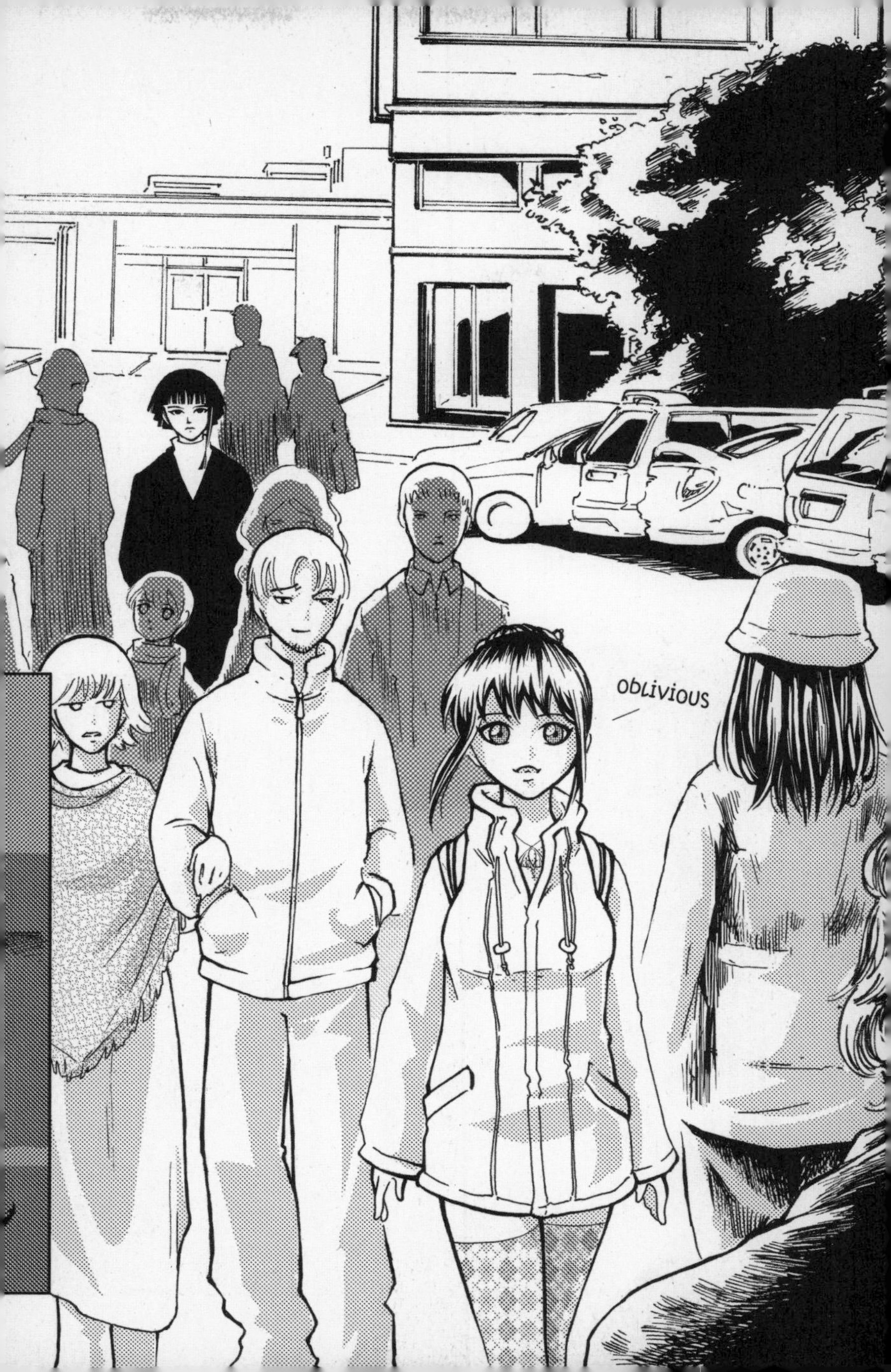
OBLIVIOUS

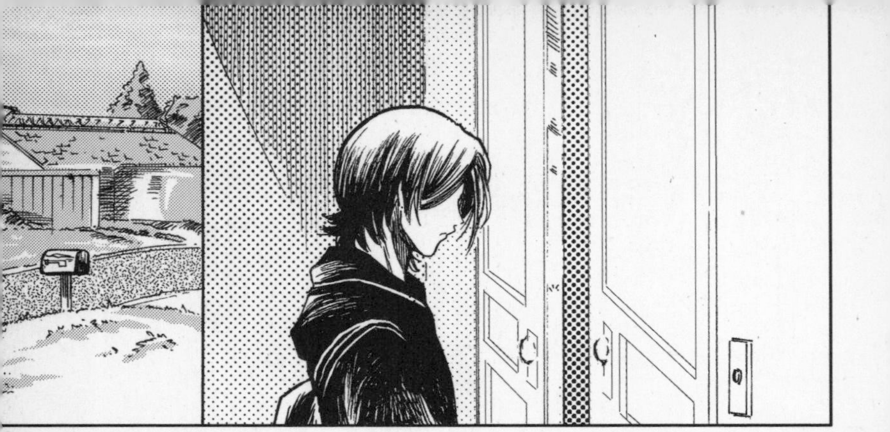

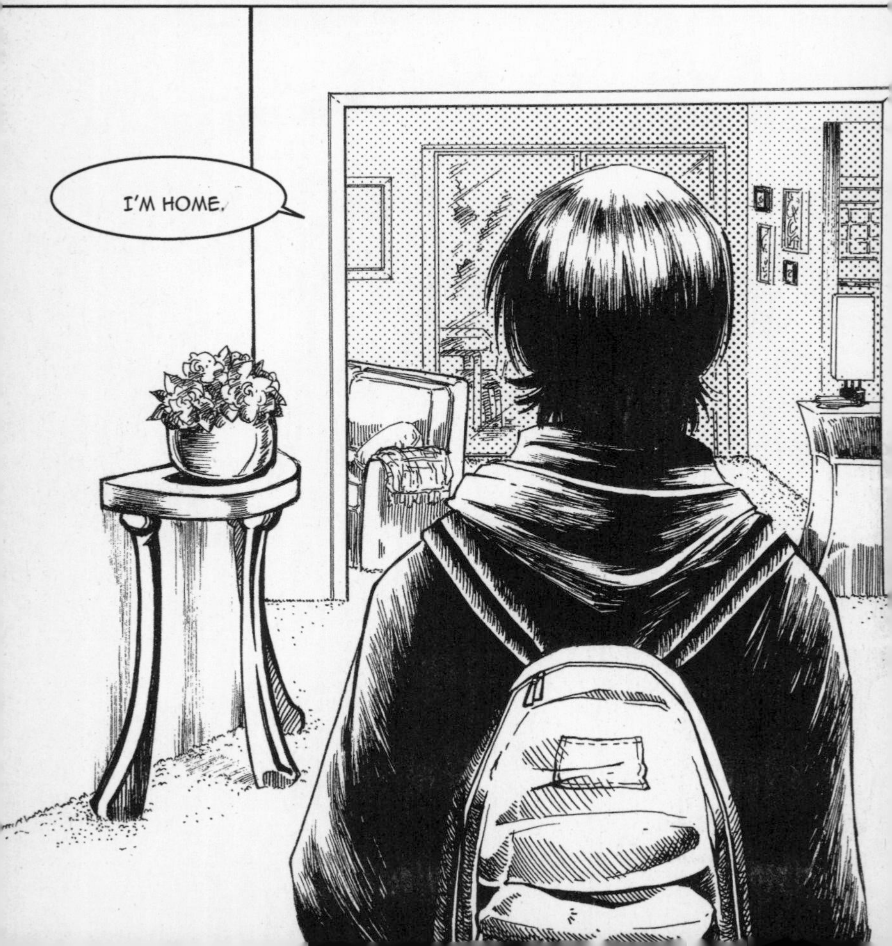
I'M HOME.

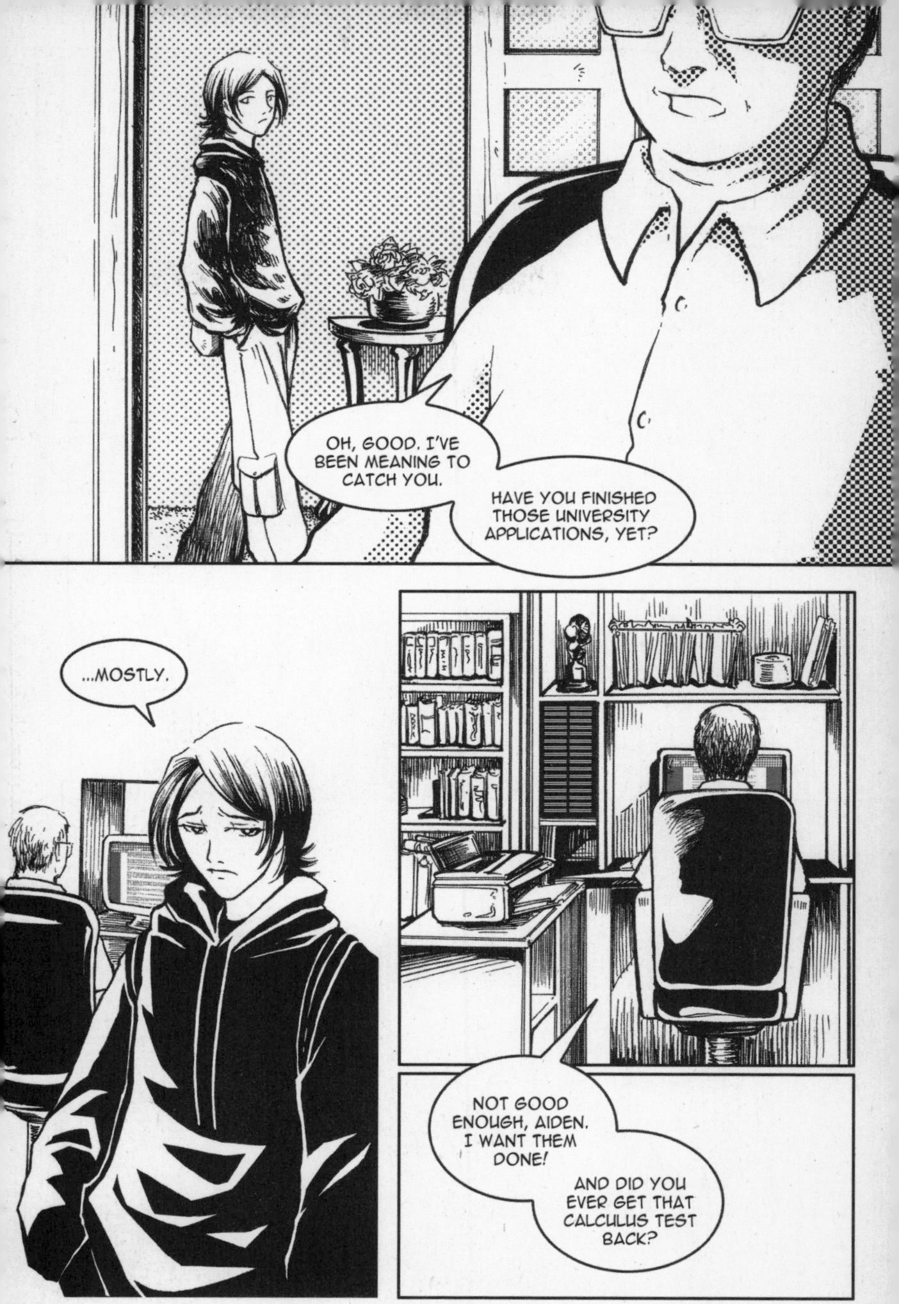
OH, GOOD. I'VE BEEN MEANING TO CATCH YOU.
HAVE YOU FINISHED THOSE UNIVERSITY APPLICATIONS, YET?
...MOSTLY.
NOT GOOD ENOUGH, AIDEN. I WANT THEM DONE!
AND DID YOU EVER GET THAT CALCULUS TEST BACK?

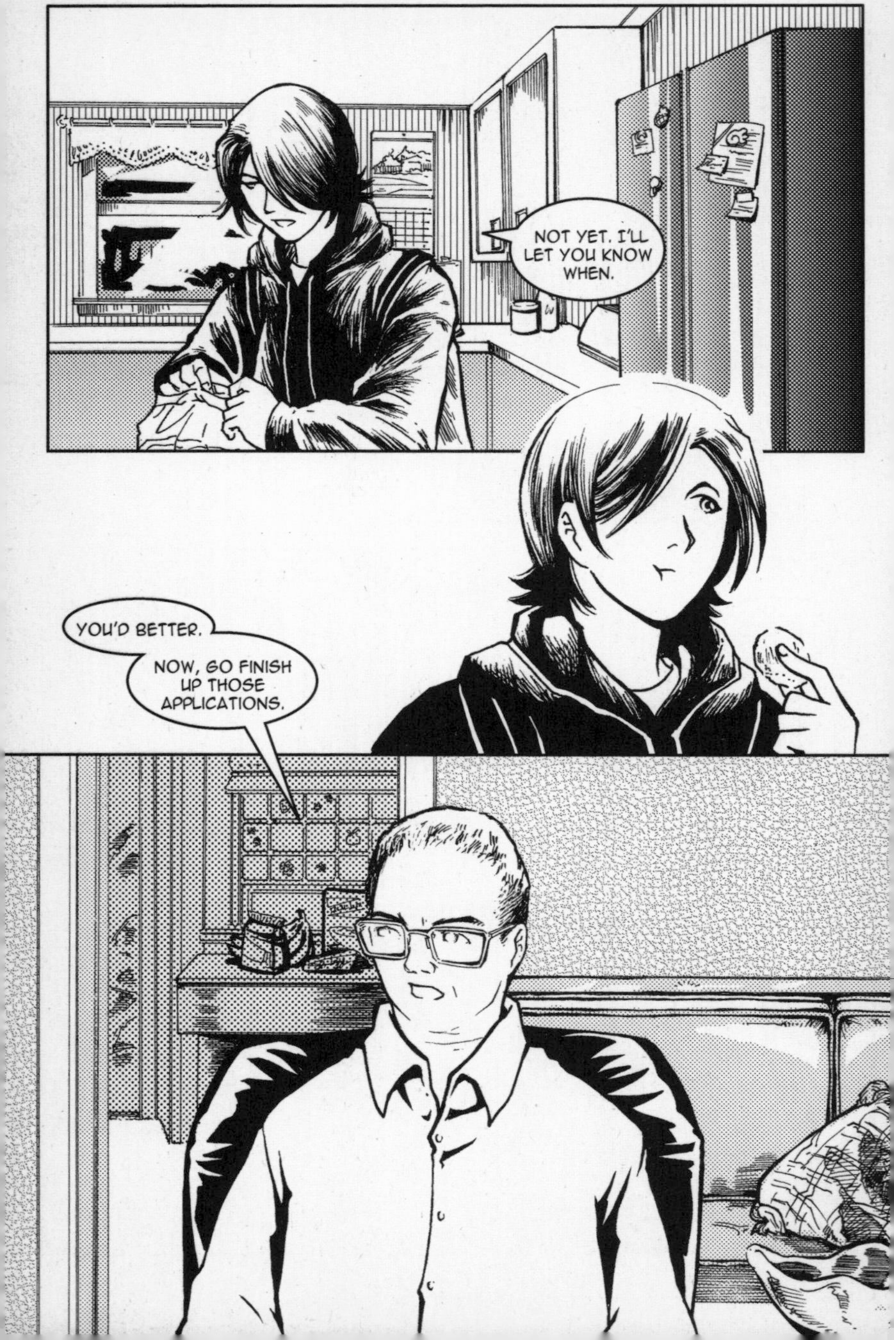
NOT YET. I'LL LET YOU KNOW WHEN.
YOU'D BETTER.
NOW, GO FINISH UP THOSE APPLICATIONS.

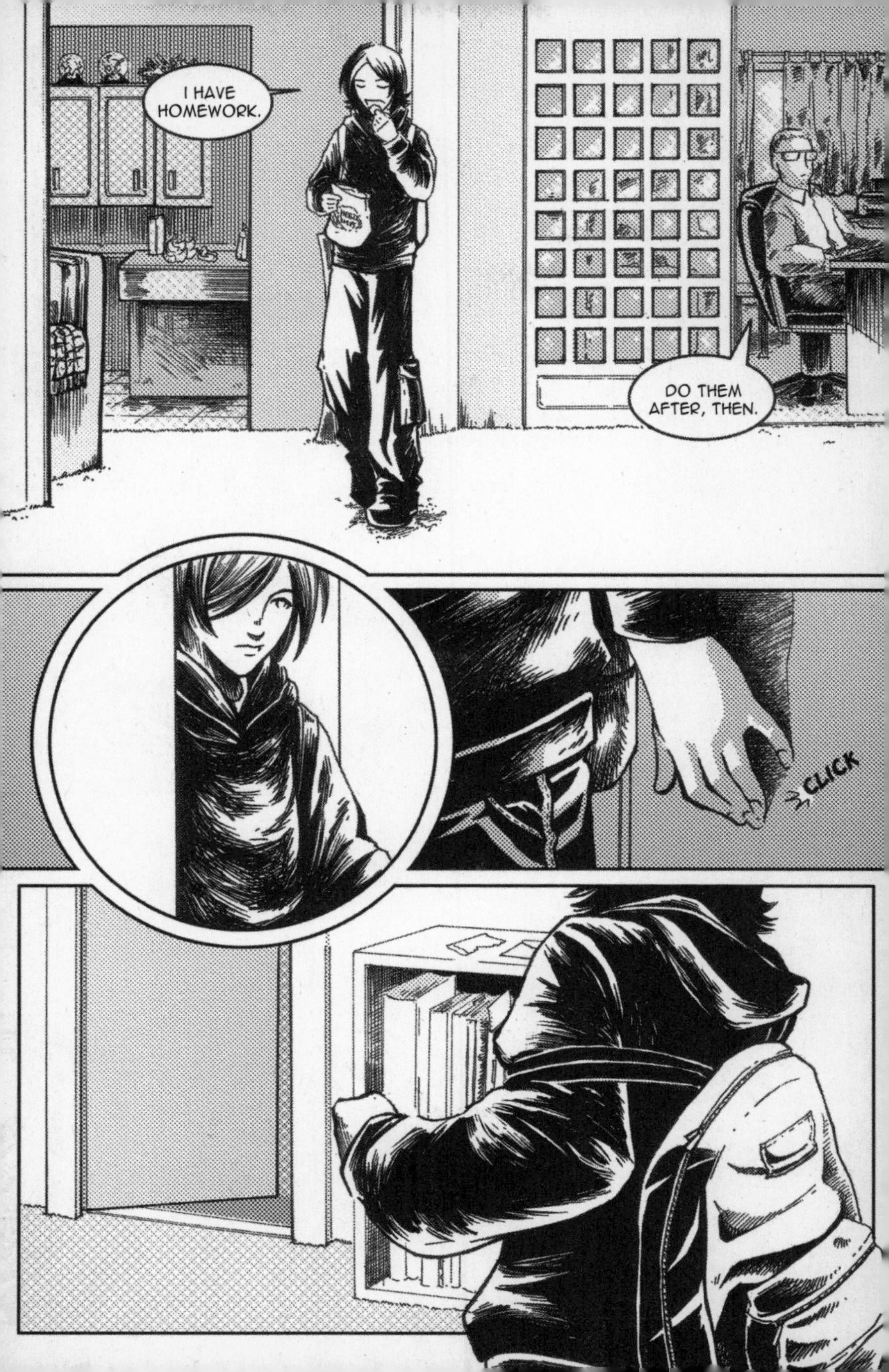
I HAVE HOMEWORK.
DO THEM AFTER, THEN.
CLICK

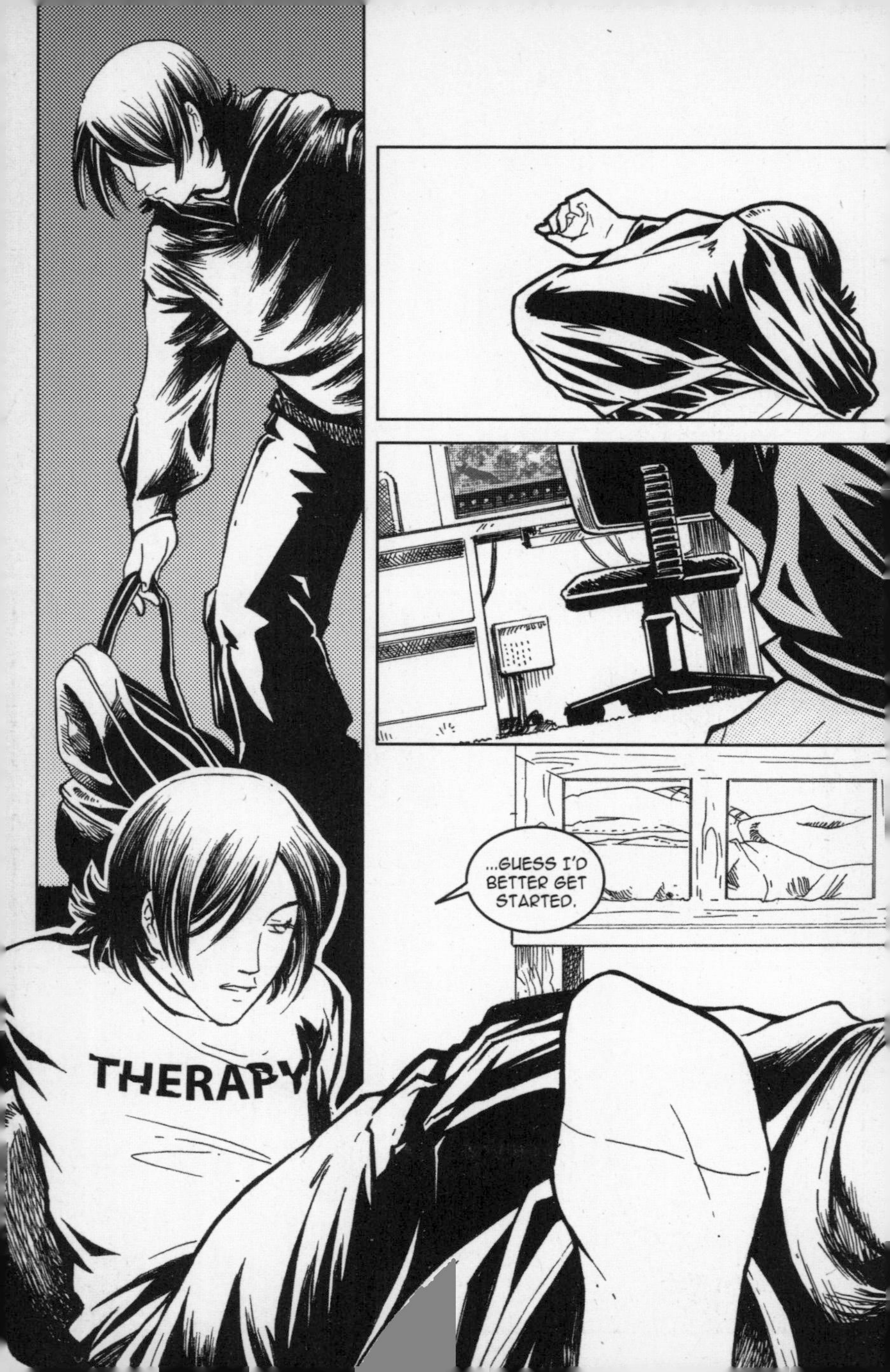
THERAPY
...GUESS I'D BETTER GET STARTED.

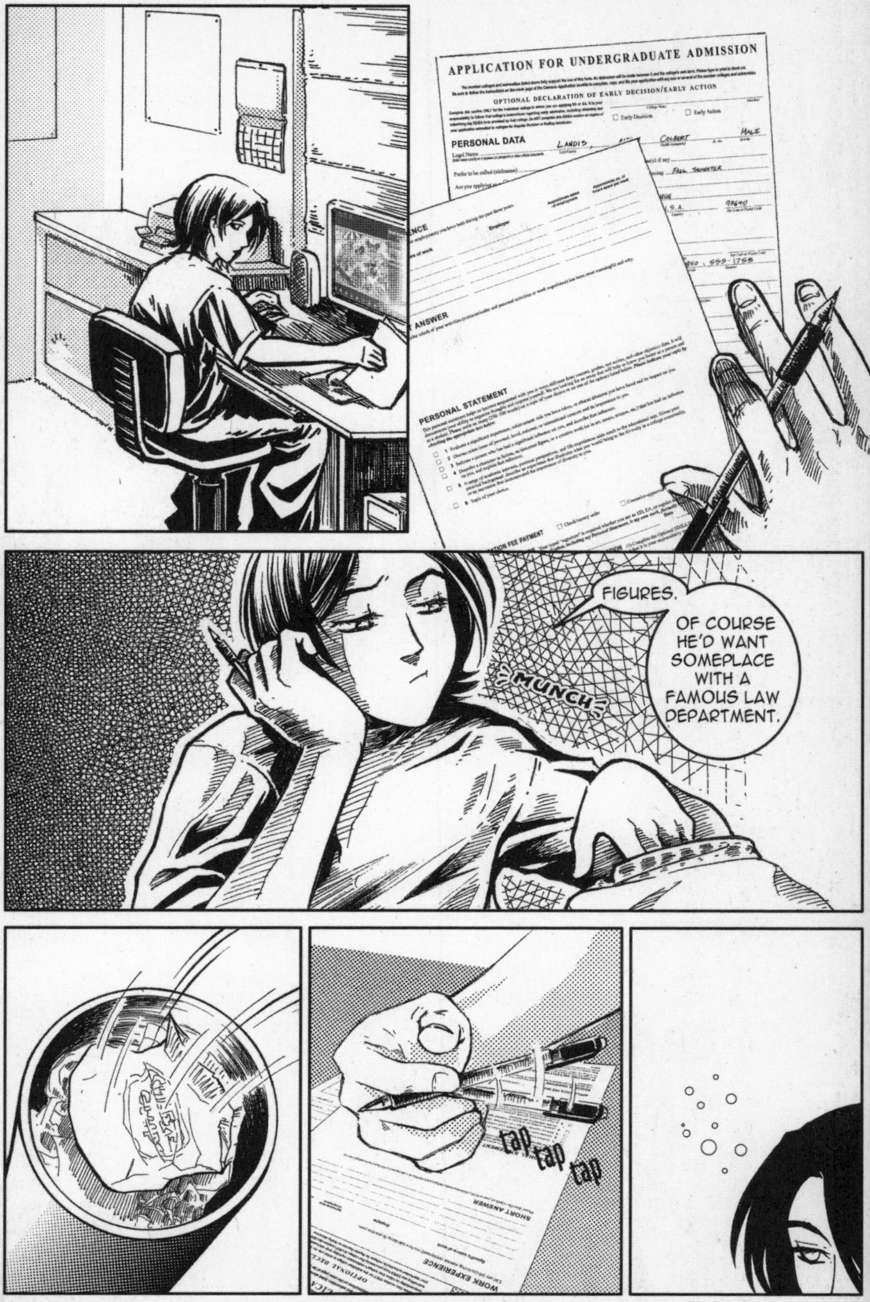
APPLICATION FOR UNDERGRADUATE ADMISSION
OPTIONAL DECLARATION OF EARLY DECISION/EARLY ACTION
Early Decision
Early Action
PERSONAL DATA
LANDIS
COLBERT
MALE
FALL SEMESTER
93640
U.S.A.
555-1755
PERSONAL STATEMENT
FIGURES.
OF COURSE HE'D WANT SOMEPLACE WITH A FAMOUS LAW DEPARTMENT.
MUNCH
tap
tap
tap
SHORT ANSWER
WORK EXPERIENCE

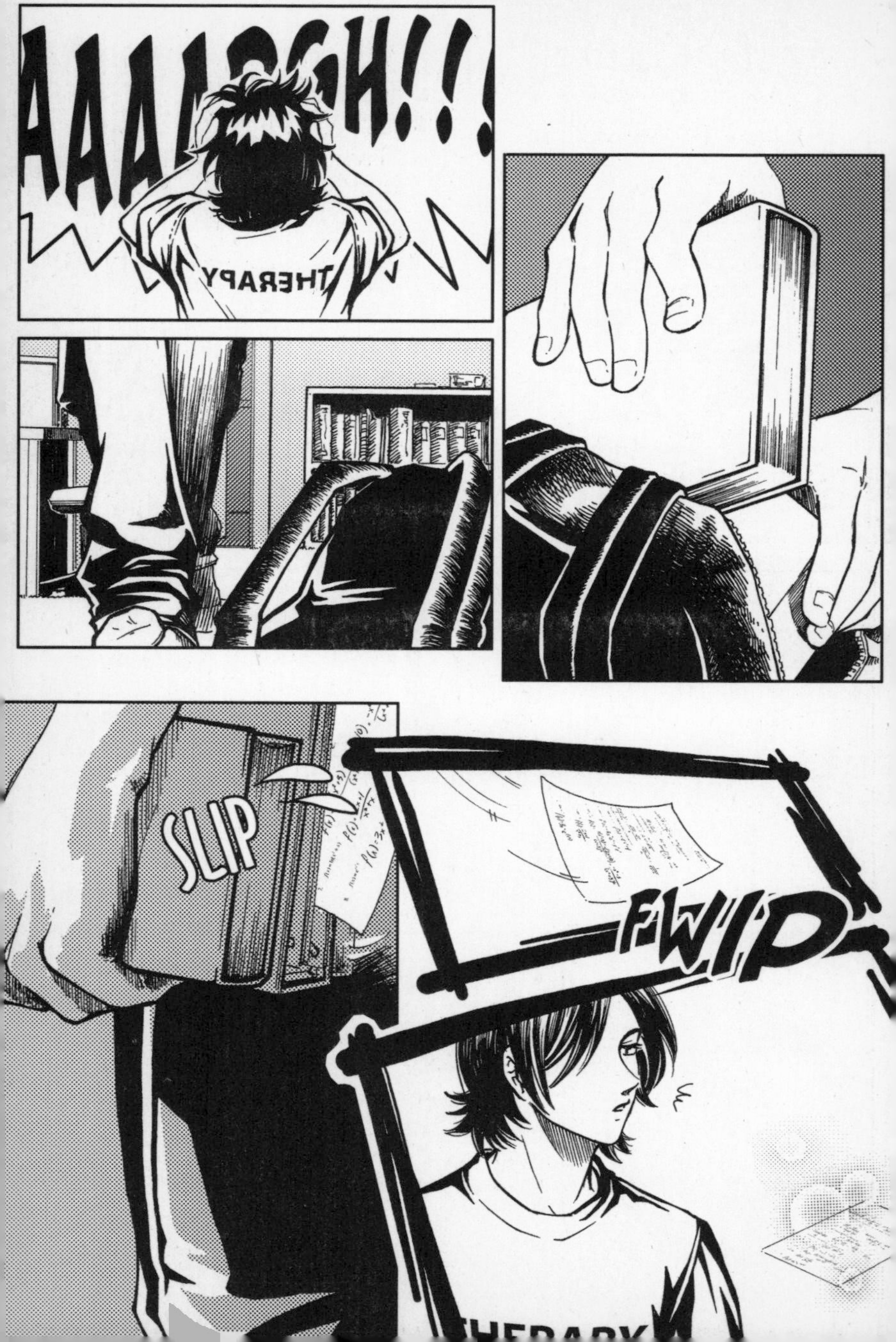
AAA GH!!
THERAPY
SLIP
FWIP

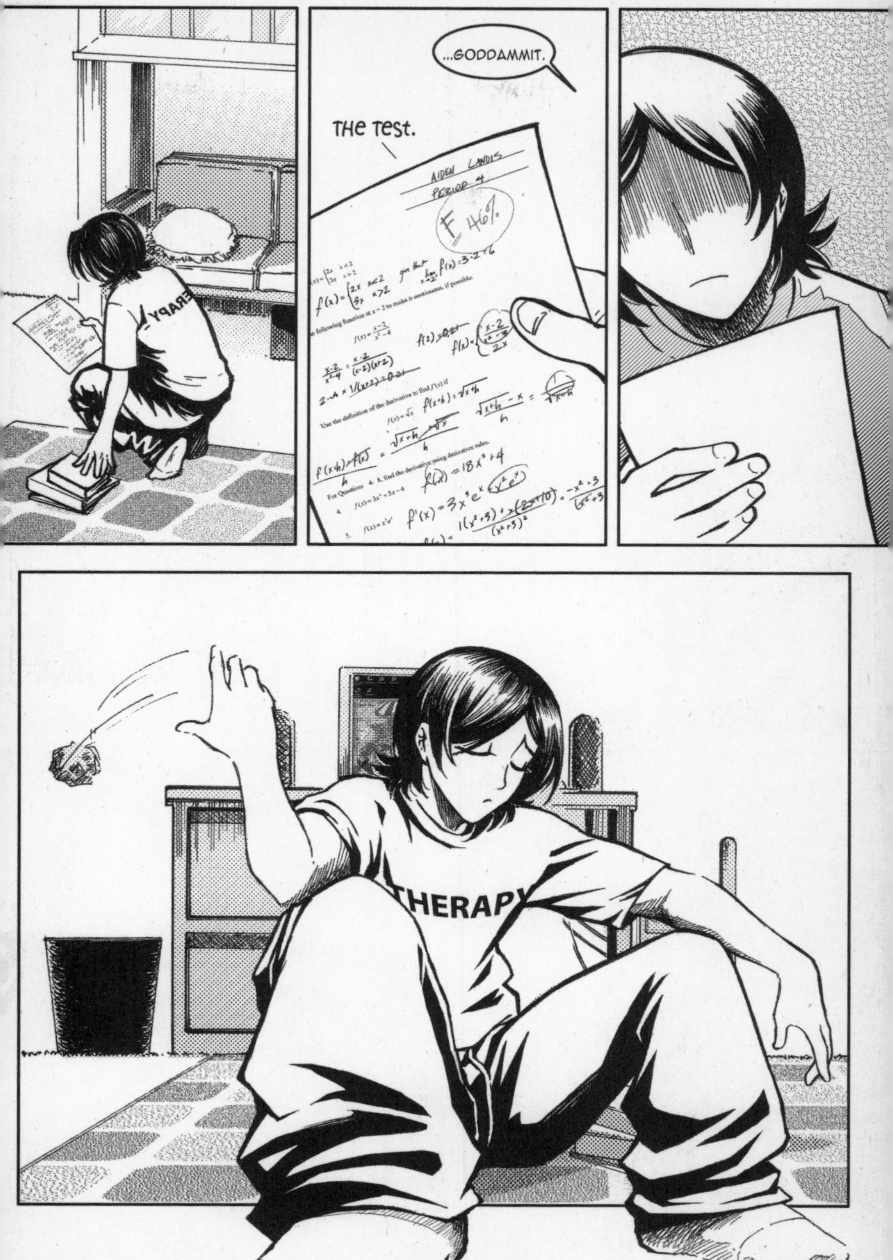

ERAPY
...GODDAMMIT.
THE TEST.
AIDEN LANDIS
PERIOD 4
F 46%
THERAPY

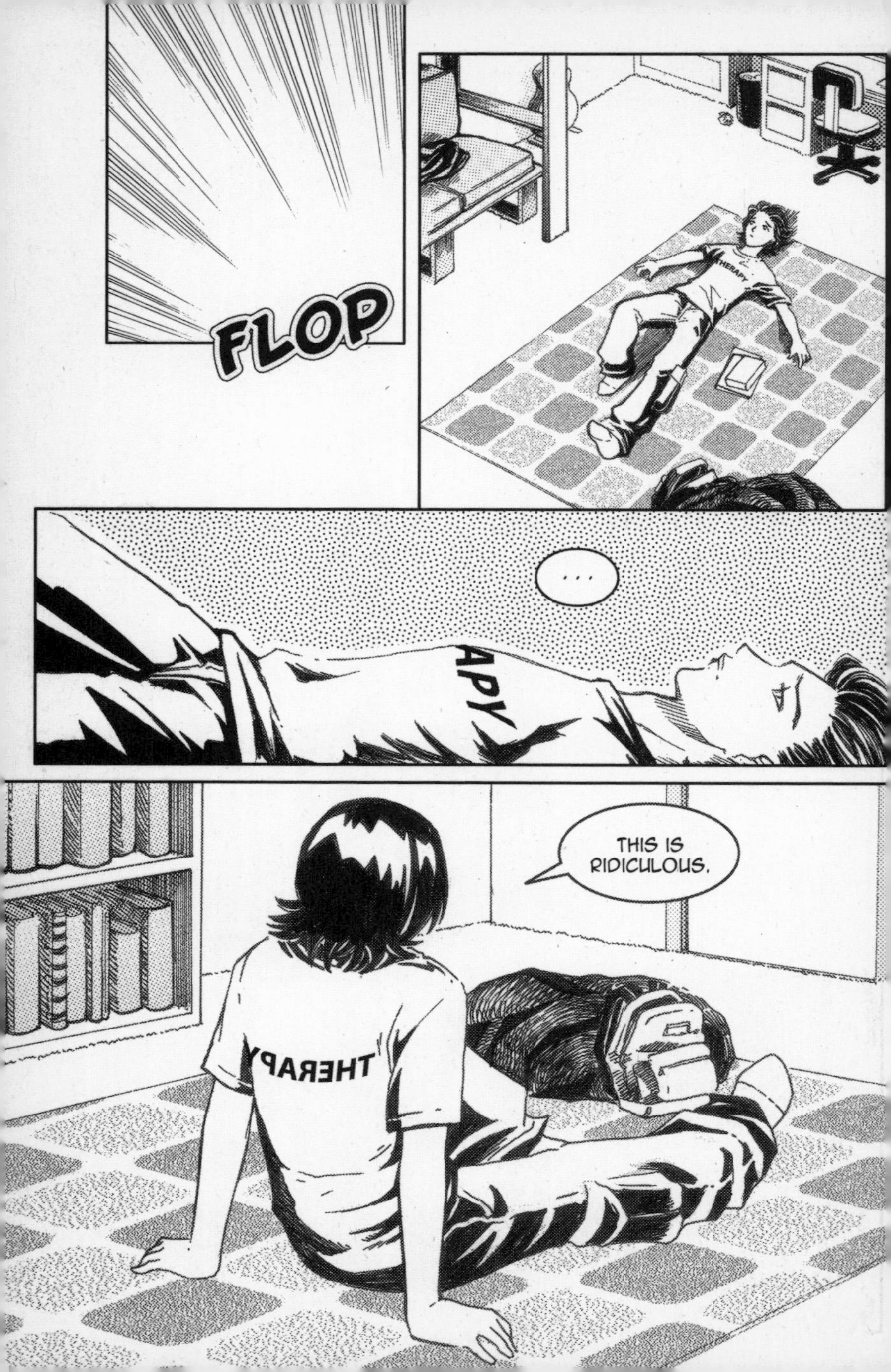
FLOP
. . .
THIS IS RIDICULOUS.

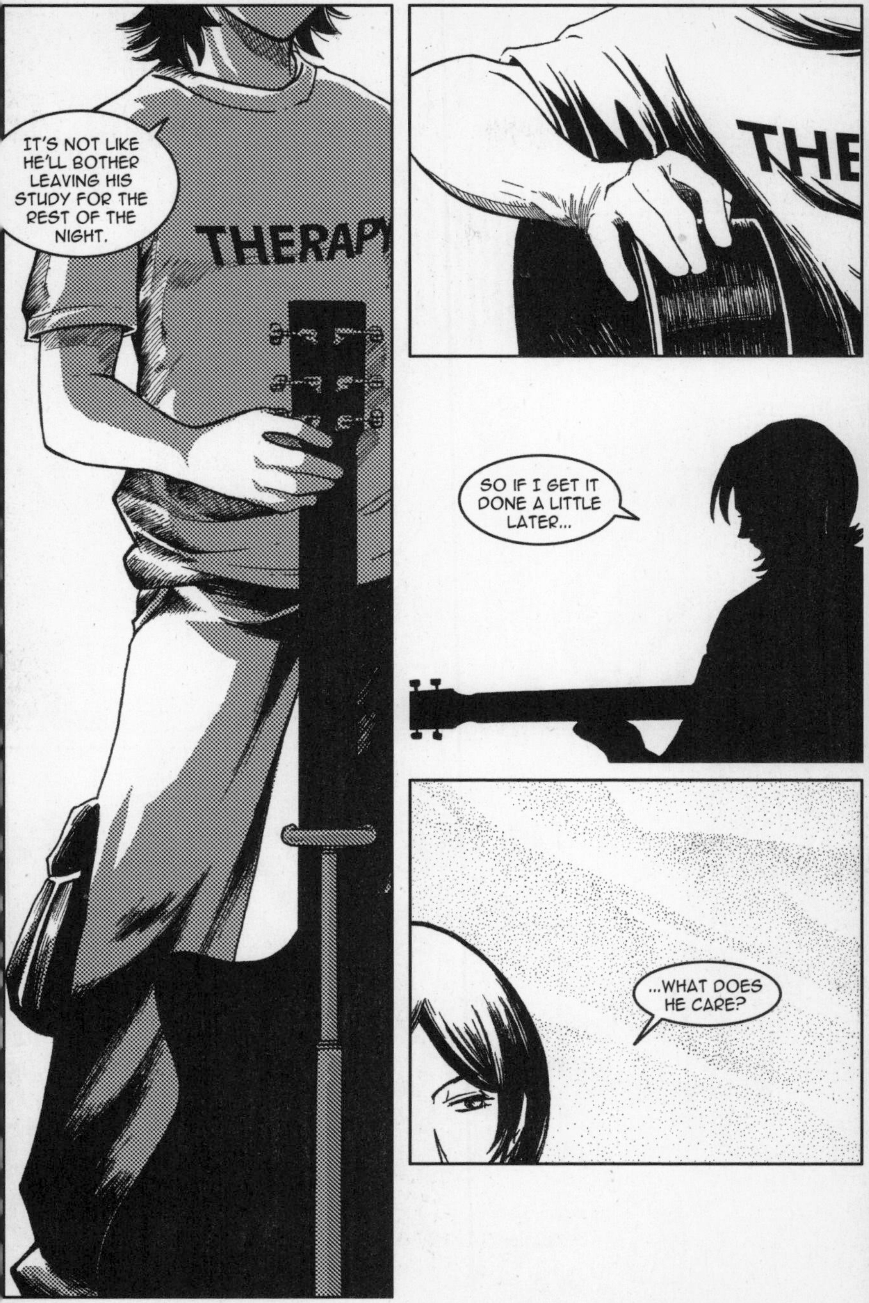
IT'S NOT LIKE HE'LL BOTHER LEAVING HIS STUDY FOR THE REST OF THE NIGHT.
THERAPY
THE
SO IF I GET IT DONE A LITTLE LATER...
...WHAT DOES HE CARE?

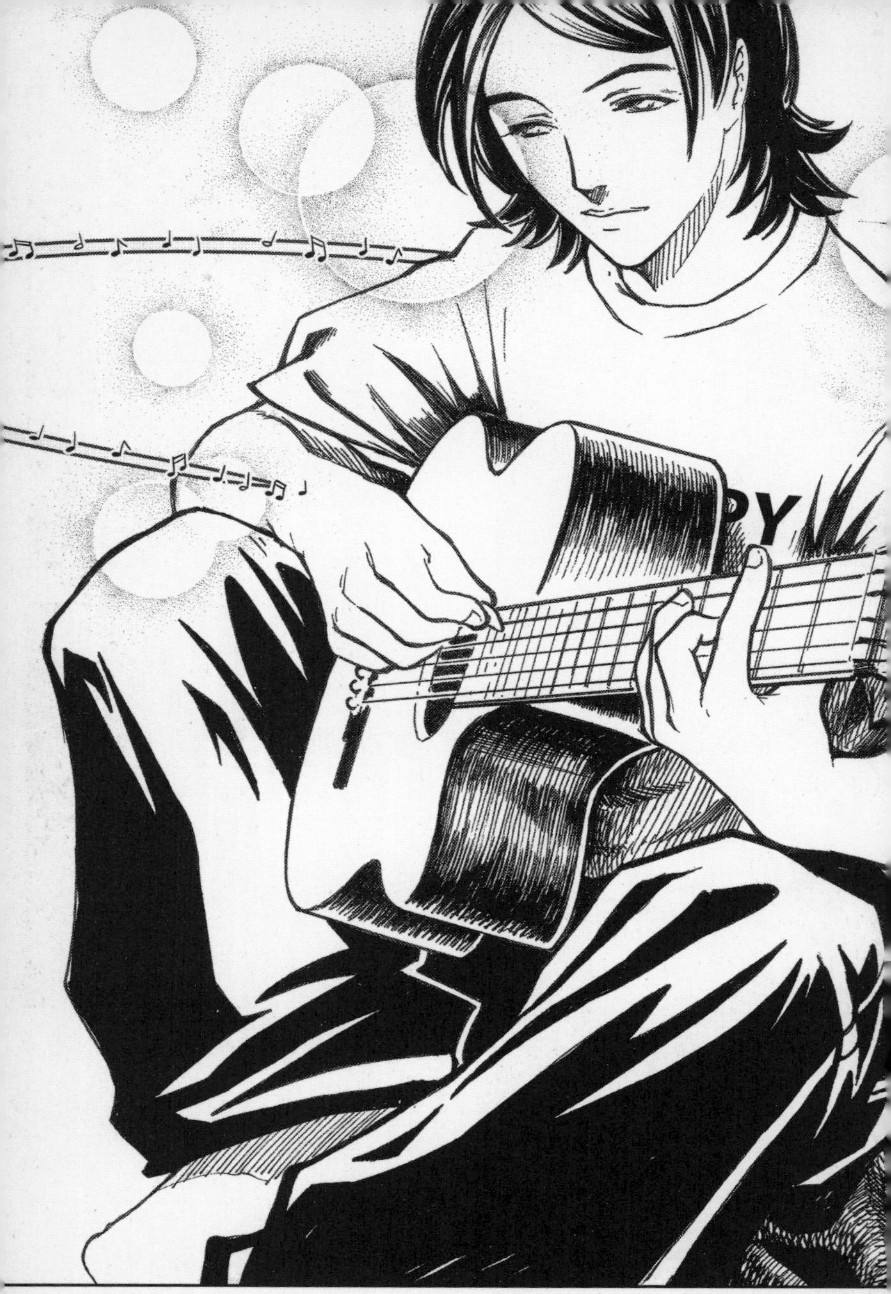

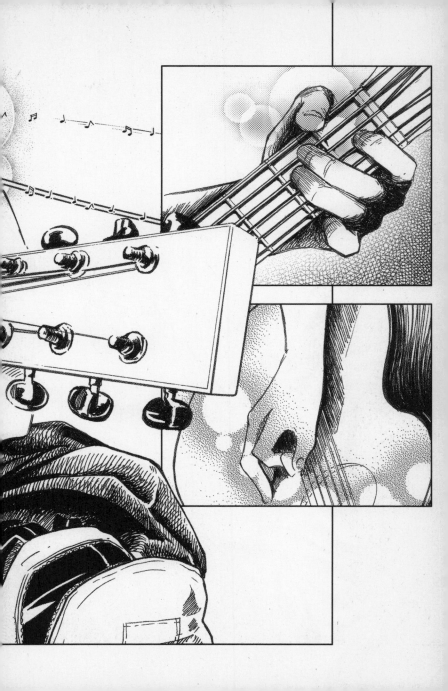

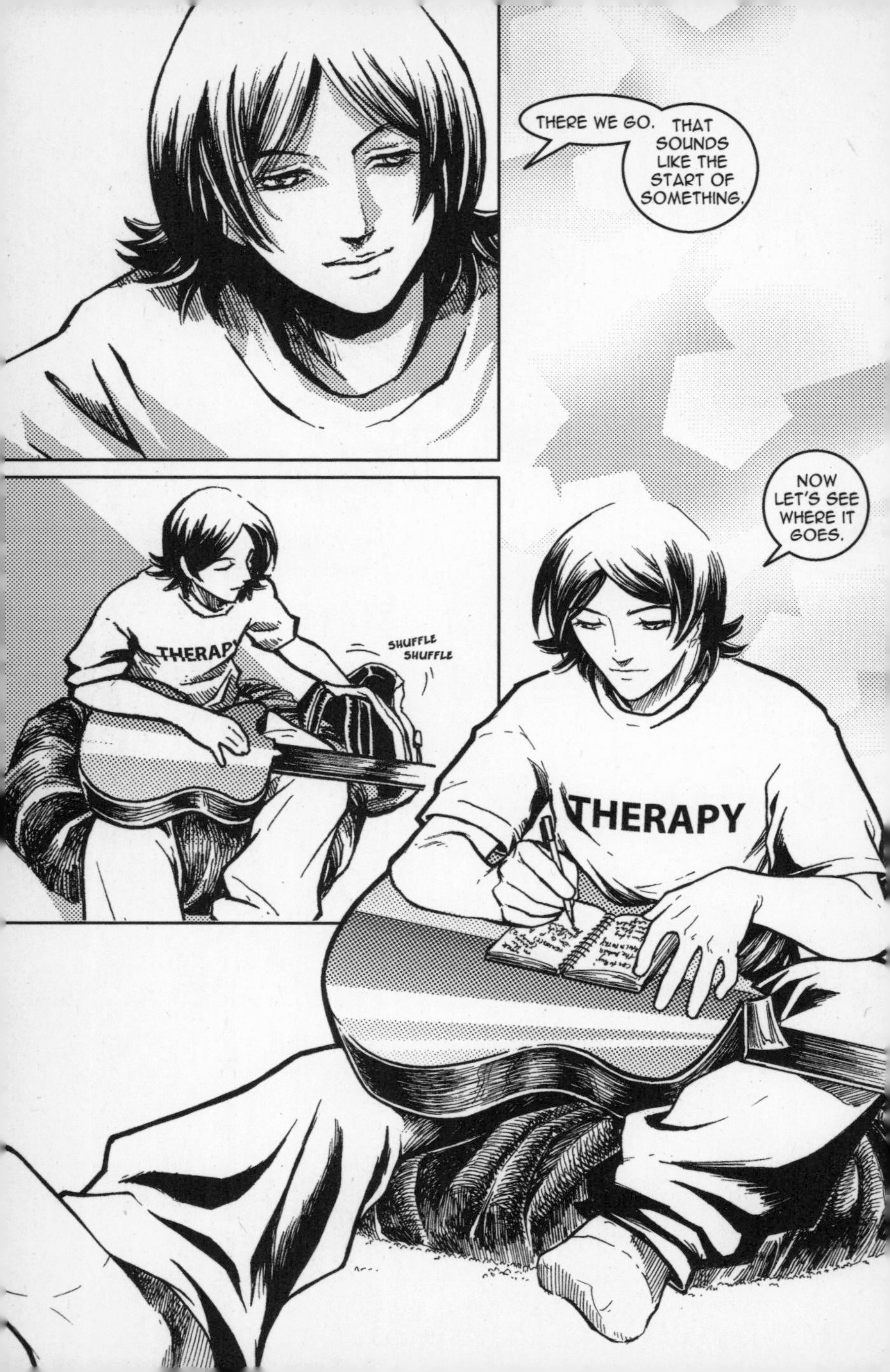
THERE WE GO. THAT SOUNDS LIKE THE START OF SOMETHING.
THERAPY
SHUFFLE SHUFFLE
NOW LET'S SEE WHERE IT GOES.
THERAPY

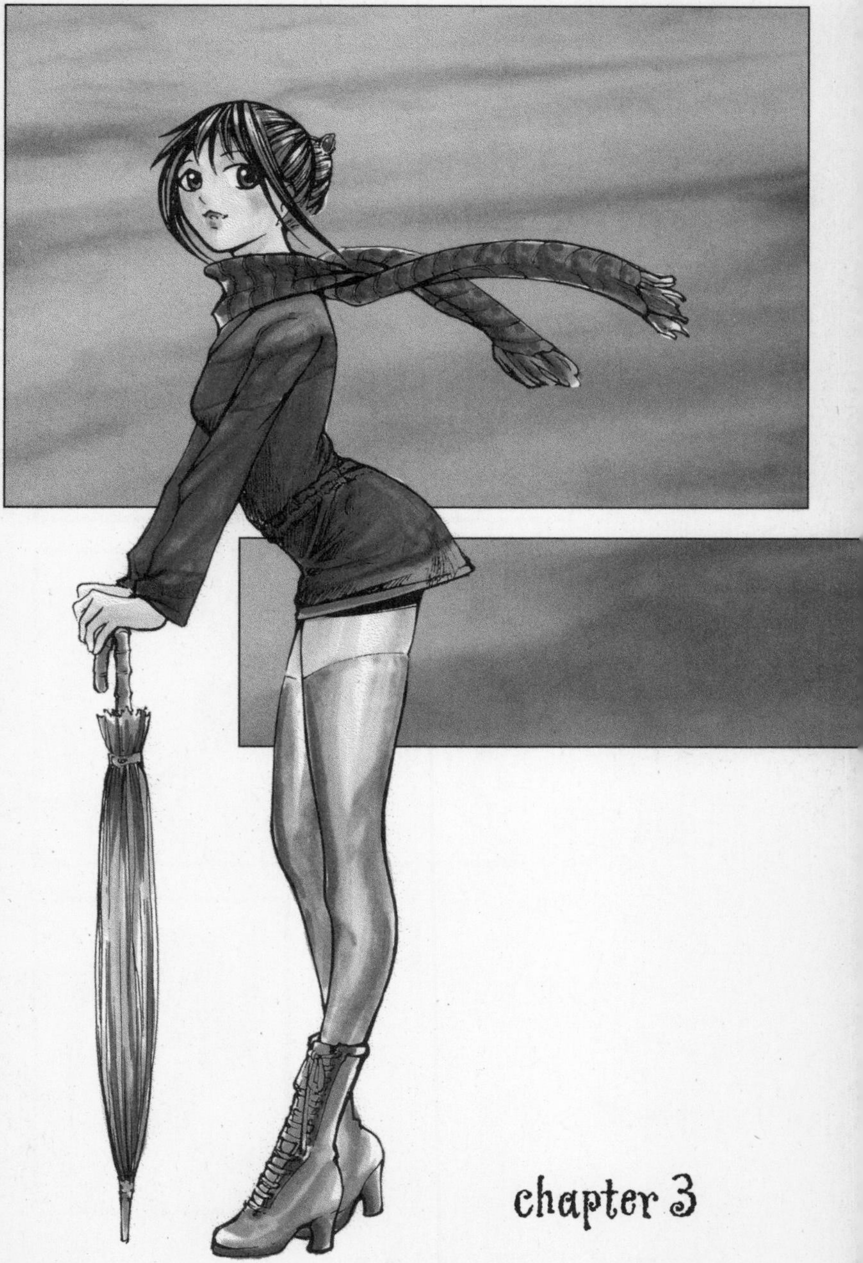

chapter 3

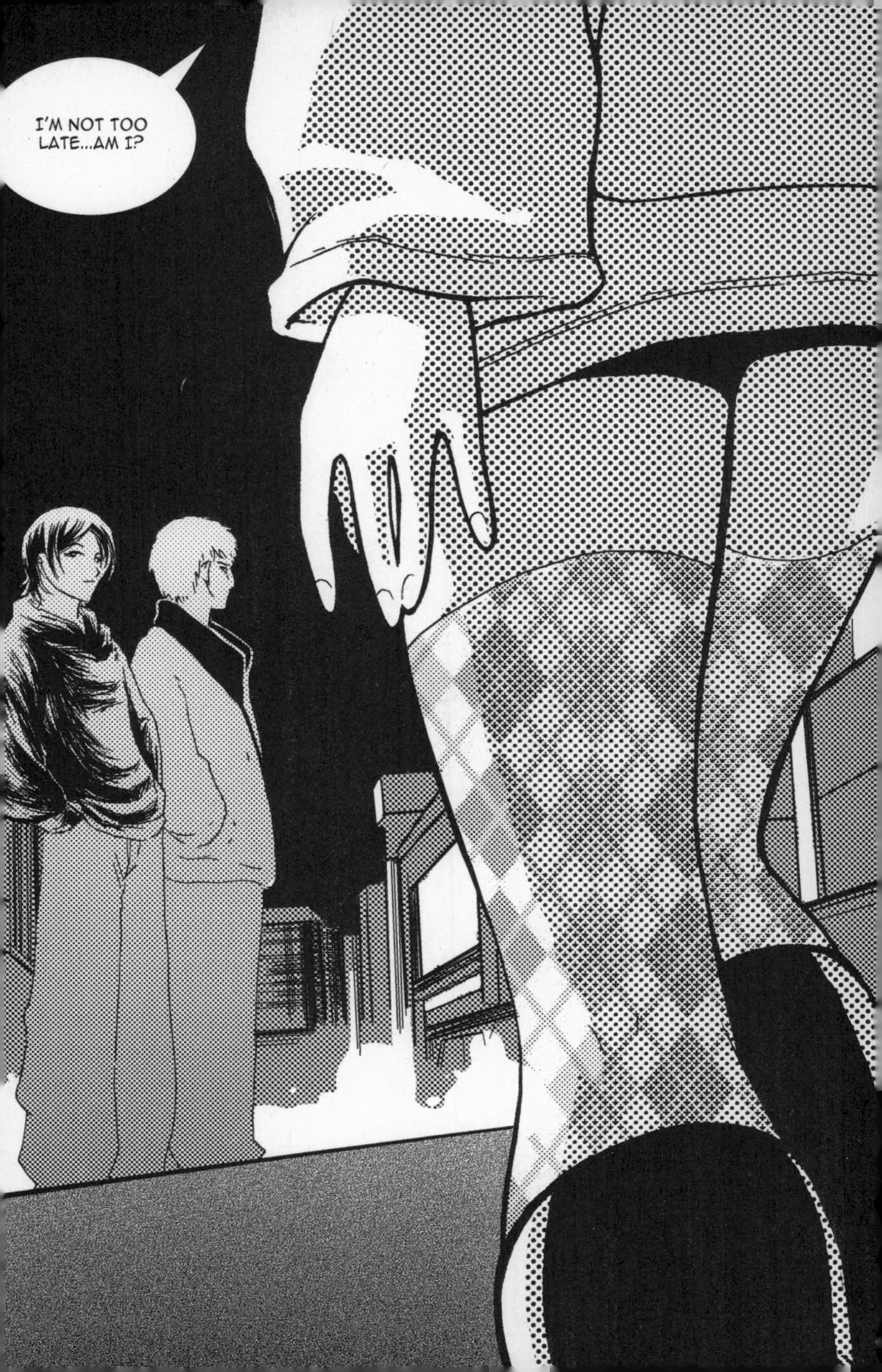
I'M NOT TOO LATE...AM I?

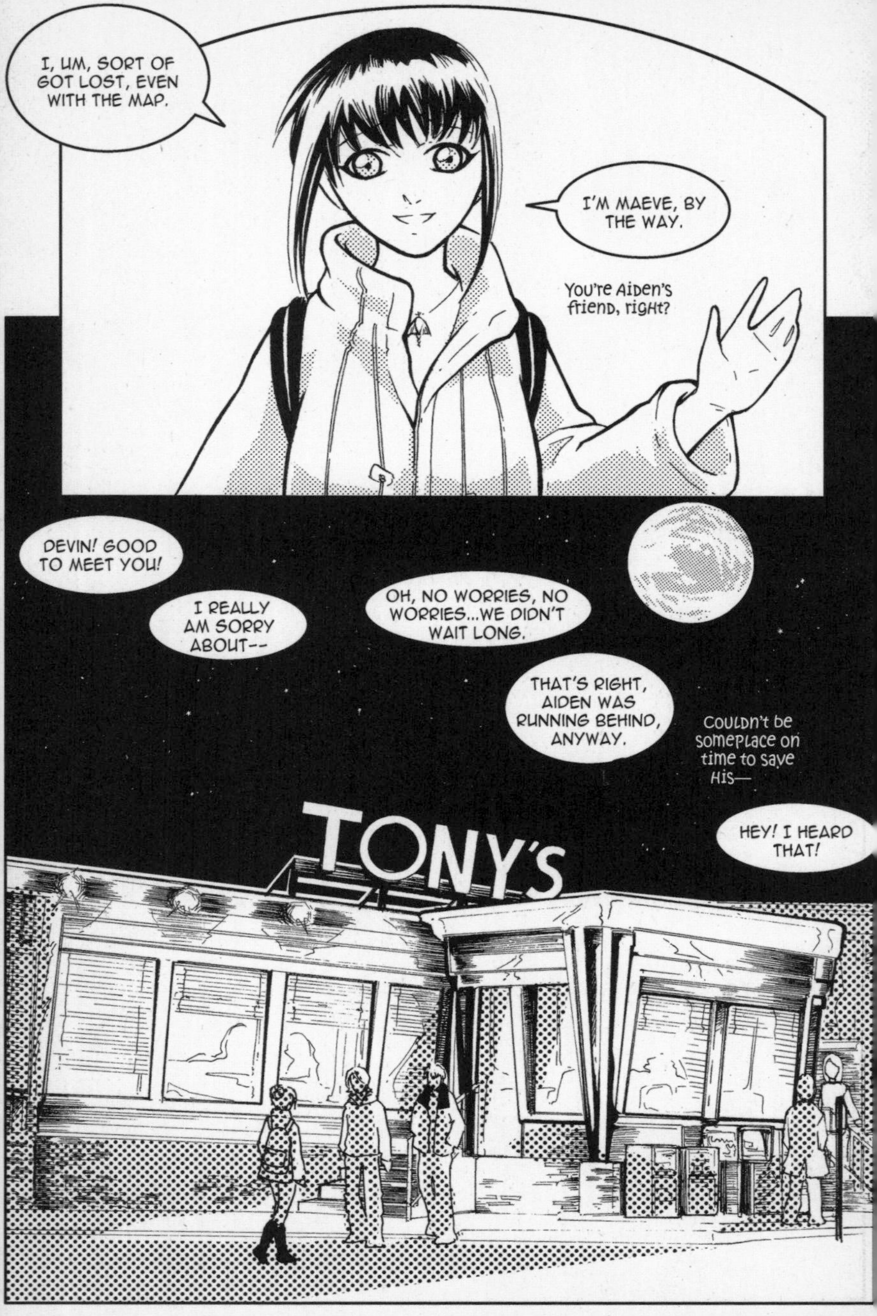
I, UM, SORT OF GOT LOST, EVEN WITH THE MAP.
I'M MAEVE, BY THE WAY.
You're Aiden's friend, right?
DEVIN! GOOD TO MEET YOU!
I REALLY AM SORRY ABOUT--
OH, NO WORRIES, NO WORRIES...WE DIDN'T WAIT LONG.
THAT'S RIGHT, AIDEN WAS RUNNING BEHIND, ANYWAY.
Couldn't be someplace on time to save his—
HEY! I HEARD THAT!
TONY'S

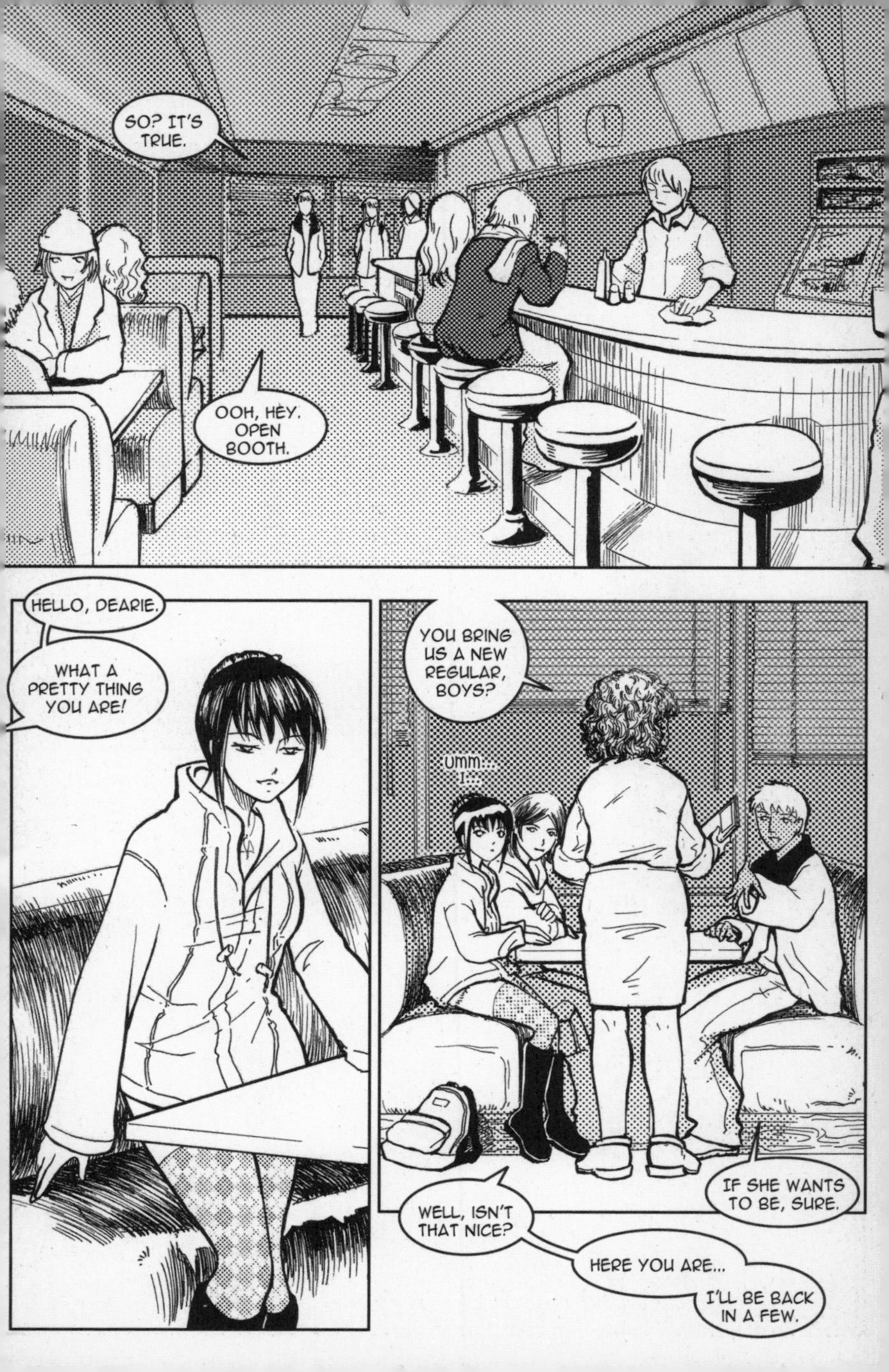
SO? IT'S TRUE.
OOH, HEY. OPEN BOOTH.
HELLO, DEARIE.
WHAT A PRETTY THING YOU ARE!
YOU BRING US A NEW REGULAR, BOYS?
UMM... I...
IF SHE WANTS TO BE, SURE.
WELL, ISN'T THAT NICE?
HERE YOU ARE...
I'LL BE BACK IN A FEW.

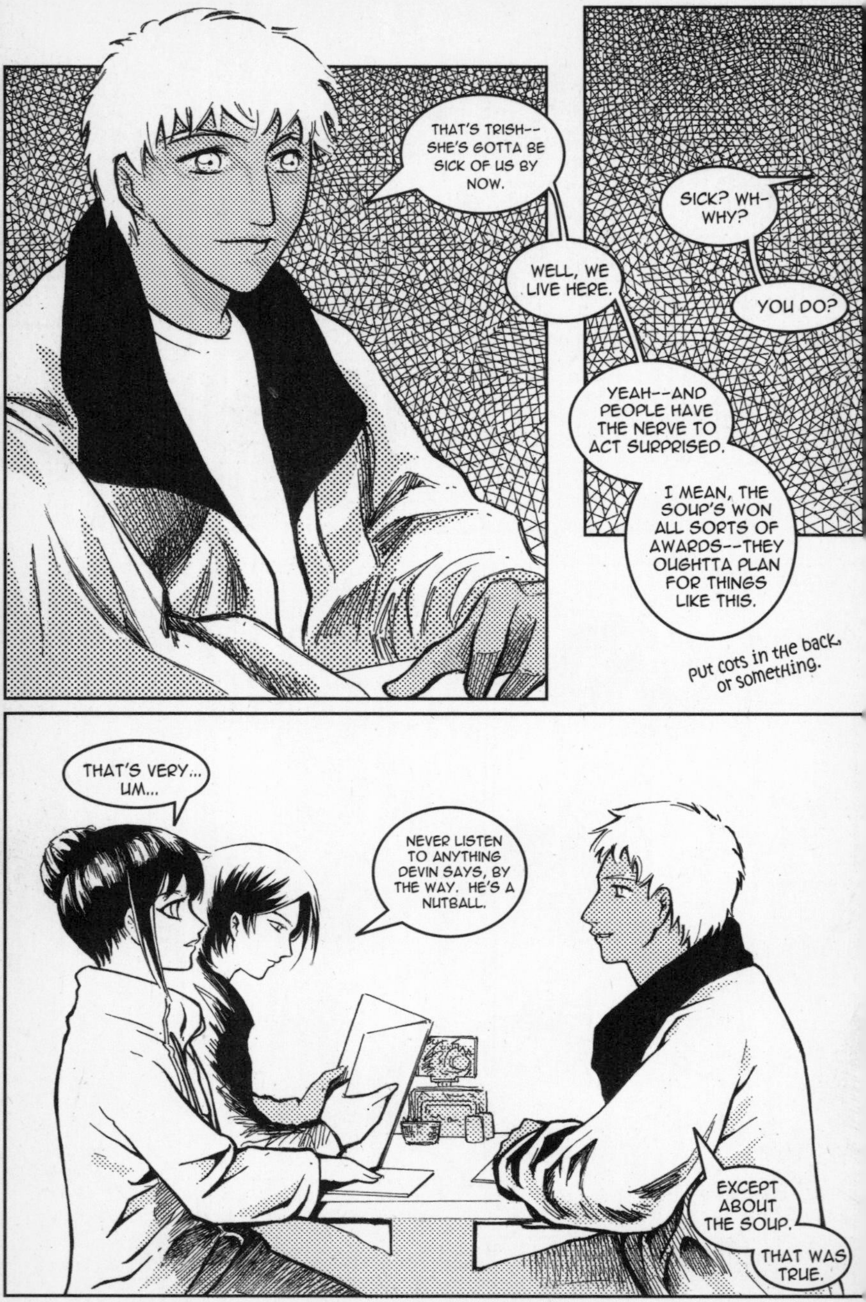

THAT'S TRISH--SHE'S GOTTA BE SICK OF US BY NOW.
SICK? WH-WHY?
WELL, WE LIVE HERE.
YOU DO?
YEAH--AND PEOPLE HAVE THE NERVE TO ACT SURPRISED.
I MEAN, THE SOUP'S WON ALL SORTS OF AWARDS--THEY OUGHTTA PLAN FOR THINGS LIKE THIS.
Put cots in the back, or something.
THAT'S VERY... UM...
NEVER LISTEN TO ANYTHING DEVIN SAYS, BY THE WAY. HE'S A NUTBALL.
EXCEPT ABOUT THE SOUP.
THAT WAS TRUE.

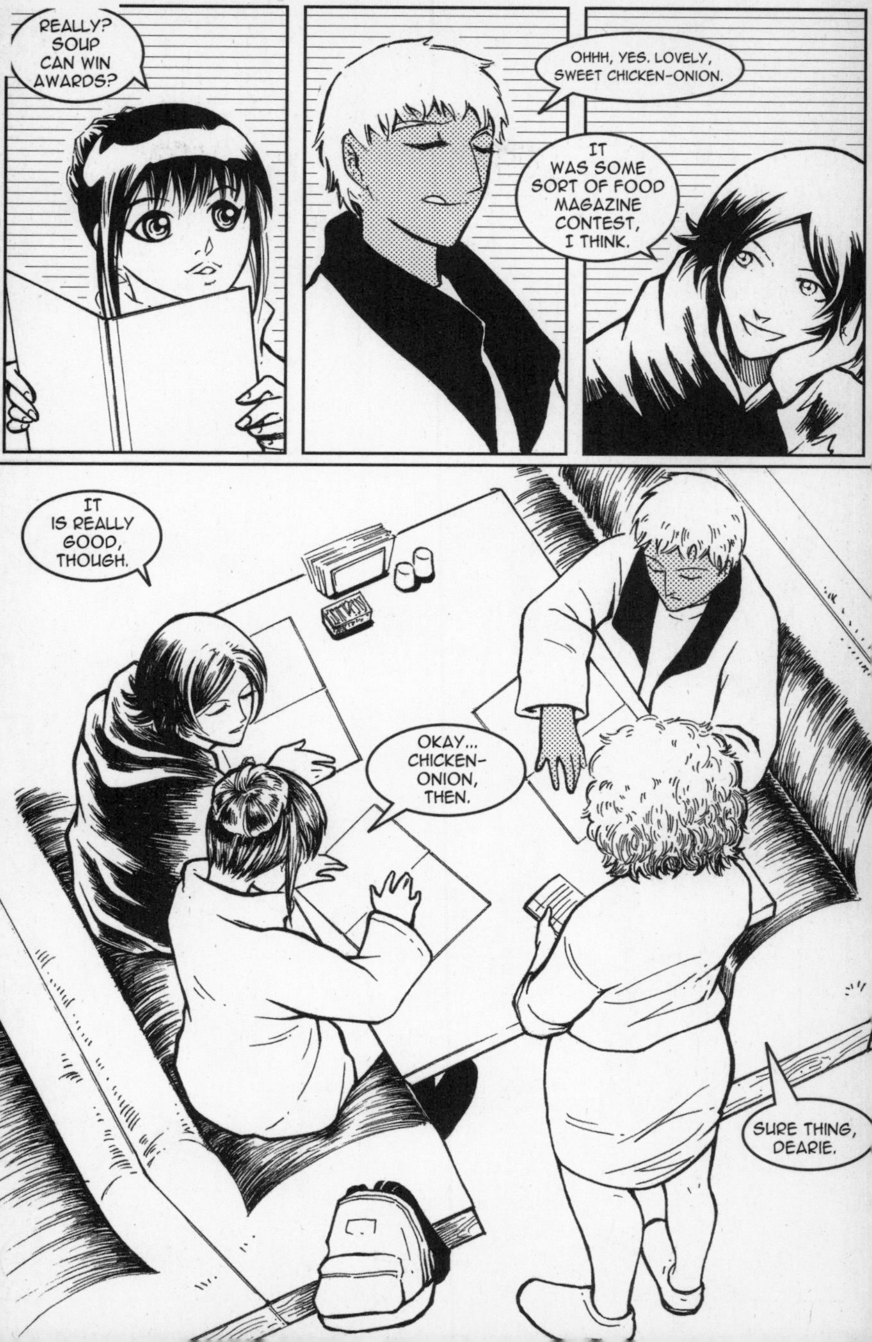
REALLY? SOUP CAN WIN AWARDS?
OHHH, YES. LOVELY, SWEET CHICKEN-ONION.
IT WAS SOME SORT OF FOOD MAGAZINE CONTEST, I THINK.
IT IS REALLY GOOD, THOUGH.
OKAY... CHICKEN-ONION, THEN.
SURE THING, DEARIE.

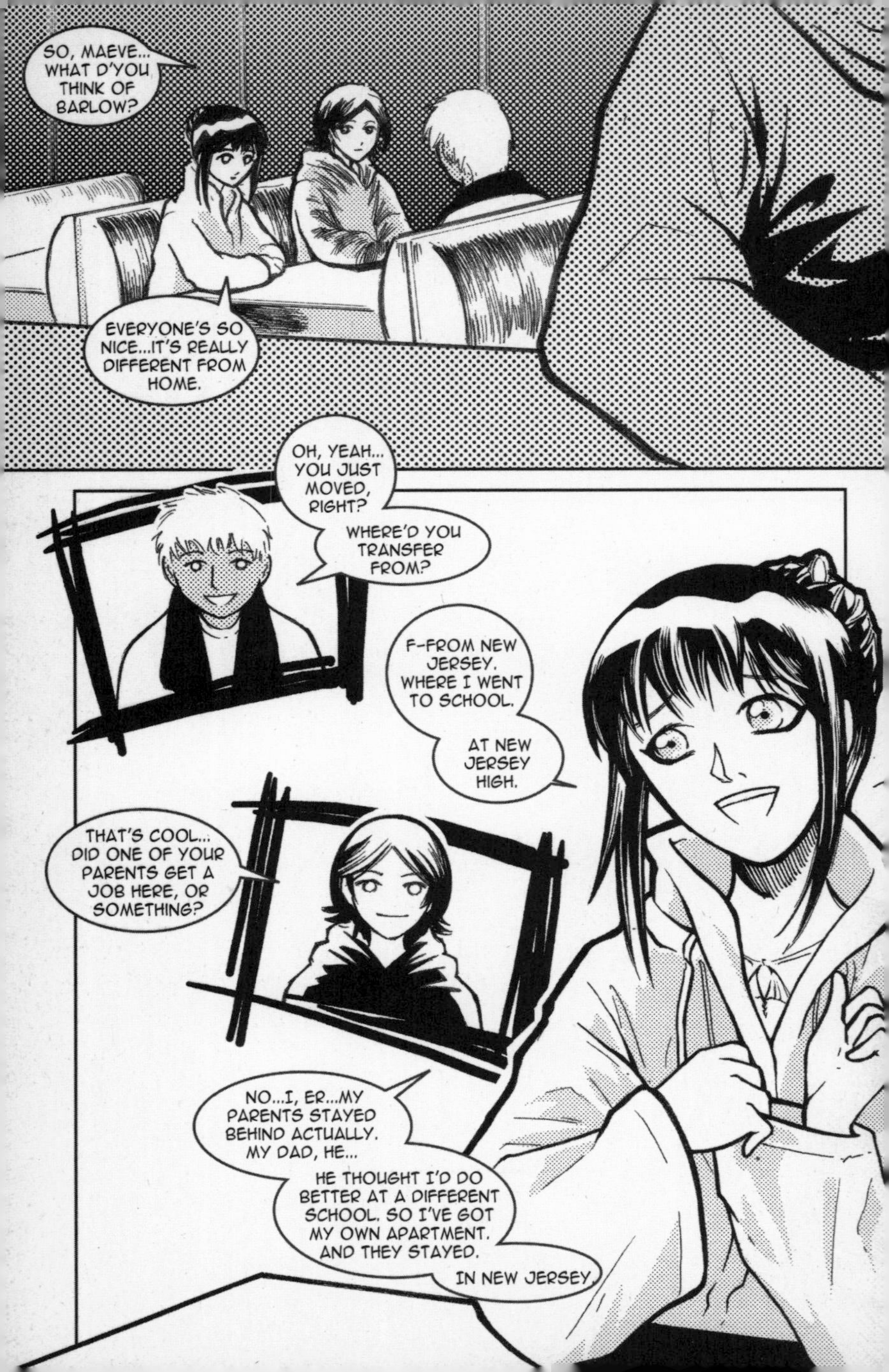

SO, MAEVE... WHAT D'YOU THINK OF BARLOW?
EVERYONE'S SO NICE...IT'S REALLY DIFFERENT FROM HOME.
OH, YEAH... YOU JUST MOVED, RIGHT?
WHERE'D YOU TRANSFER FROM?
F-FROM NEW JERSEY. WHERE I WENT TO SCHOOL.
AT NEW JERSEY HIGH.
THAT'S COOL... DID ONE OF YOUR PARENTS GET A JOB HERE, OR SOMETHING?
NO...I, ER...MY PARENTS STAYED BEHIND ACTUALLY. MY DAD, HE...
HE THOUGHT I'D DO BETTER AT A DIFFERENT SCHOOL. SO I'VE GOT MY OWN APARTMENT. AND THEY STAYED.
IN NEW JERSEY.

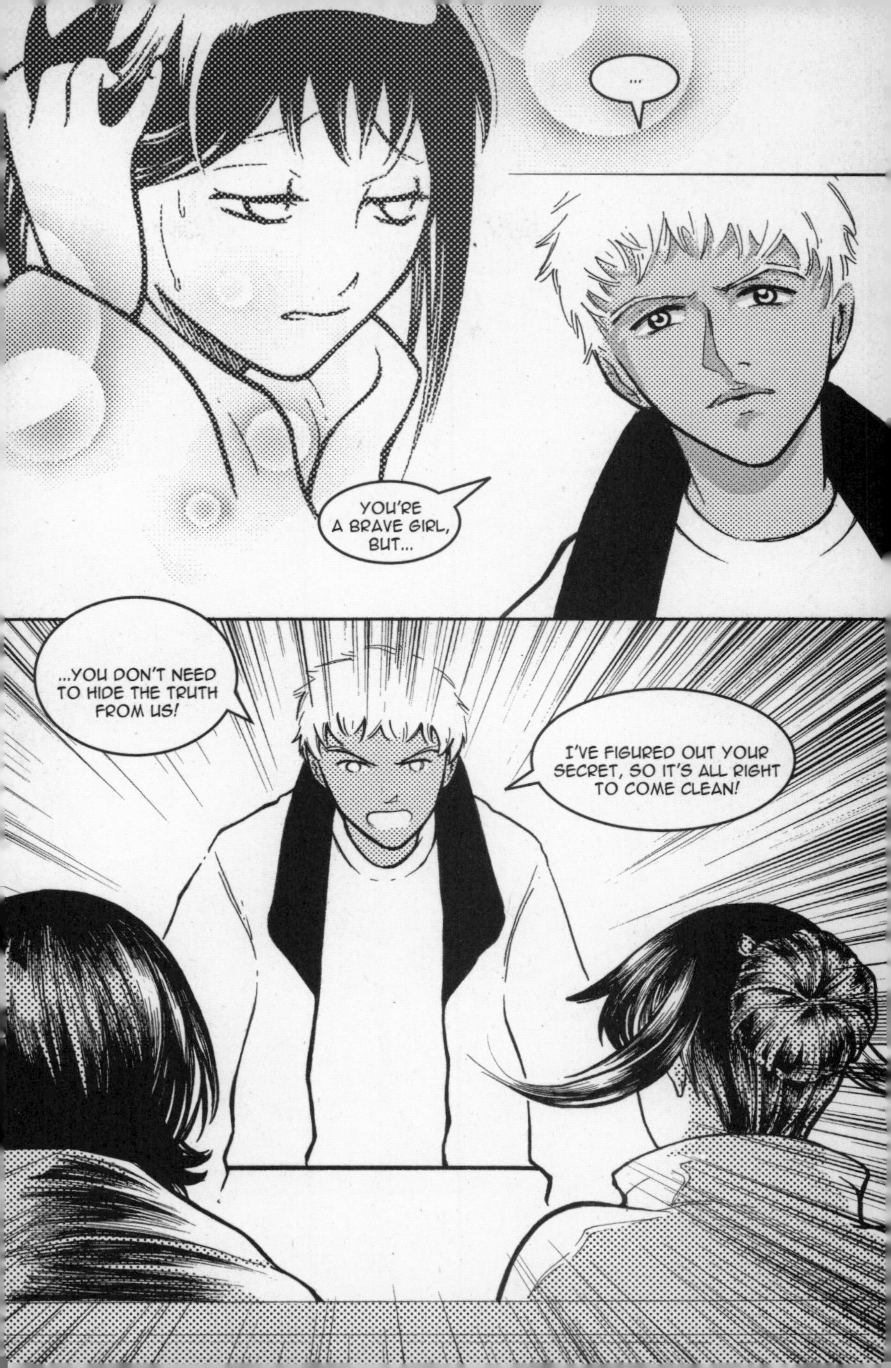
...
YOU'RE A BRAVE GIRL, BUT...
...YOU DON'T NEED TO HIDE THE TRUTH FROM US!
I'VE FIGURED OUT YOUR SECRET, SO IT'S ALL RIGHT TO COME CLEAN!

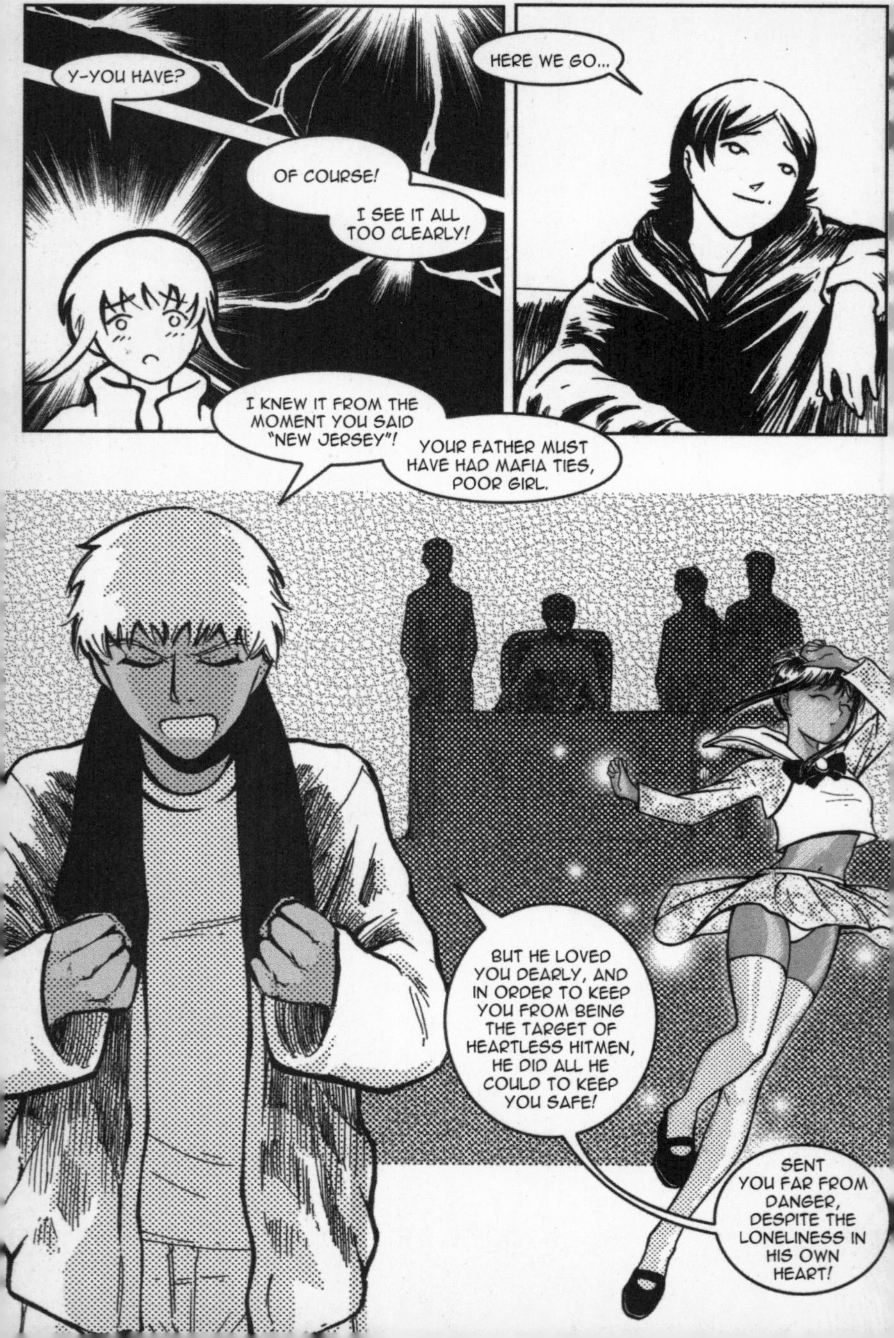
Y-YOU HAVE?
OF COURSE!
I SEE IT ALL TOO CLEARLY!
HERE WE GO...
I KNEW IT FROM THE MOMENT YOU SAID "NEW JERSEY"!
YOUR FATHER MUST HAVE HAD MAFIA TIES, POOR GIRL.
BUT HE LOVED YOU DEARLY, AND IN ORDER TO KEEP YOU FROM BEING THE TARGET OF HEARTLESS HITMEN, HE DID ALL HE COULD TO KEEP YOU SAFE!
SENT YOU FAR FROM DANGER, DESPITE THE LONELINESS IN HIS OWN HEART!

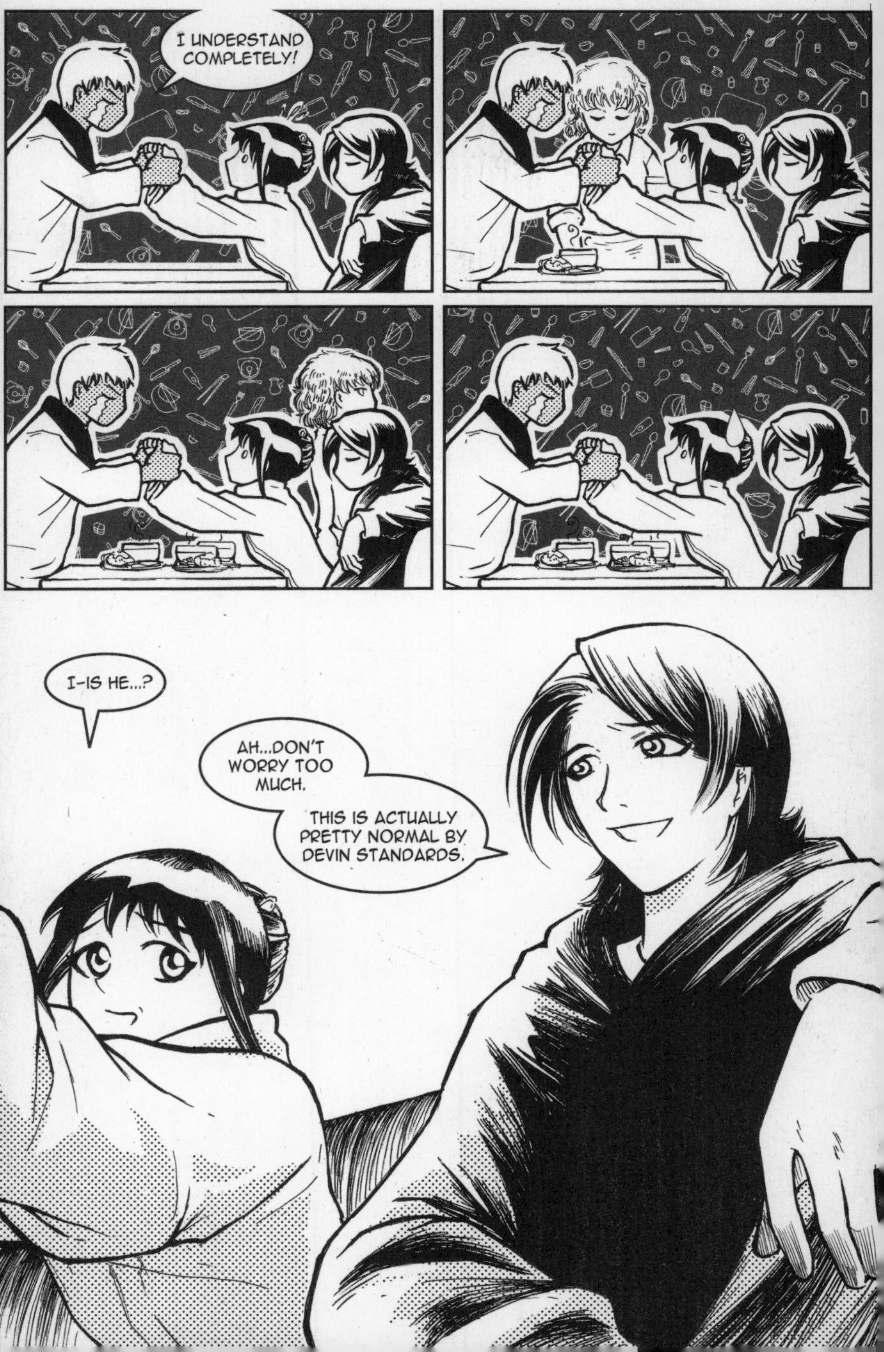
I UNDERSTAND COMPLETELY!
I-IS HE...?
AH...DON'T WORRY TOO MUCH.
THIS IS ACTUALLY PRETTY NORMAL BY DEVIN STANDARDS.

Erebus, the demon world.

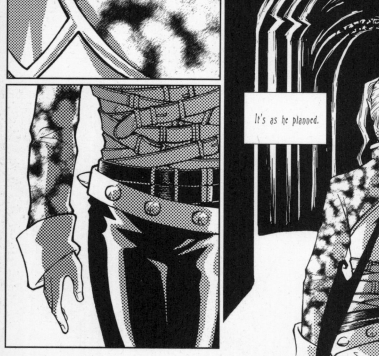

The halls are empty here, silent.

It's as he planned.

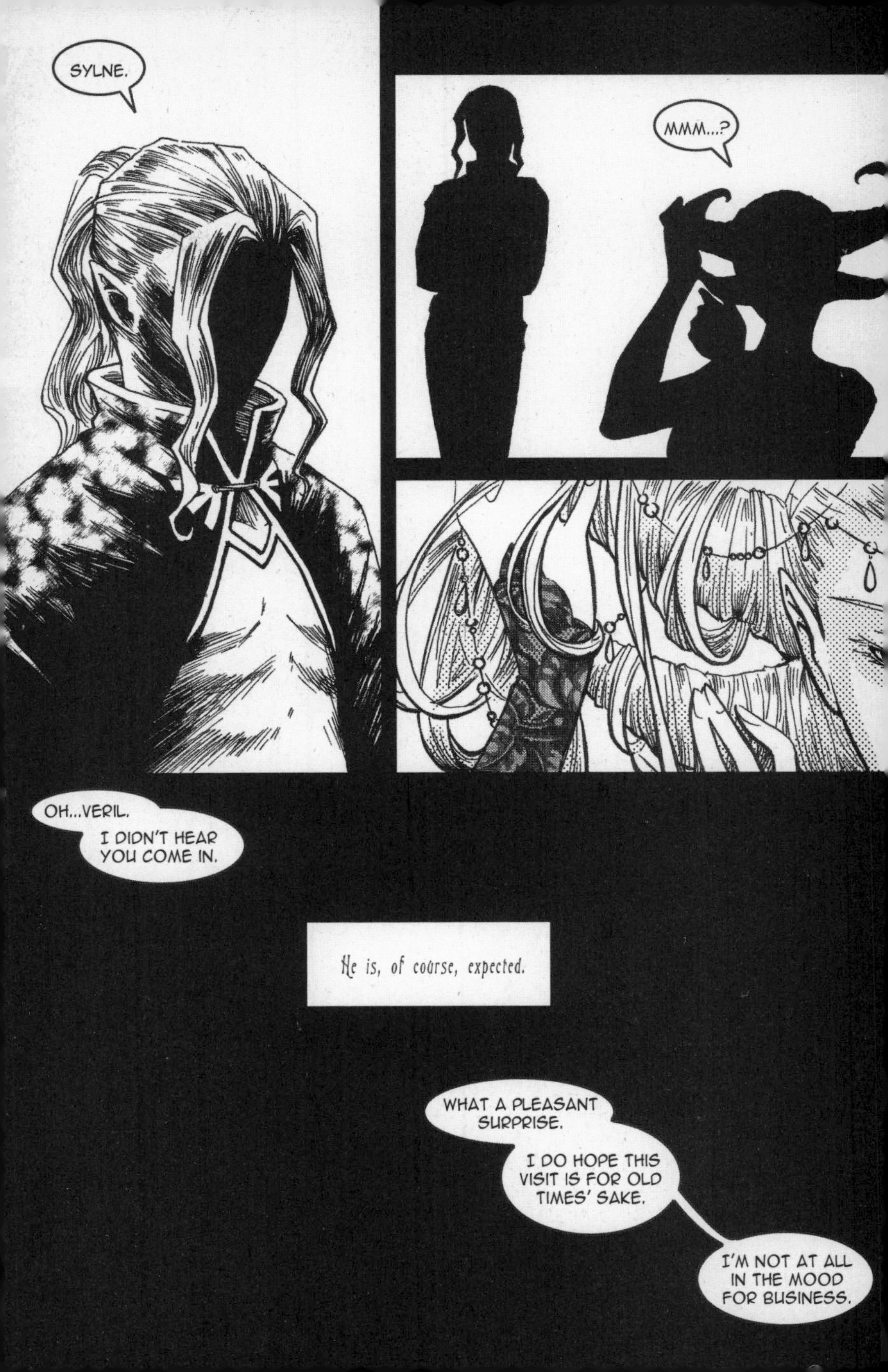
SYLNE.
MMM...?
OH...VERIL.
I DIDN'T HEAR YOU COME IN.
He is, of course, expected.
WHAT A PLEASANT SURPRISE.
I DO HOPE THIS VISIT IS FOR OLD TIMES' SAKE.
I'M NOT AT ALL IN THE MOOD FOR BUSINESS.

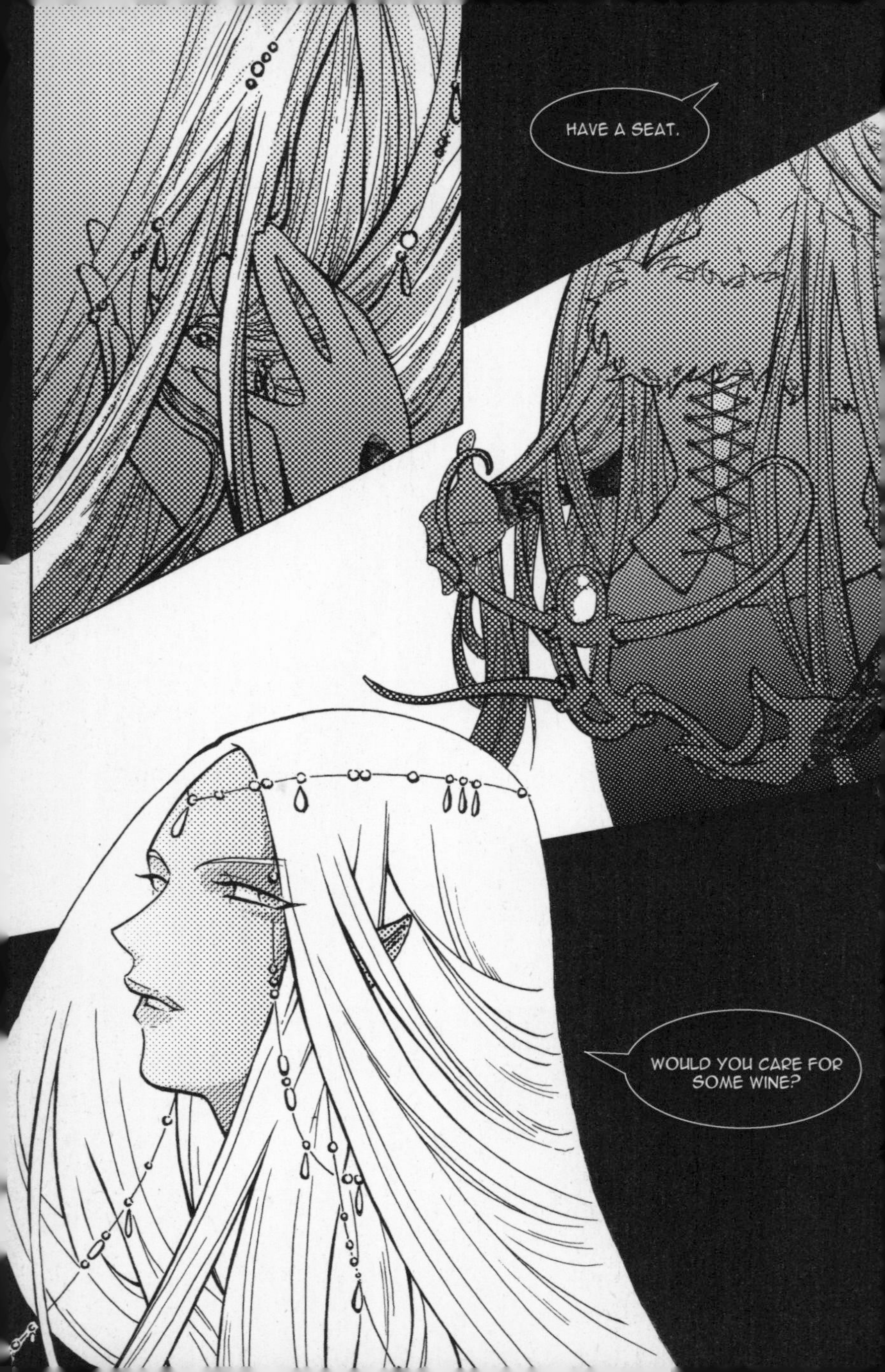
HAVE A SEAT.
WOULD YOU CARE FOR SOME WINE?

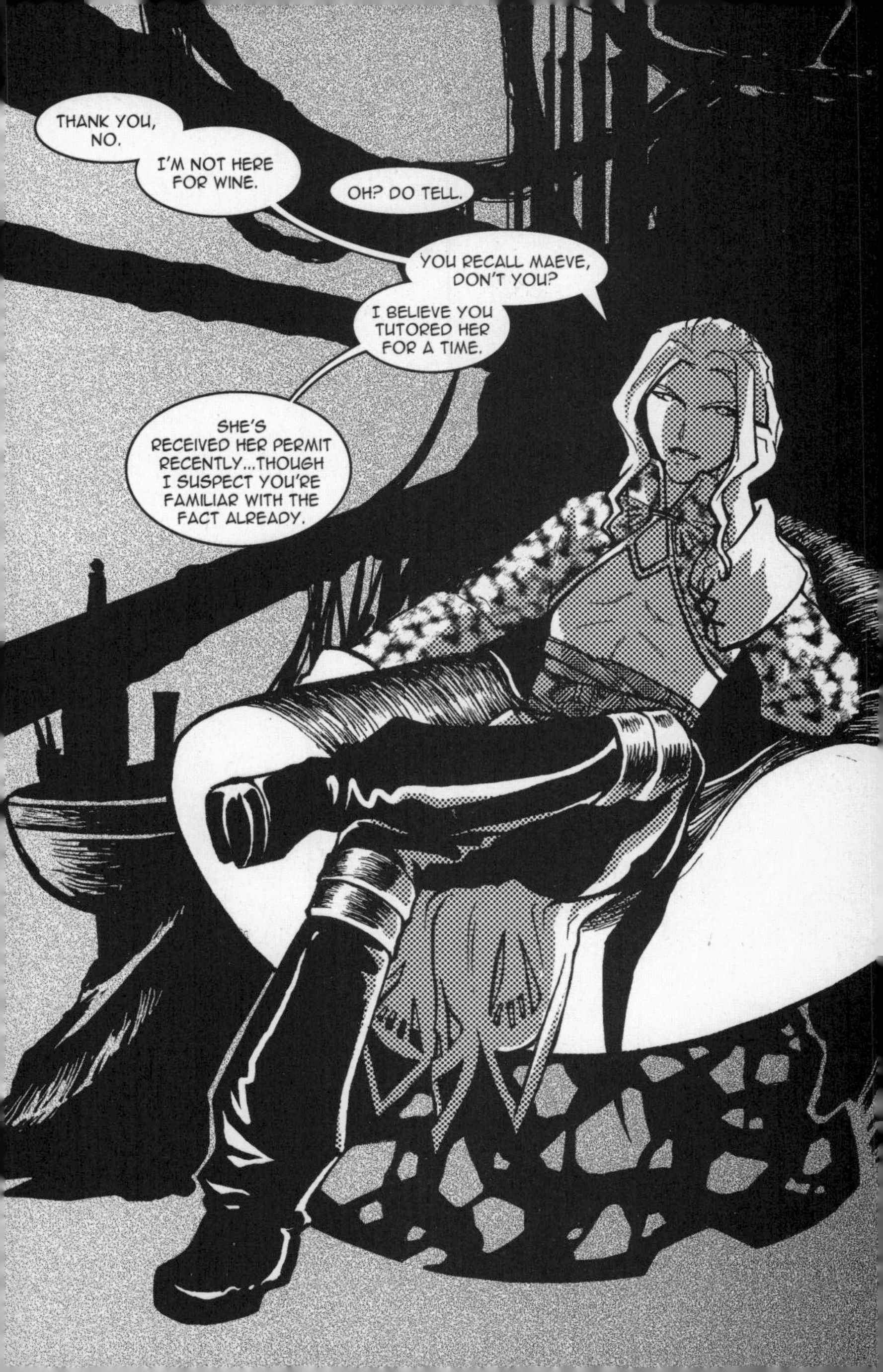
THANK YOU, NO.
I'M NOT HERE FOR WINE.
OH? DO TELL.
YOU RECALL MAEVE, DON'T YOU?
I BELIEVE YOU TUTORED HER FOR A TIME.
SHE'S RECEIVED HER PERMIT RECENTLY...THOUGH I SUSPECT YOU'RE FAMILIAR WITH THE FACT ALREADY.

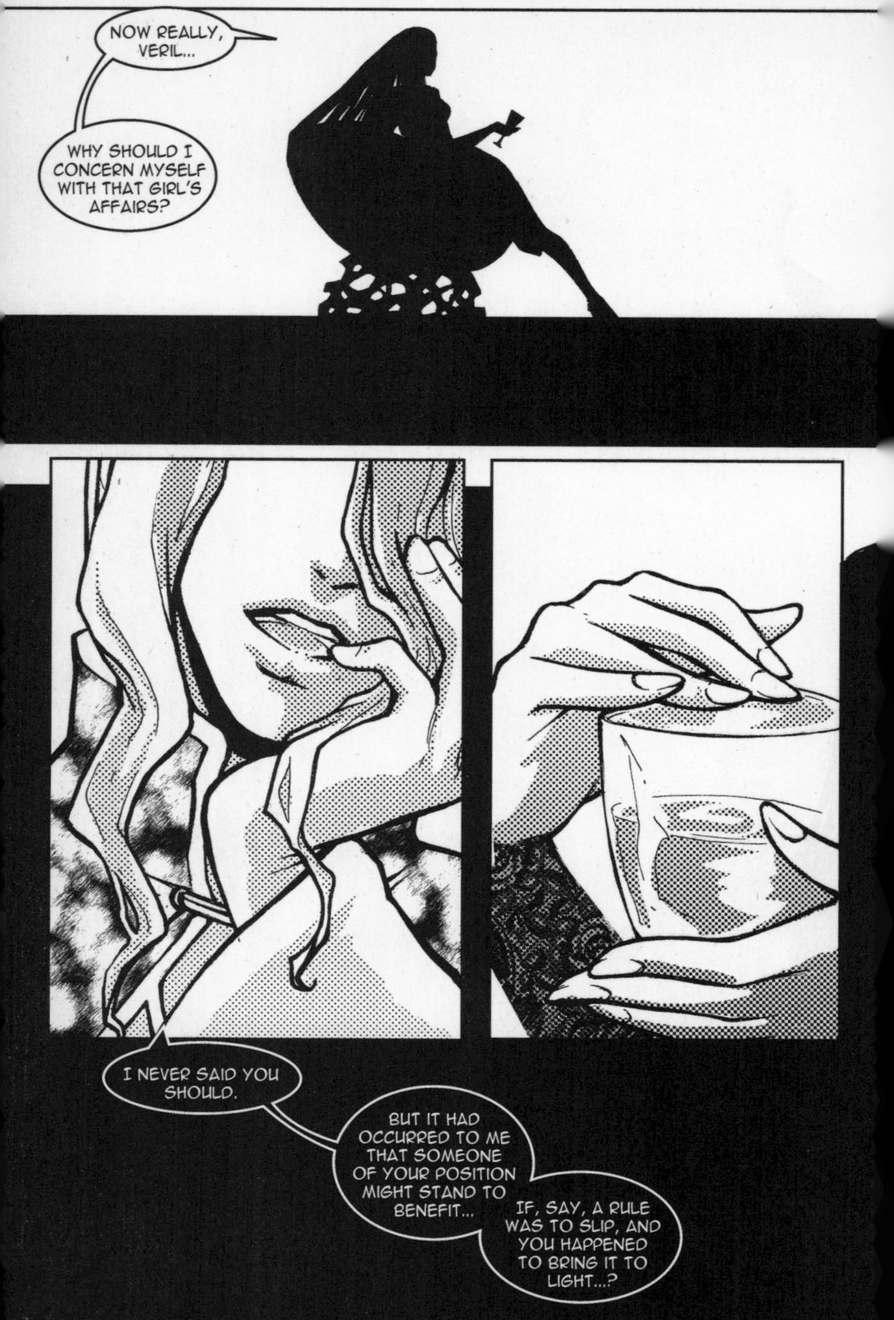
NOW REALLY, VERIL...
WHY SHOULD I CONCERN MYSELF WITH THAT GIRL'S AFFAIRS?
I NEVER SAID YOU SHOULD.
BUT IT HAD OCCURRED TO ME THAT SOMEONE OF YOUR POSITION MIGHT STAND TO BENEFIT...
IF, SAY, A RULE WAS TO SLIP, AND YOU HAPPENED TO BRING IT TO LIGHT...?

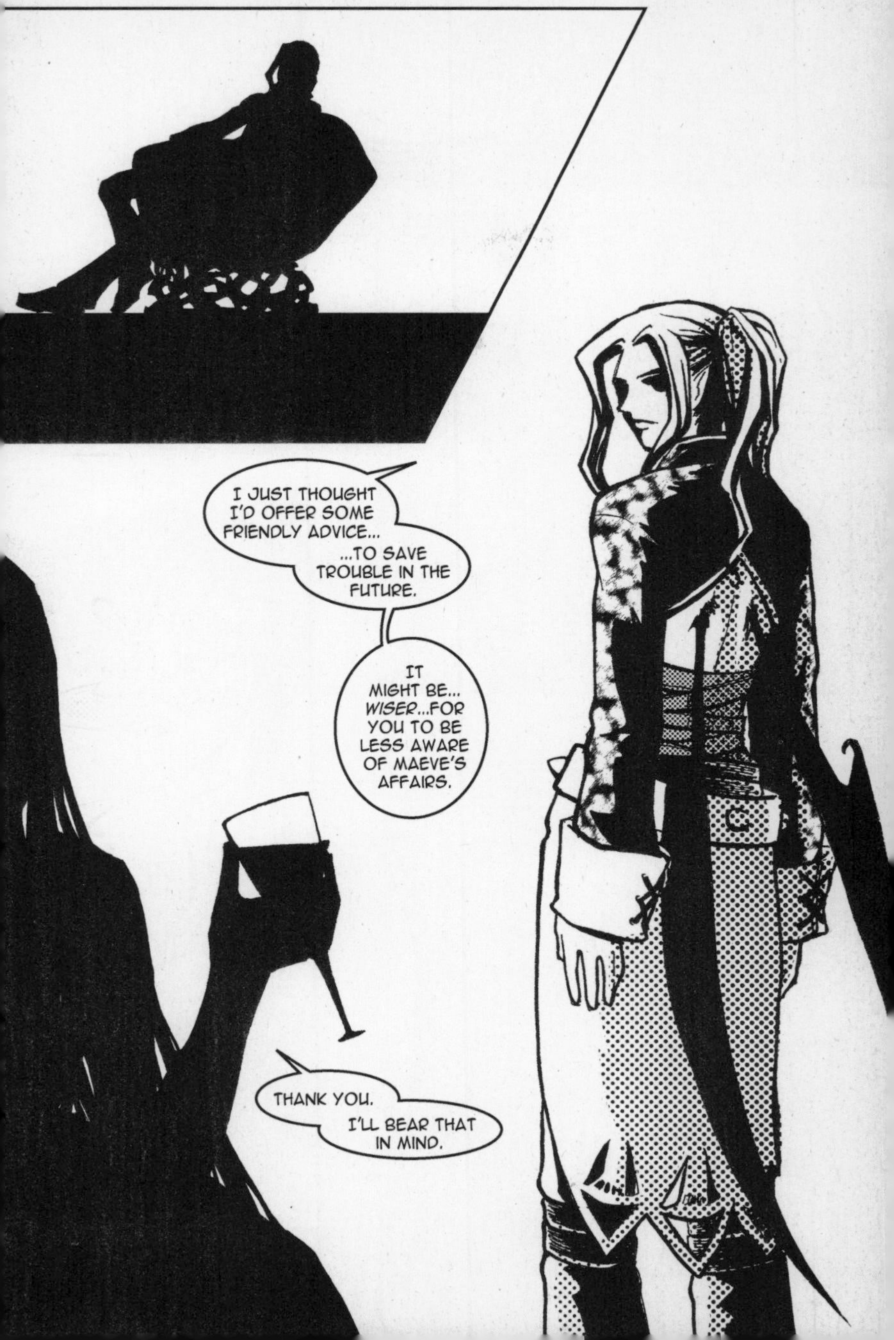
I JUST THOUGHT I'D OFFER SOME FRIENDLY ADVICE...
...TO SAVE TROUBLE IN THE FUTURE.
IT MIGHT BE... *WISER*...FOR YOU TO BE LESS AWARE OF MAEVE'S AFFAIRS.
THANK YOU.
I'LL BEAR THAT IN MIND.

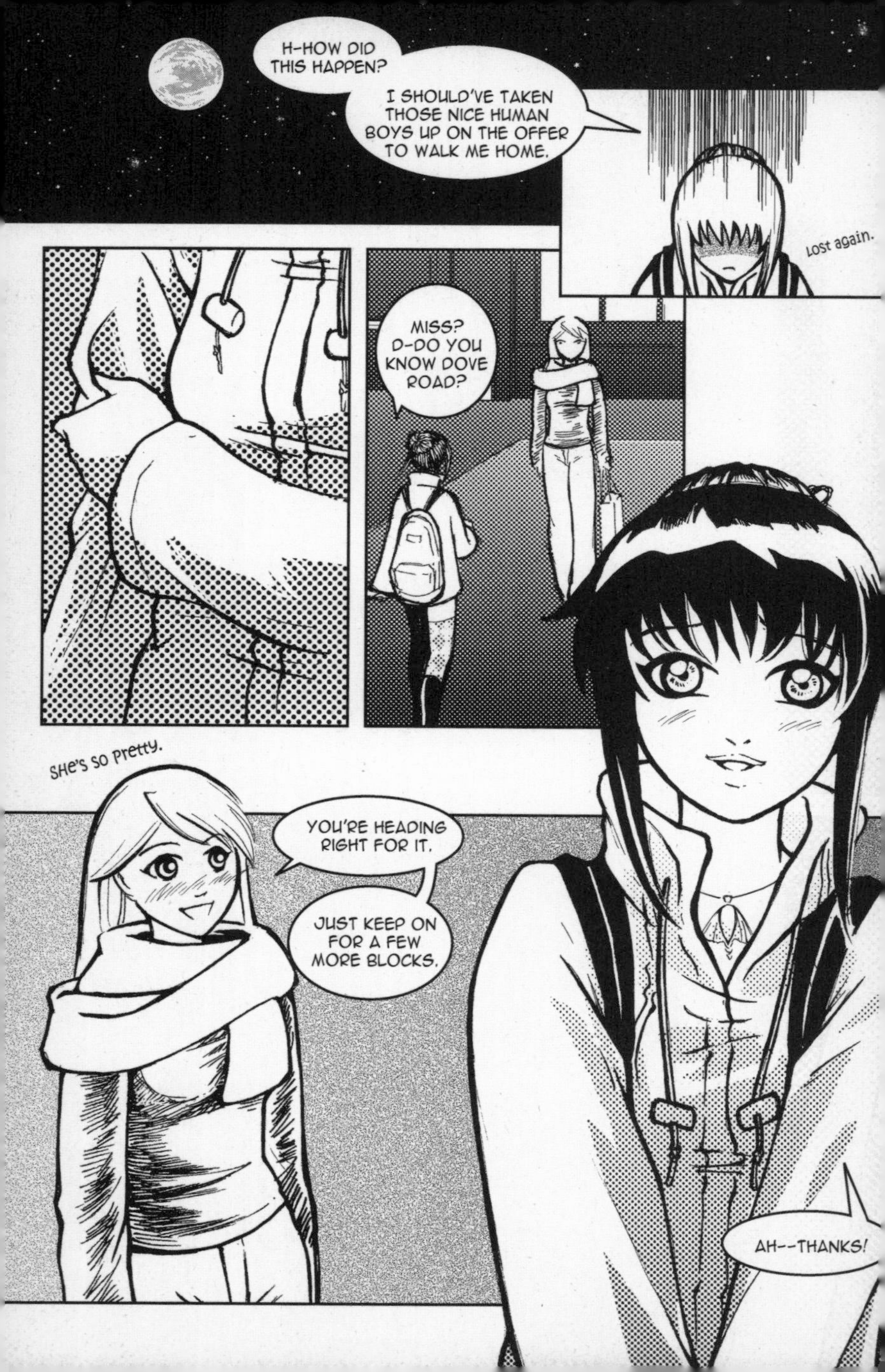
H-HOW DID THIS HAPPEN?
I SHOULD'VE TAKEN THOSE NICE HUMAN BOYS UP ON THE OFFER TO WALK ME HOME.
Lost again.
MISS? D-DO YOU KNOW DOVE ROAD?
SHE's so Pretty.
YOU'RE HEADING RIGHT FOR IT.
JUST KEEP ON FOR A FEW MORE BLOCKS.
AH--THANKS!

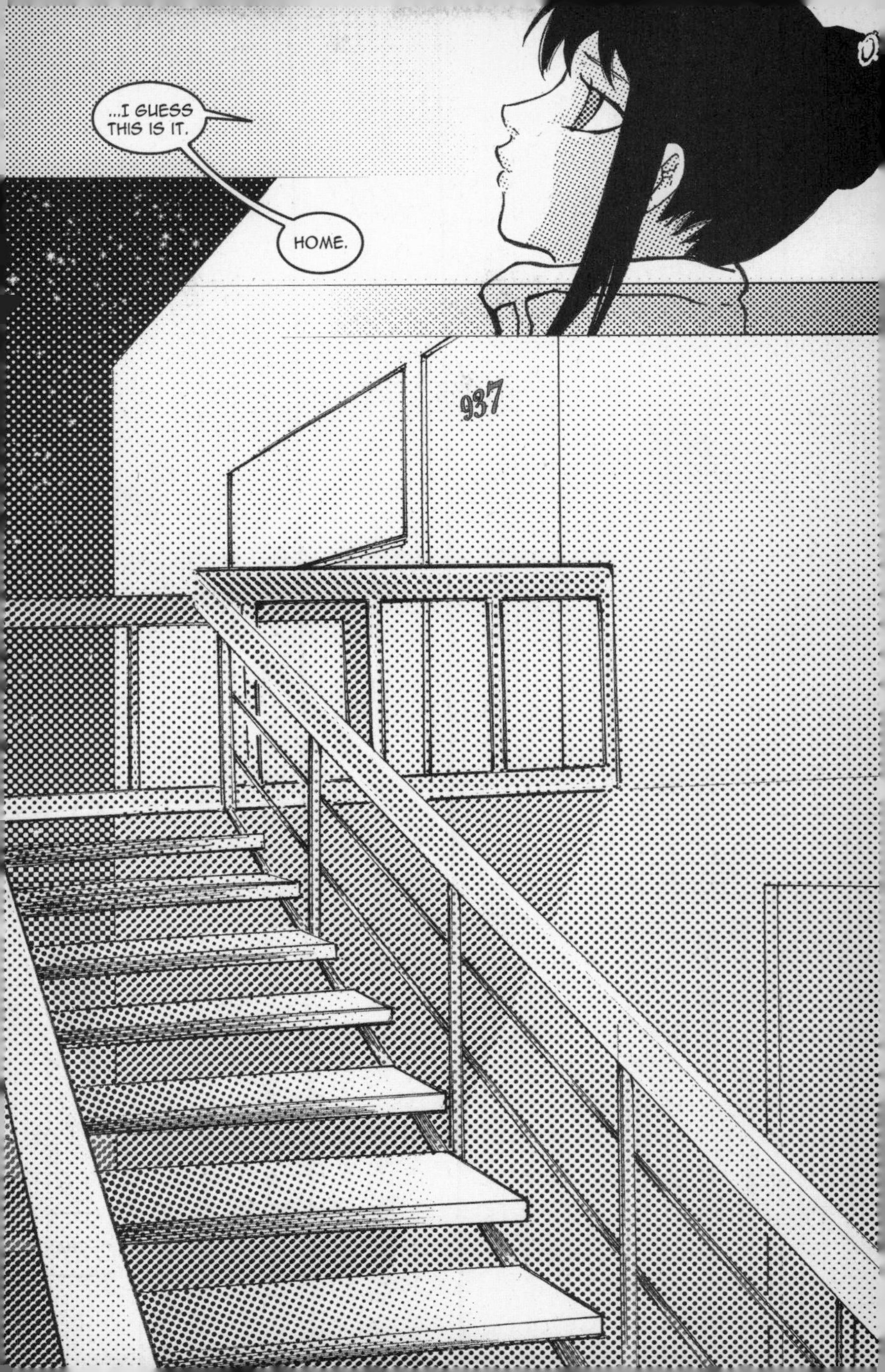
...I GUESS THIS IS IT.
HOME.
937

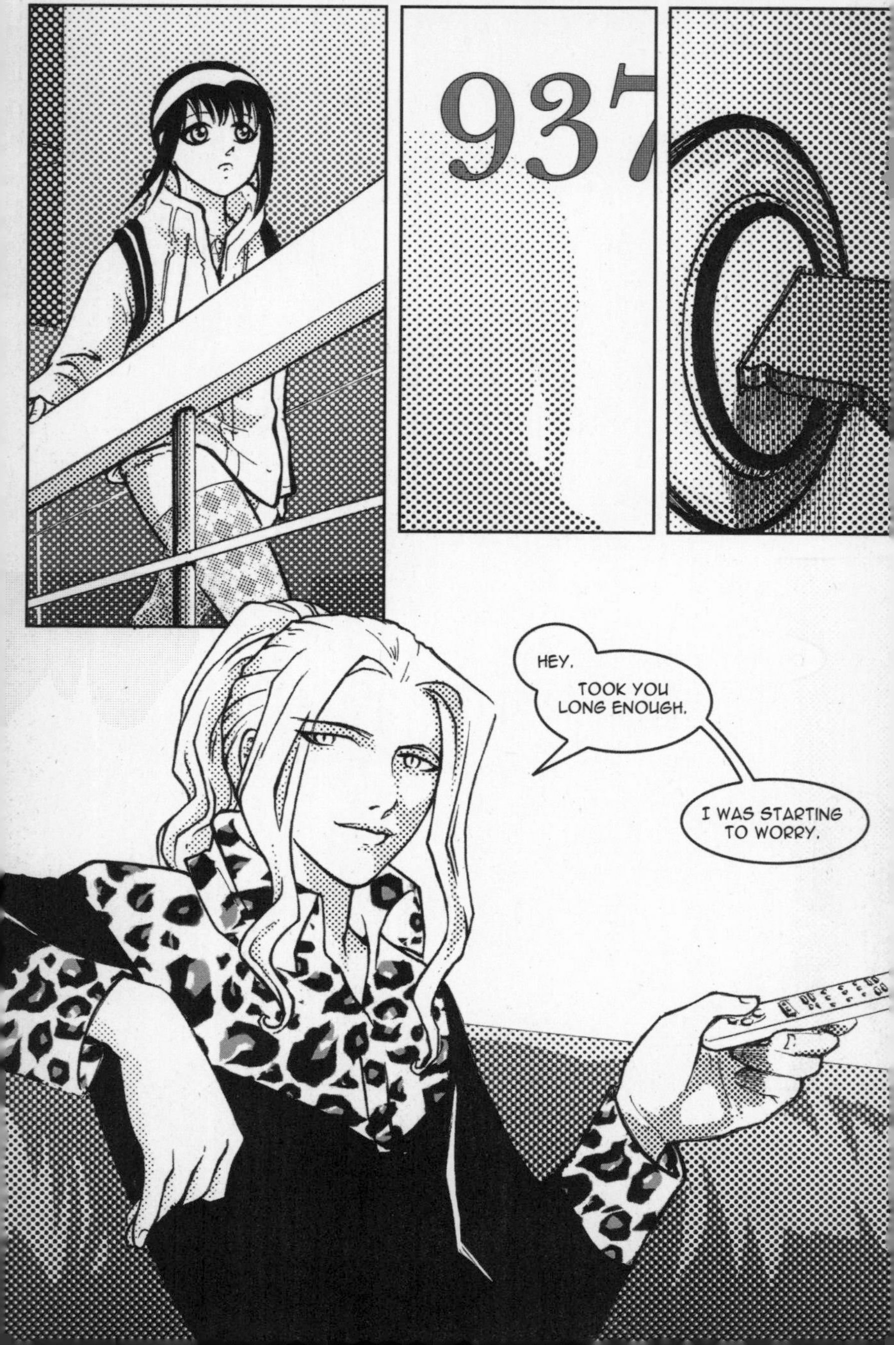
937
HEY.
TOOK YOU LONG ENOUGH.
I WAS STARTING TO WORRY.

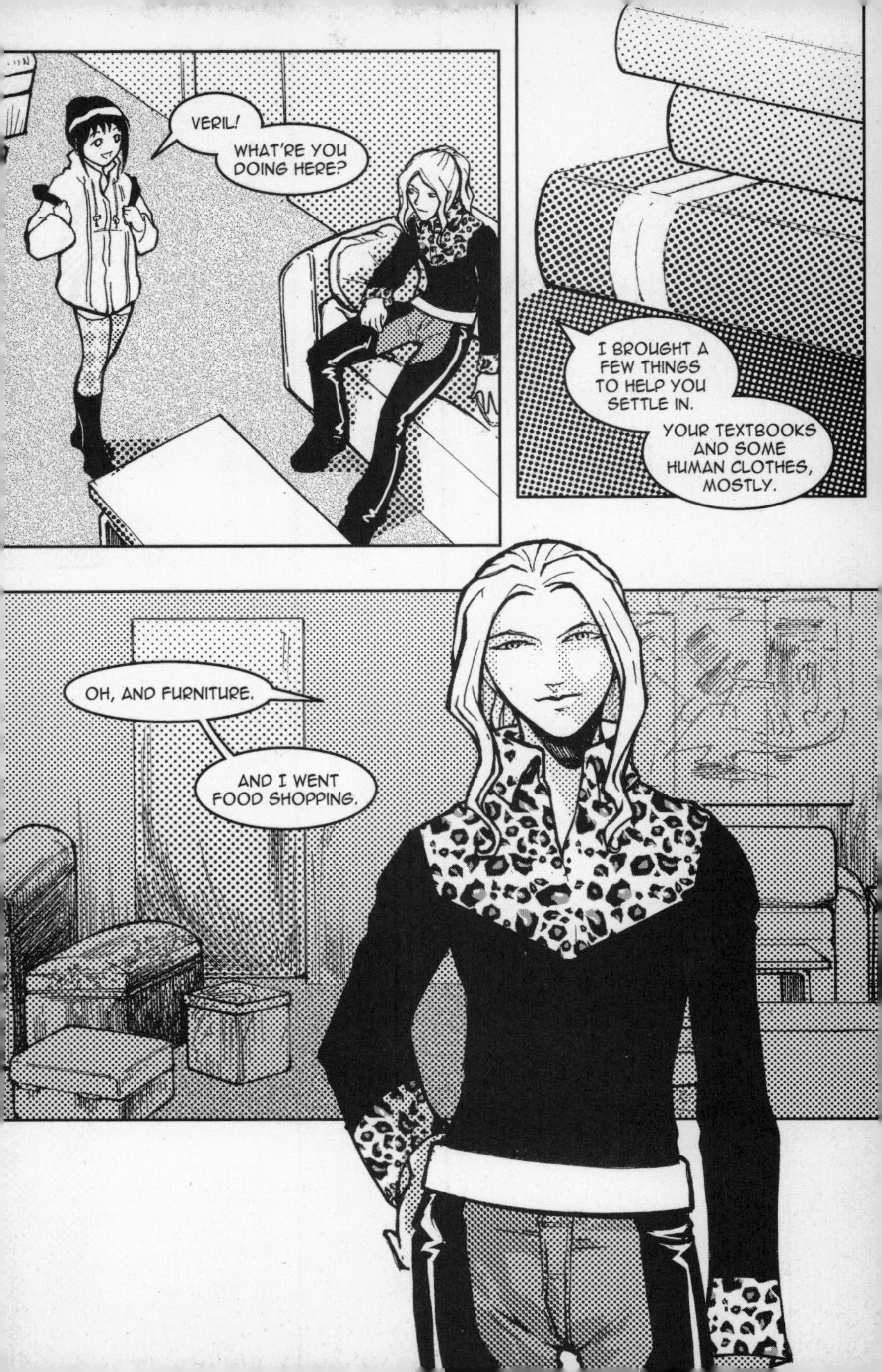
VERIL!
WHAT'RE YOU DOING HERE?
I BROUGHT A FEW THINGS TO HELP YOU SETTLE IN.
YOUR TEXTBOOKS AND SOME HUMAN CLOTHES, MOSTLY.
OH, AND FURNITURE.
AND I WENT FOOD SHOPPING.

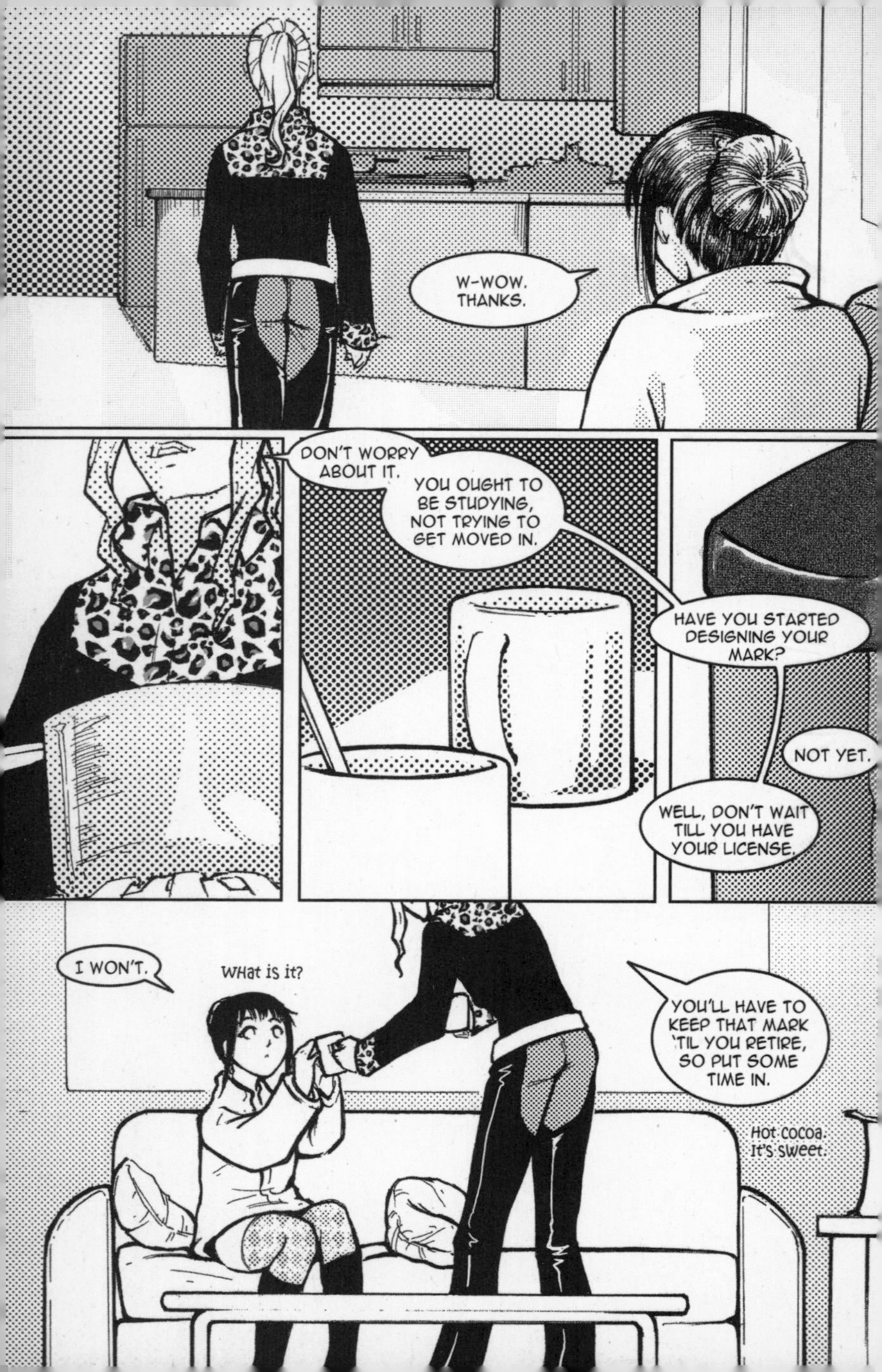
W-WOW. THANKS.
DON'T WORRY ABOUT IT.
YOU OUGHT TO BE STUDYING, NOT TRYING TO GET MOVED IN.
HAVE YOU STARTED DESIGNING YOUR MARK?
NOT YET.
WELL, DON'T WAIT TILL YOU HAVE YOUR LICENSE.
I WON'T.
What is it?
YOU'LL HAVE TO KEEP THAT MARK 'TIL YOU RETIRE, SO PUT SOME TIME IN.
Hot cocoa. It's sweet.

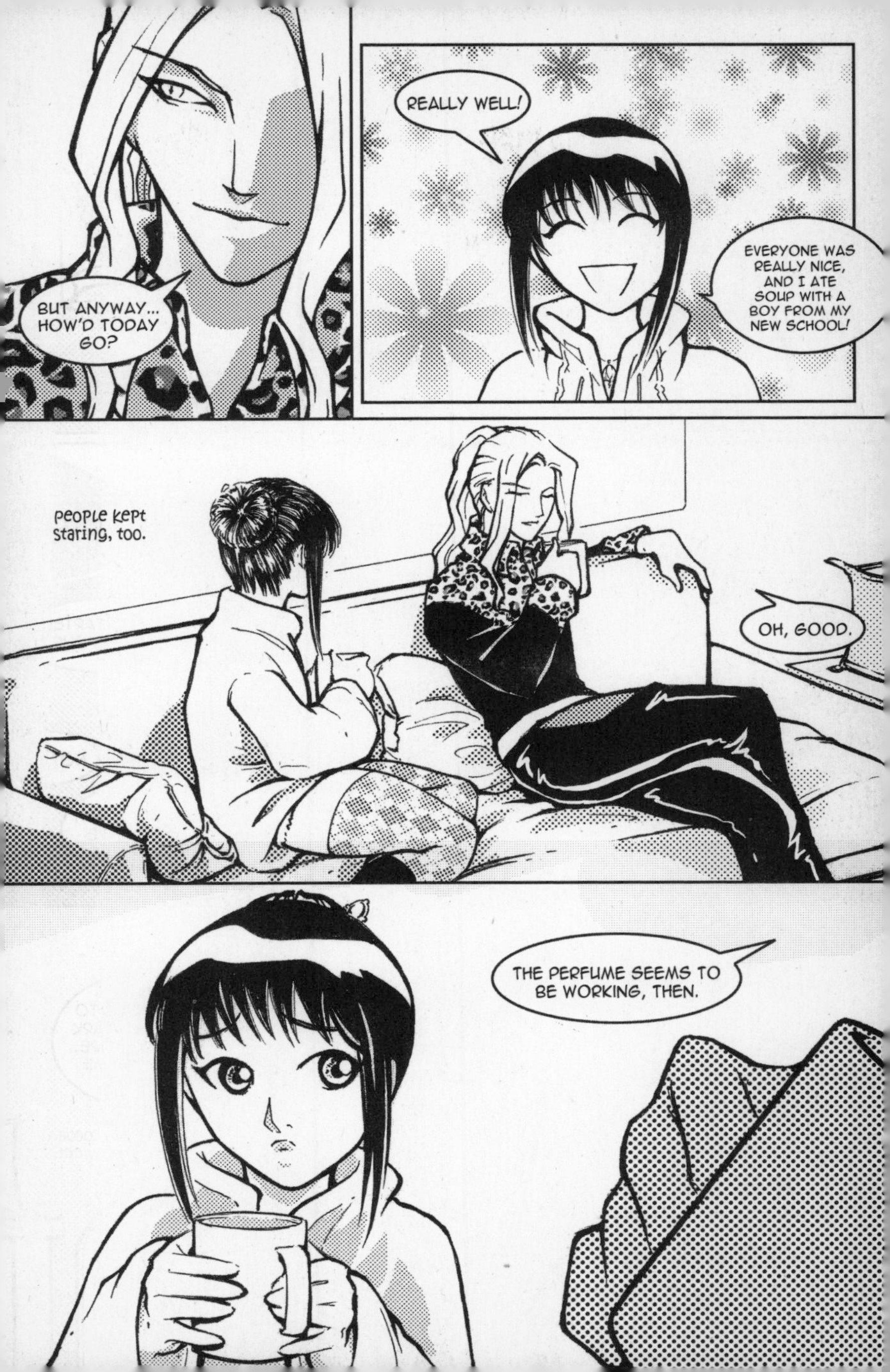
BUT ANYWAY... HOW'D TODAY GO?
REALLY WELL!
EVERYONE WAS REALLY NICE, AND I ATE SOUP WITH A BOY FROM MY NEW SCHOOL!
people kept staring, too.
OH, GOOD.
THE PERFUME SEEMS TO BE WORKING, THEN.

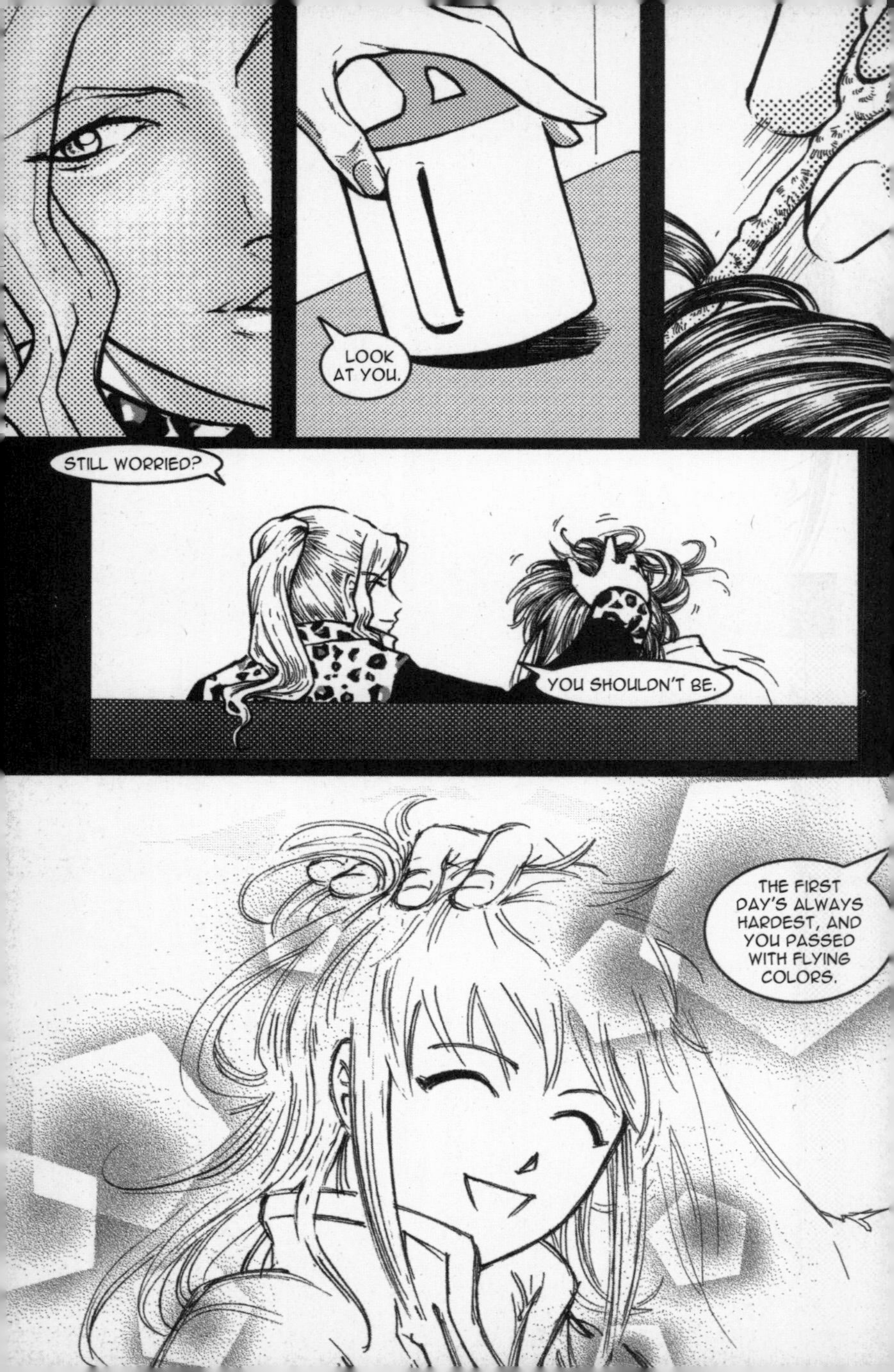
LOOK AT YOU.
STILL WORRIED?
YOU SHOULDN'T BE.
THE FIRST DAY'S ALWAYS HARDEST, AND YOU PASSED WITH FLYING COLORS.

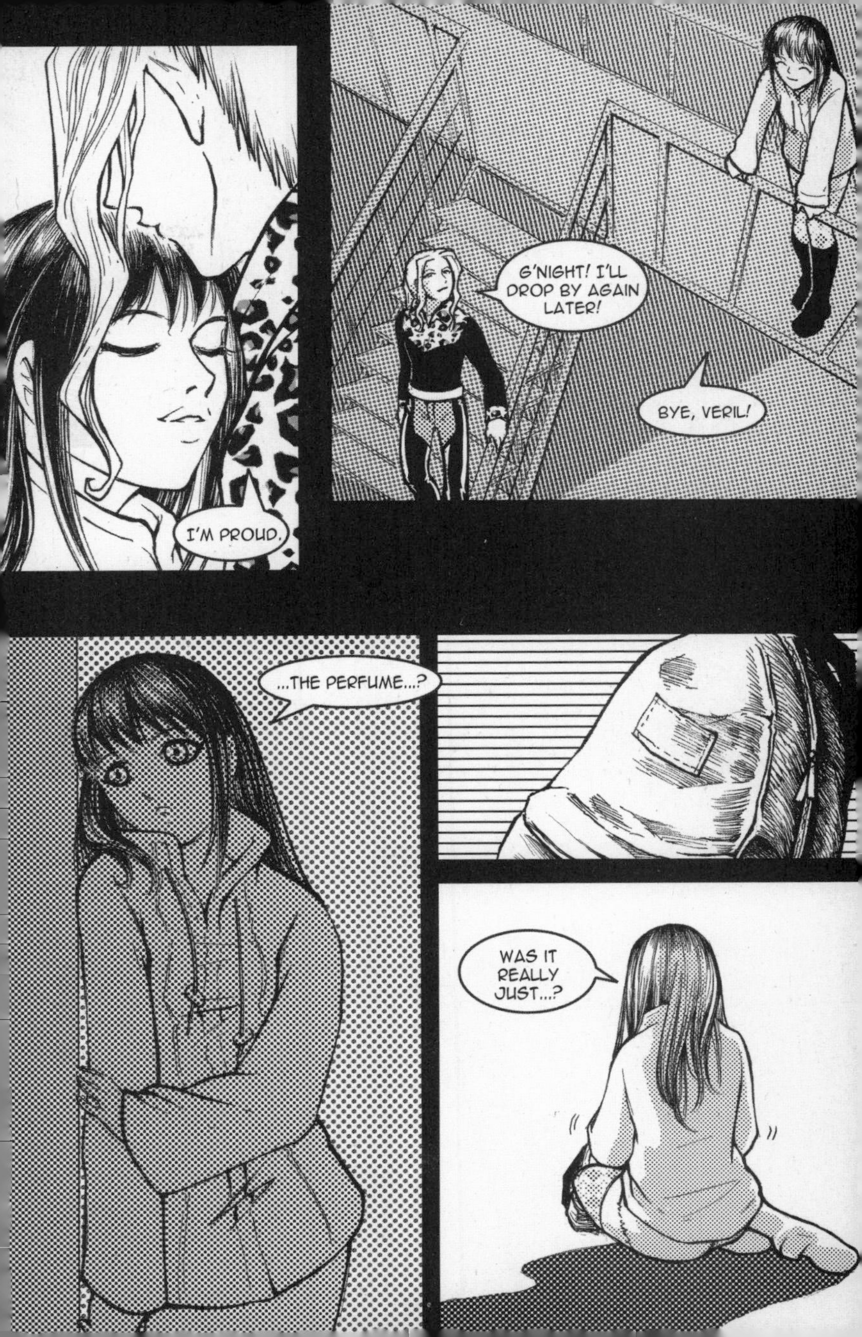
I'M PROUD.
G'NIGHT! I'LL DROP BY AGAIN LATER!
BYE, VERIL!
...THE PERFUME...?
WAS IT REALLY JUST...?

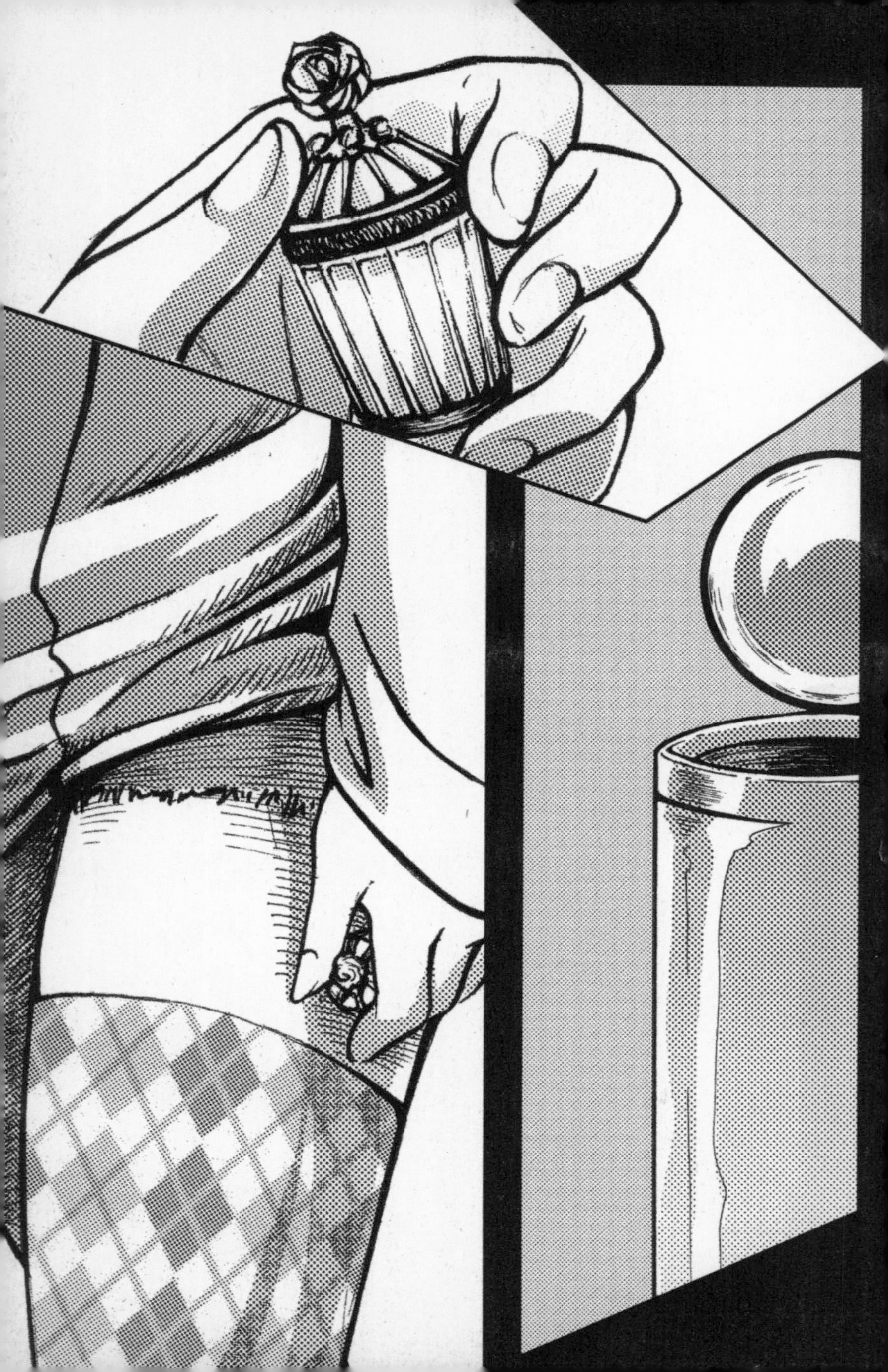

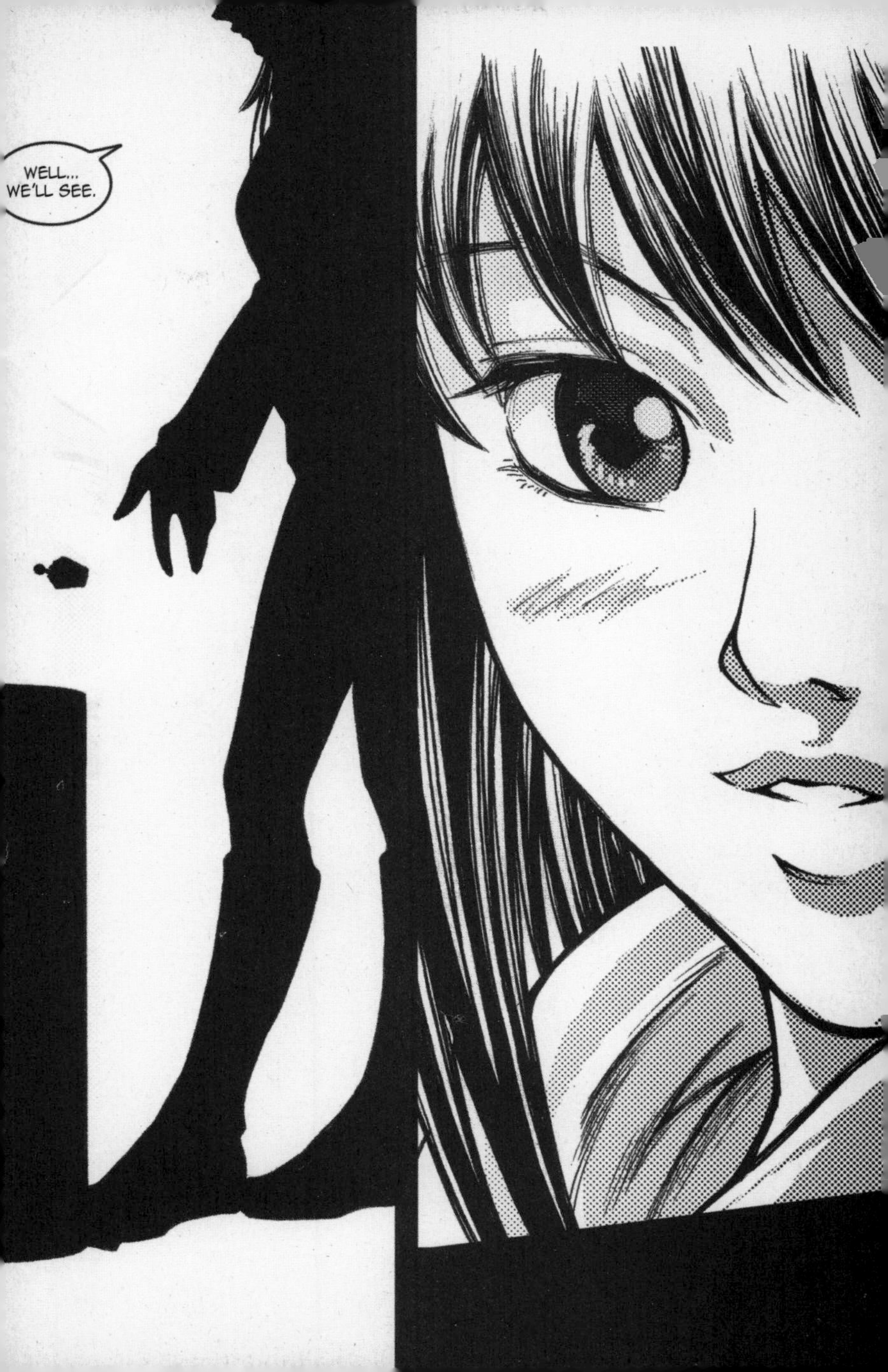
WELL... WE'LL SEE.

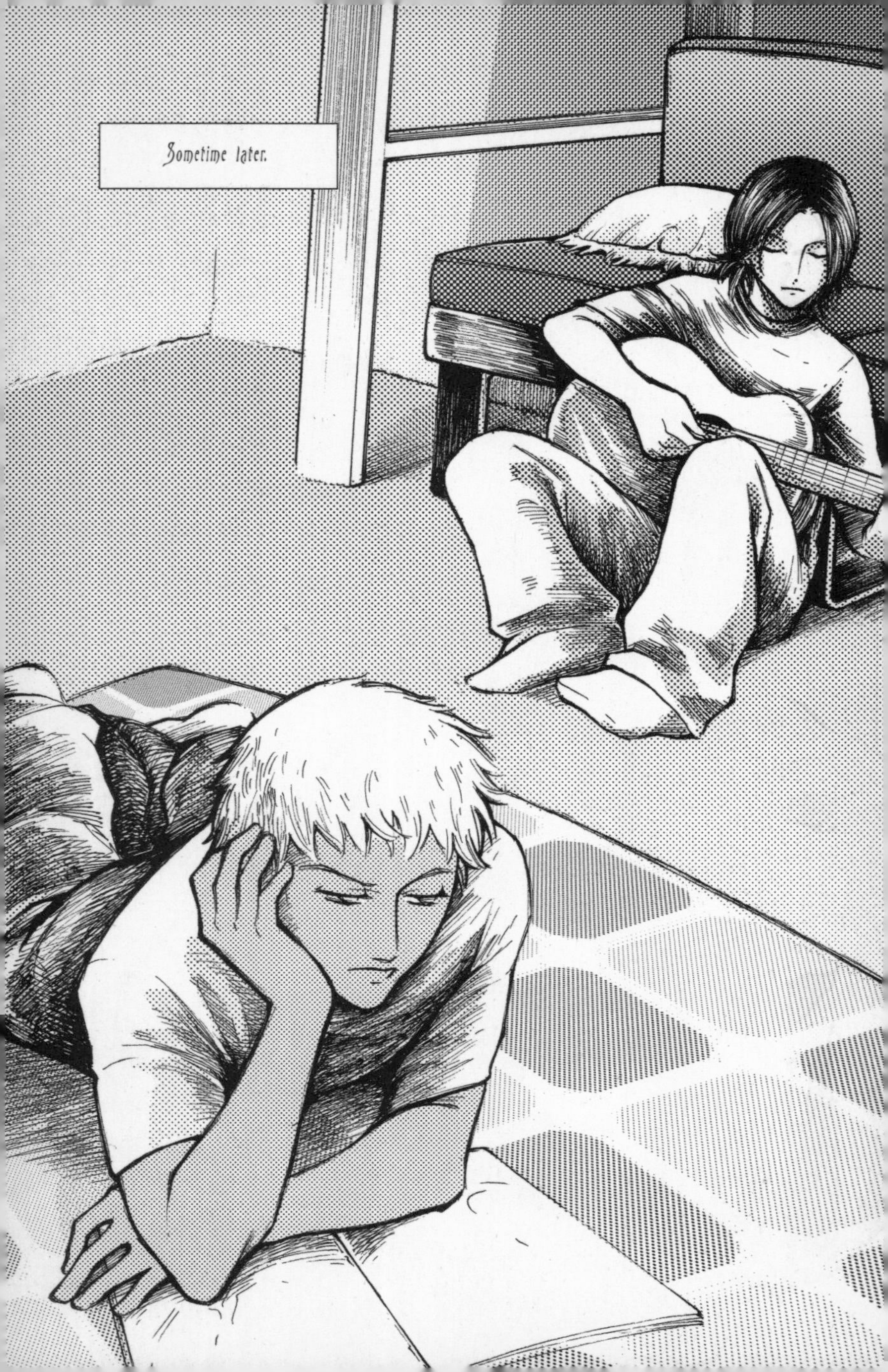
Sometime later.

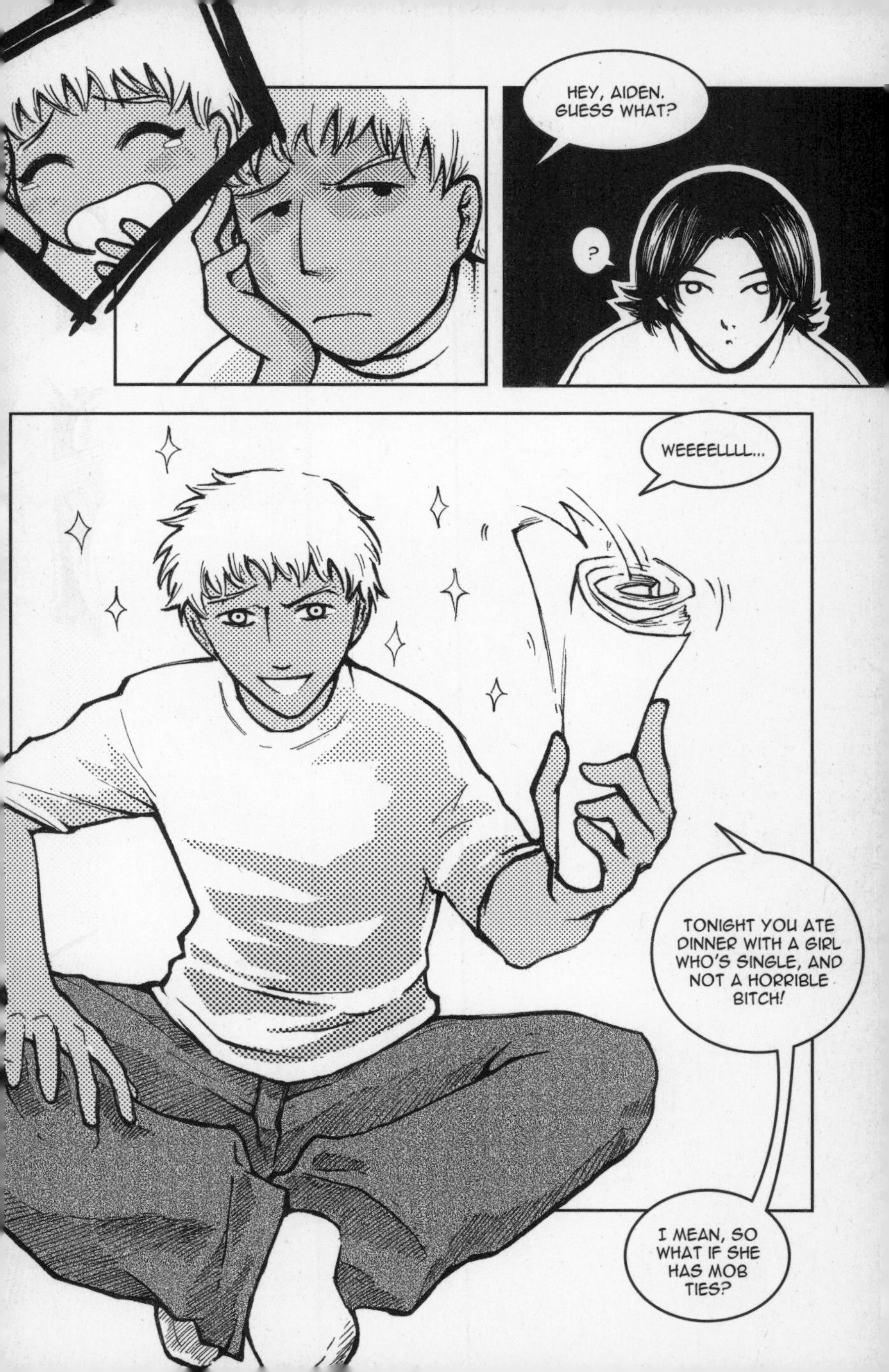
HEY, AIDEN. GUESS WHAT?
?
WEEEELLLL...
TONIGHT YOU ATE DINNER WITH A GIRL WHO'S SINGLE, AND NOT A HORRIBLE BITCH!
I MEAN, SO WHAT IF SHE HAS MOB TIES?

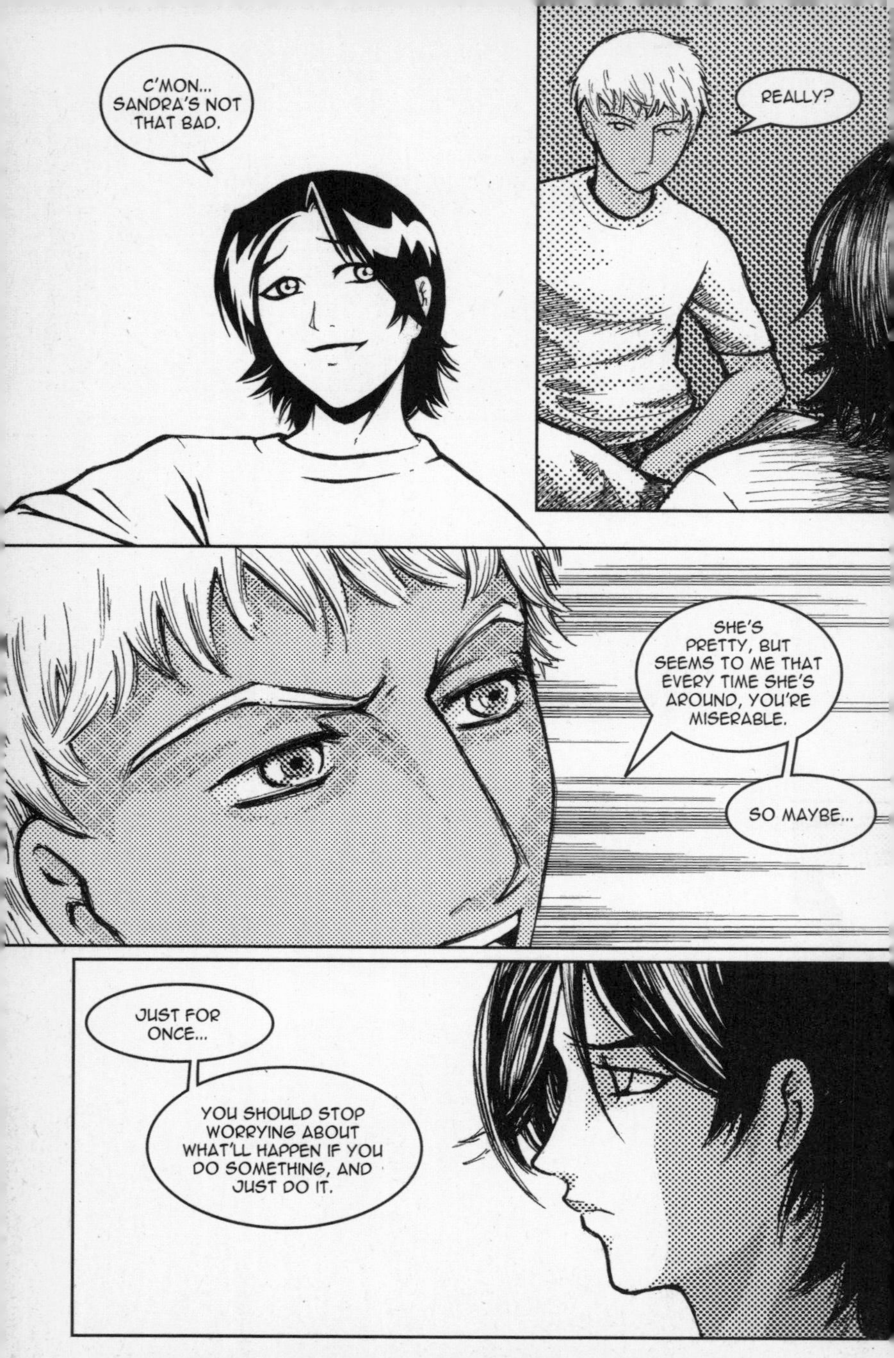
C'MON... SANDRA'S NOT THAT BAD.
REALLY?
SHE'S PRETTY, BUT SEEMS TO ME THAT EVERY TIME SHE'S AROUND, YOU'RE MISERABLE.
SO MAYBE...
JUST FOR ONCE...
YOU SHOULD STOP WORRYING ABOUT WHAT'LL HAPPEN IF YOU DO SOMETHING, AND JUST DO IT.

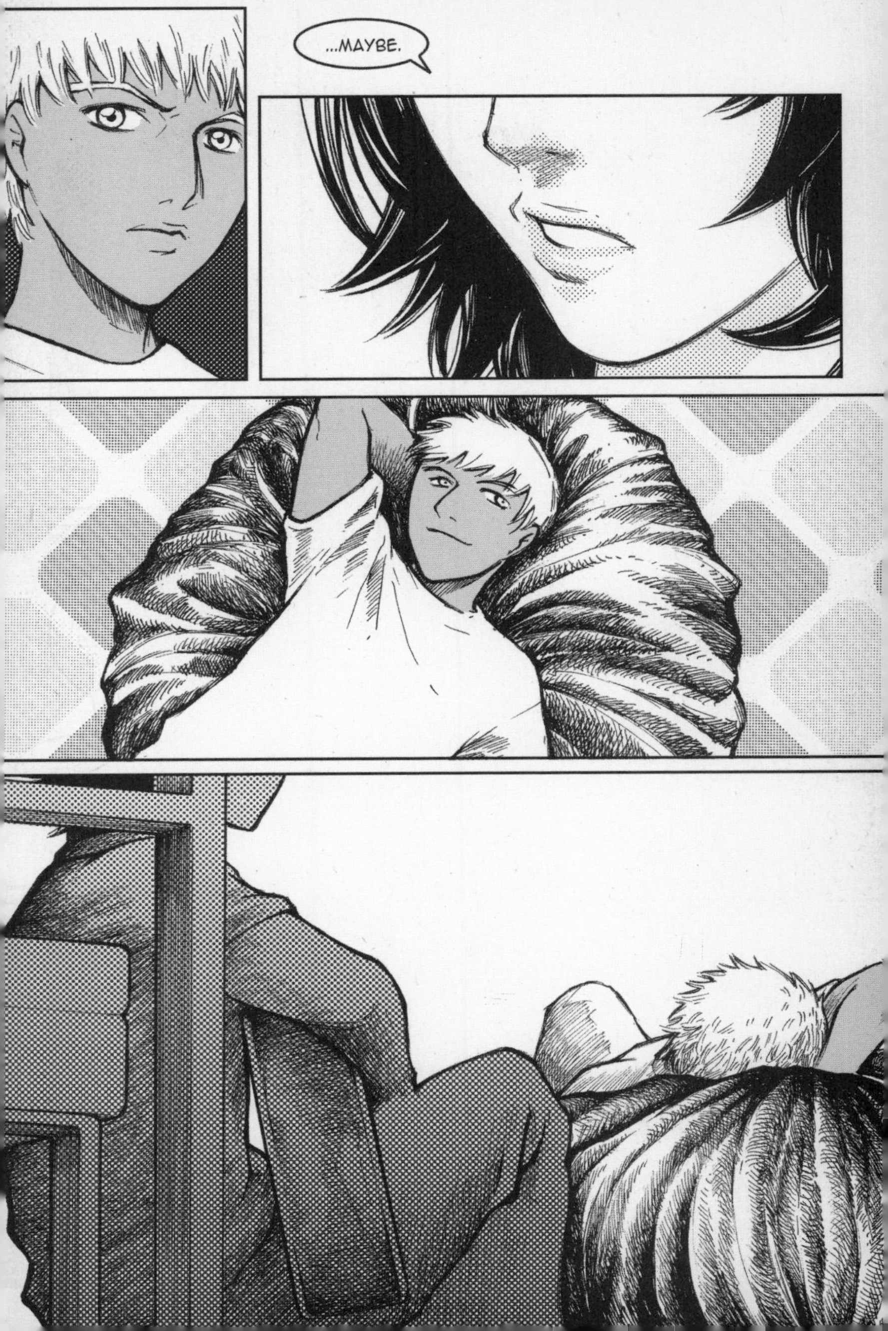
...MAYBE.

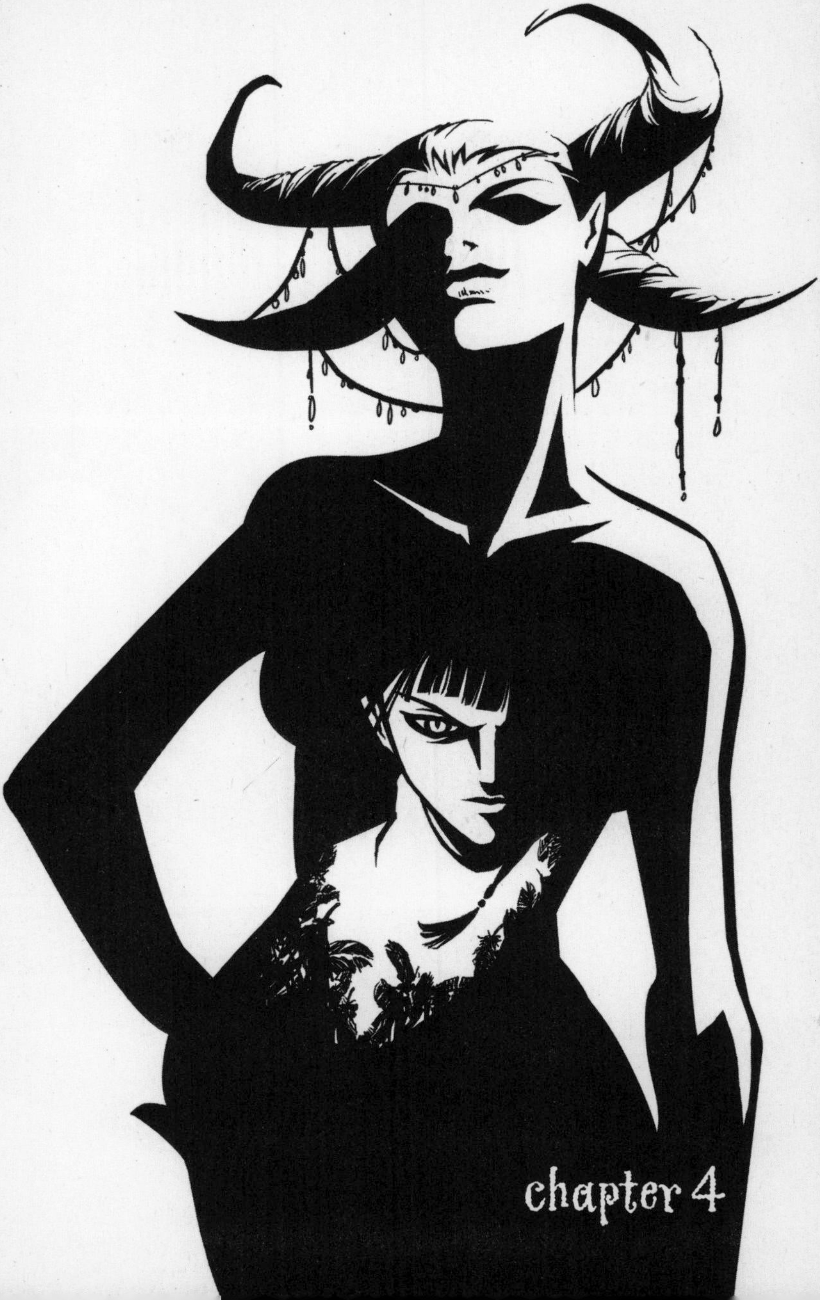

chapter 4

Erebus.

YES, OF COURSE. NOT AT ALL.

COME OUT, LITTLE IMP.

I HAVE TIME FOR YOU NOW.

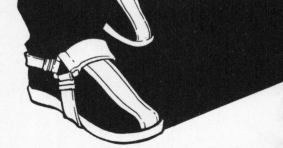

Two weeks later.

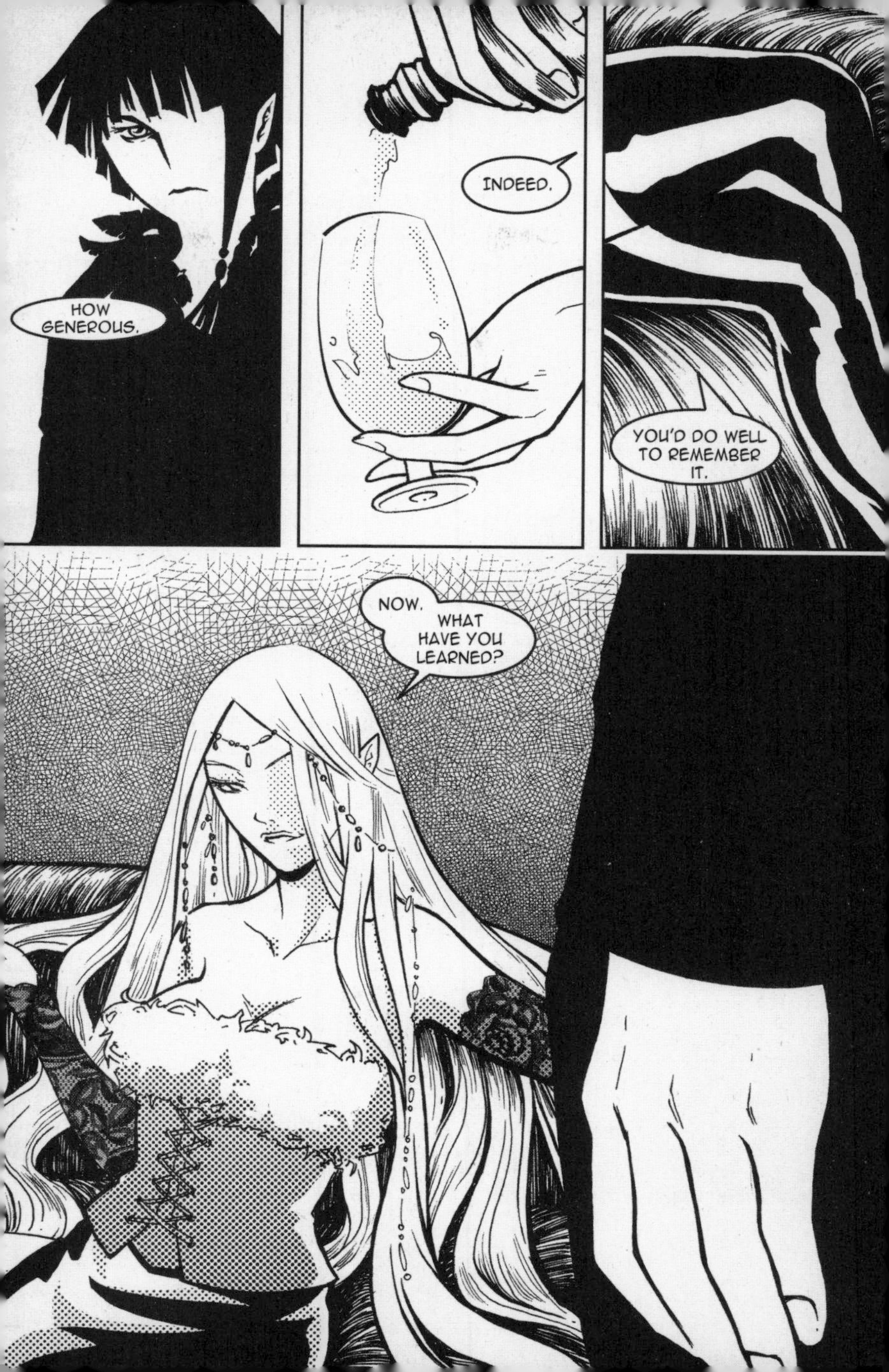
HOW GENEROUS.
INDEED.
YOU'D DO WELL TO REMEMBER IT.
NOW.
WHAT HAVE YOU LEARNED?

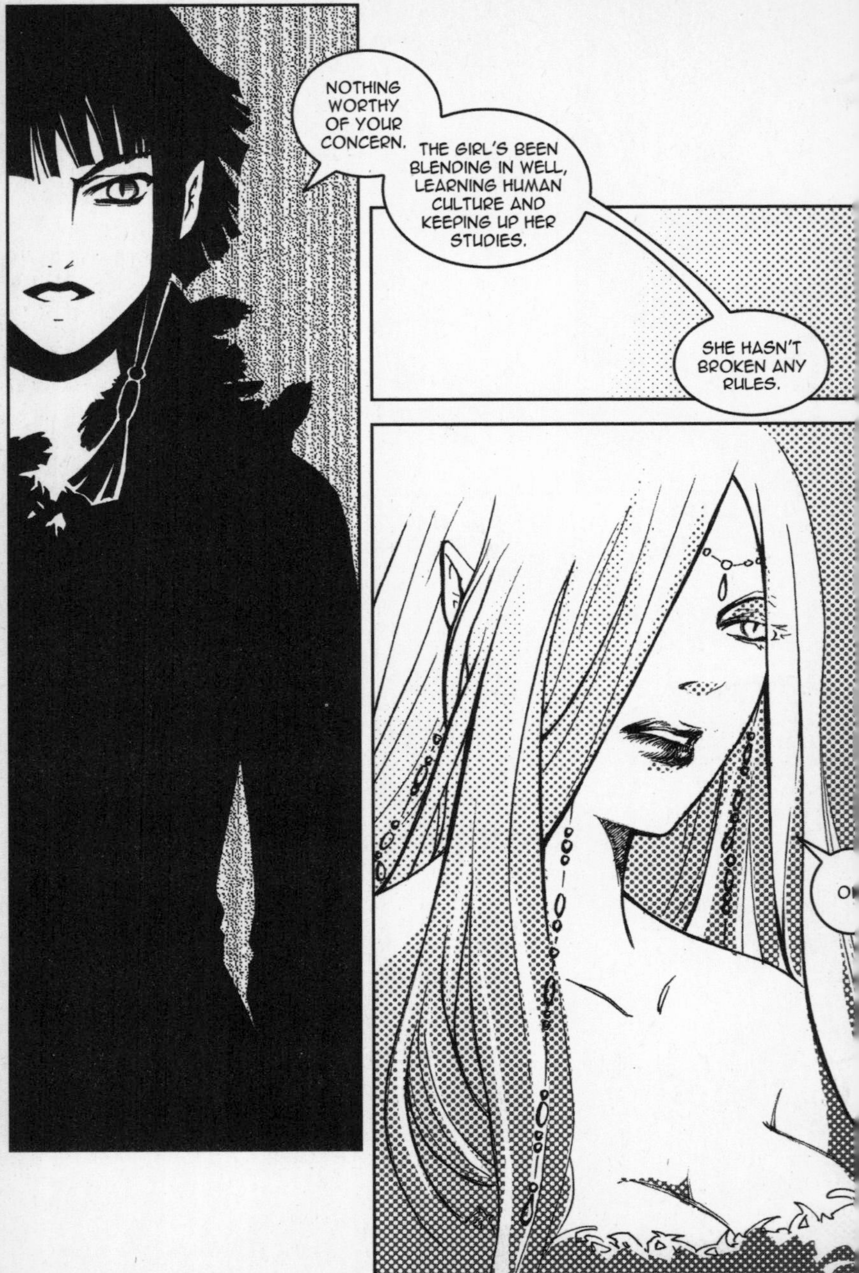
NOTHING WORTHY OF YOUR CONCERN.
THE GIRL'S BEEN BLENDING IN WELL, LEARNING HUMAN CULTURE AND KEEPING UP HER STUDIES.
SHE HASN'T BROKEN ANY RULES.

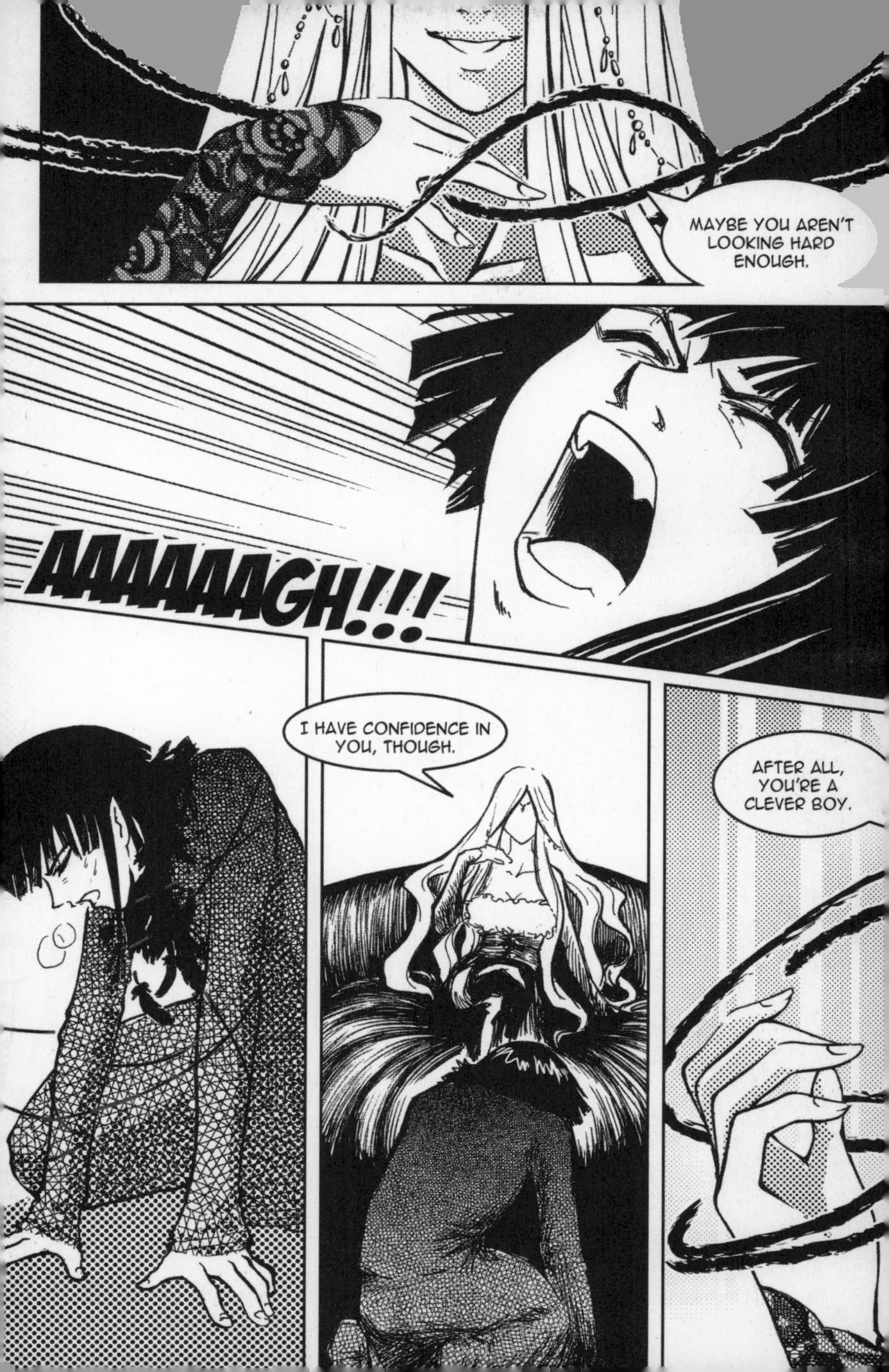
MAYBE YOU AREN'T LOOKING HARD ENOUGH.
AAAAAAAGH!!!
I HAVE CONFIDENCE IN YOU, THOUGH.
AFTER ALL, YOU'RE A CLEVER BOY.

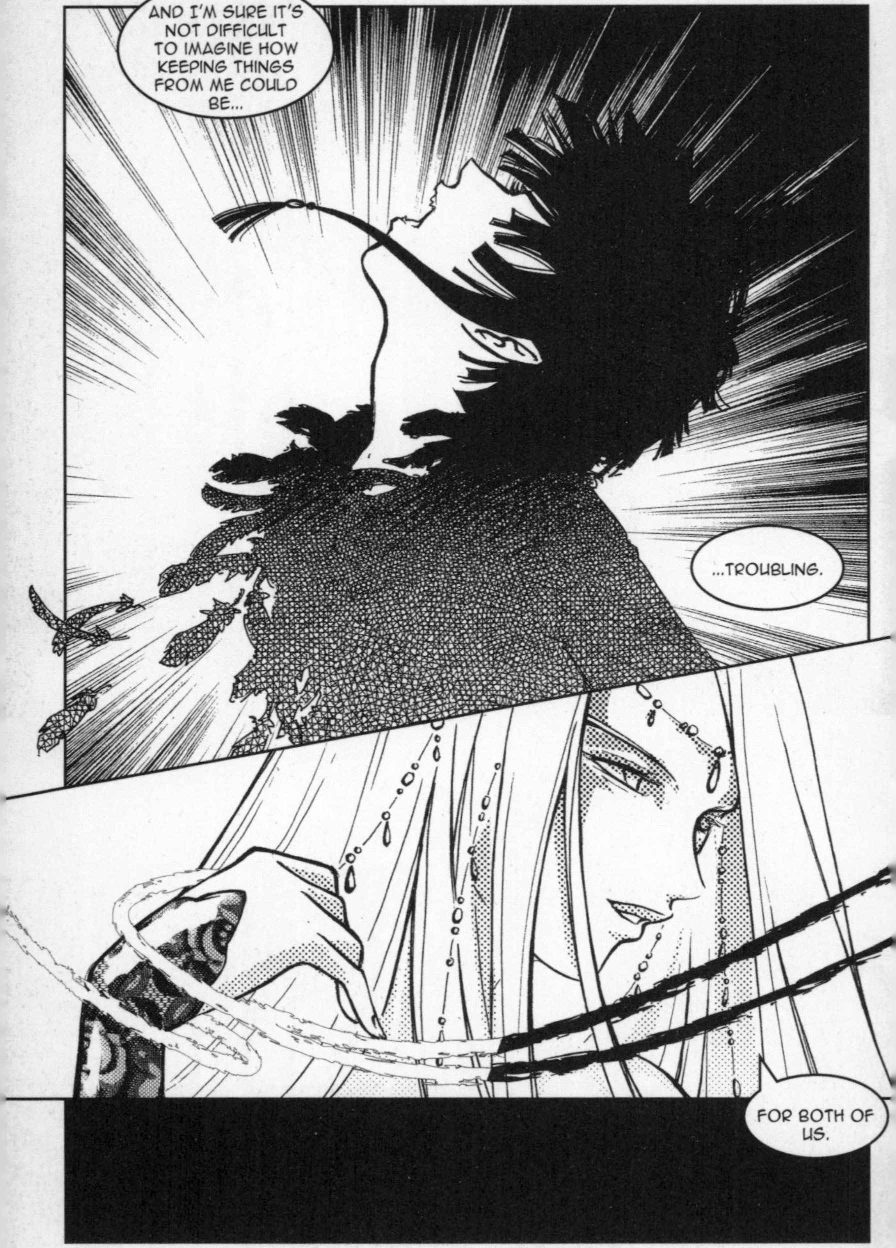

AND I'M SURE IT'S NOT DIFFICULT TO IMAGINE HOW KEEPING THINGS FROM ME COULD BE...
...TROUBLING.
FOR BOTH OF US.

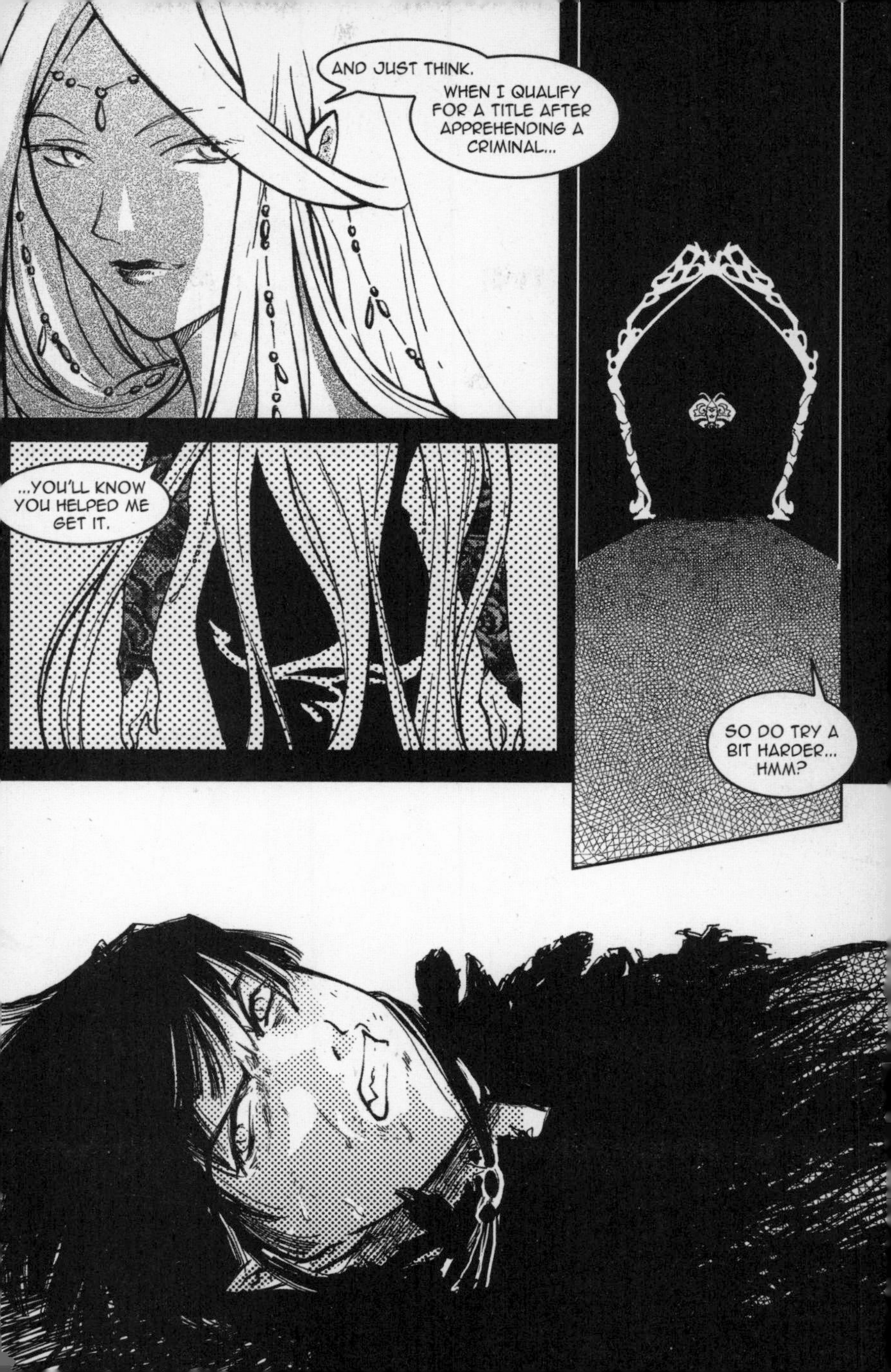
AND JUST THINK.
WHEN I QUALIFY FOR A TITLE AFTER APPREHENDING A CRIMINAL...
...YOU'LL KNOW YOU HELPED ME GET IT.
SO DO TRY A BIT HARDER... HMM?

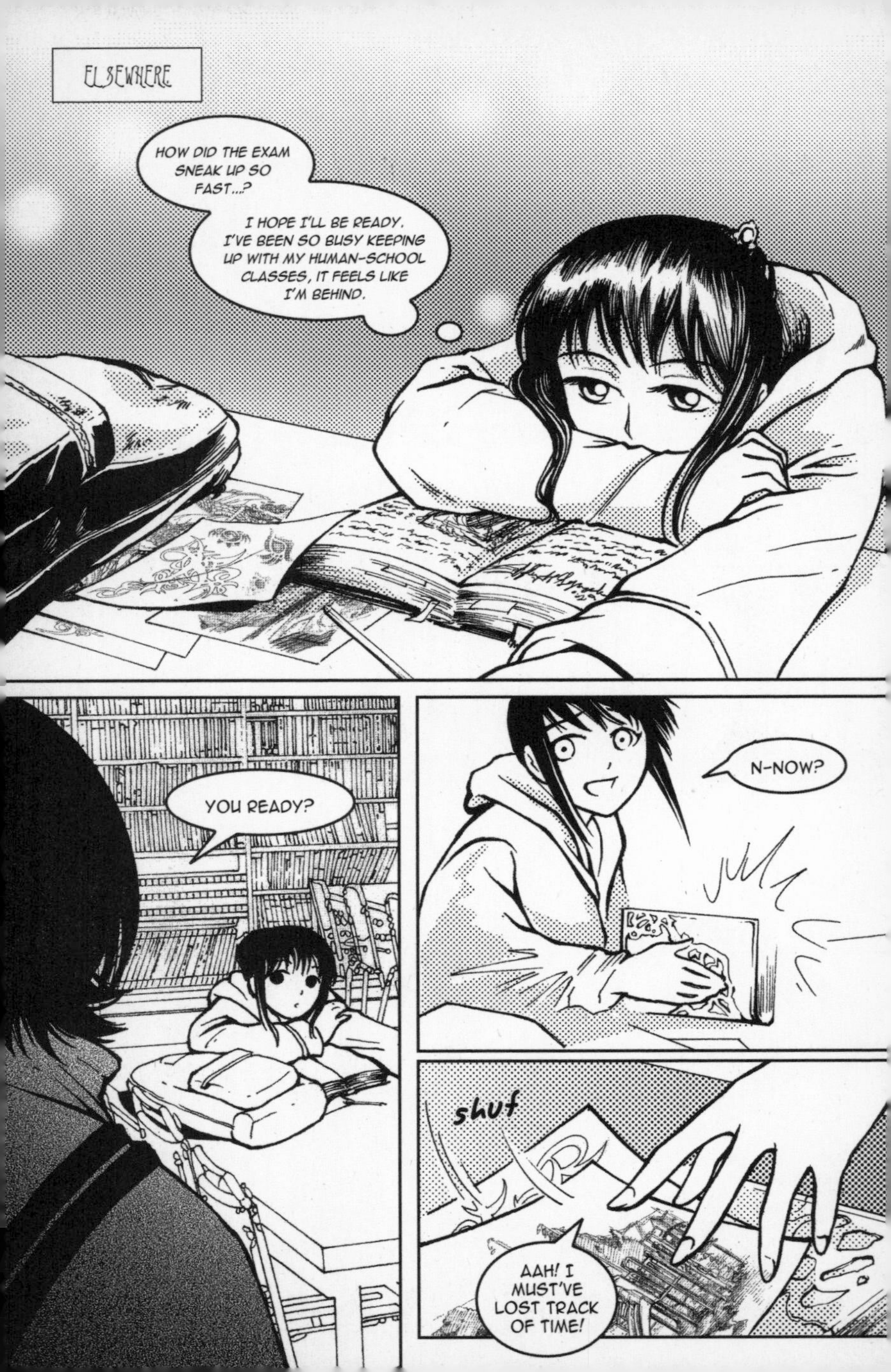
ELSEWHERE
HOW DID THE EXAM SNEAK UP SO FAST...?
I HOPE I'LL BE READY. I'VE BEEN SO BUSY KEEPING UP WITH MY HUMAN-SCHOOL CLASSES, IT FEELS LIKE I'M BEHIND.
YOU READY?
N-NOW?
shuf
AAH! I MUST'VE LOST TRACK OF TIME!

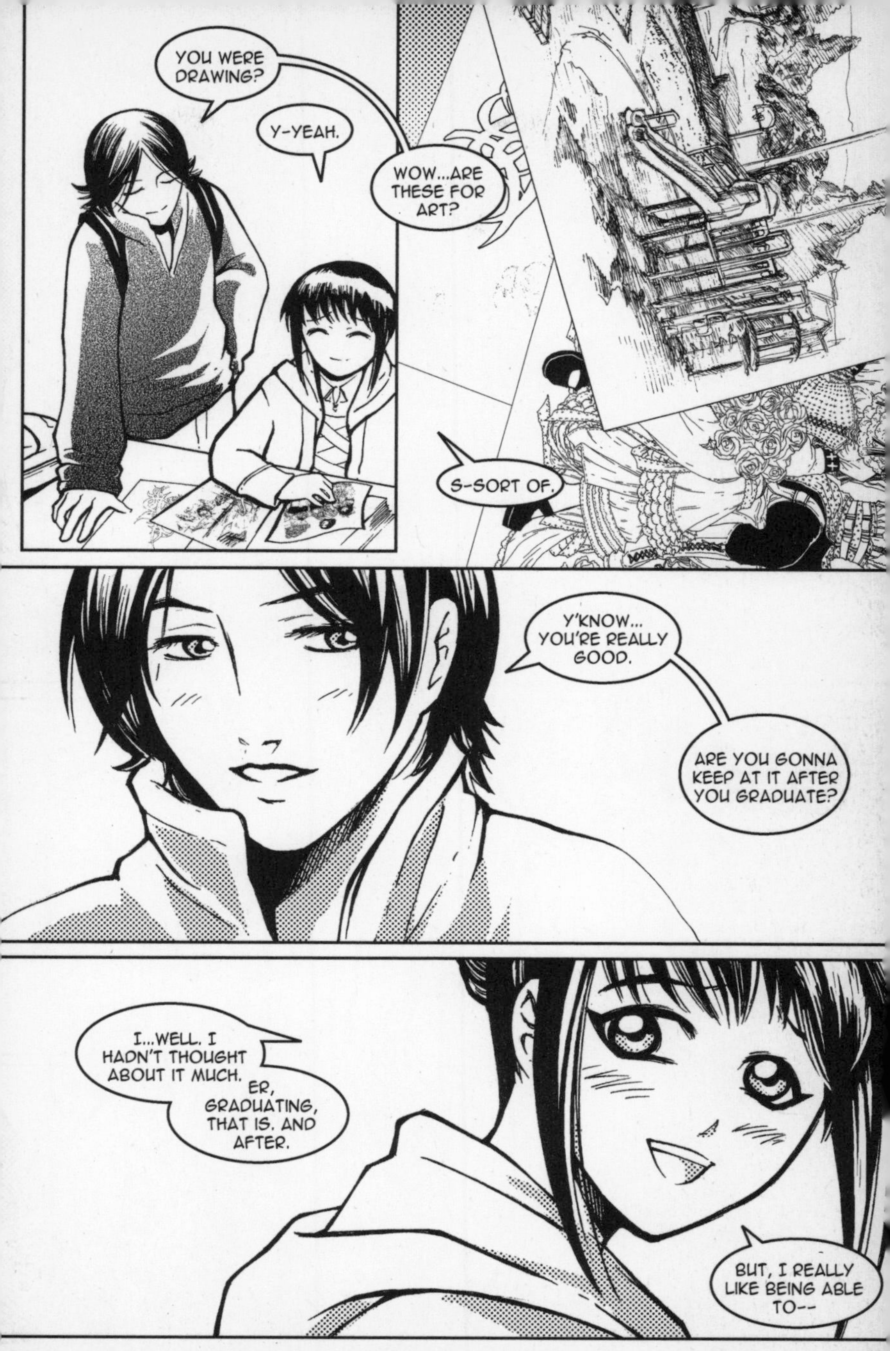
YOU WERE DRAWING?
Y-YEAH.
WOW...ARE THESE FOR ART?
S-SORT OF.
Y'KNOW... YOU'RE REALLY GOOD.
ARE YOU GONNA KEEP AT IT AFTER YOU GRADUATE?
I...WELL. I HADN'T THOUGHT ABOUT IT MUCH.
ER, GRADUATING, THAT IS. AND AFTER.
BUT, I REALLY LIKE BEING ABLE TO--

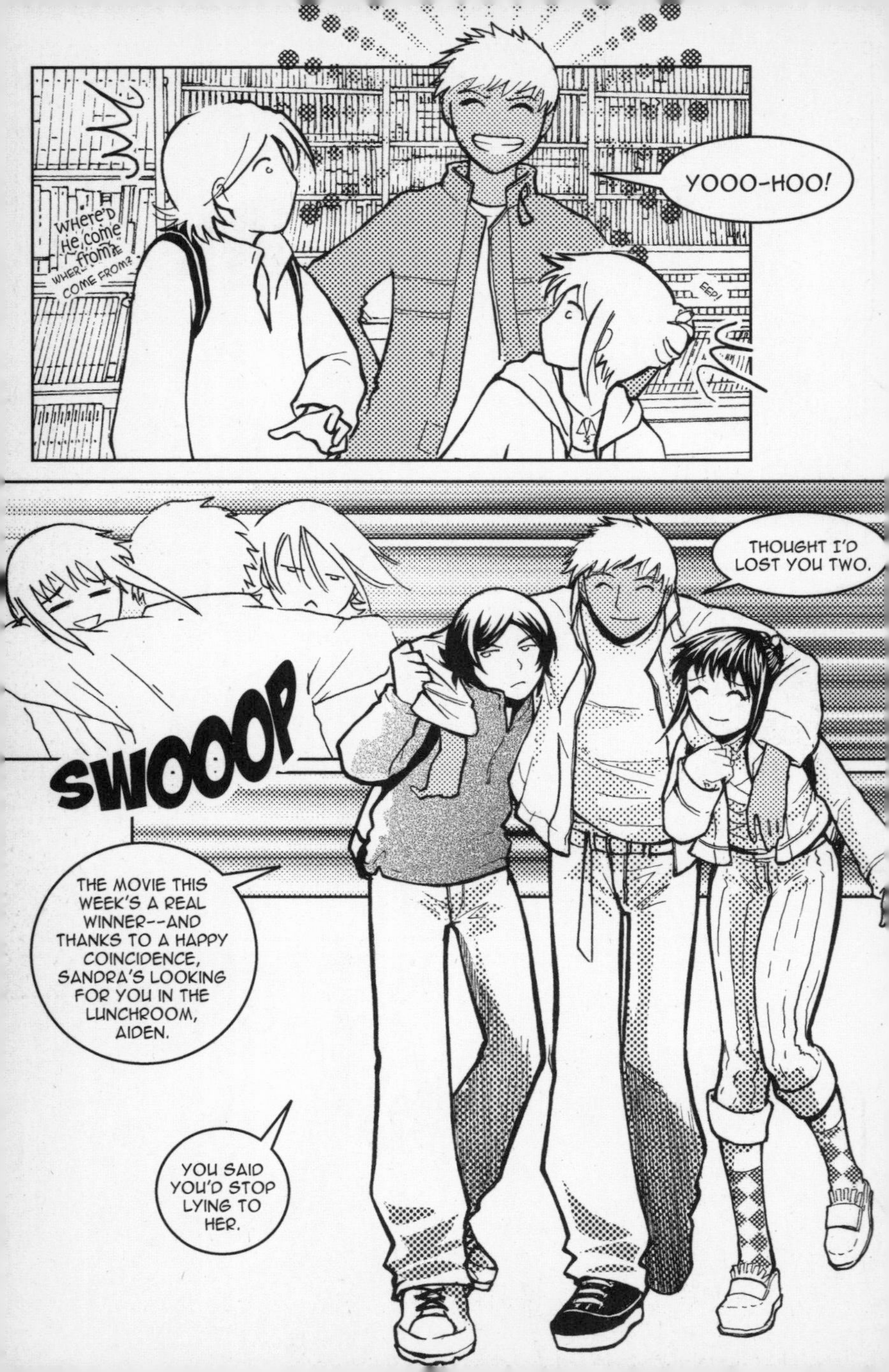

WHERE'D HE COME FROM?
WHERE'D HE COME FROM?
YOOO-HOO!
EEP!
THOUGHT I'D LOST YOU TWO.
SWOOOP
THE MOVIE THIS WEEK'S A REAL WINNER--AND THANKS TO A HAPPY COINCIDENCE, SANDRA'S LOOKING FOR YOU IN THE LUNCHROOM, AIDEN.
YOU SAID YOU'D STOP LYING TO HER.

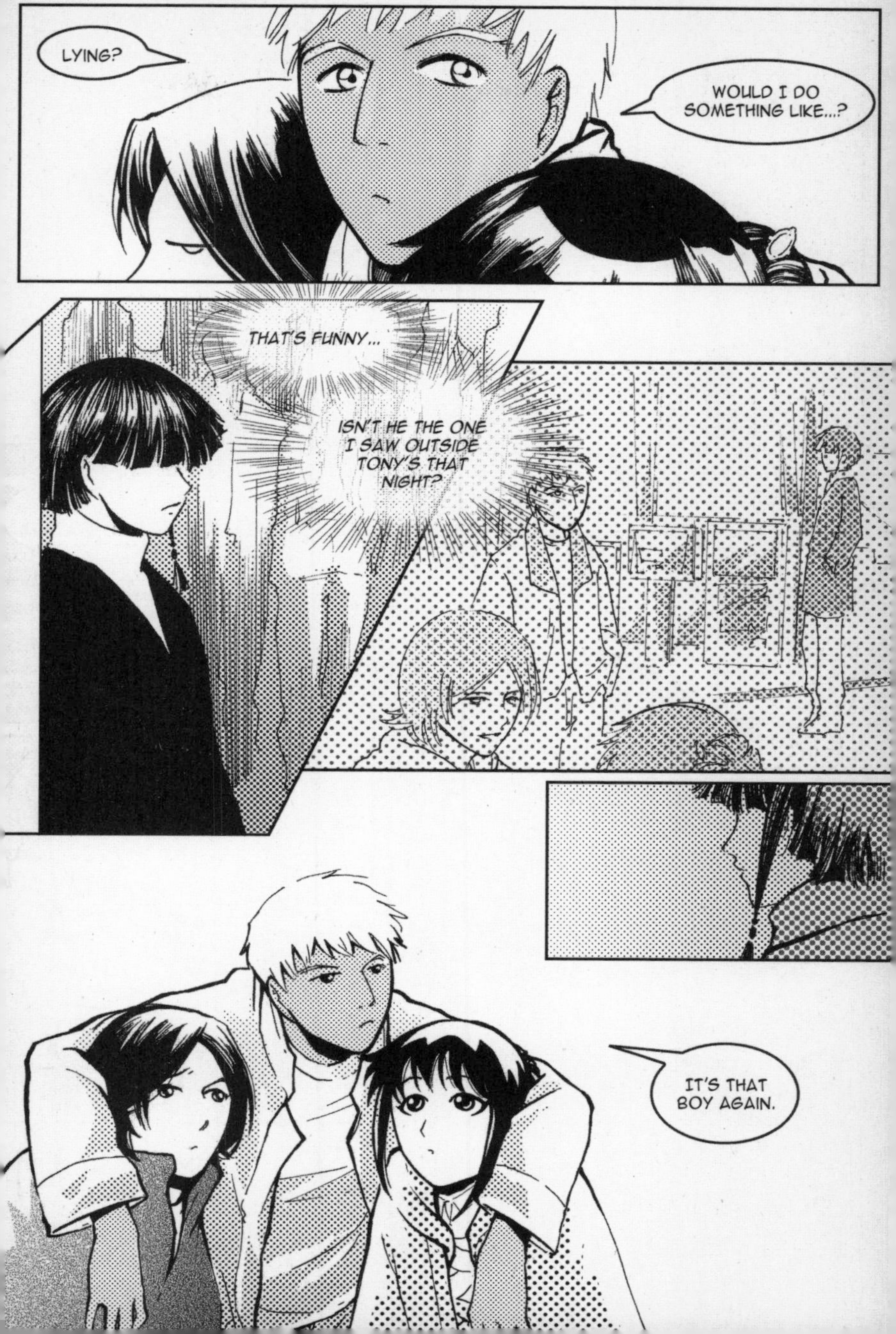
LYING?
WOULD I DO SOMETHING LIKE...?
THAT'S FUNNY...
ISN'T HE THE ONE I SAW OUTSIDE TONY'S THAT NIGHT?
IT'S THAT BOY AGAIN.

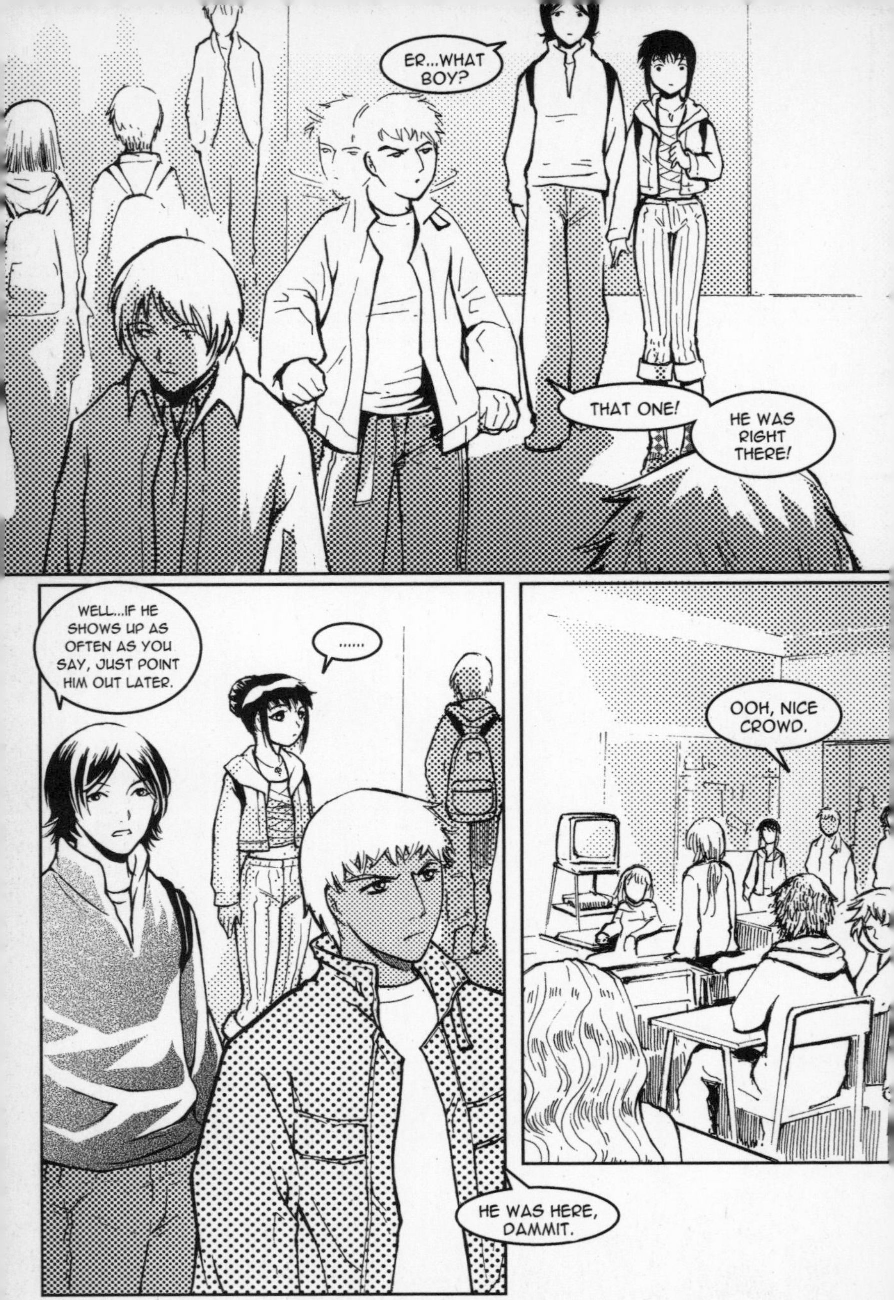
ER...WHAT BOY?
THAT ONE!
HE WAS RIGHT THERE!
WELL...IF HE SHOWS UP AS OFTEN AS YOU SAY, JUST POINT HIM OUT LATER.
......
HE WAS HERE, DAMMIT.
OOH, NICE CROWD.

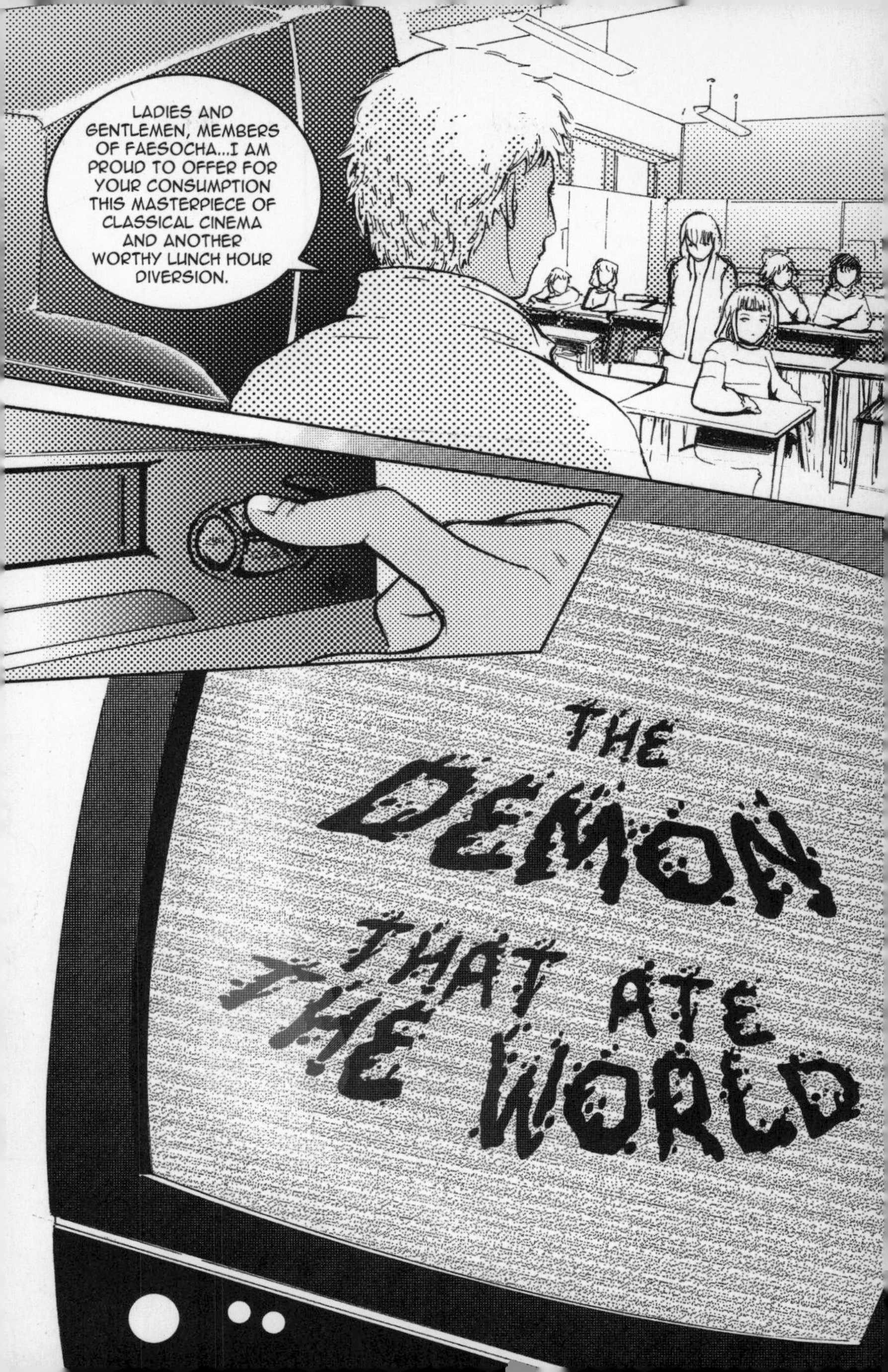
LADIES AND GENTLEMEN, MEMBERS OF FAESOCHA...I AM PROUD TO OFFER FOR YOUR CONSUMPTION THIS MASTERPIECE OF CLASSICAL CINEMA AND ANOTHER WORTHY LUNCH HOUR DIVERSION.
THE DEMON THAT ATE THE WORLD

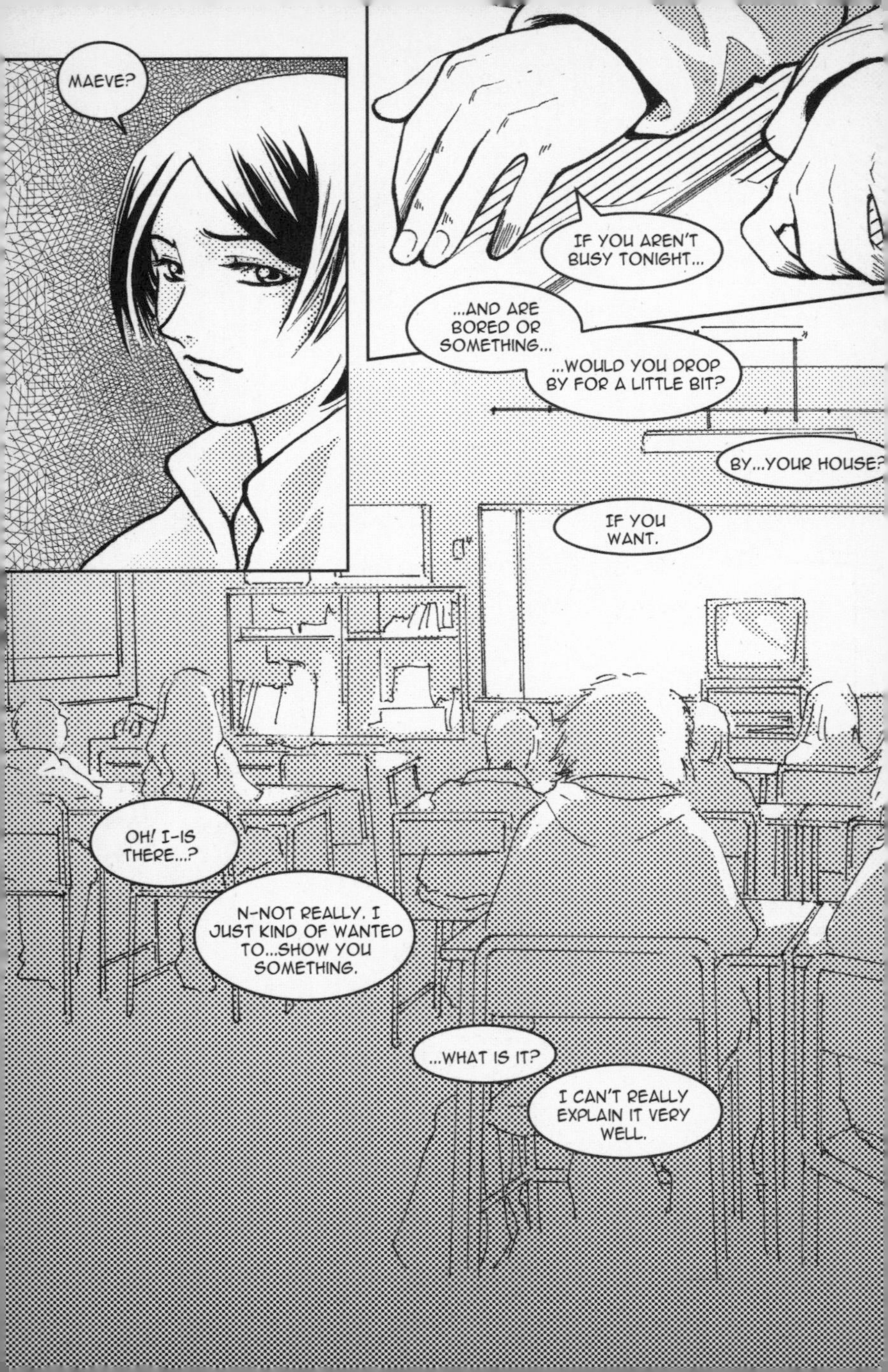
MAEVE?
IF YOU AREN'T BUSY TONIGHT...
...AND ARE BORED OR SOMETHING...
...WOULD YOU DROP BY FOR A LITTLE BIT?
BY...YOUR HOUSE?
IF YOU WANT.
OH! I-IS THERE...?
N-NOT REALLY. I JUST KIND OF WANTED TO...SHOW YOU SOMETHING.
...WHAT IS IT?
I CAN'T REALLY EXPLAIN IT VERY WELL.

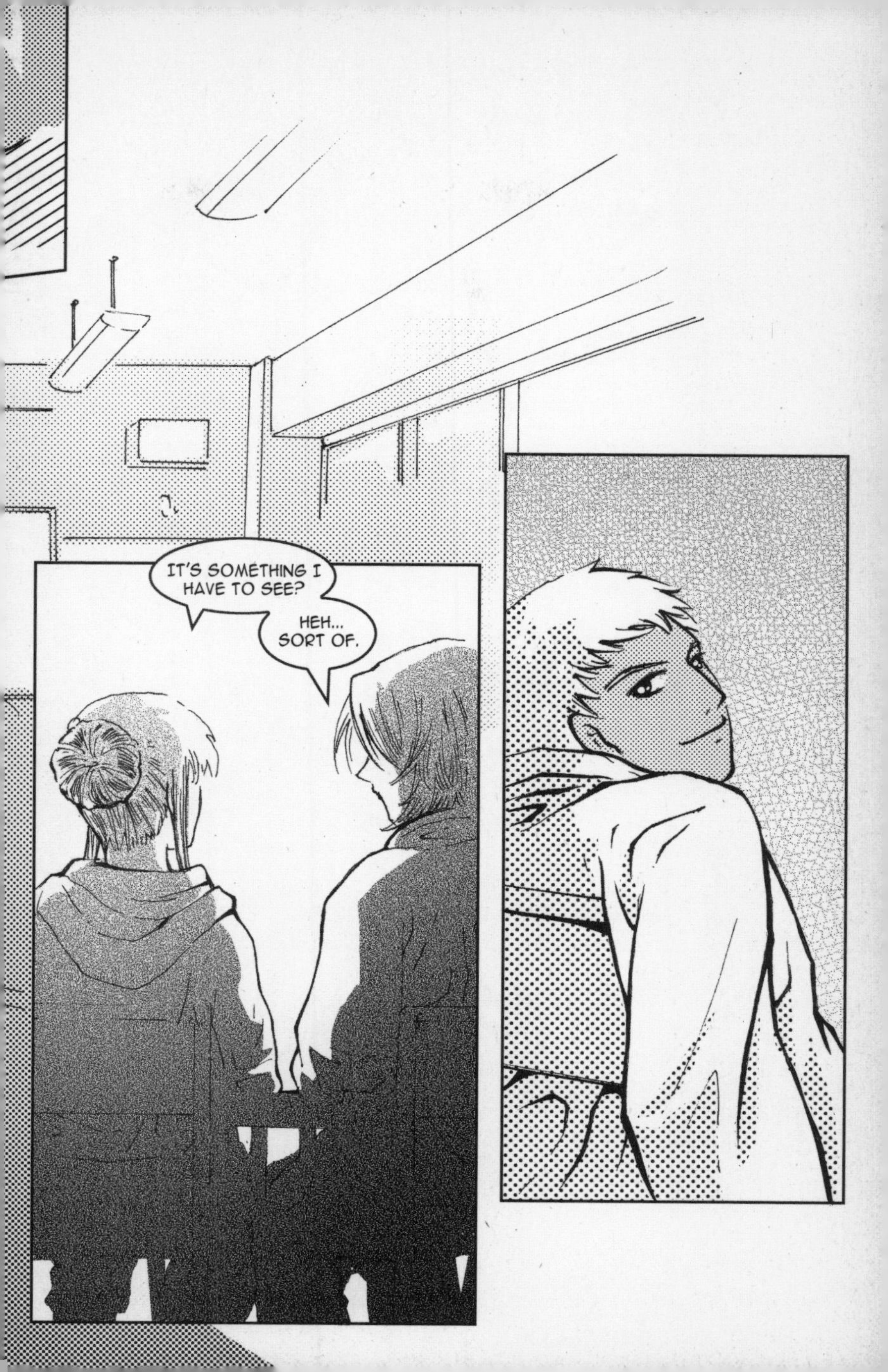
IT'S SOMETHING I HAVE TO SEE?
HEH... SORT OF.

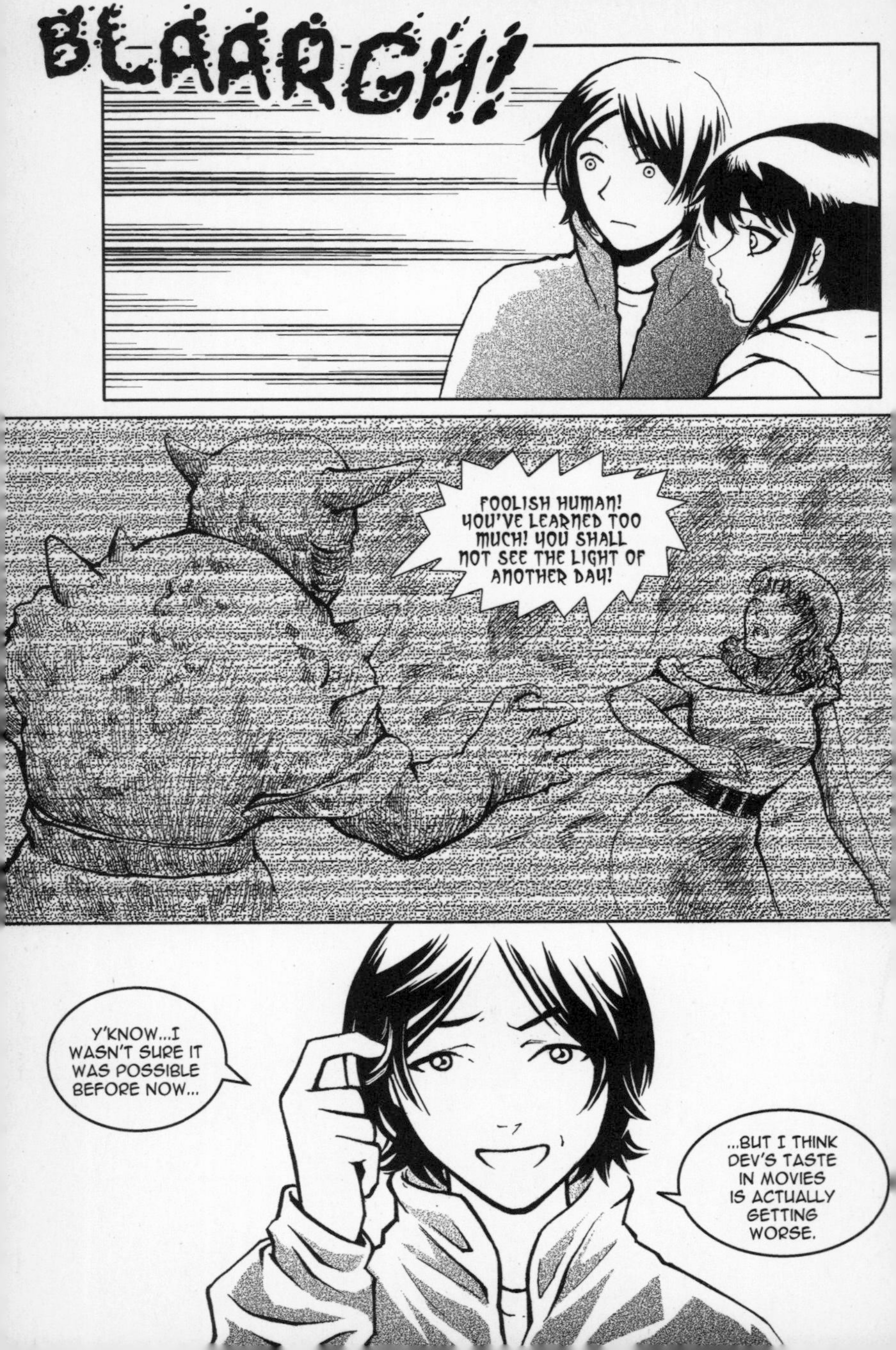
BLAARGH!
FOOLISH HUMAN! YOU'VE LEARNED TOO MUCH! YOU SHALL NOT SEE THE LIGHT OF ANOTHER DAY!
Y'KNOW...I WASN'T SURE IT WAS POSSIBLE BEFORE NOW...
...BUT I THINK DEV'S TASTE IN MOVIES IS ACTUALLY GETTING WORSE.

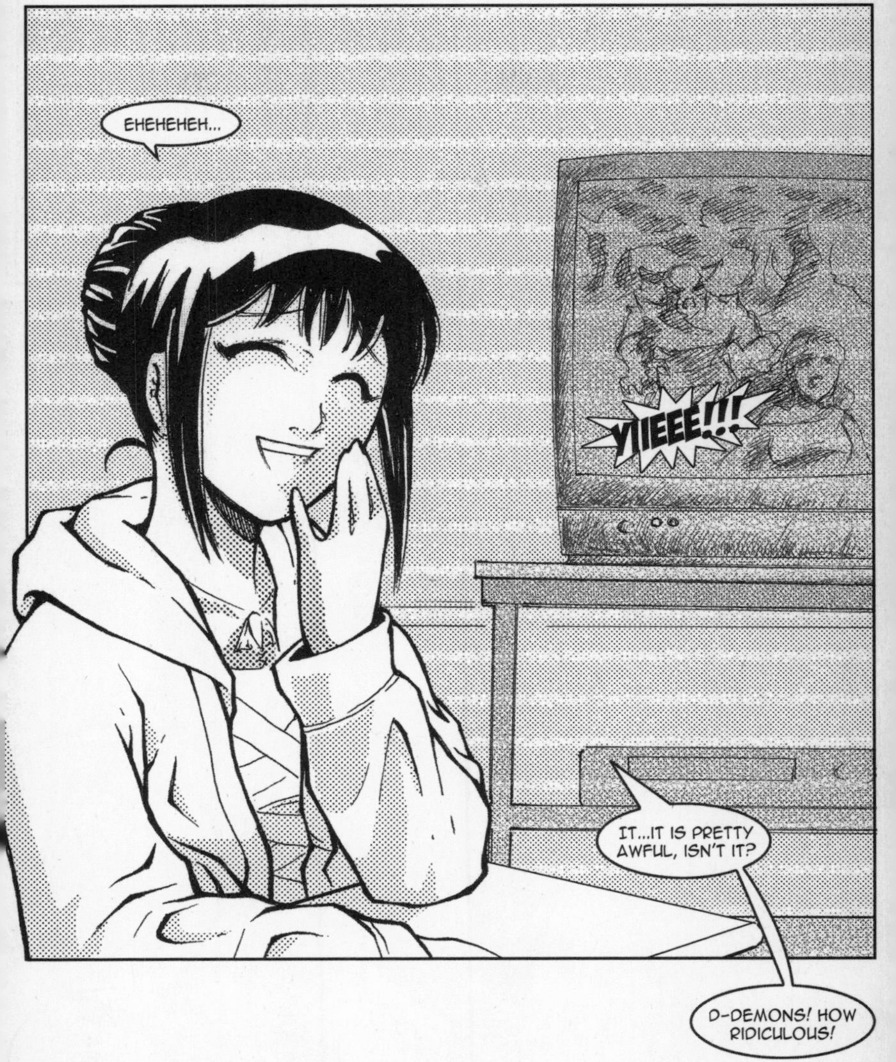
EHEHEHEH...
YIIEEE!!!
IT...IT IS PRETTY AWFUL, ISN'T IT?
D-DEMONS! HOW RIDICULOUS!

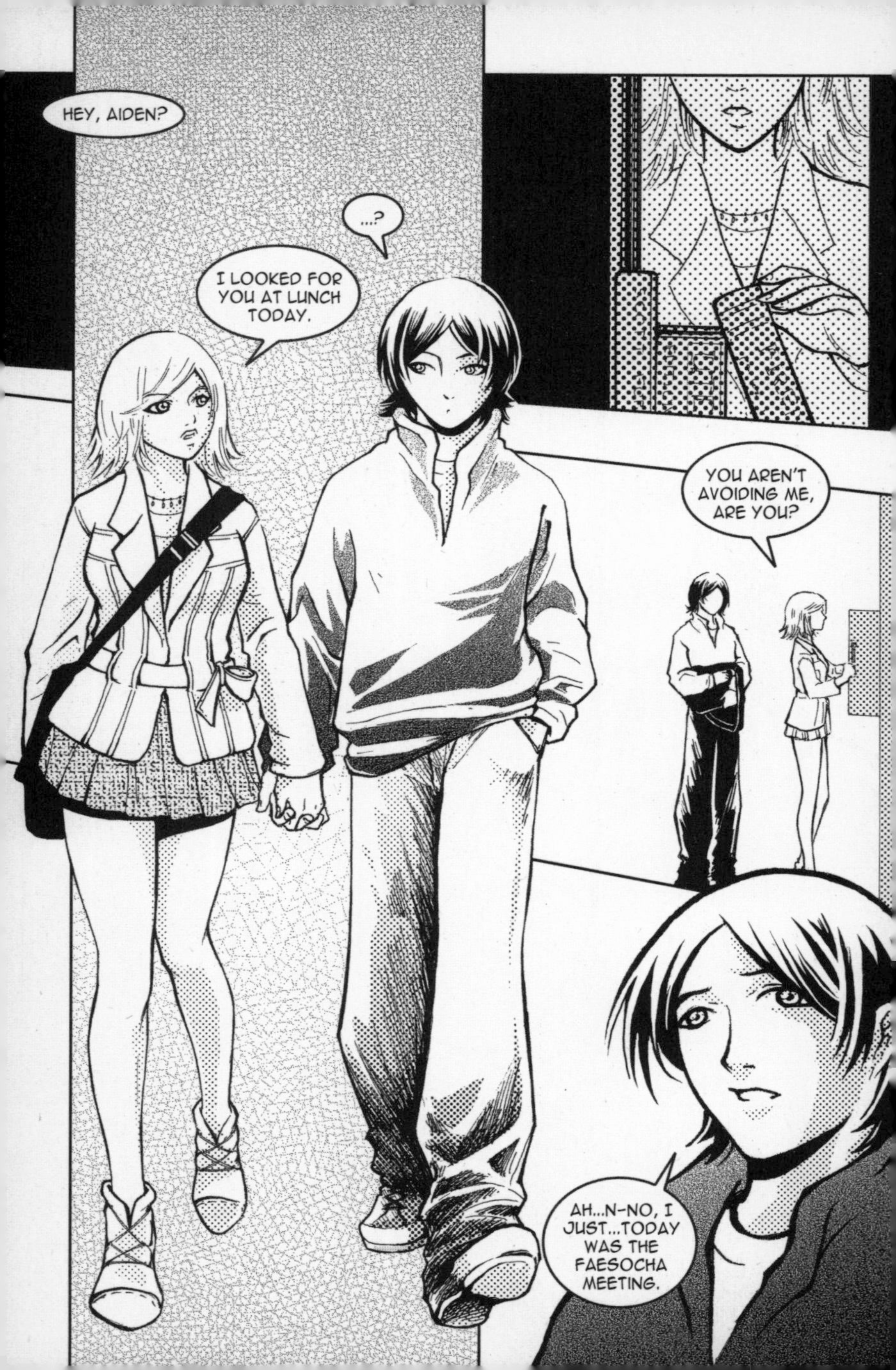
HEY, AIDEN?
...?
I LOOKED FOR YOU AT LUNCH TODAY.
YOU AREN'T AVOIDING ME, ARE YOU?
AH...N-NO, I JUST...TODAY WAS THE FAESOCHA MEETING.

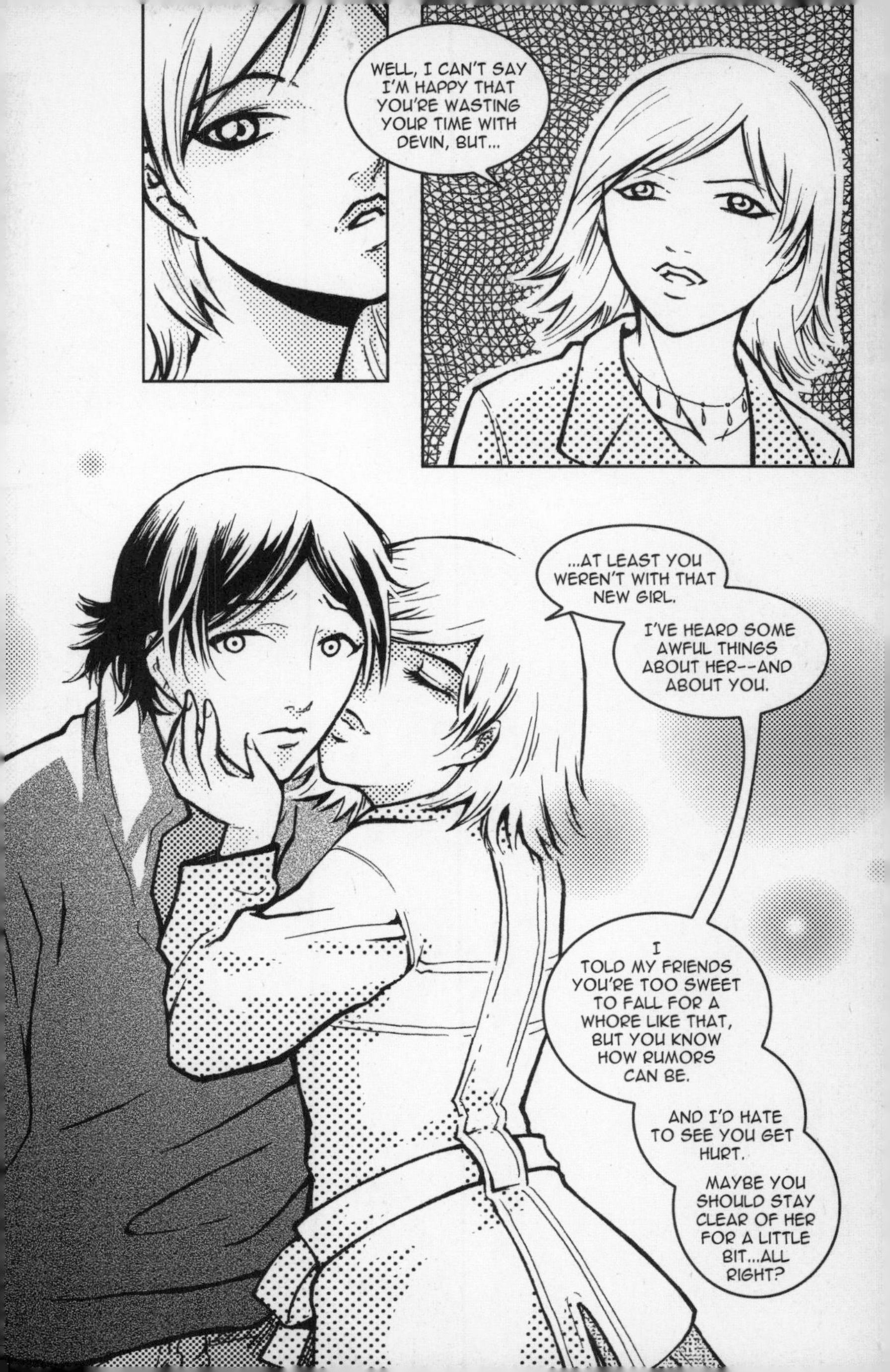
WELL, I CAN'T SAY I'M HAPPY THAT YOU'RE WASTING YOUR TIME WITH DEVIN, BUT...
...AT LEAST YOU WEREN'T WITH THAT NEW GIRL.
I'VE HEARD SOME AWFUL THINGS ABOUT HER--AND ABOUT YOU.
I TOLD MY FRIENDS YOU'RE TOO SWEET TO FALL FOR A WHORE LIKE THAT, BUT YOU KNOW HOW RUMORS CAN BE.
AND I'D HATE TO SEE YOU GET HURT.
MAYBE YOU SHOULD STAY CLEAR OF HER FOR A LITTLE BIT...ALL RIGHT?

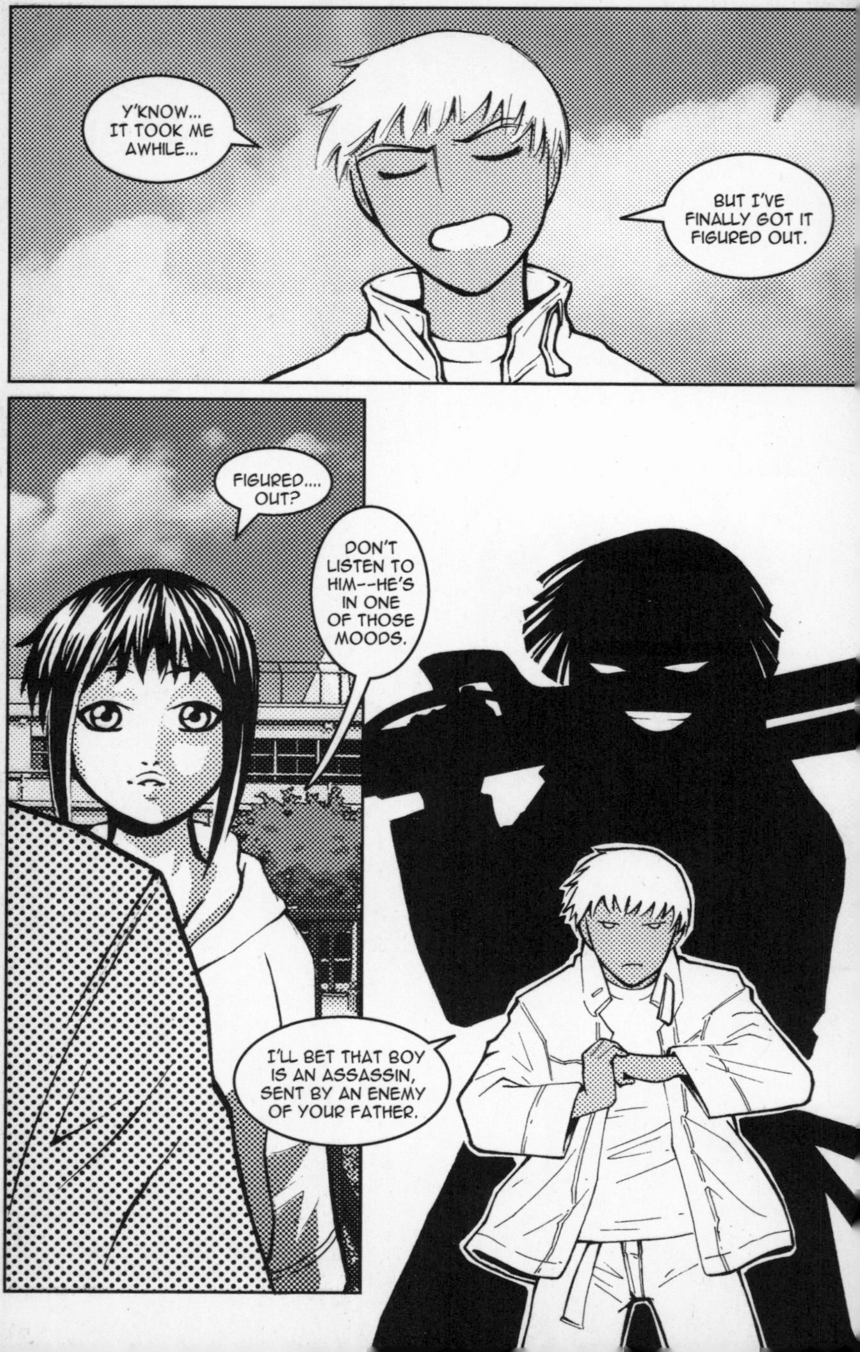
Y'KNOW... IT TOOK ME AWHILE...
BUT I'VE FINALLY GOT IT FIGURED OUT.
FIGURED.... OUT?
DON'T LISTEN TO HIM--HE'S IN ONE OF THOSE MOODS.
I'LL BET THAT BOY IS AN ASSASSIN, SENT BY AN ENEMY OF YOUR FATHER.

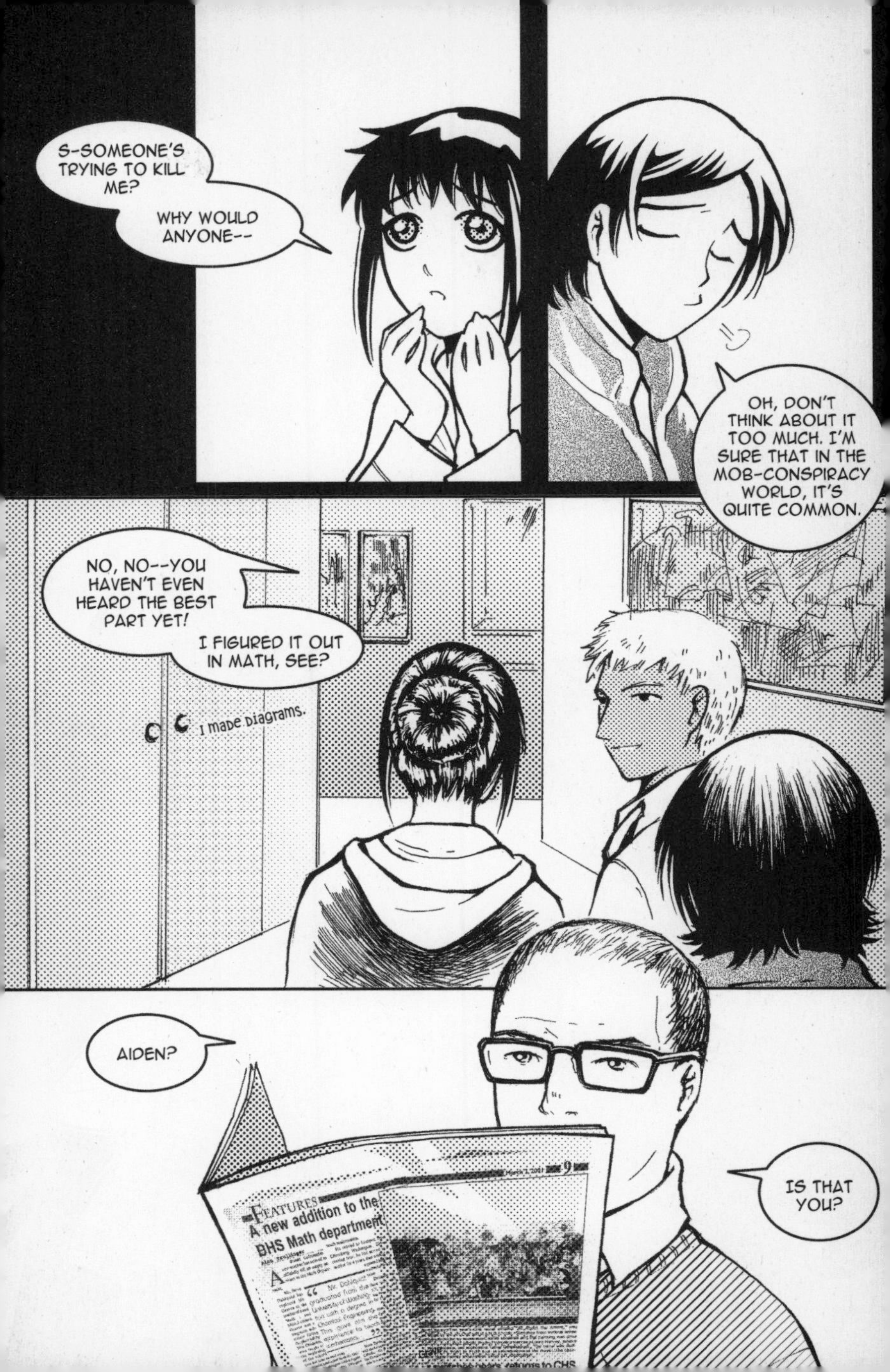
S-SOMEONE'S TRYING TO KILL ME?
WHY WOULD ANYONE--
OH, DON'T THINK ABOUT IT TOO MUCH. I'M SURE THAT IN THE MOB-CONSPIRACY WORLD, IT'S QUITE COMMON.
NO, NO--YOU HAVEN'T EVEN HEARD THE BEST PART YET!
I FIGURED IT OUT IN MATH, SEE?
I made diagrams.
AIDEN?
FEATURES
A new addition to the BHS Math department
IS THAT YOU?

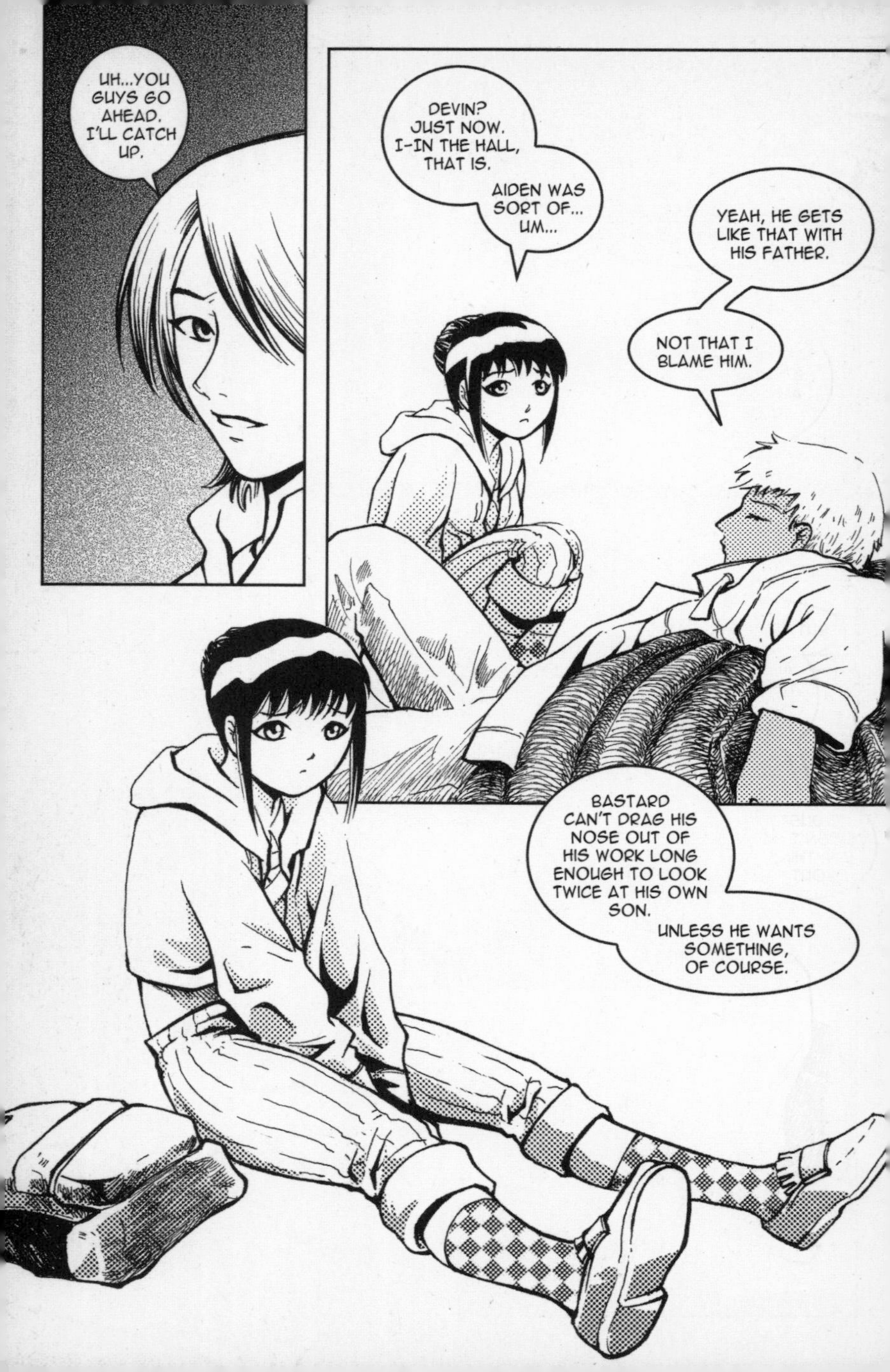
UH...YOU GUYS GO AHEAD. I'LL CATCH UP.
DEVIN? JUST NOW. I-IN THE HALL, THAT IS.
AIDEN WAS SORT OF... UM...
YEAH, HE GETS LIKE THAT WITH HIS FATHER.
NOT THAT I BLAME HIM.
BASTARD CAN'T DRAG HIS NOSE OUT OF HIS WORK LONG ENOUGH TO LOOK TWICE AT HIS OWN SON.
UNLESS HE WANTS SOMETHING, OF COURSE.

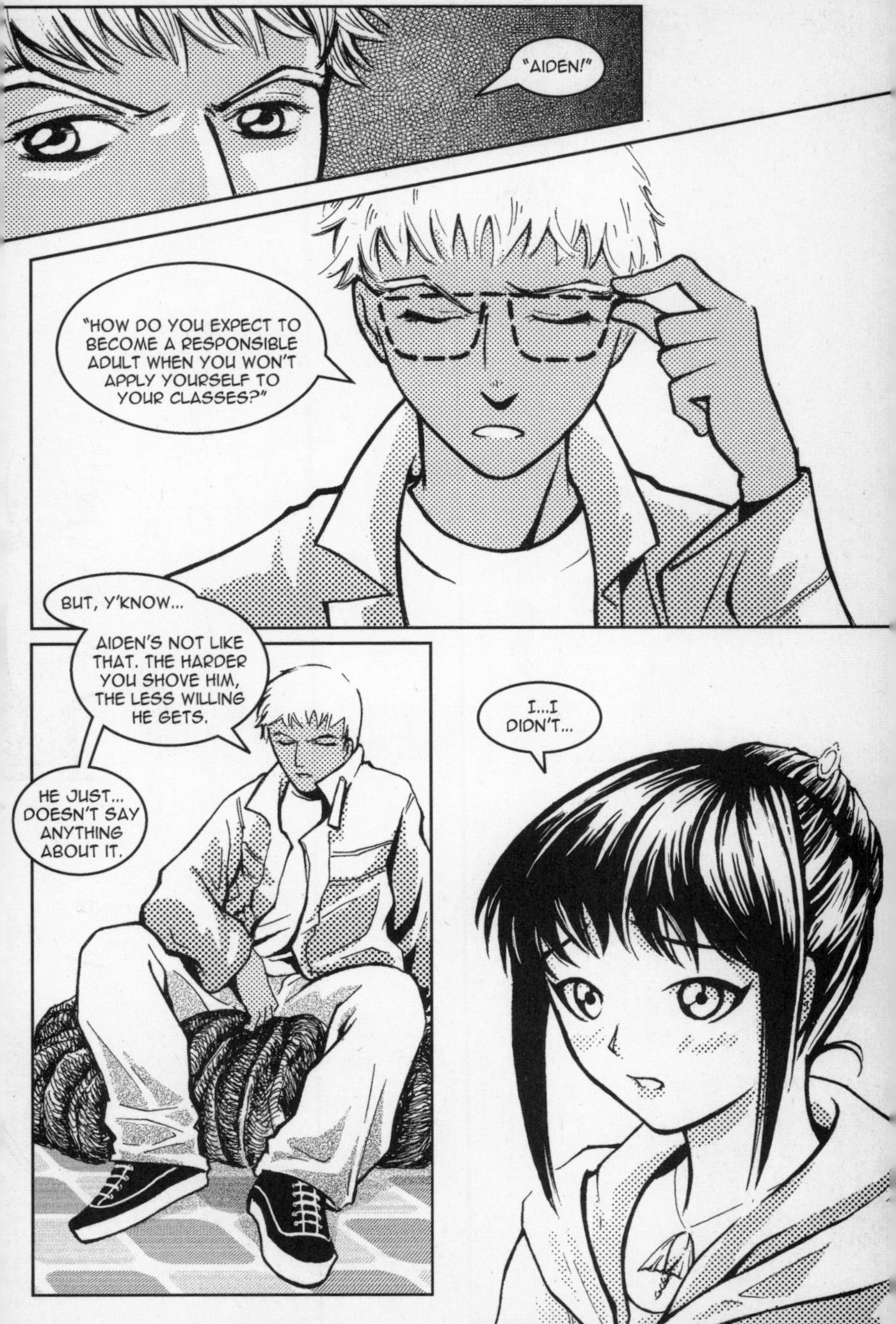
"AIDEN!"
"HOW DO YOU EXPECT TO BECOME A RESPONSIBLE ADULT WHEN YOU WON'T APPLY YOURSELF TO YOUR CLASSES?"
I...I DIDN'T...
BUT, Y'KNOW...
AIDEN'S NOT LIKE THAT. THE HARDER YOU SHOVE HIM, THE LESS WILLING HE GETS.
HE JUST... DOESN'T SAY ANYTHING ABOUT IT.

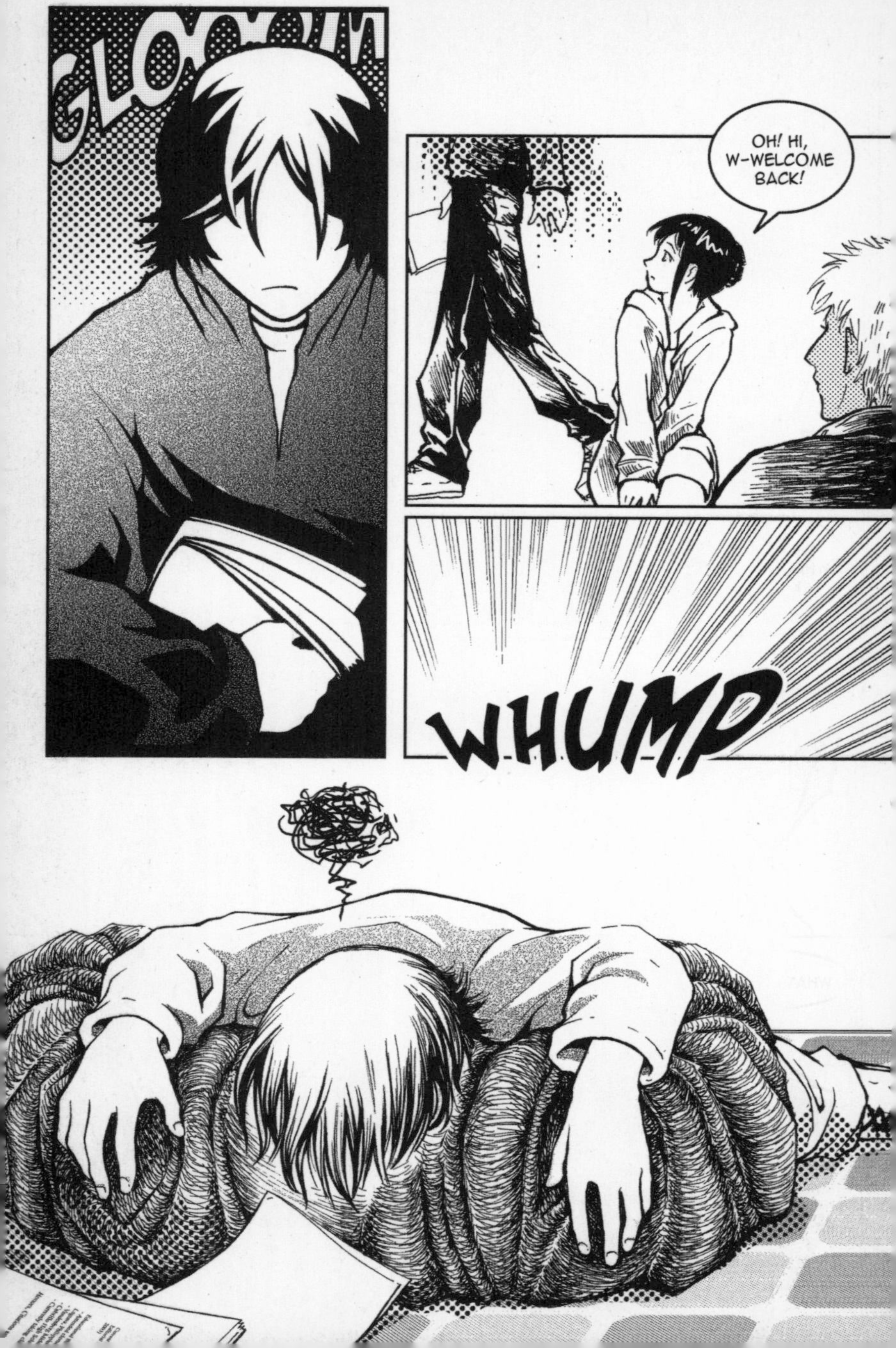
GLOOOM
OH! HI, W-WELCOME BACK!
WHUMP

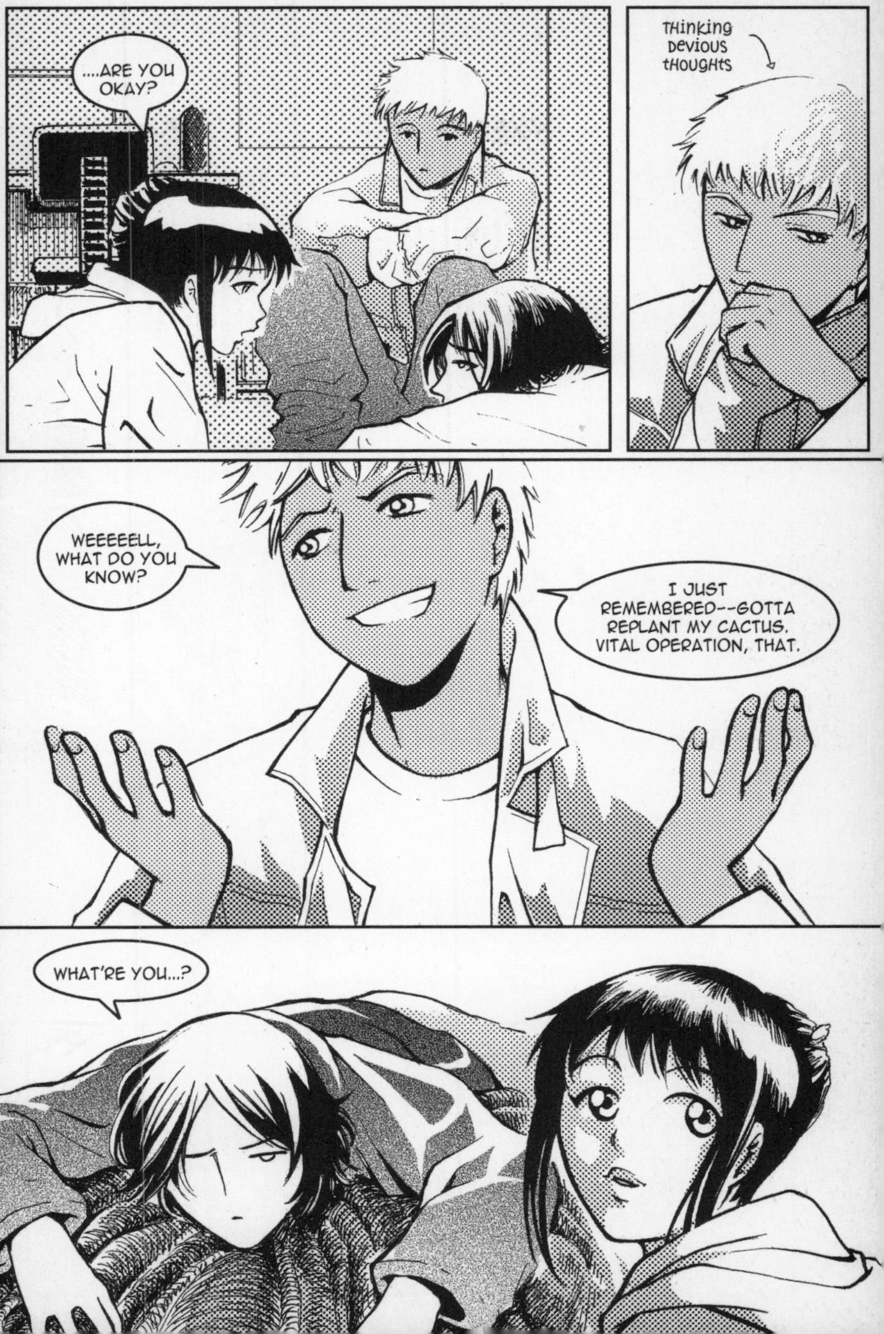
....ARE YOU OKAY?
THINKING DEVIOUS THOUGHTS
WEEEEELL, WHAT DO YOU KNOW?
I JUST REMEMBERED--GOTTA REPLANT MY CACTUS. VITAL OPERATION, THAT.
WHAT'RE YOU...?

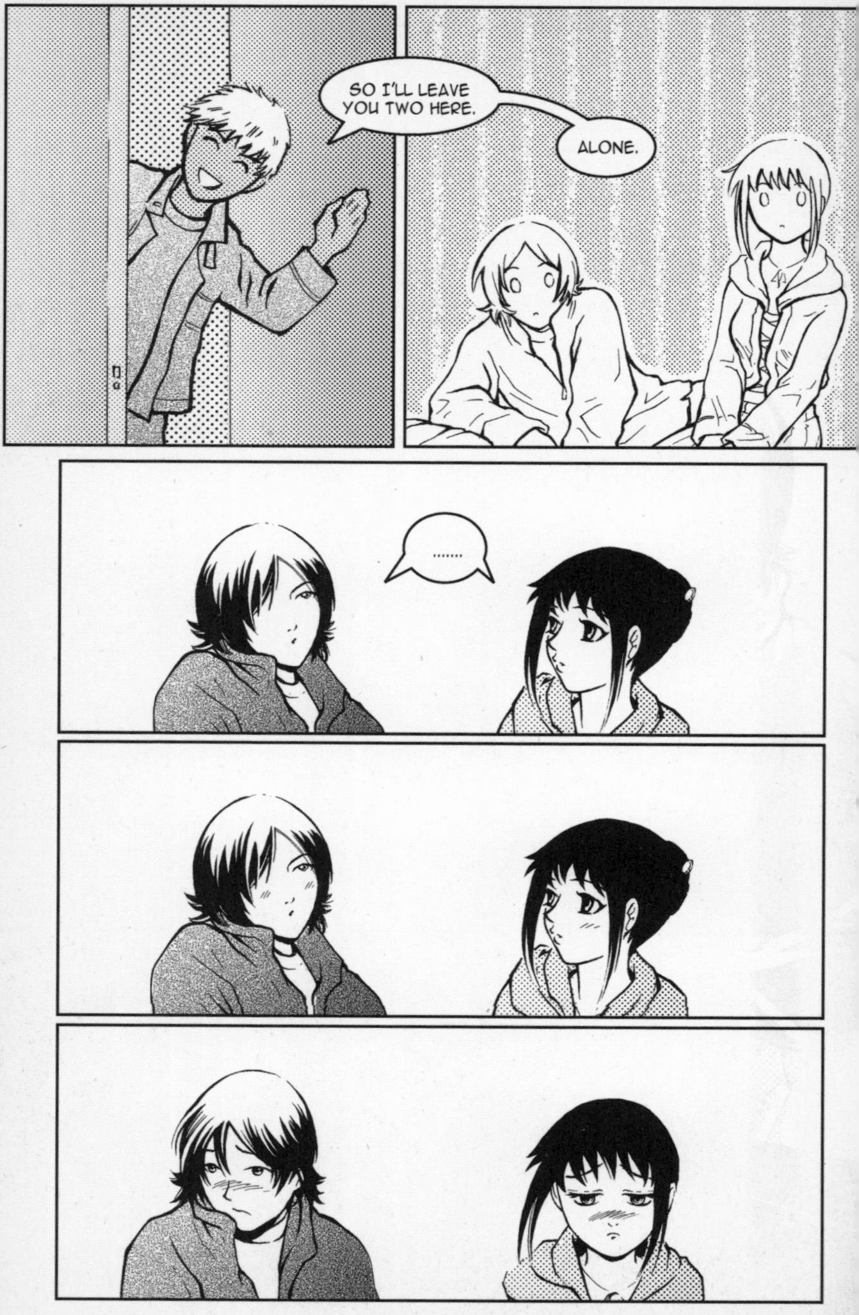
SO I'LL LEAVE YOU TWO HERE.
ALONE.
....

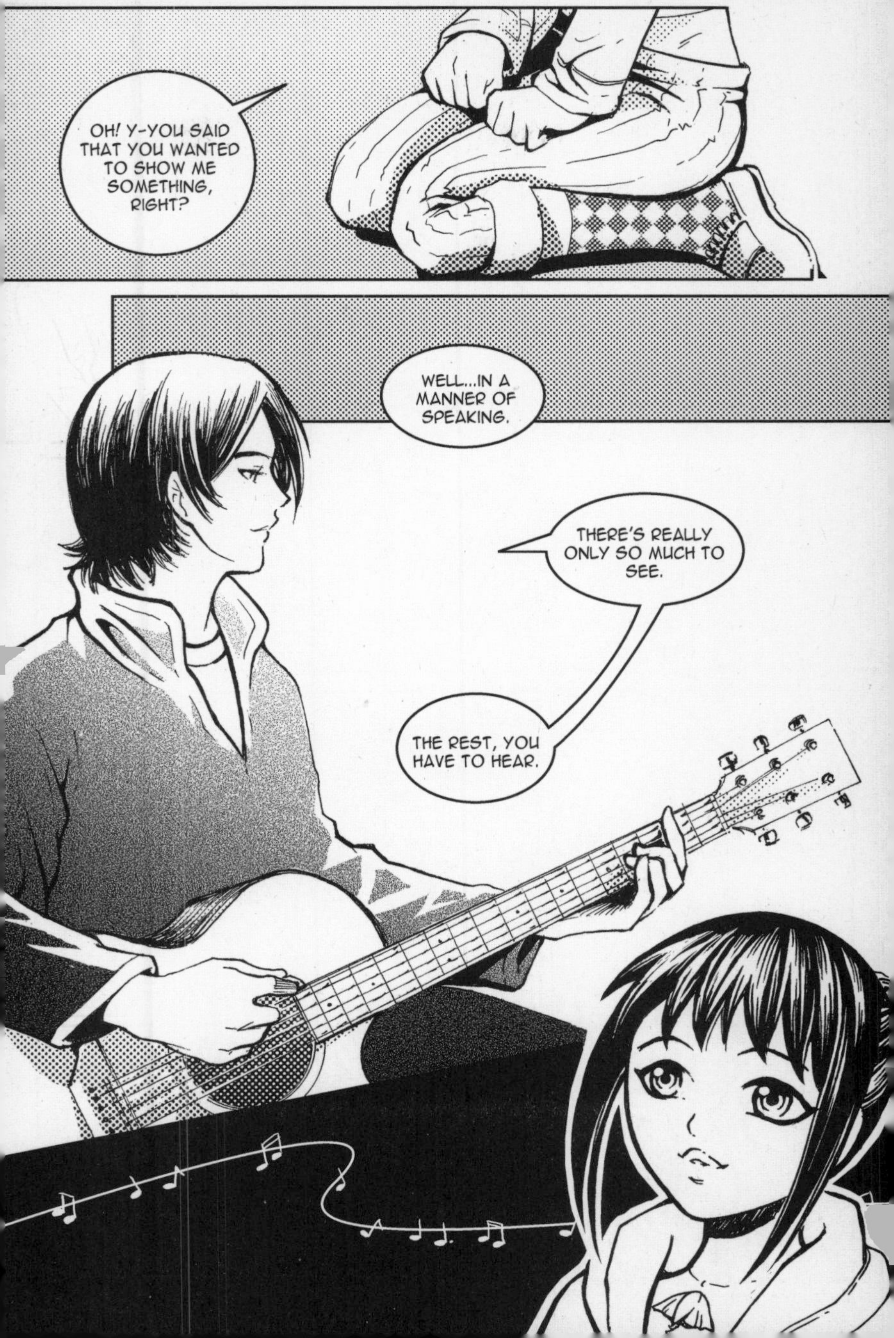
OH! Y-YOU SAID THAT YOU WANTED TO SHOW ME SOMETHING, RIGHT?
WELL...IN A MANNER OF SPEAKING.
THERE'S REALLY ONLY SO MUCH TO SEE.
THE REST, YOU HAVE TO HEAR.

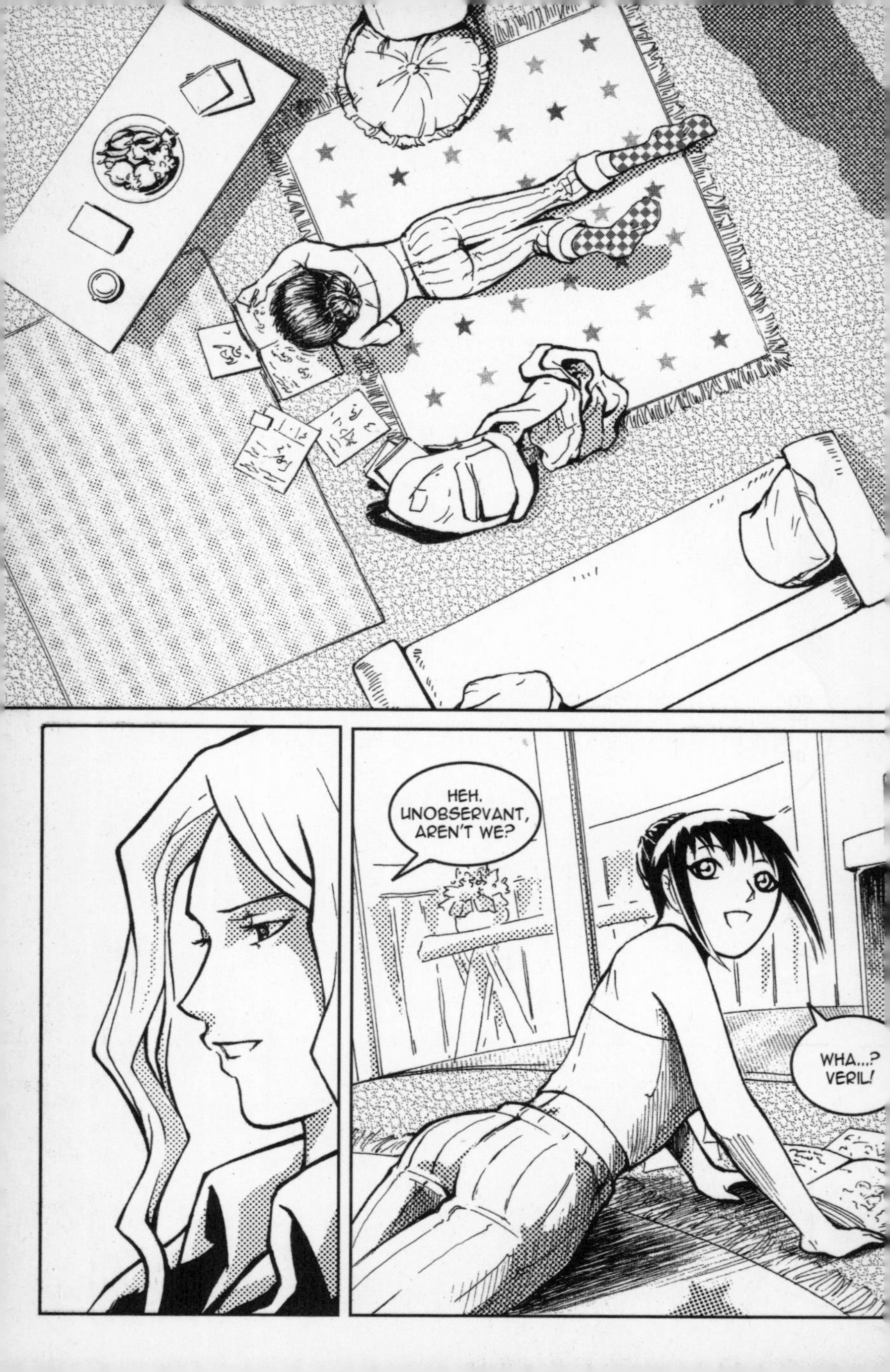
HEH. UNOBSERVANT, AREN'T WE?
WHA...? VERIL!

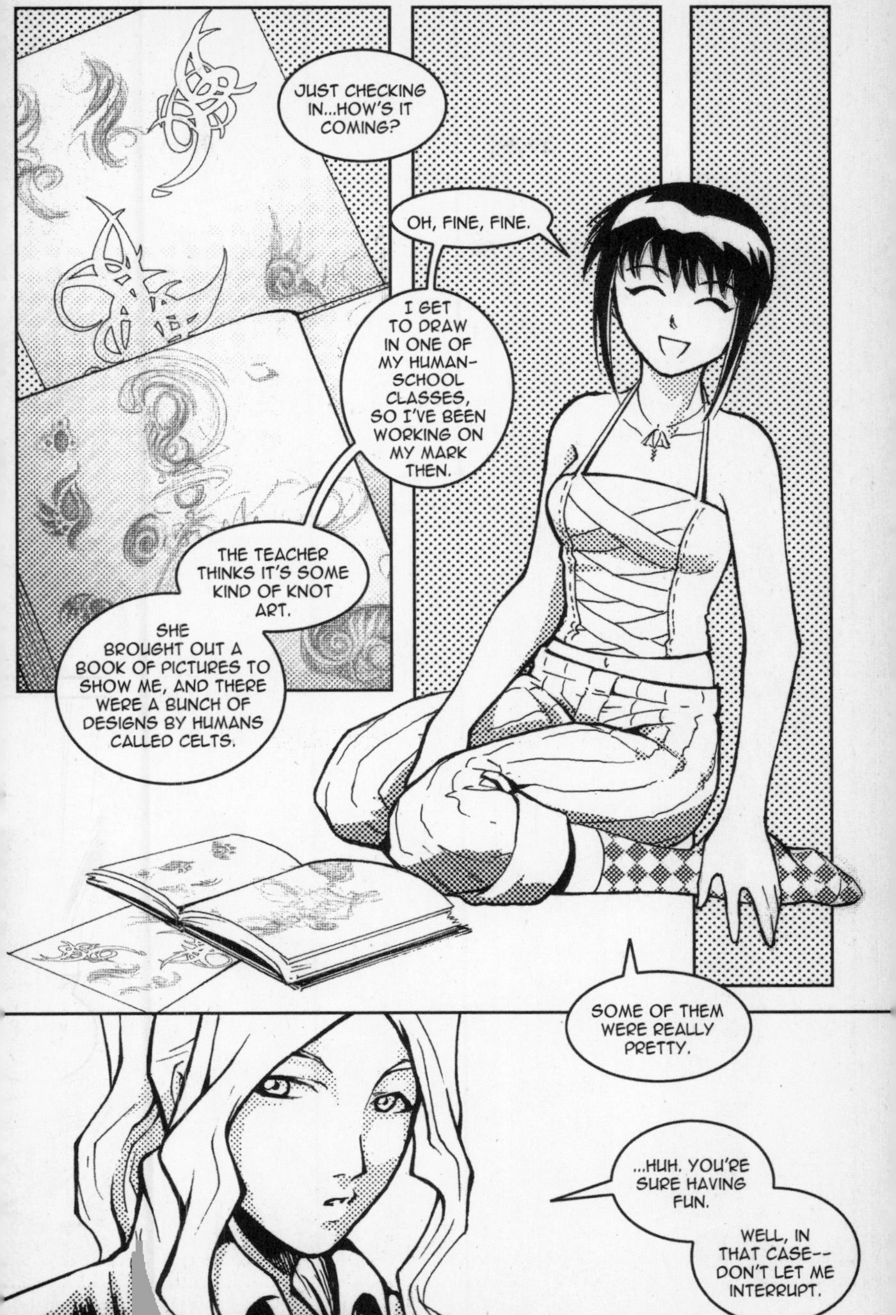
JUST CHECKING IN...HOW'S IT COMING?
OH, FINE, FINE.
I GET TO DRAW IN ONE OF MY HUMAN-SCHOOL CLASSES, SO I'VE BEEN WORKING ON MY MARK THEN.
THE TEACHER THINKS IT'S SOME KIND OF KNOT ART.
SHE BROUGHT OUT A BOOK OF PICTURES TO SHOW ME, AND THERE WERE A BUNCH OF DESIGNS BY HUMANS CALLED CELTS.
SOME OF THEM WERE REALLY PRETTY.
...HUH. YOU'RE SURE HAVING FUN.
WELL, IN THAT CASE-- DON'T LET ME INTERRUPT.

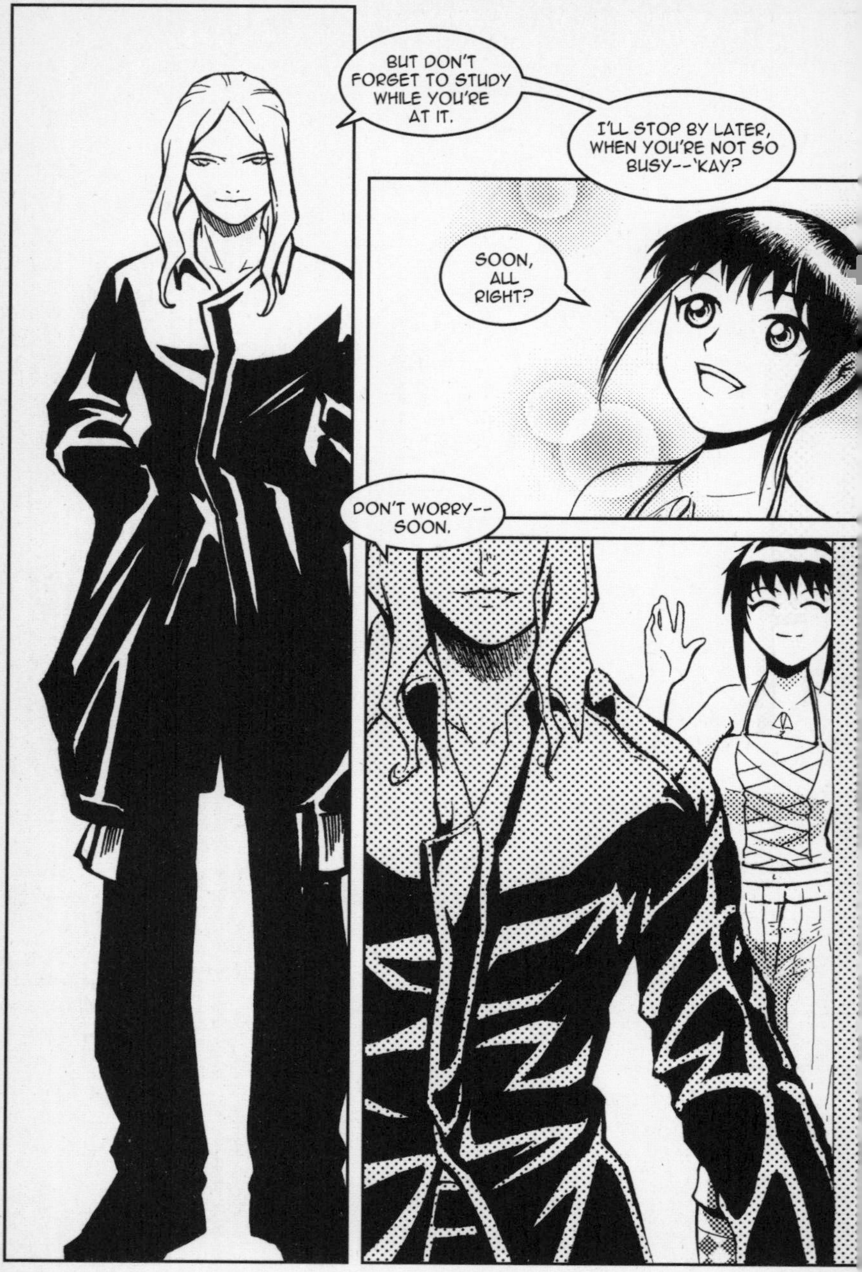
BUT DON'T FORGET TO STUDY WHILE YOU'RE AT IT.
I'LL STOP BY LATER, WHEN YOU'RE NOT SO BUSY--'KAY?
SOON, ALL RIGHT?
DON'T WORRY-- SOON.

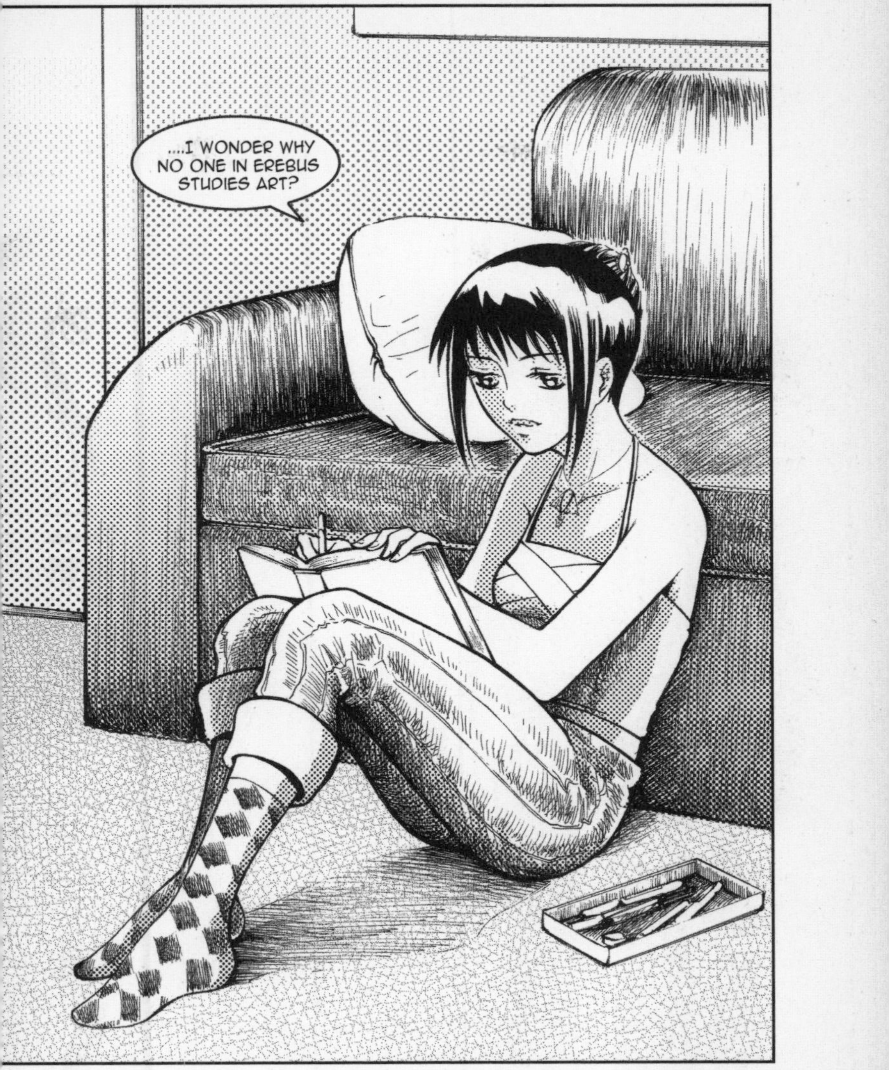
....I WONDER WHY NO ONE IN EREBUS STUDIES ART?

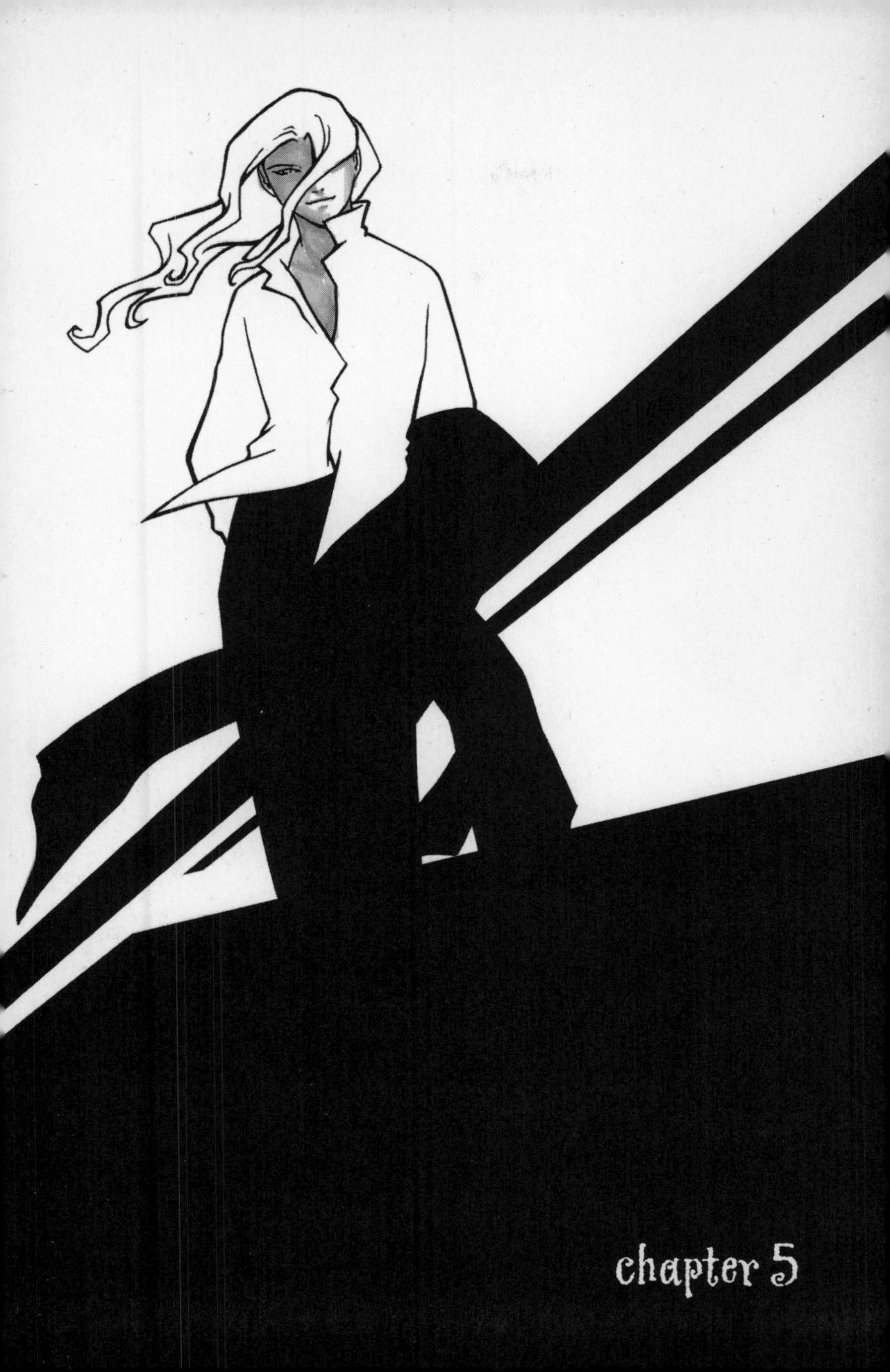
chapter 5

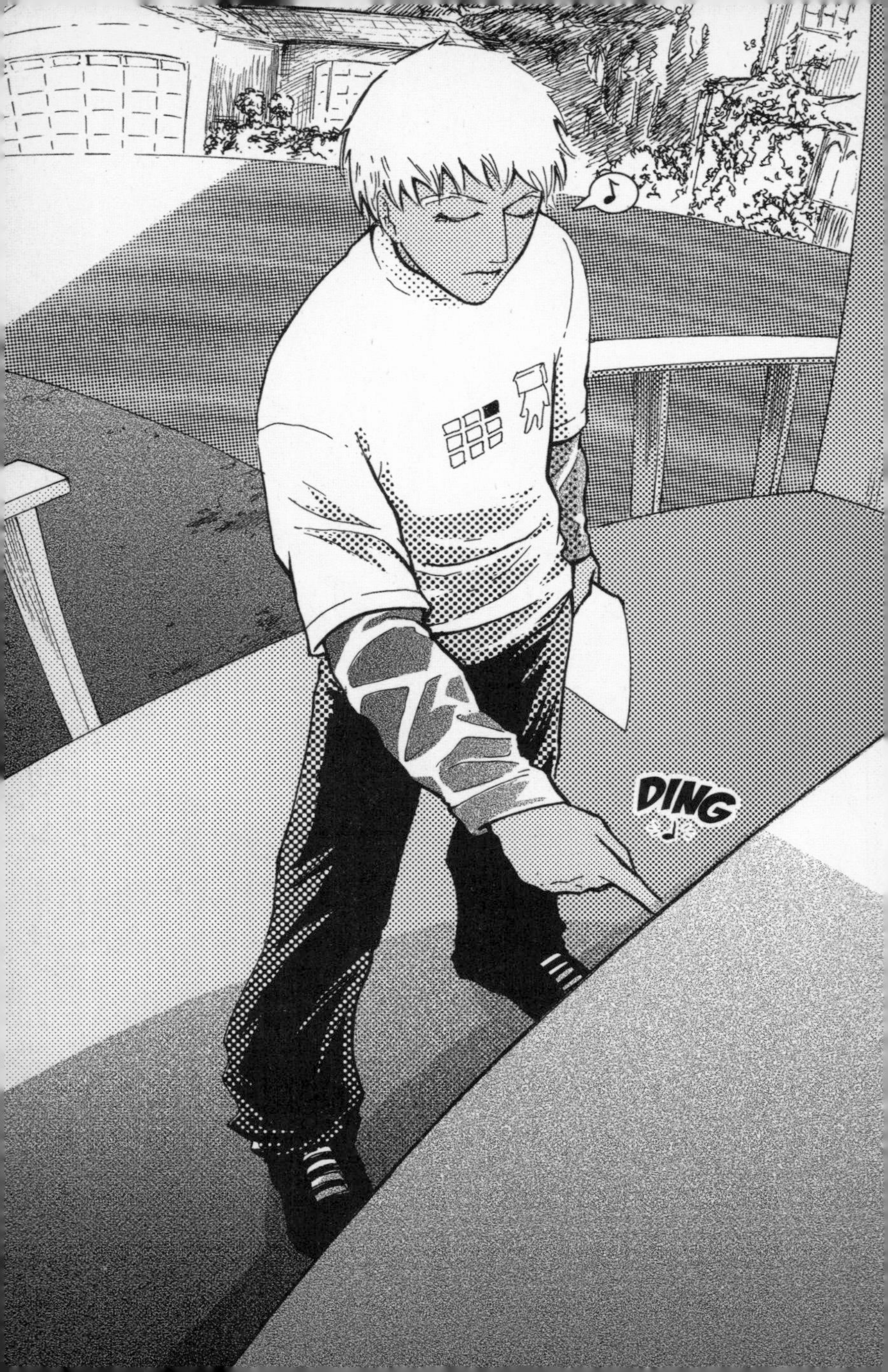
DING

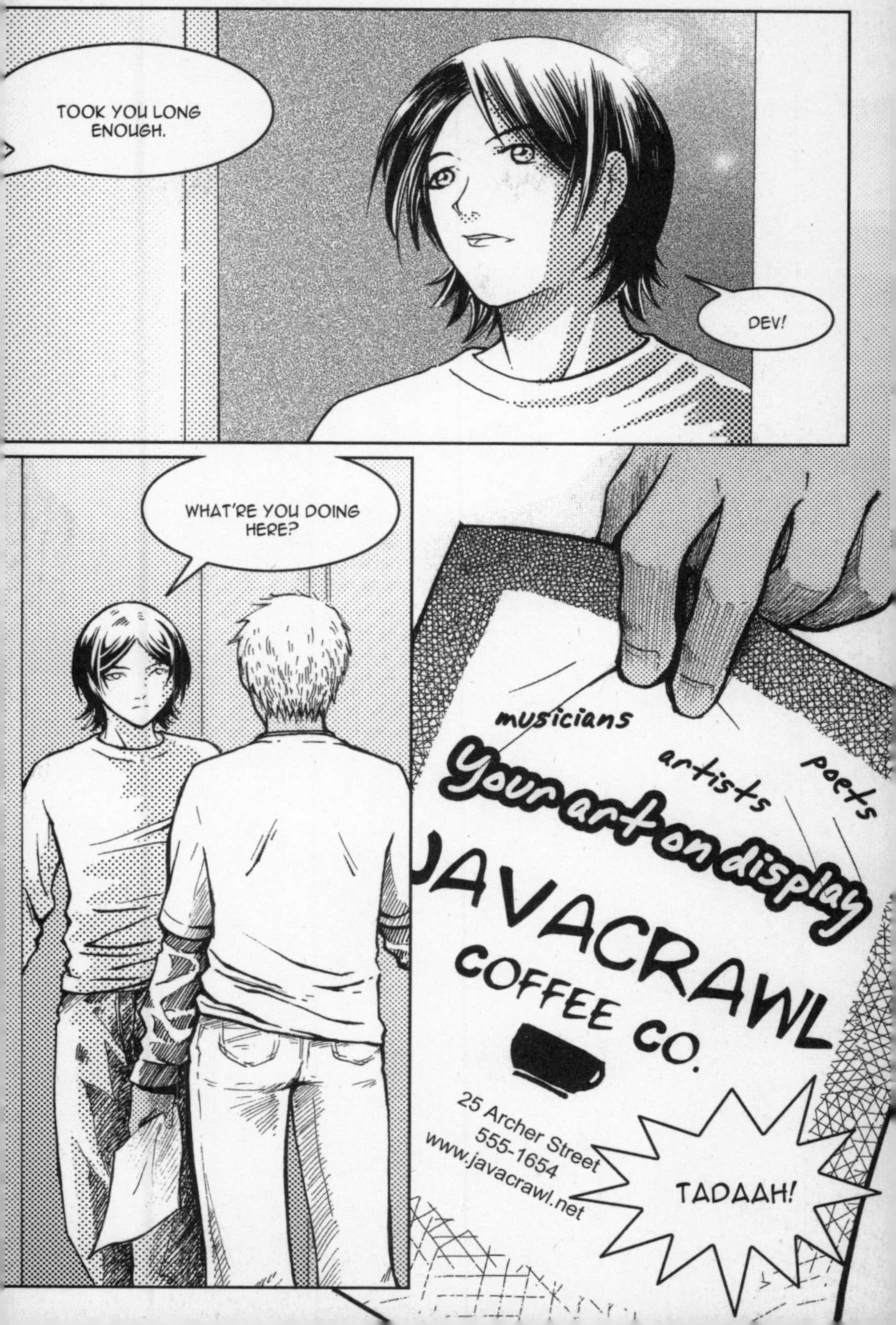
TOOK YOU LONG ENOUGH.
DEV!
WHAT'RE YOU DOING HERE?
musicians
artists
poets
your art on display
JAVACRAWL
COFFEE CO.
25 Archer Street
555-1654
www.javacrawl.net
TADAAH!

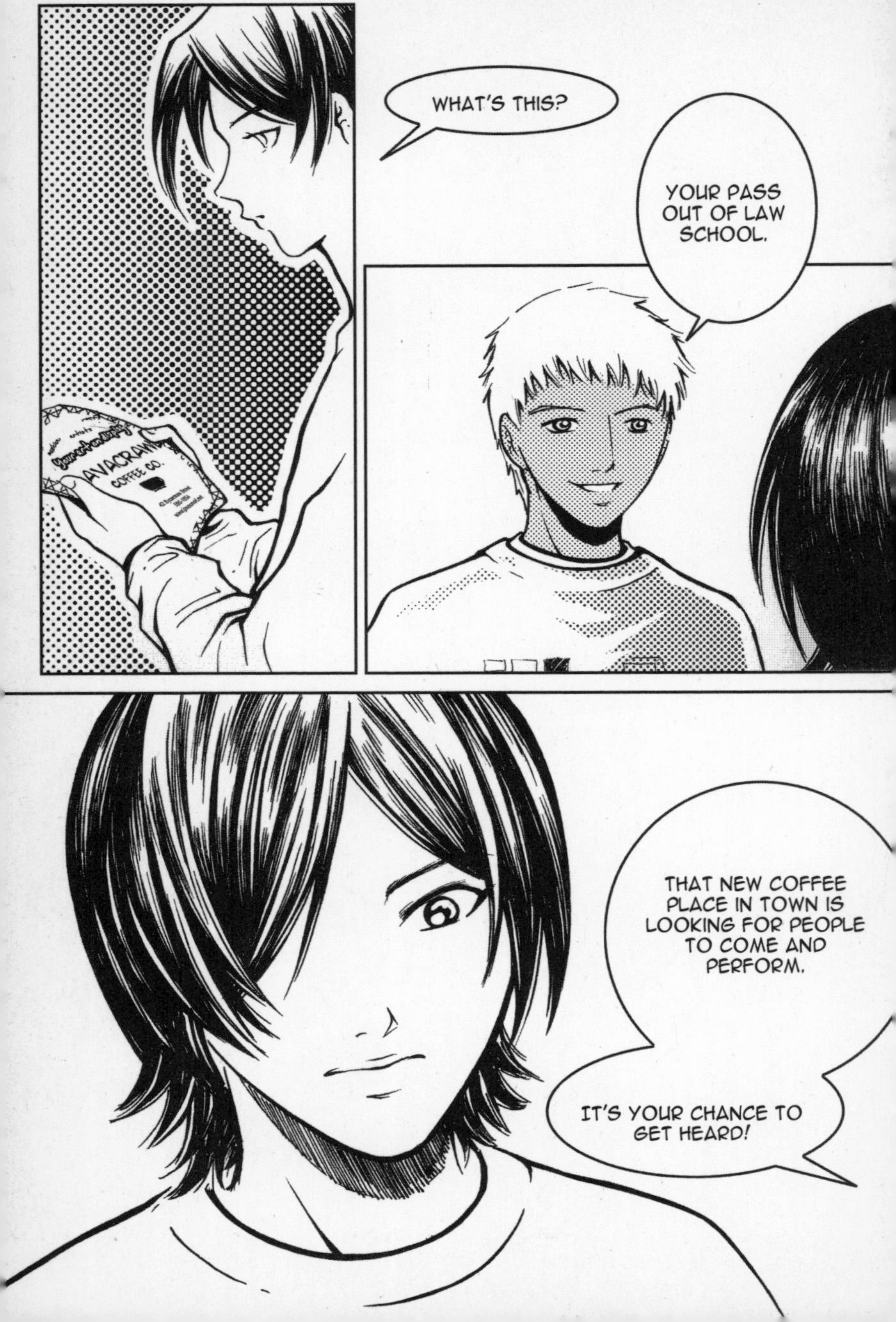
WHAT'S THIS?
COFFEE CO.
YOUR PASS OUT OF LAW SCHOOL.
THAT NEW COFFEE PLACE IN TOWN IS LOOKING FOR PEOPLE TO COME AND PERFORM.
IT'S YOUR CHANCE TO GET HEARD!

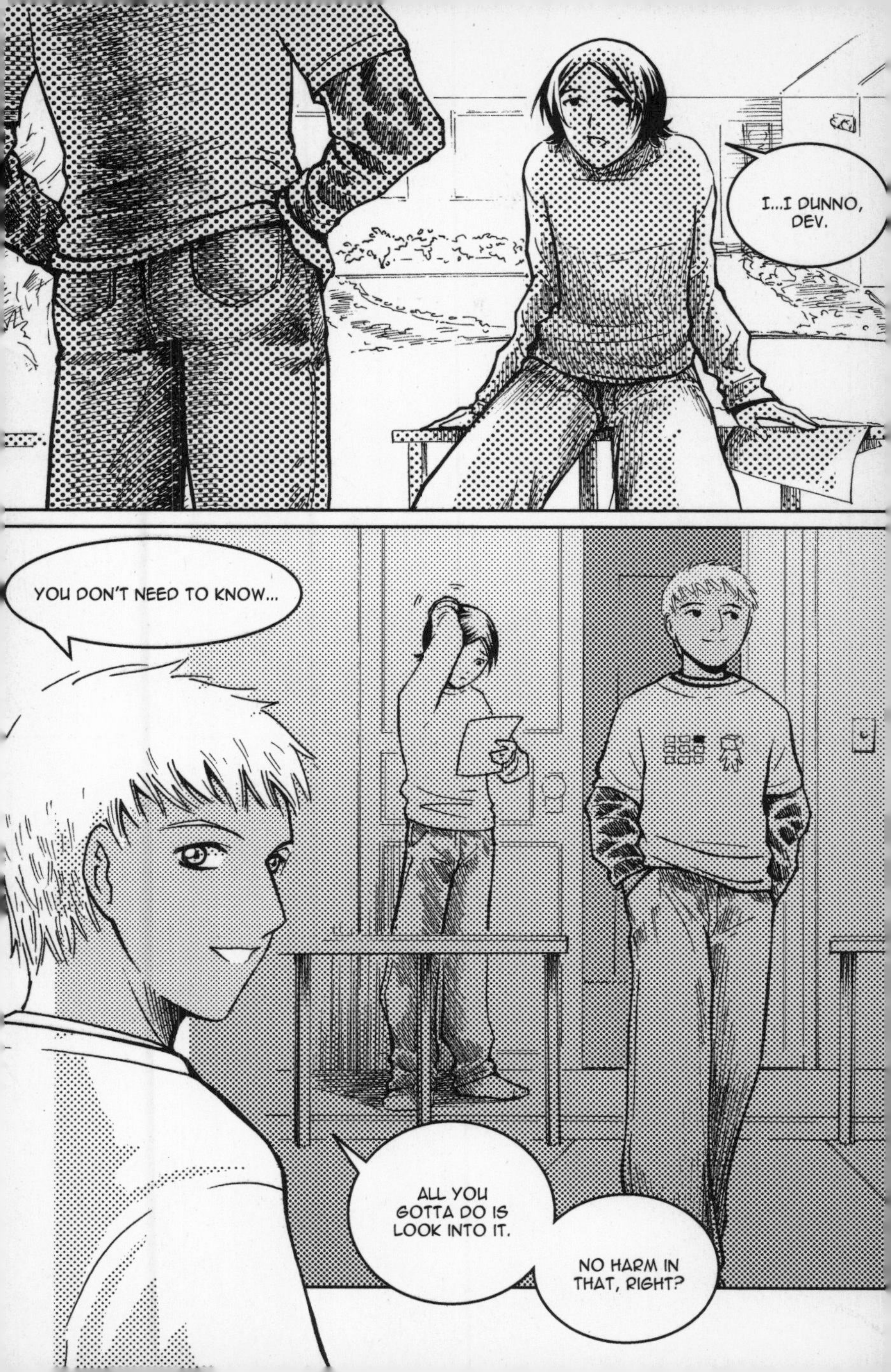
I...I DUNNO, DEV.
YOU DON'T NEED TO KNOW...
ALL YOU GOTTA DO IS LOOK INTO IT.
NO HARM IN THAT, RIGHT?

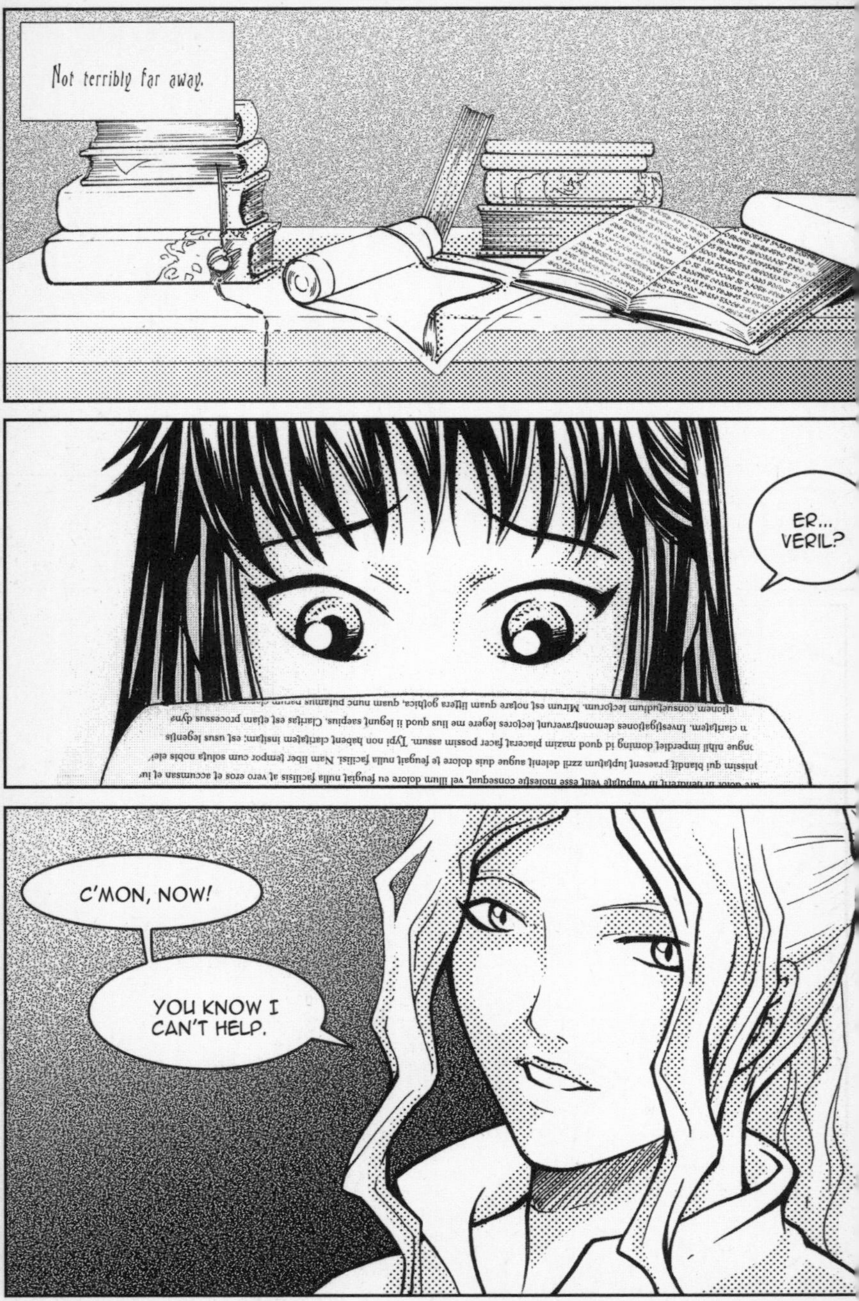
Not terribly far away.
ER... VERIL?
C'MON, NOW!
YOU KNOW I CAN'T HELP.

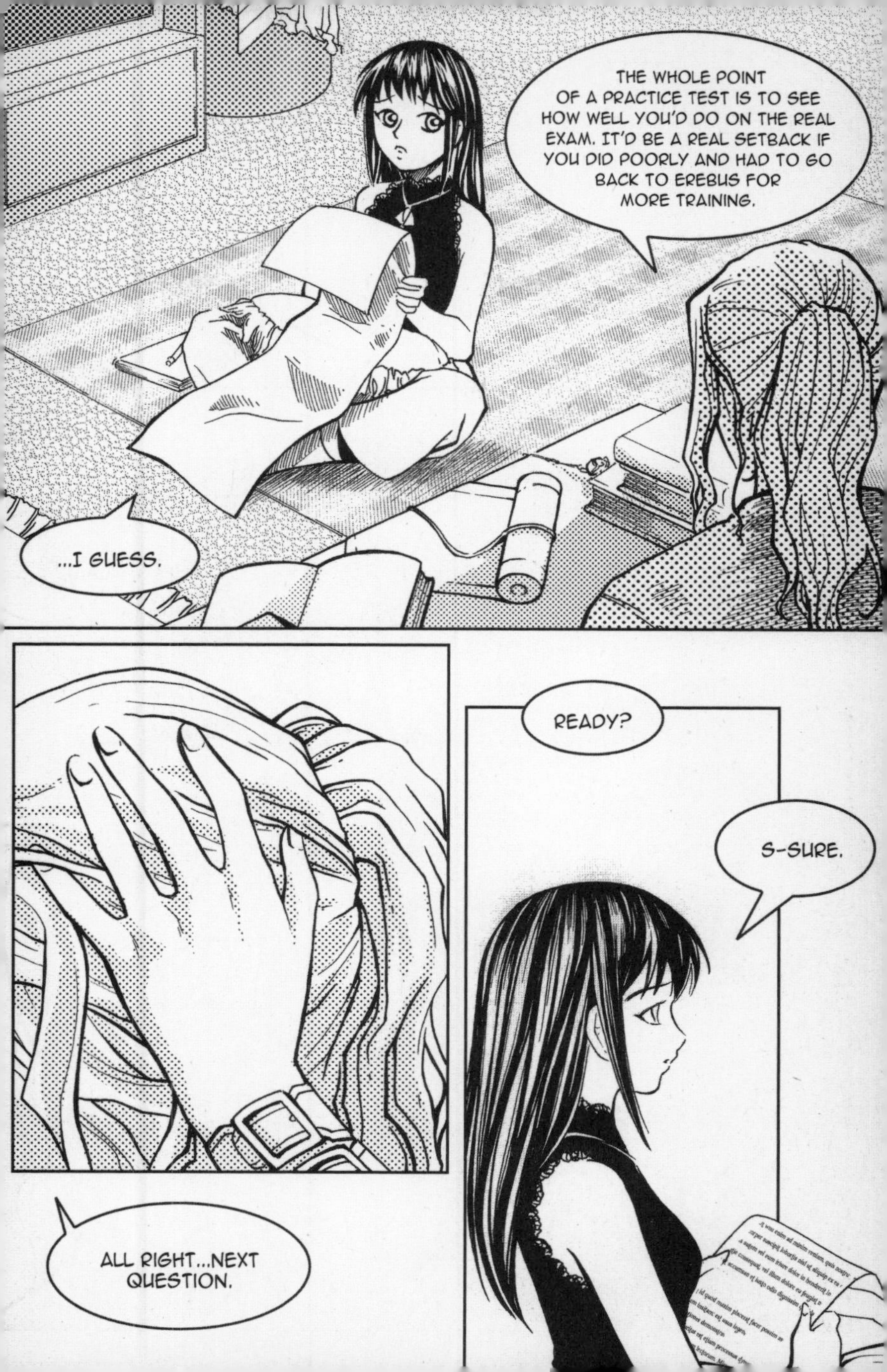
THE WHOLE POINT OF A PRACTICE TEST IS TO SEE HOW WELL YOU'D DO ON THE REAL EXAM. IT'D BE A REAL SETBACK IF YOU DID POORLY AND HAD TO GO BACK TO EREBUS FOR MORE TRAINING.
...I GUESS.
ALL RIGHT...NEXT QUESTION.
READY?
S-SURE.

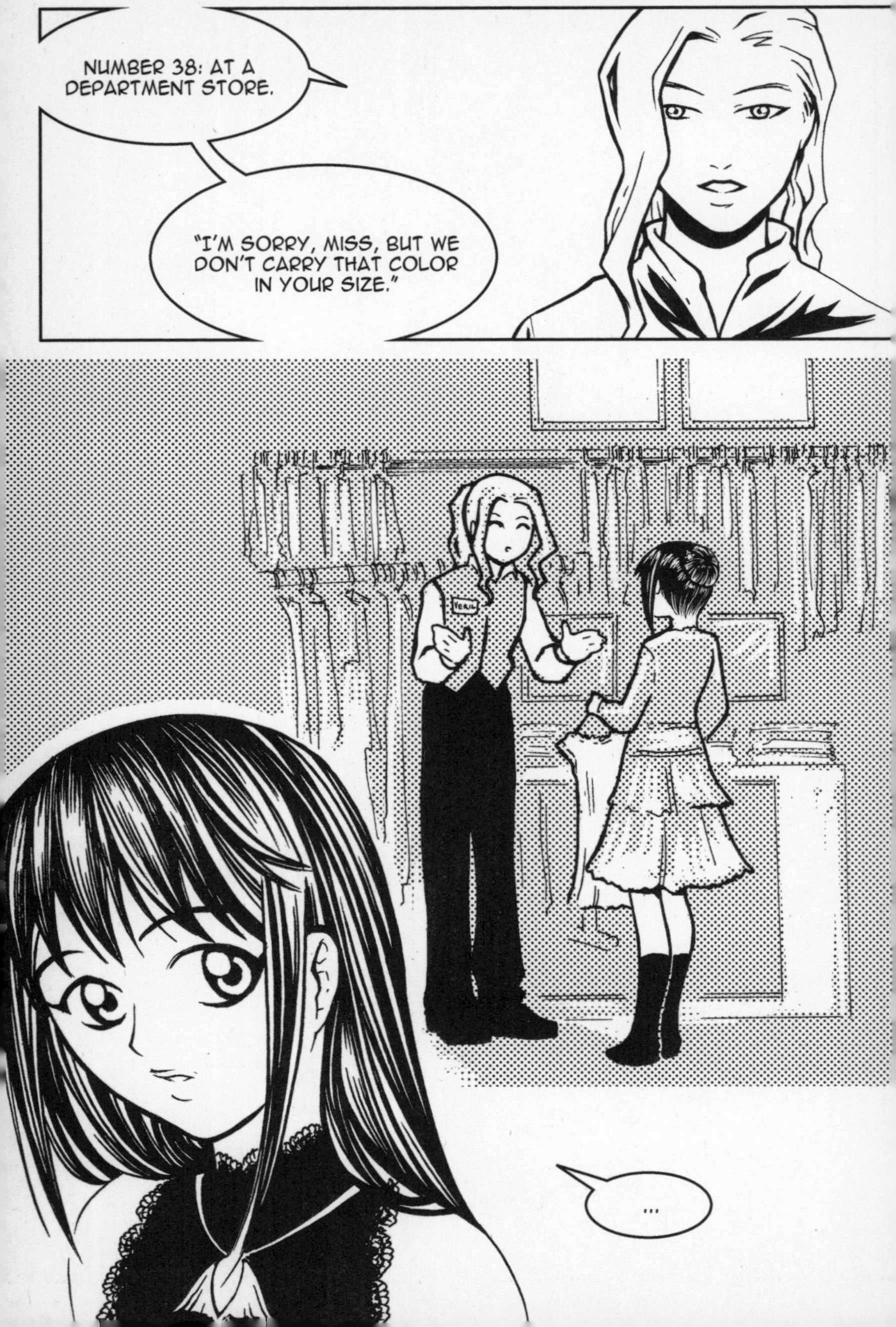
NUMBER 38: AT A DEPARTMENT STORE.
"I'M SORRY, MISS, BUT WE DON'T CARRY THAT COLOR IN YOUR SIZE."
...

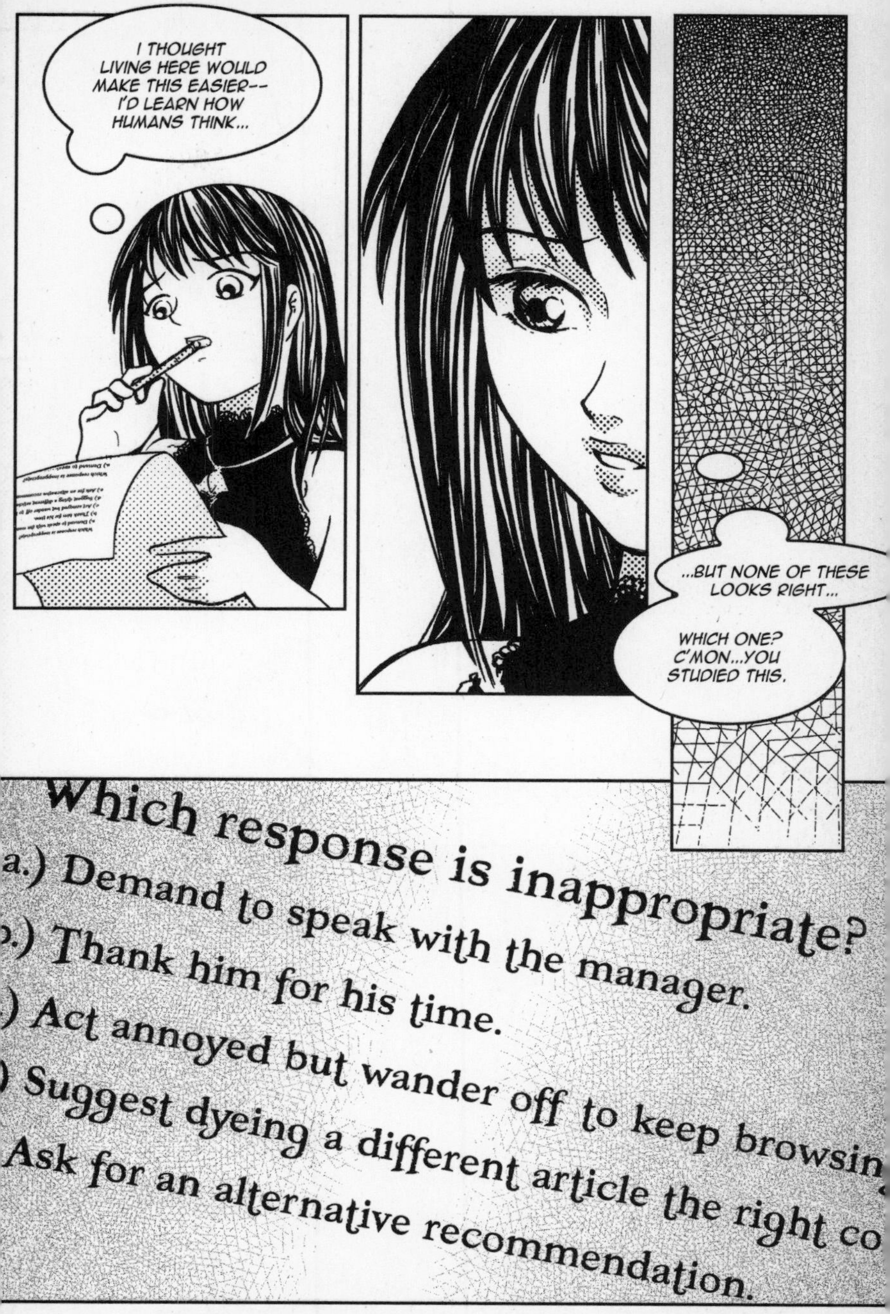

I THOUGHT LIVING HERE WOULD MAKE THIS EASIER-- I'D LEARN HOW HUMANS THINK...
...BUT NONE OF THESE LOOKS RIGHT...
WHICH ONE? C'MON...YOU STUDIED THIS.
Which response is inappropriate?
a.) Demand to speak with the manager.
.) Thank him for his time.
) Act annoyed but wander off to keep browsin
Suggest dyeing a different article the right co
Ask for an alternative recommendation.

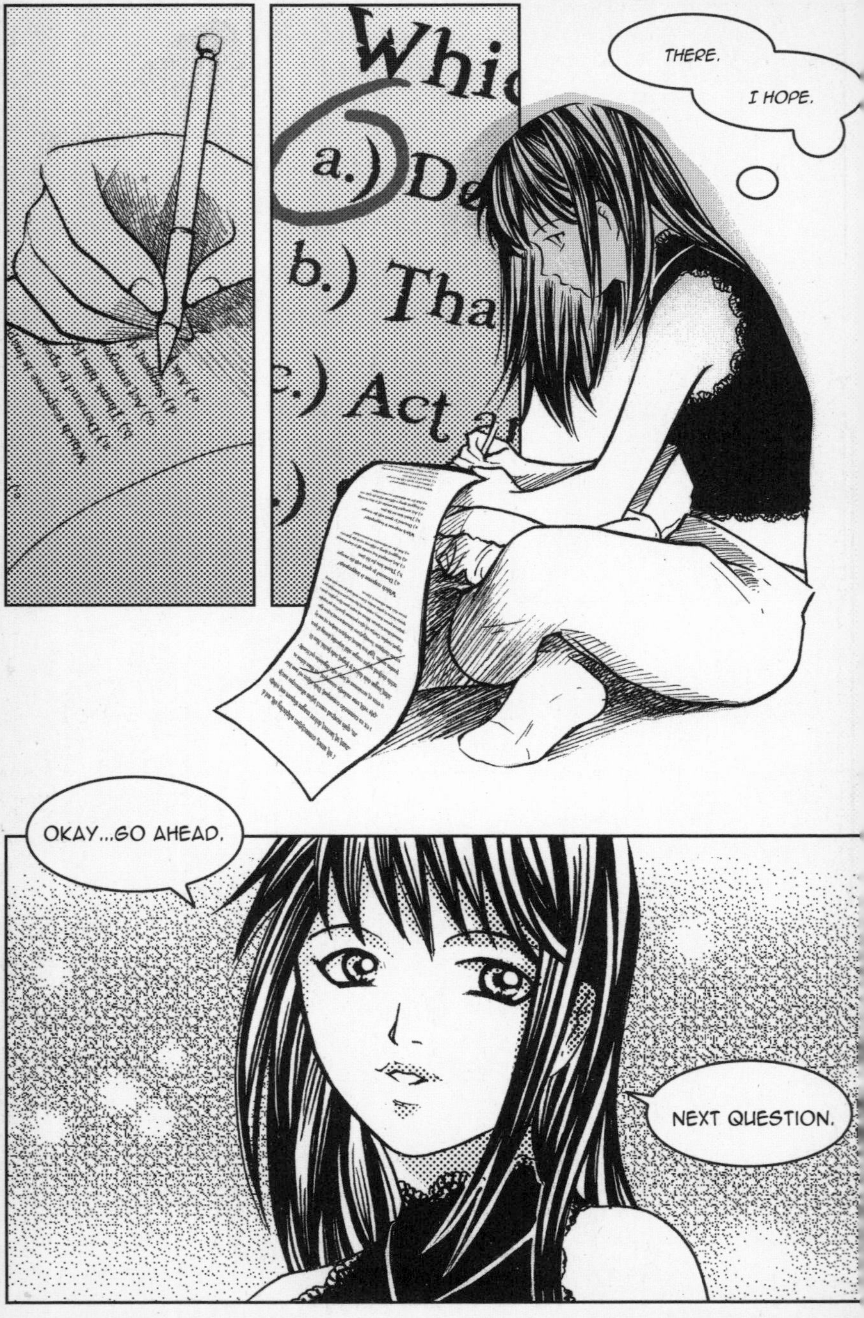
Whic
a.) De
b.) Tha
c.) Act ar
THERE.
I HOPE.
OKAY...GO AHEAD.
NEXT QUESTION.

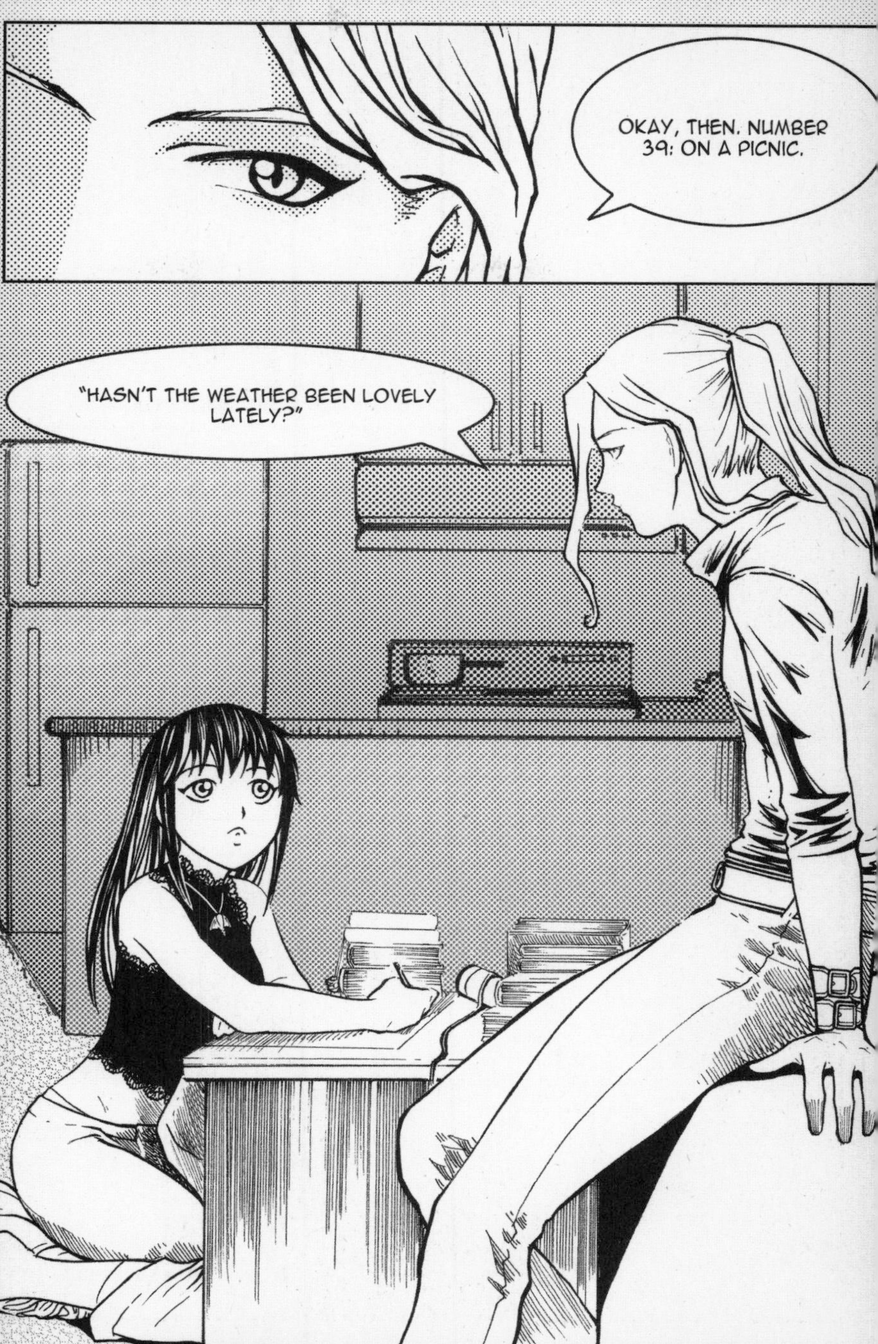
OKAY, THEN. NUMBER 39: ON A PICNIC.
"HASN'T THE WEATHER BEEN LOVELY LATELY?"

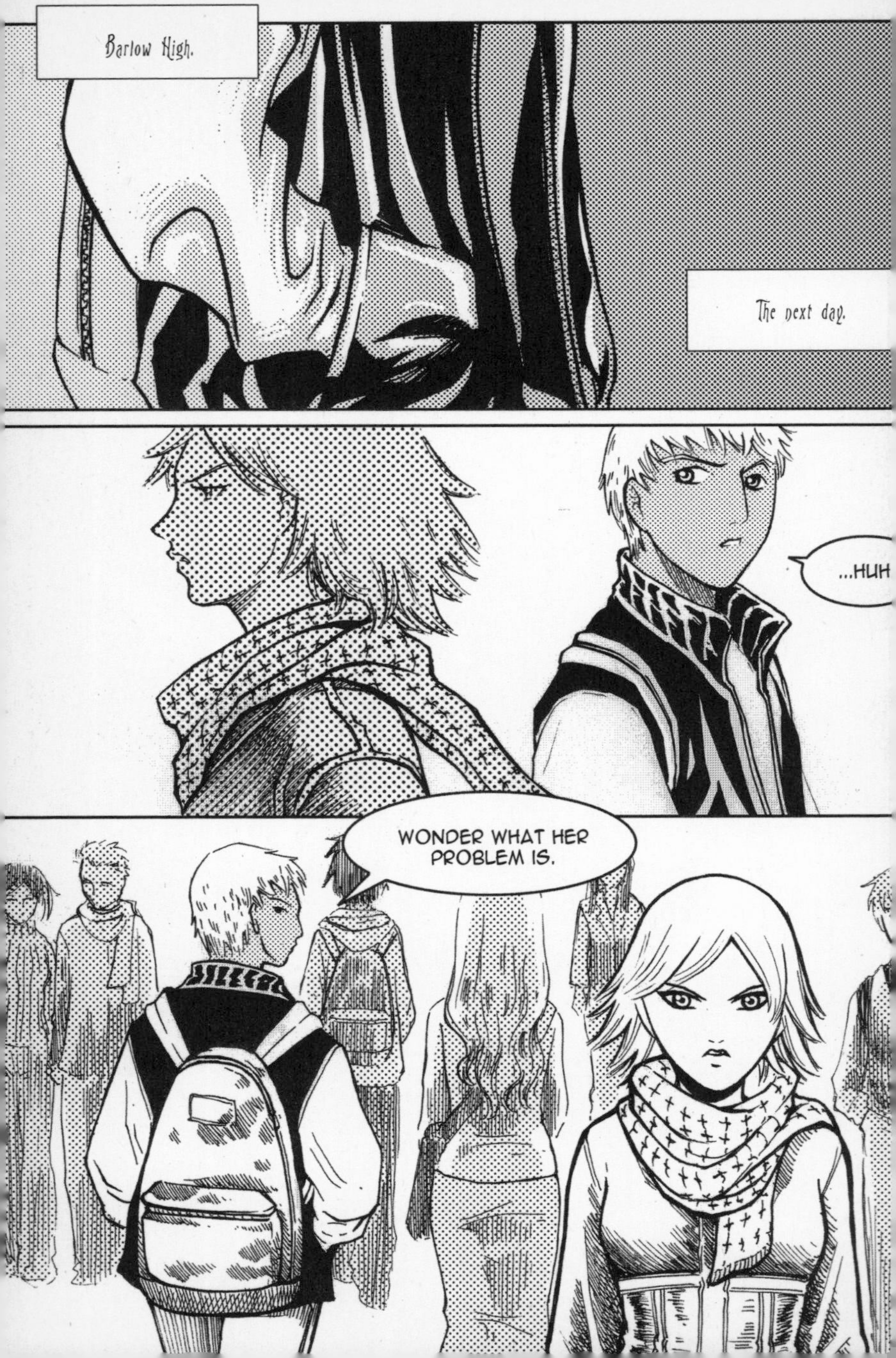
Barlow High.
The next day.
...HUH
WONDER WHAT HER PROBLEM IS.

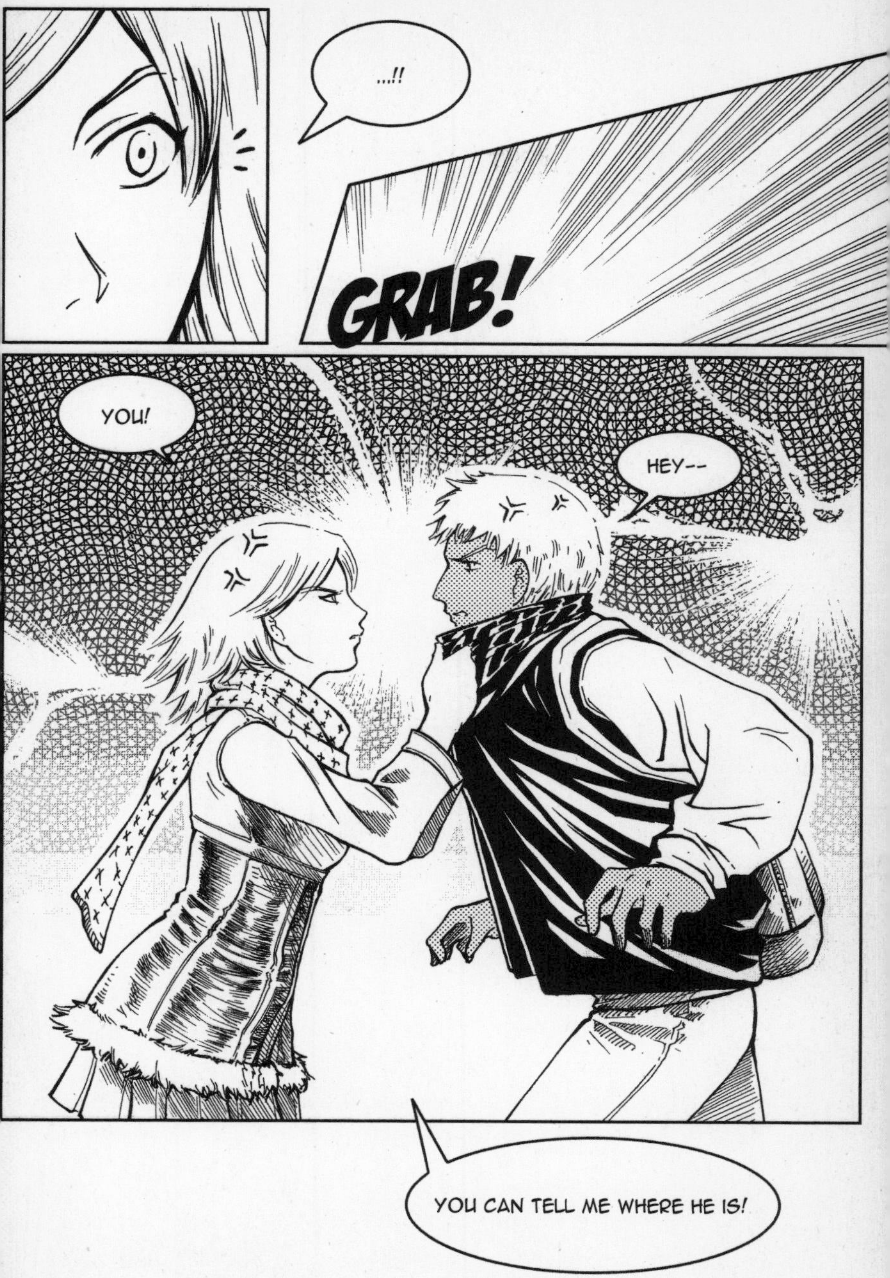
...!!
GRAB!
YOU!
HEY--
YOU CAN TELL ME WHERE HE IS!

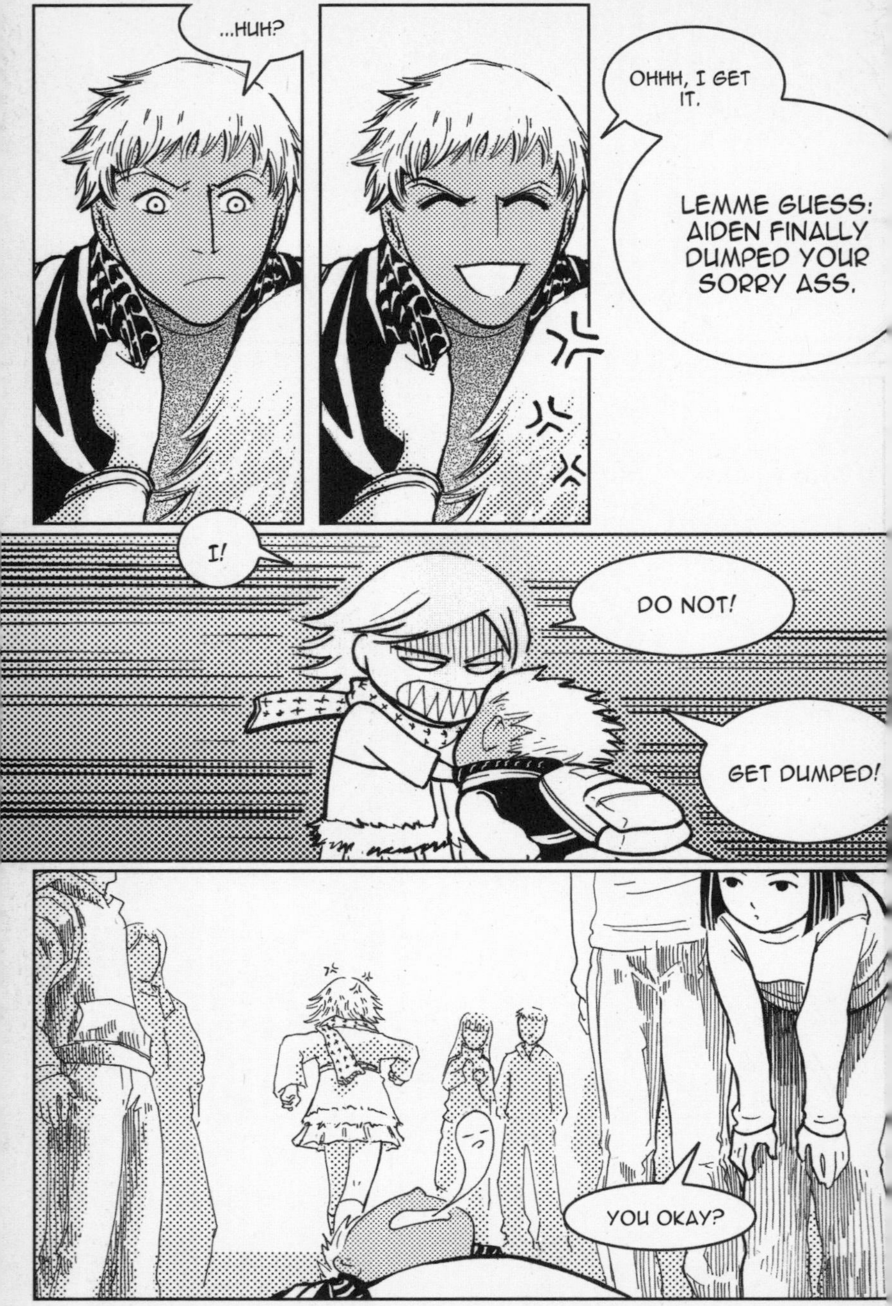
...HUH?
OHHH, I GET IT.
LEMME GUESS: AIDEN FINALLY DUMPED YOUR SORRY ASS.
I!
DO NOT!
GET DUMPED!
YOU OKAY?

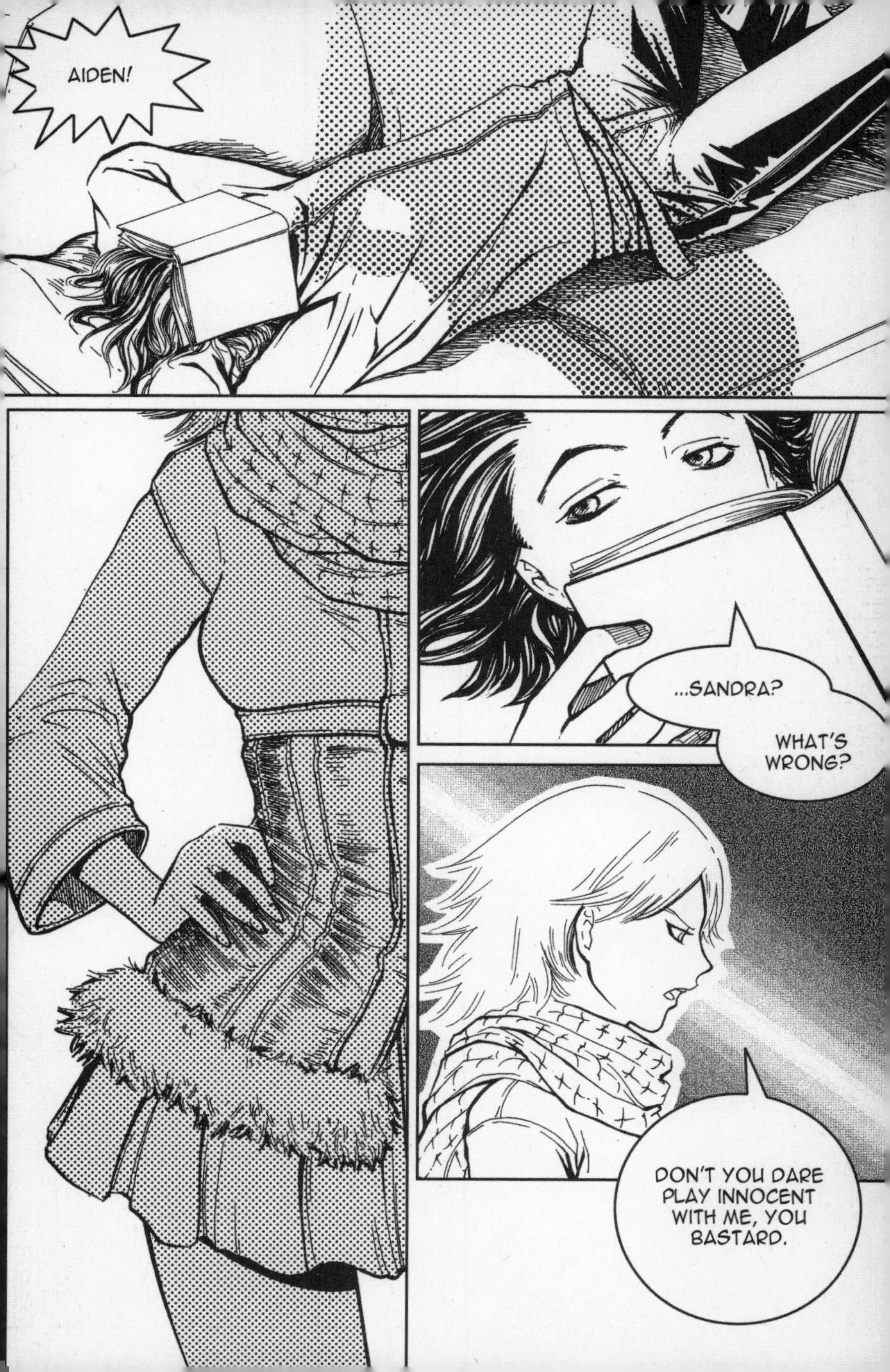
AIDEN!
...SANDRA?
WHAT'S WRONG?
DON'T YOU DARE PLAY INNOCENT WITH ME, YOU BASTARD.

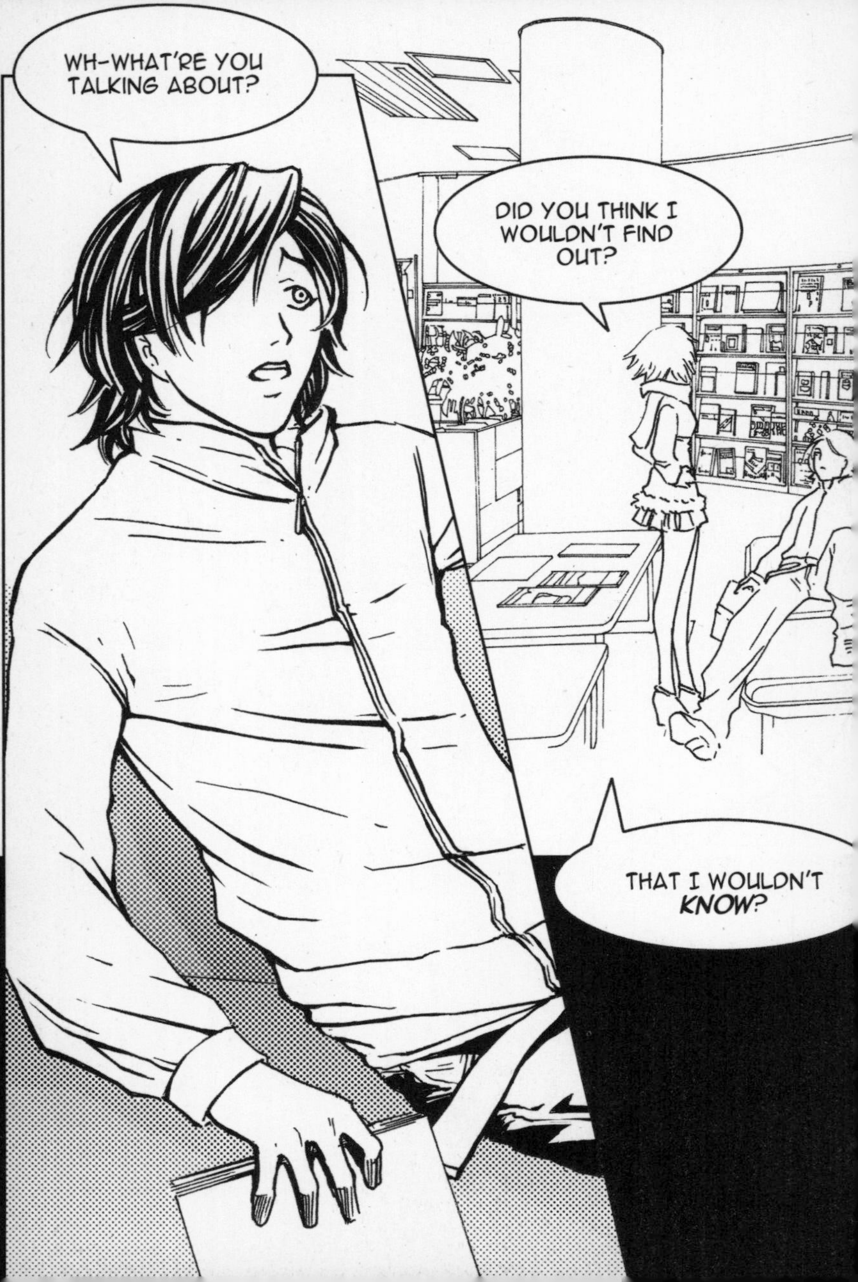
WH-WHAT'RE YOU TALKING ABOUT?
DID YOU THINK I WOULDN'T FIND OUT?
THAT I WOULDN'T *KNOW*?

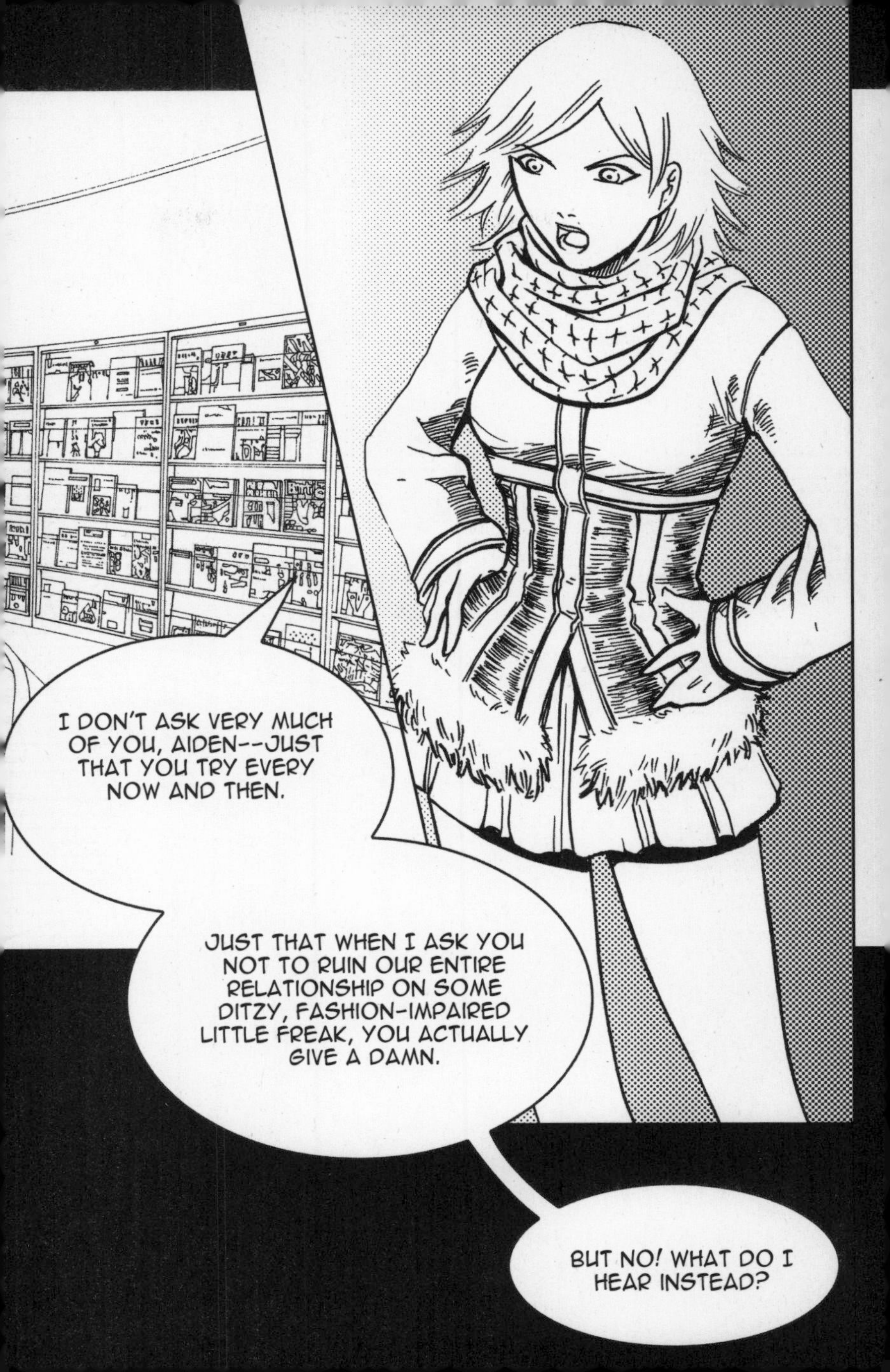
I DON'T ASK VERY MUCH OF YOU, AIDEN--JUST THAT YOU TRY EVERY NOW AND THEN.
JUST THAT WHEN I ASK YOU NOT TO RUIN OUR ENTIRE RELATIONSHIP ON SOME DITZY, FASHION-IMPAIRED LITTLE FREAK, YOU ACTUALLY GIVE A DAMN.
BUT NO! WHAT DO I HEAR INSTEAD?

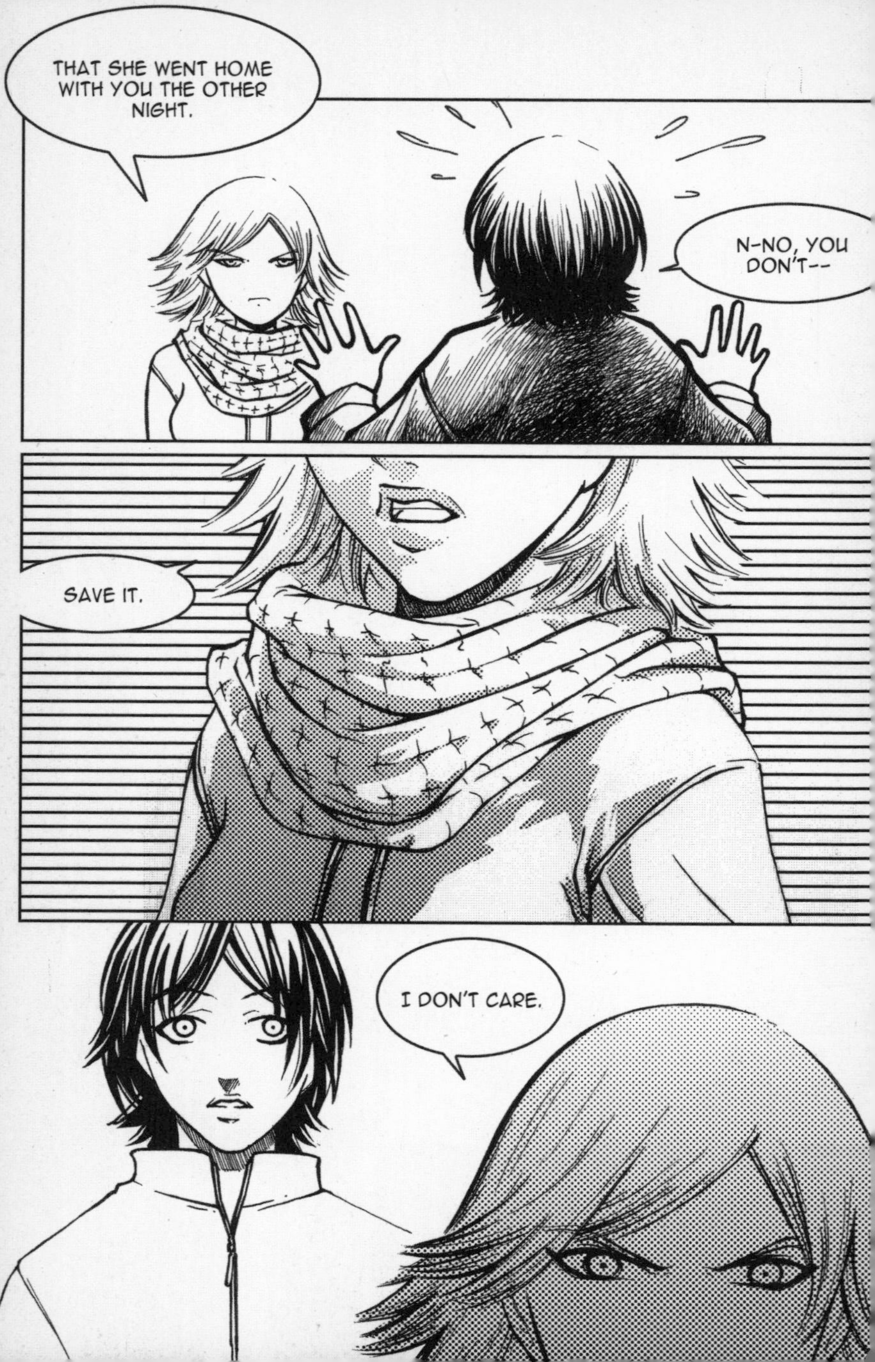
THAT SHE WENT HOME WITH YOU THE OTHER NIGHT.
N-NO, YOU DON'T--
SAVE IT.
I DON'T CARE.

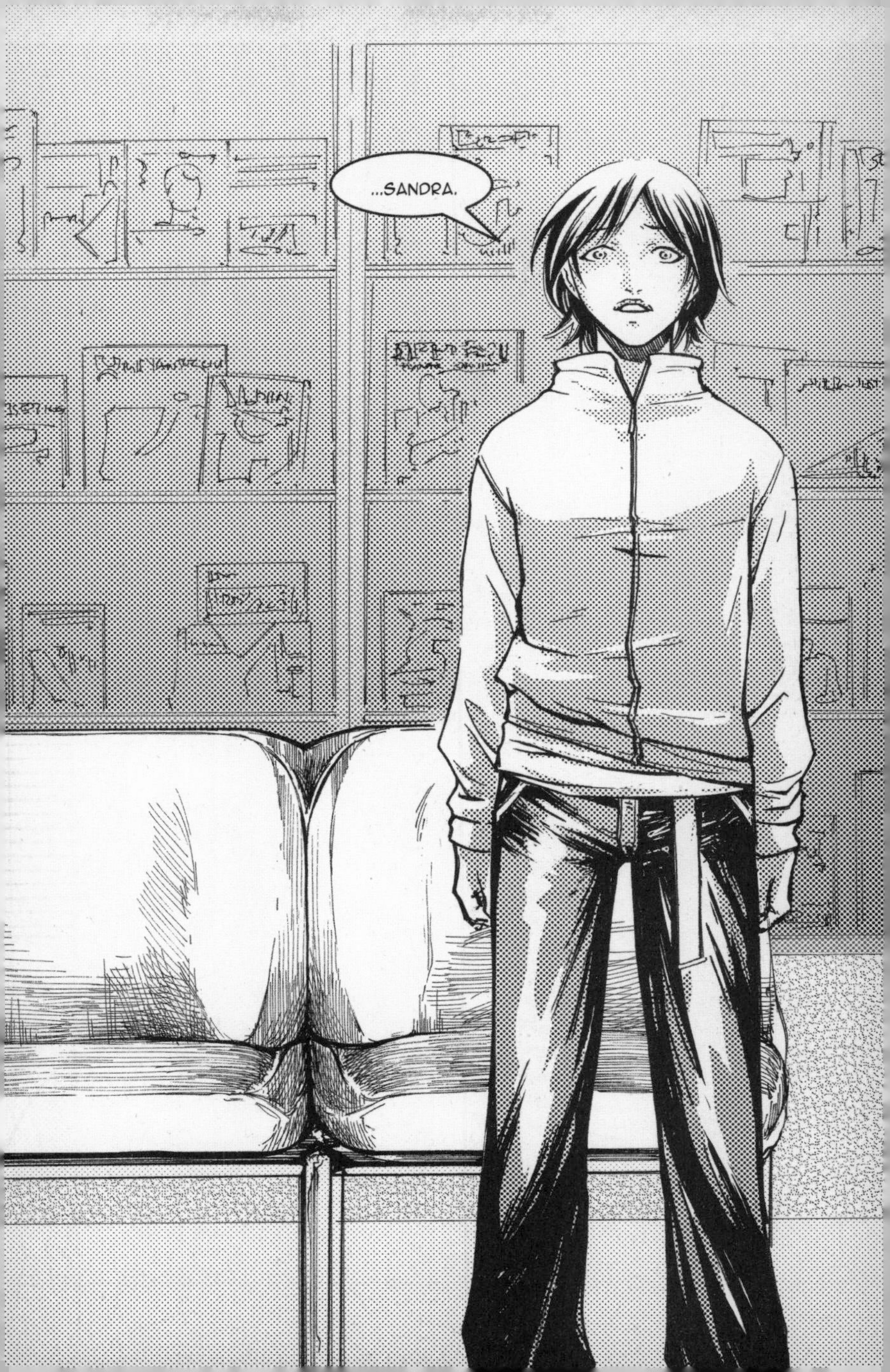
...SANDRA.

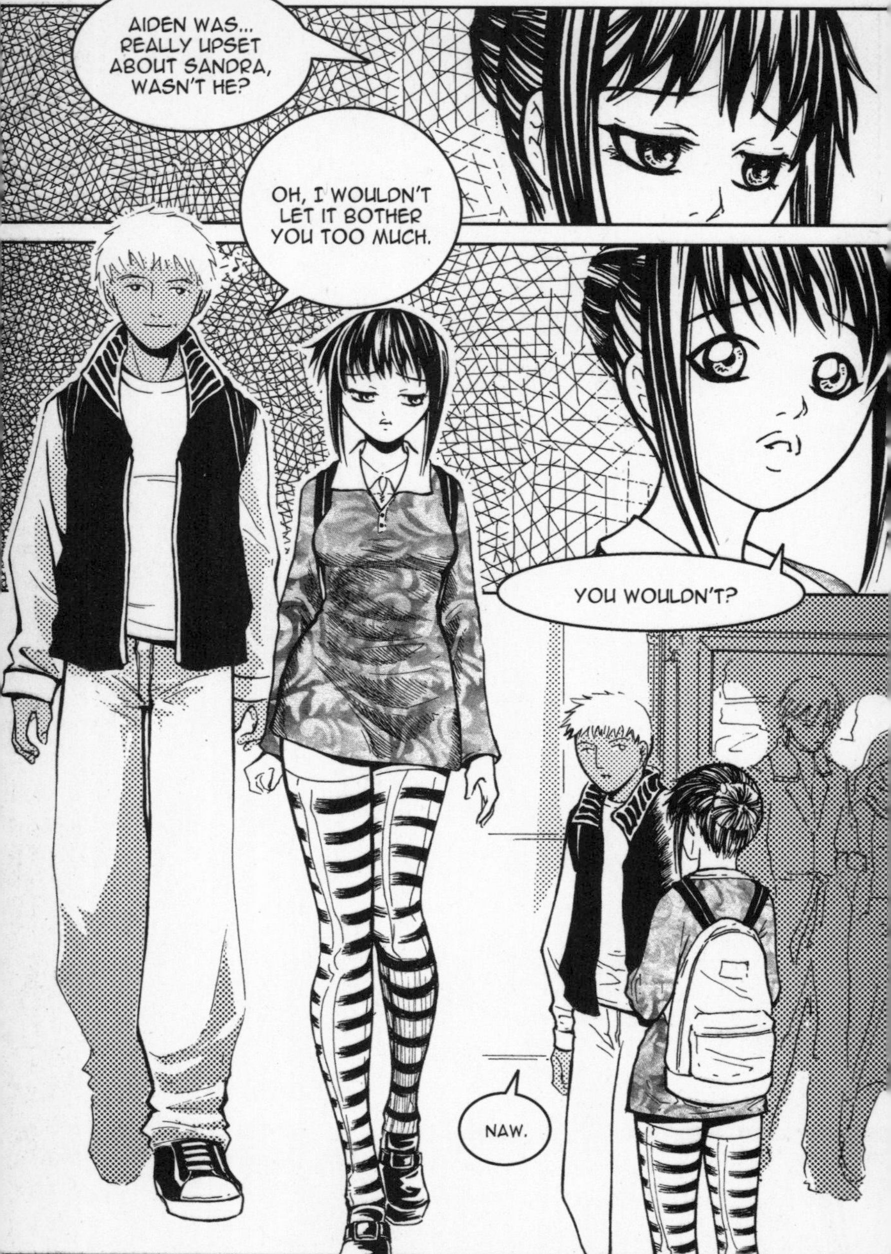
AIDEN WAS... REALLY UPSET ABOUT SANDRA, WASN'T HE?
OH, I WOULDN'T LET IT BOTHER YOU TOO MUCH.
YOU WOULDN'T?
NAW.

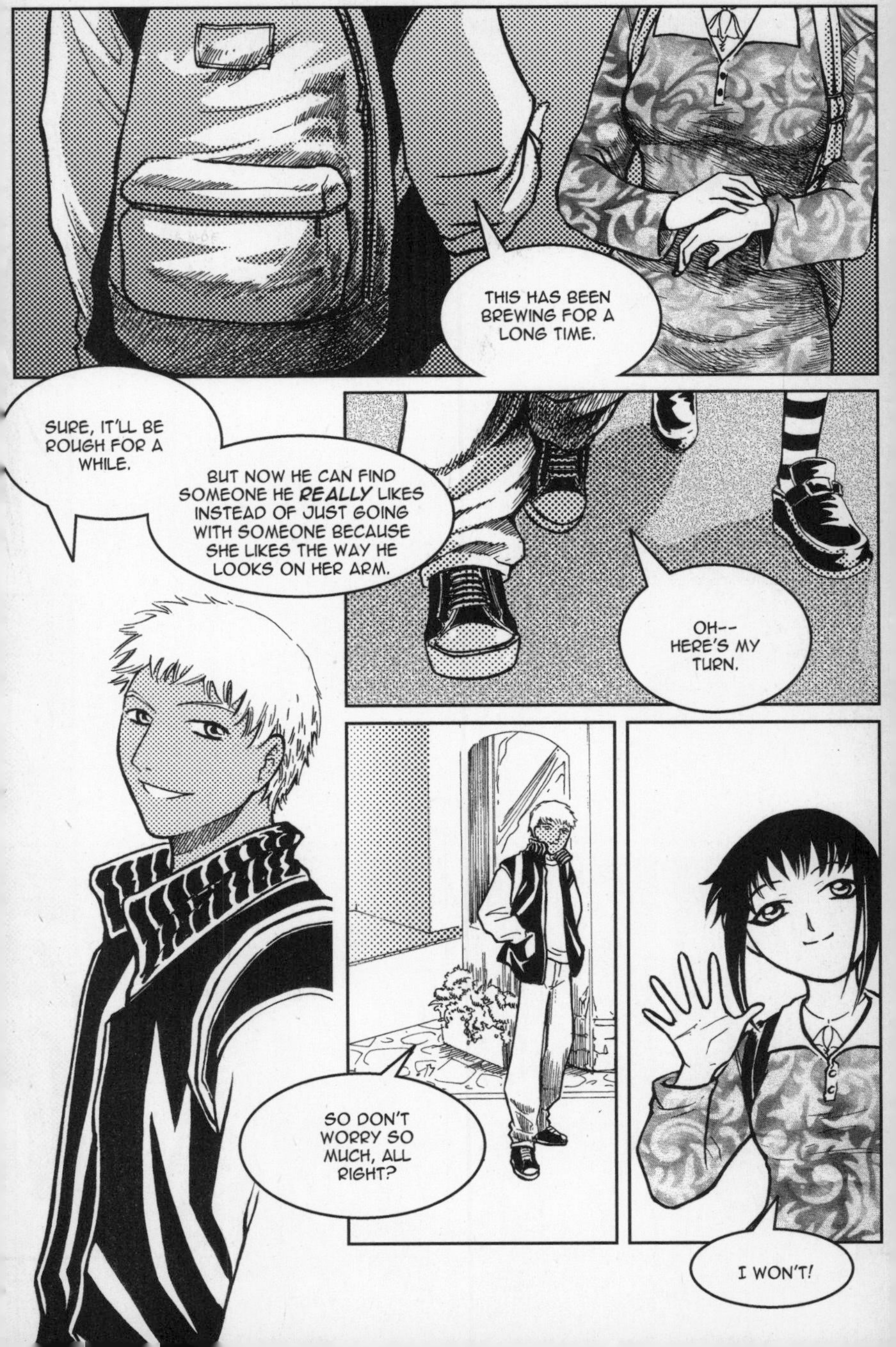
THIS HAS BEEN BREWING FOR A LONG TIME.
SURE, IT'LL BE ROUGH FOR A WHILE.
BUT NOW HE CAN FIND SOMEONE HE *REALLY* LIKES INSTEAD OF JUST GOING WITH SOMEONE BECAUSE SHE LIKES THE WAY HE LOOKS ON HER ARM.
OH-- HERE'S MY TURN.
SO DON'T WORRY SO MUCH, ALL RIGHT?
I WON'T!

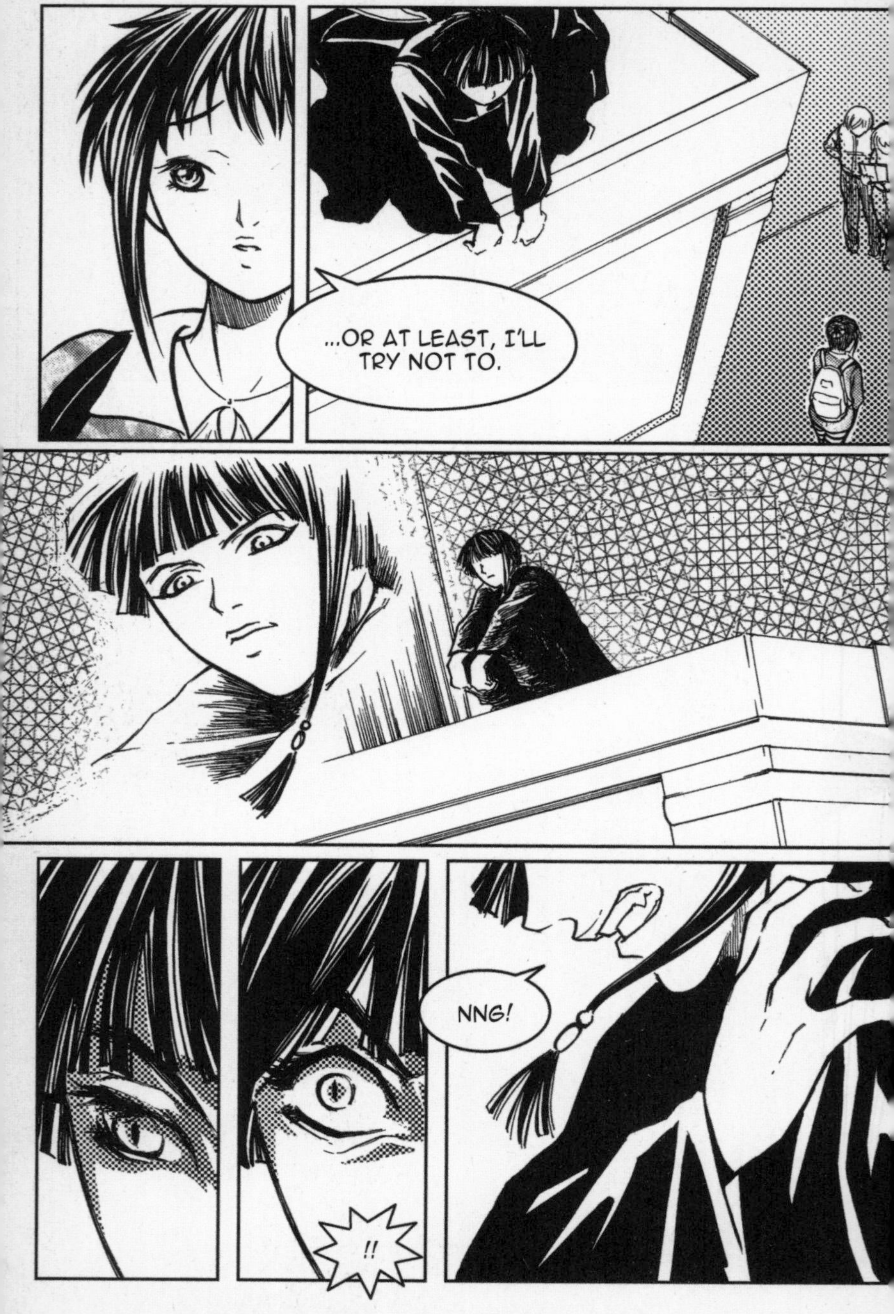
...OR AT LEAST, I'LL TRY NOT TO.
NNG!
!!

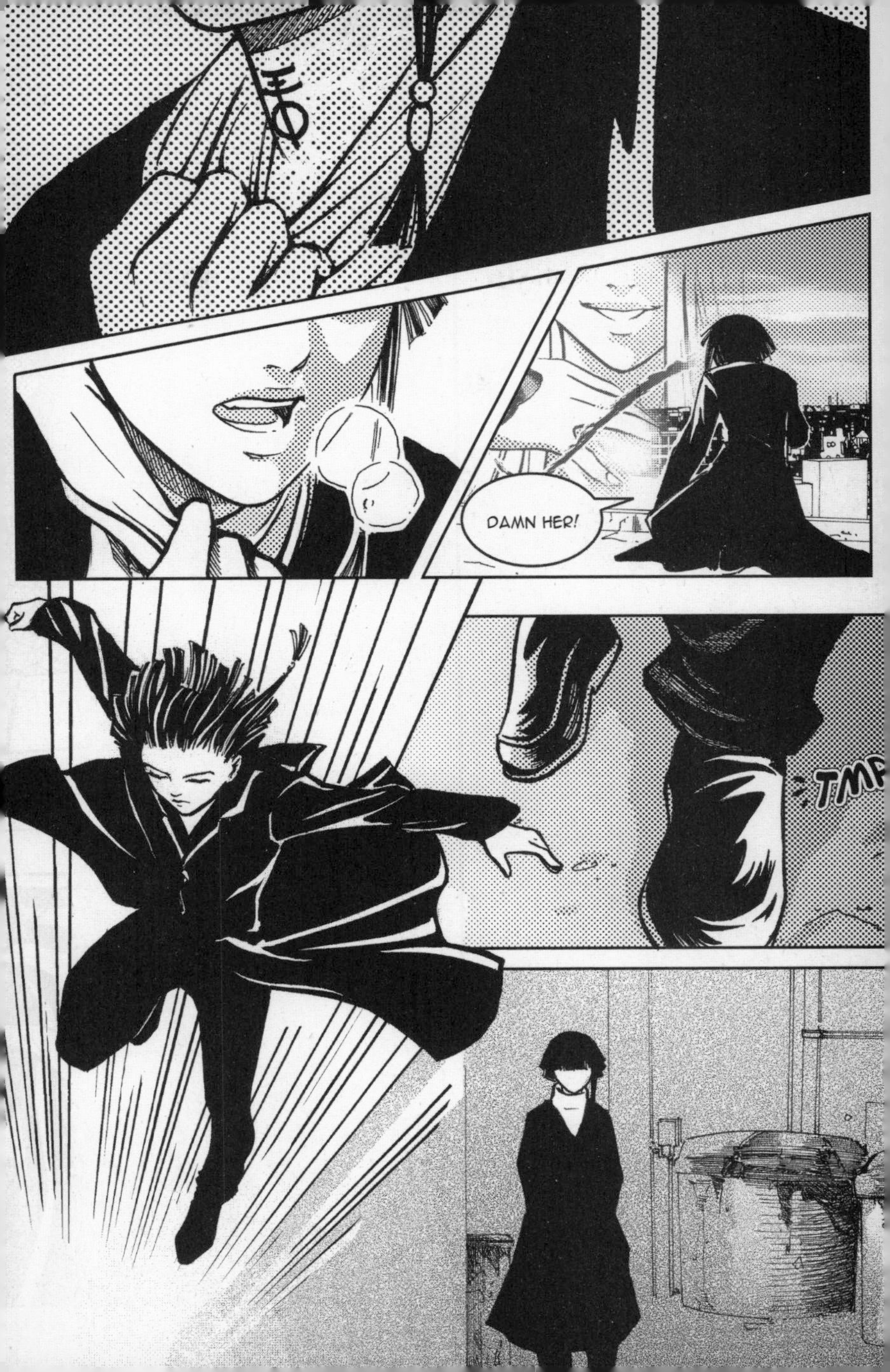
DAMN HER!
TMP

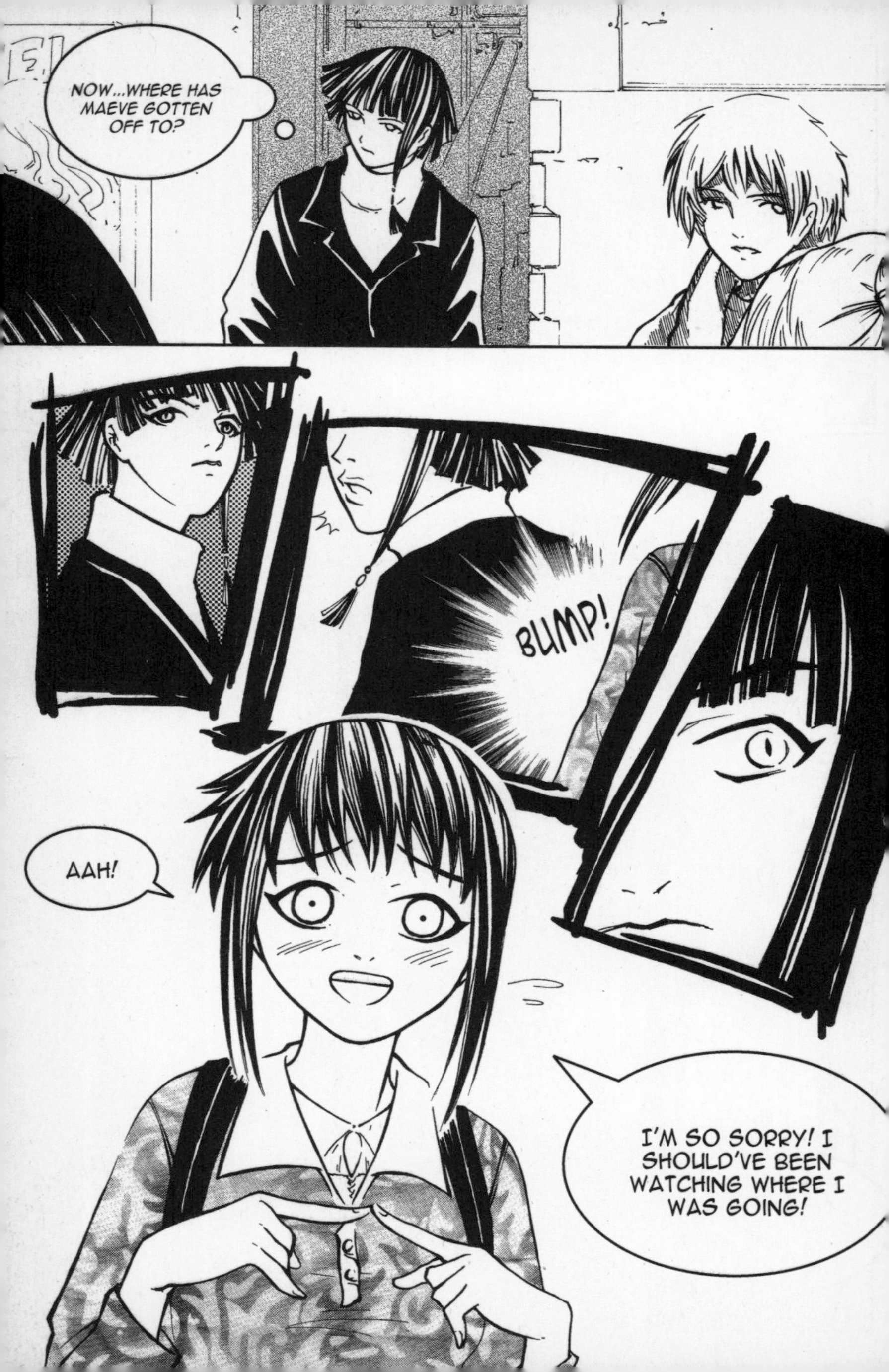
NOW...WHERE HAS MAEVE GOTTEN OFF TO?
BUMP!
AAH!
I'M SO SORRY! I SHOULD'VE BEEN WATCHING WHERE I WAS GOING!

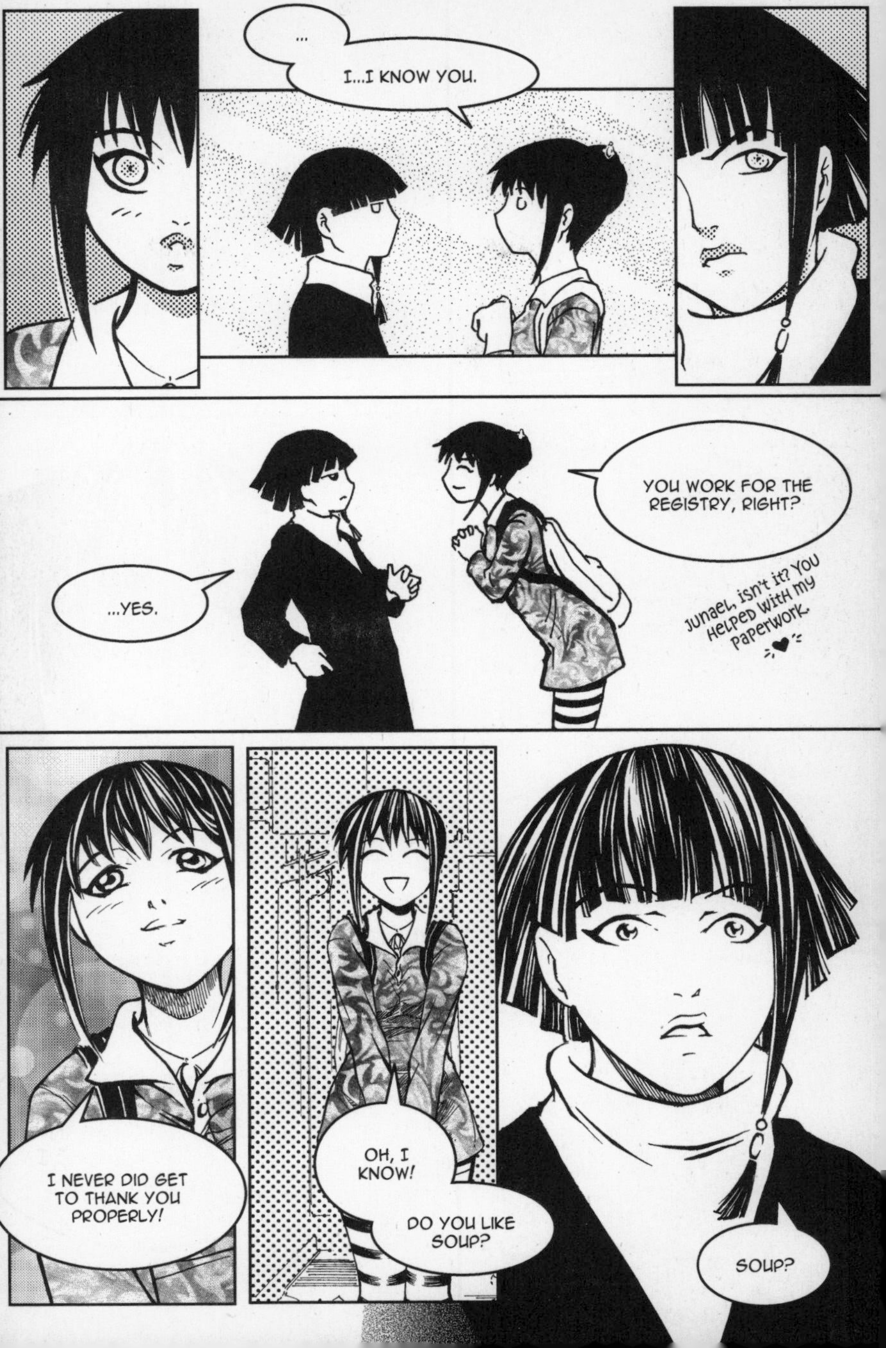
...
I...I KNOW YOU.
YOU WORK FOR THE REGISTRY, RIGHT?
...YES.
Junael, isn't it? You helped with my paperwork.
I NEVER DID GET TO THANK YOU PROPERLY!
OH, I KNOW!
DO YOU LIKE SOUP?
SOUP?

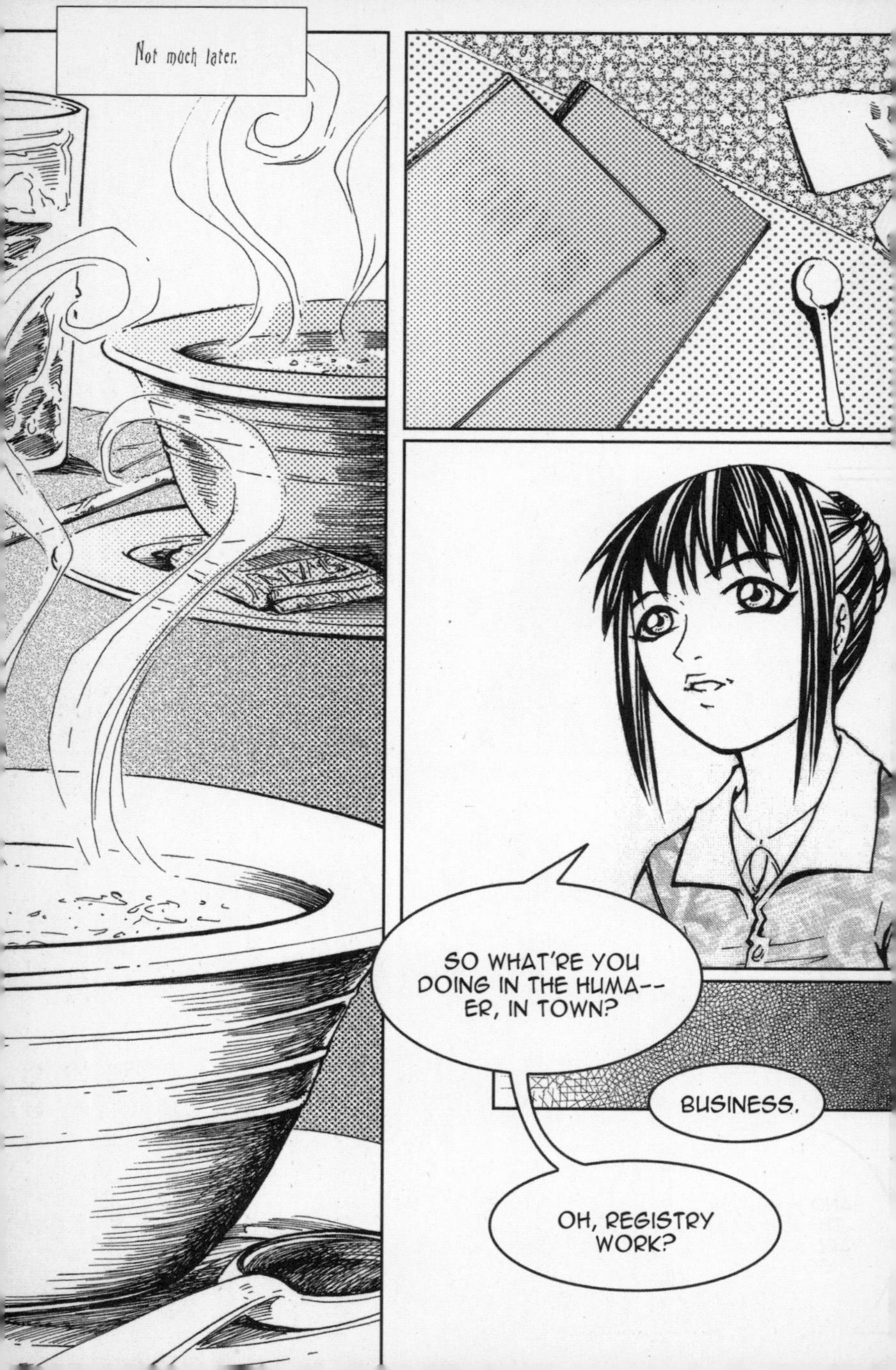
Not much later.
SO WHAT'RE YOU DOING IN THE HUMA-- ER, IN TOWN?
BUSINESS.
OH, REGISTRY WORK?

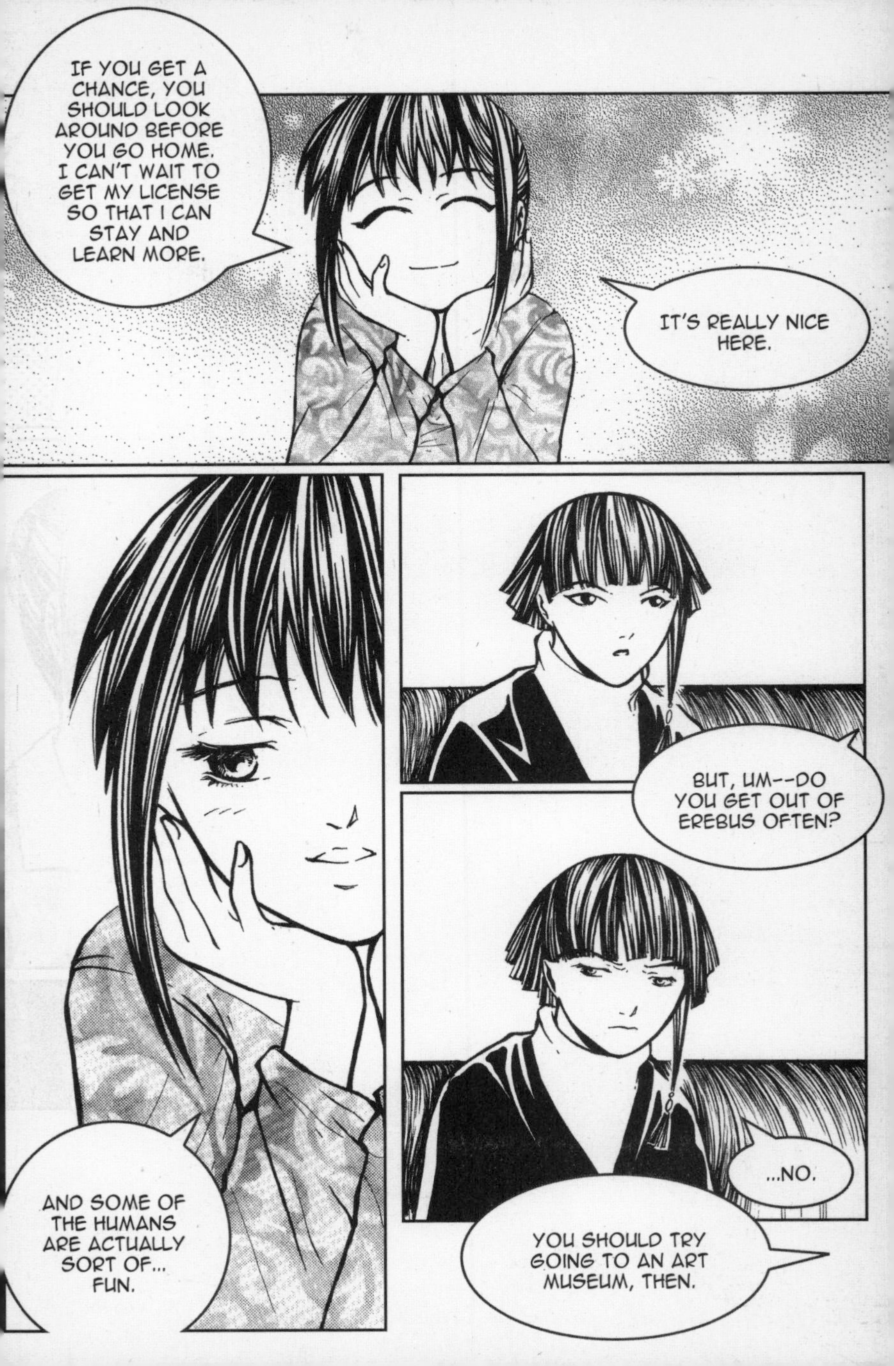
IF YOU GET A CHANCE, YOU SHOULD LOOK AROUND BEFORE YOU GO HOME. I CAN'T WAIT TO GET MY LICENSE SO THAT I CAN STAY AND LEARN MORE.
IT'S REALLY NICE HERE.
AND SOME OF THE HUMANS ARE ACTUALLY SORT OF... FUN.
BUT, UM--DO YOU GET OUT OF EREBUS OFTEN?
...NO.
YOU SHOULD TRY GOING TO AN ART MUSEUM, THEN.

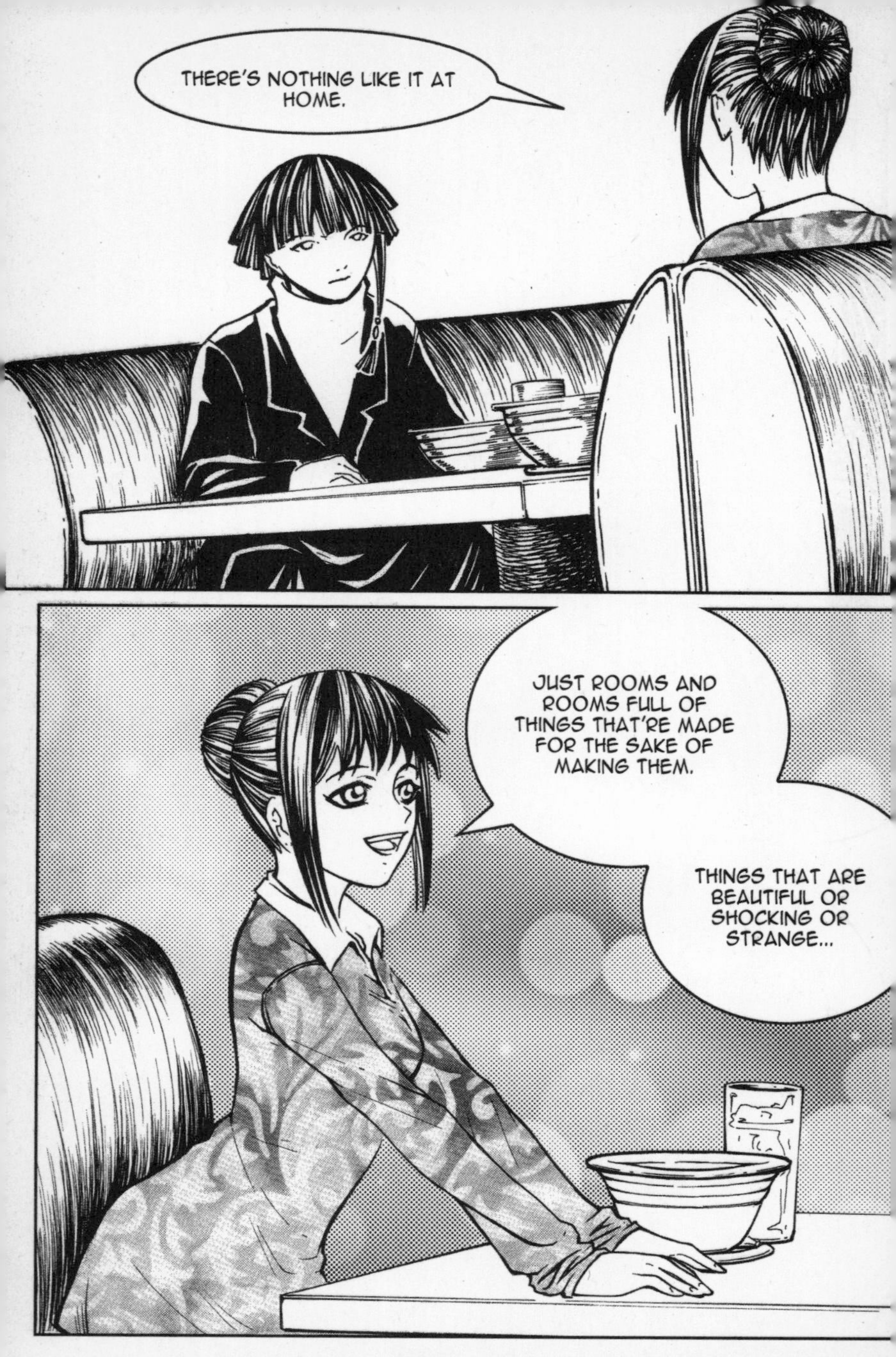
THERE'S NOTHING LIKE IT AT HOME.
JUST ROOMS AND ROOMS FULL OF THINGS THAT'RE MADE FOR THE SAKE OF MAKING THEM.
THINGS THAT ARE BEAUTIFUL OR SHOCKING OR STRANGE...

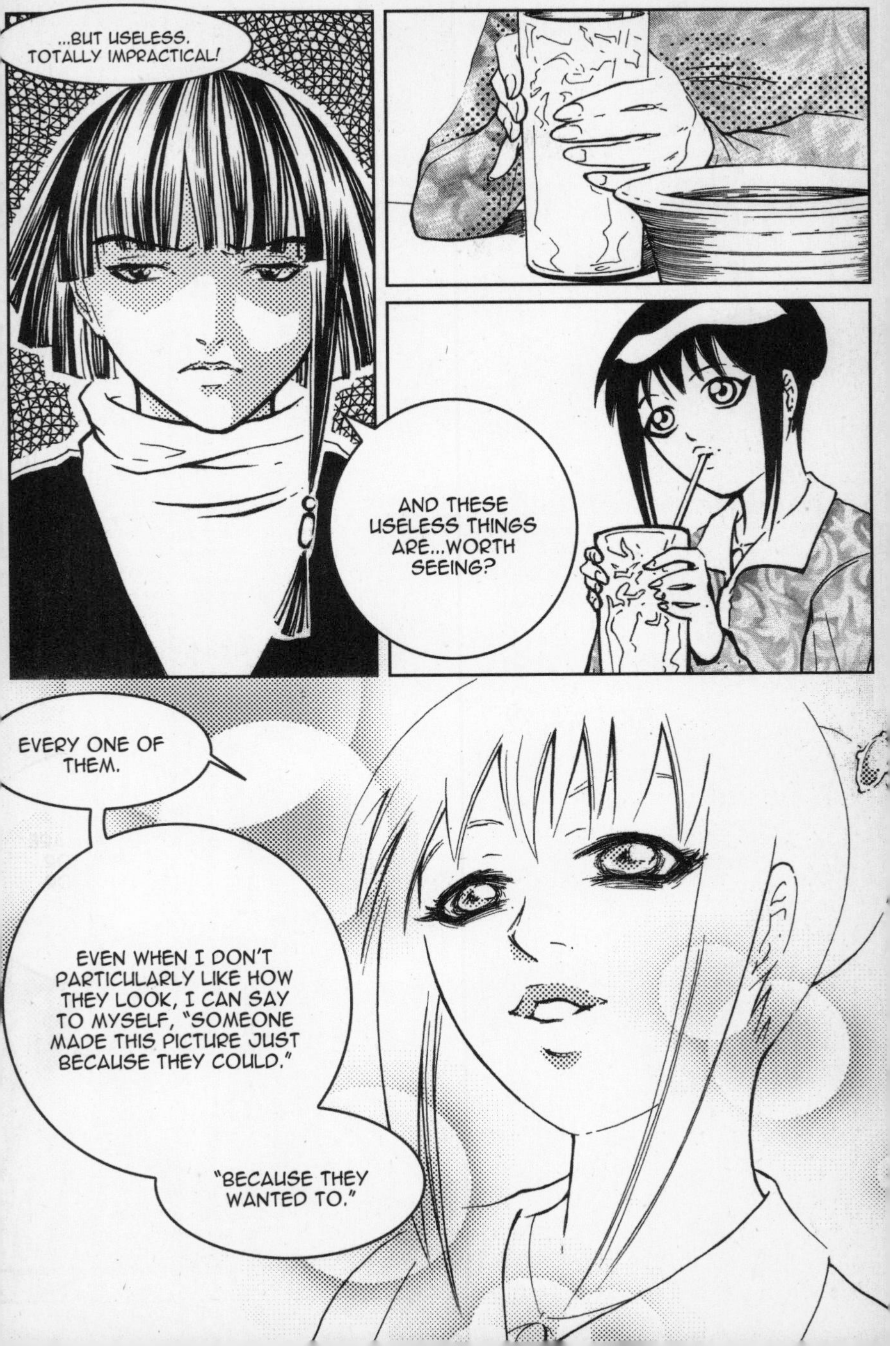
...BUT USELESS. TOTALLY IMPRACTICAL!
AND THESE USELESS THINGS ARE...WORTH SEEING?
EVERY ONE OF THEM.
EVEN WHEN I DON'T PARTICULARLY LIKE HOW THEY LOOK, I CAN SAY TO MYSELF, "SOMEONE MADE THIS PICTURE JUST BECAUSE THEY COULD."
"BECAUSE THEY WANTED TO."

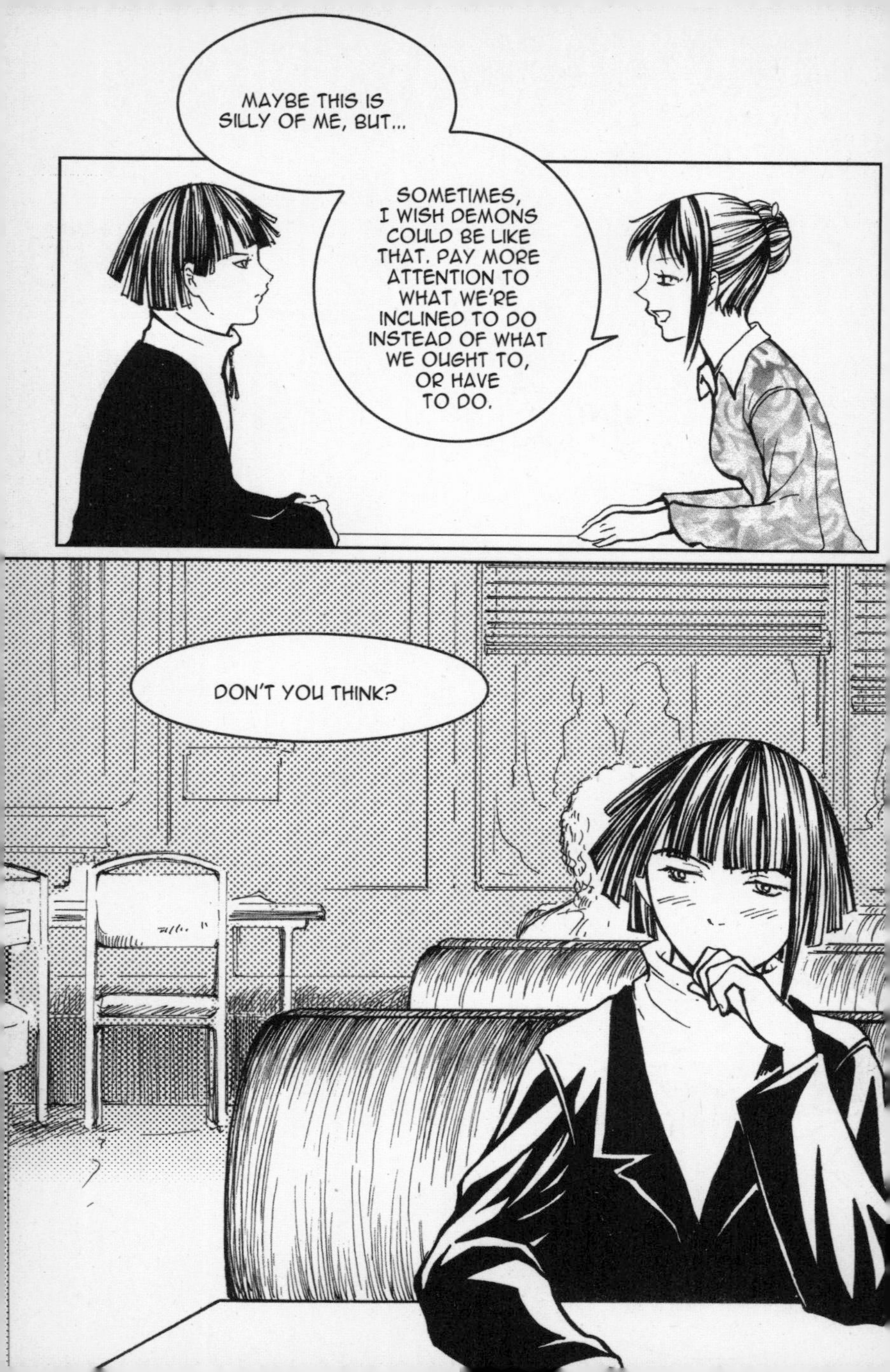
MAYBE THIS IS SILLY OF ME, BUT...
SOMETIMES, I WISH DEMONS COULD BE LIKE THAT. PAY MORE ATTENTION TO WHAT WE'RE INCLINED TO DO INSTEAD OF WHAT WE OUGHT TO, OR HAVE TO DO.
DON'T YOU THINK?

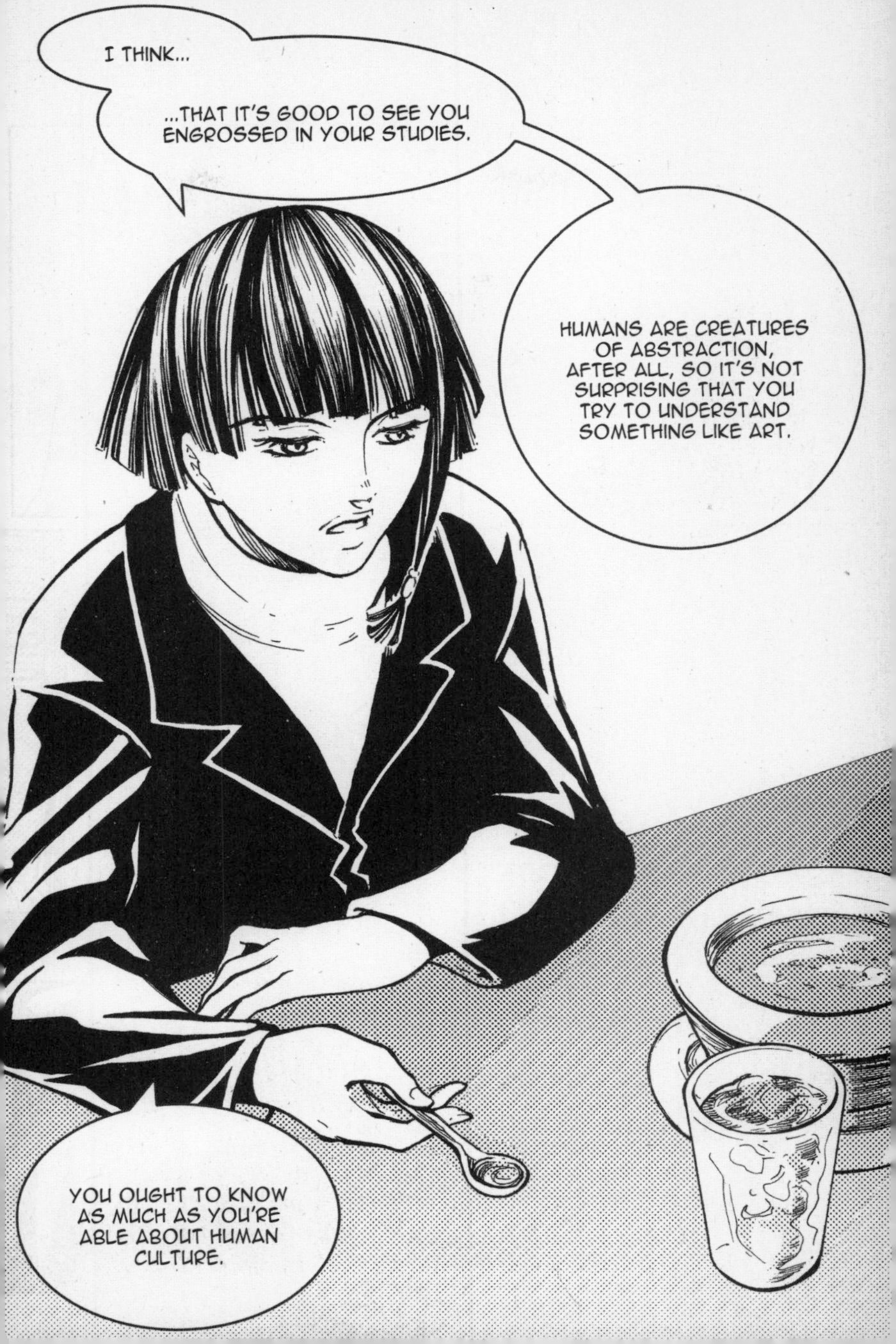
I THINK...
...THAT IT'S GOOD TO SEE YOU ENGROSSED IN YOUR STUDIES.
HUMANS ARE CREATURES OF ABSTRACTION, AFTER ALL, SO IT'S NOT SURPRISING THAT YOU TRY TO UNDERSTAND SOMETHING LIKE ART.
YOU OUGHT TO KNOW AS MUCH AS YOU'RE ABLE ABOUT HUMAN CULTURE.

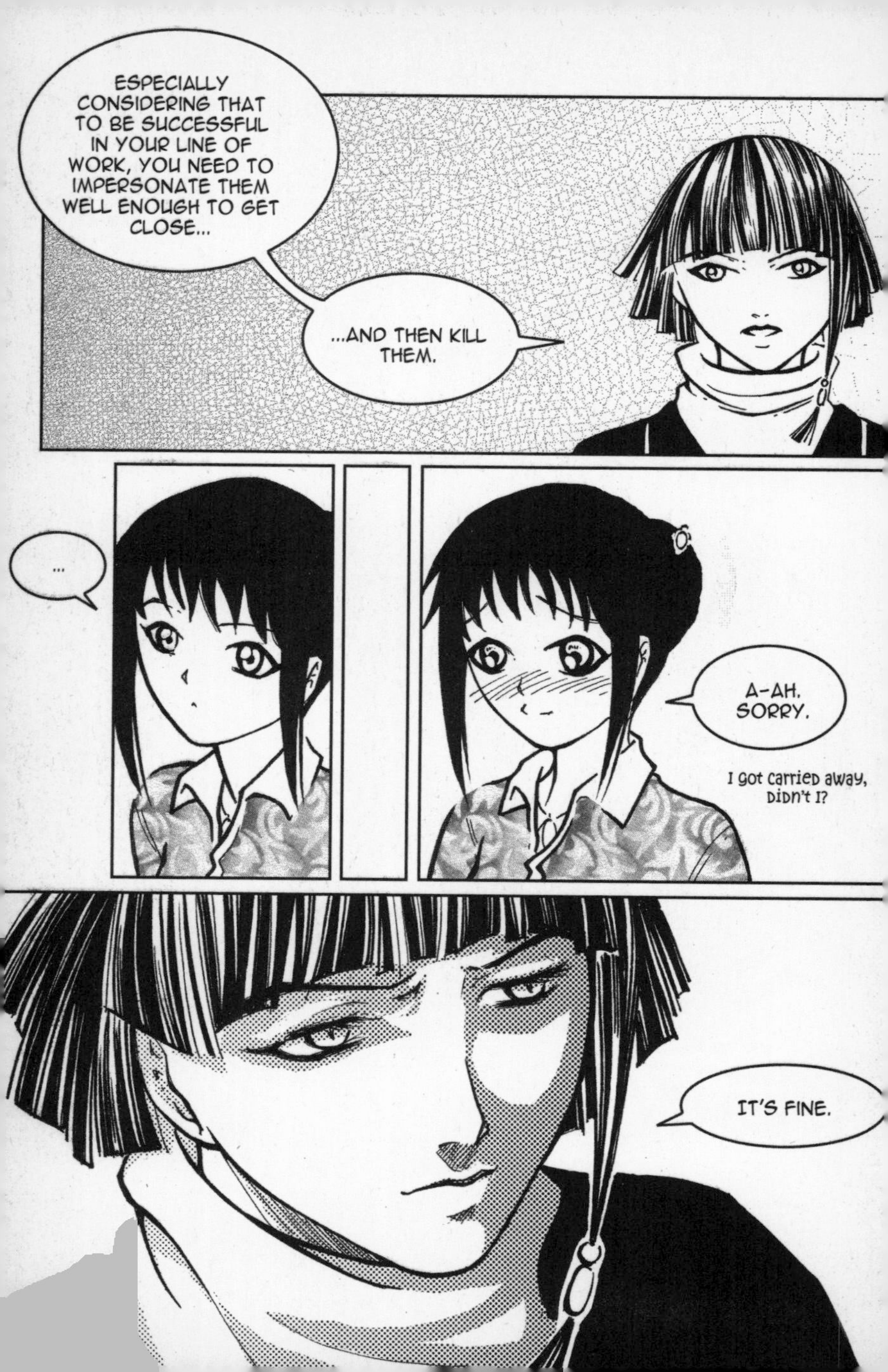
ESPECIALLY CONSIDERING THAT TO BE SUCCESSFUL IN YOUR LINE OF WORK, YOU NEED TO IMPERSONATE THEM WELL ENOUGH TO GET CLOSE...
...AND THEN KILL THEM.
...
A-AH. SORRY.
I got carried away, didn't I?
IT'S FINE.

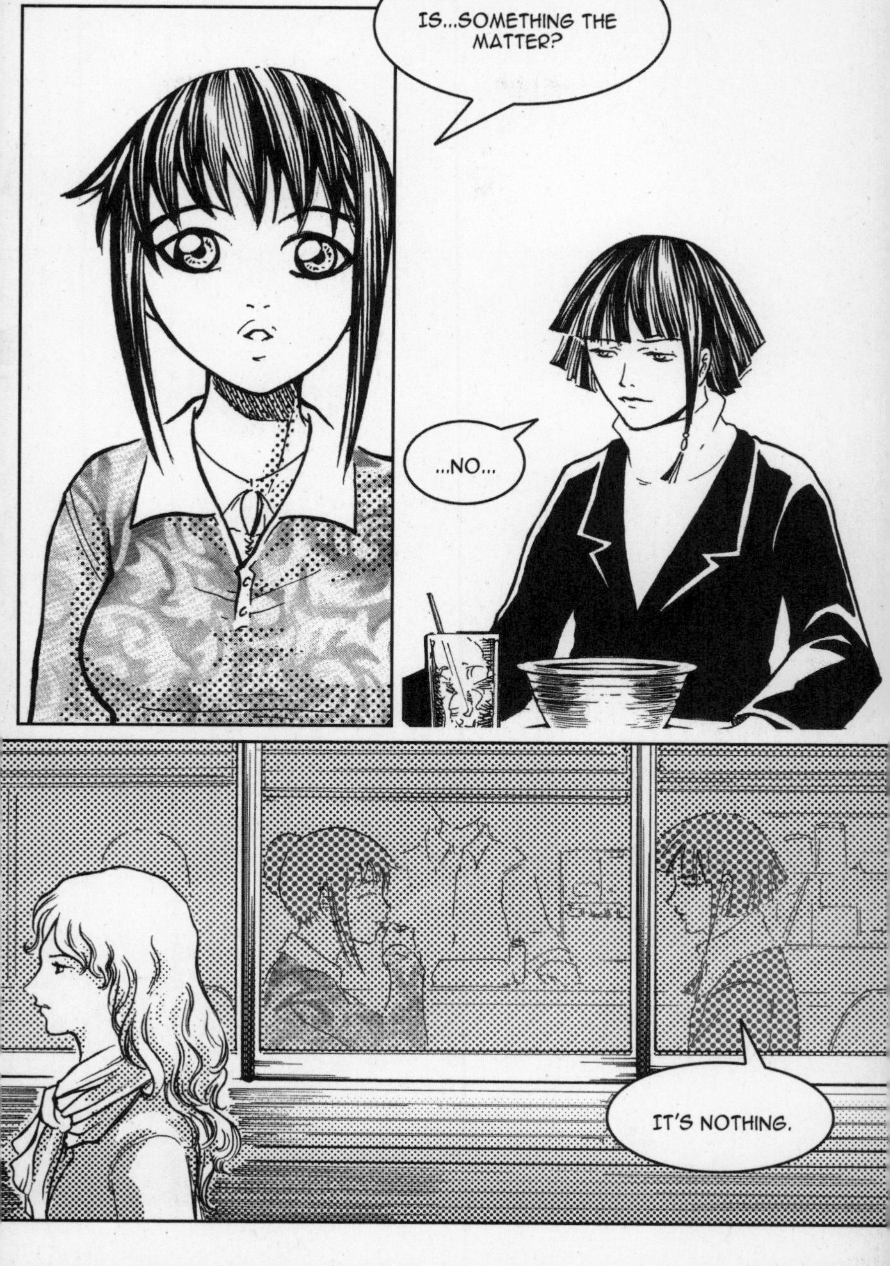
IS...SOMETHING THE MATTER?
...NO...
IT'S NOTHING.

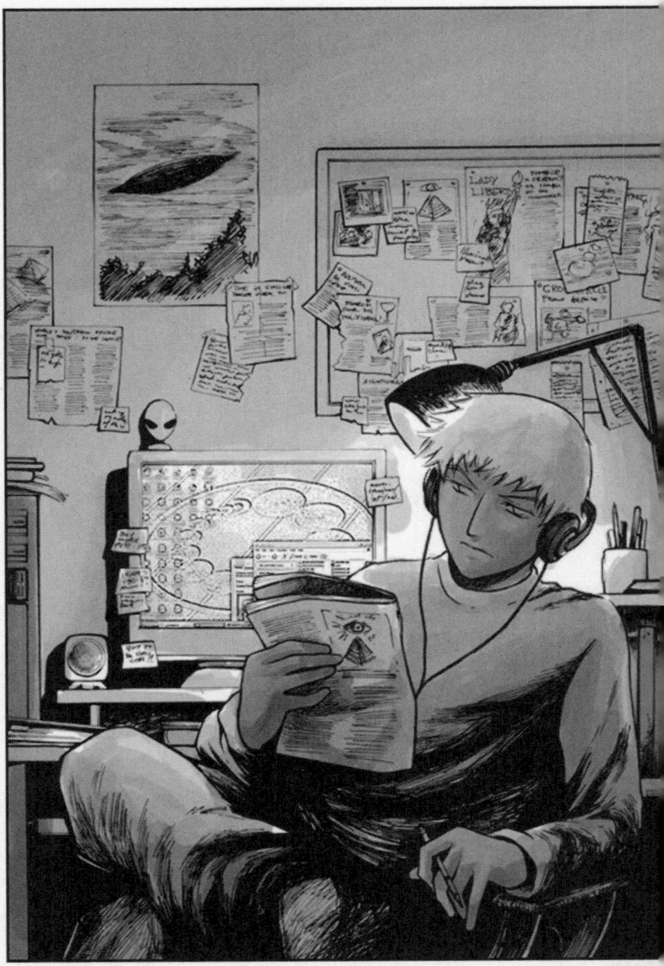
LADY

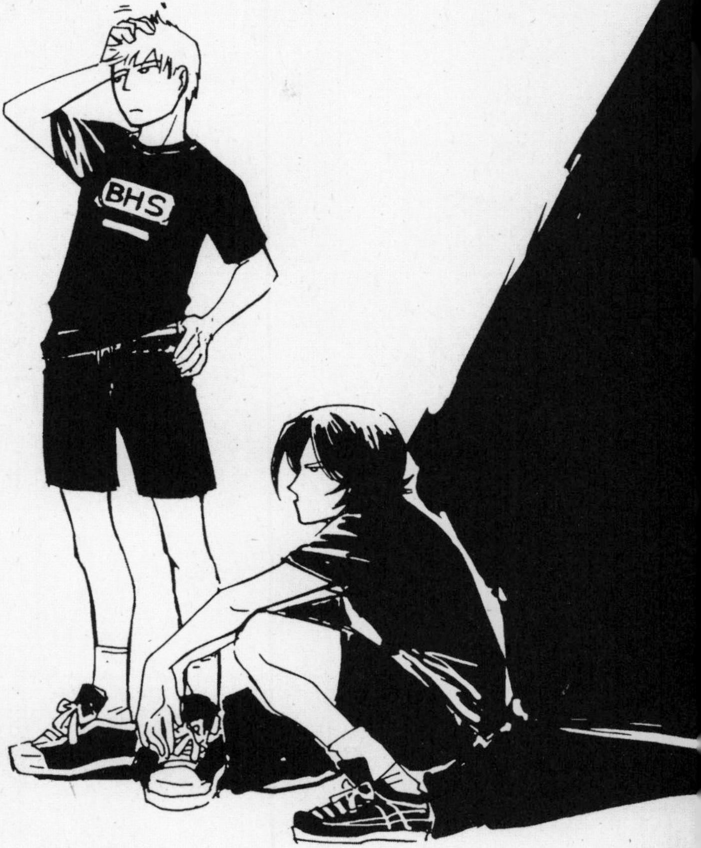
BHS

chapter 6

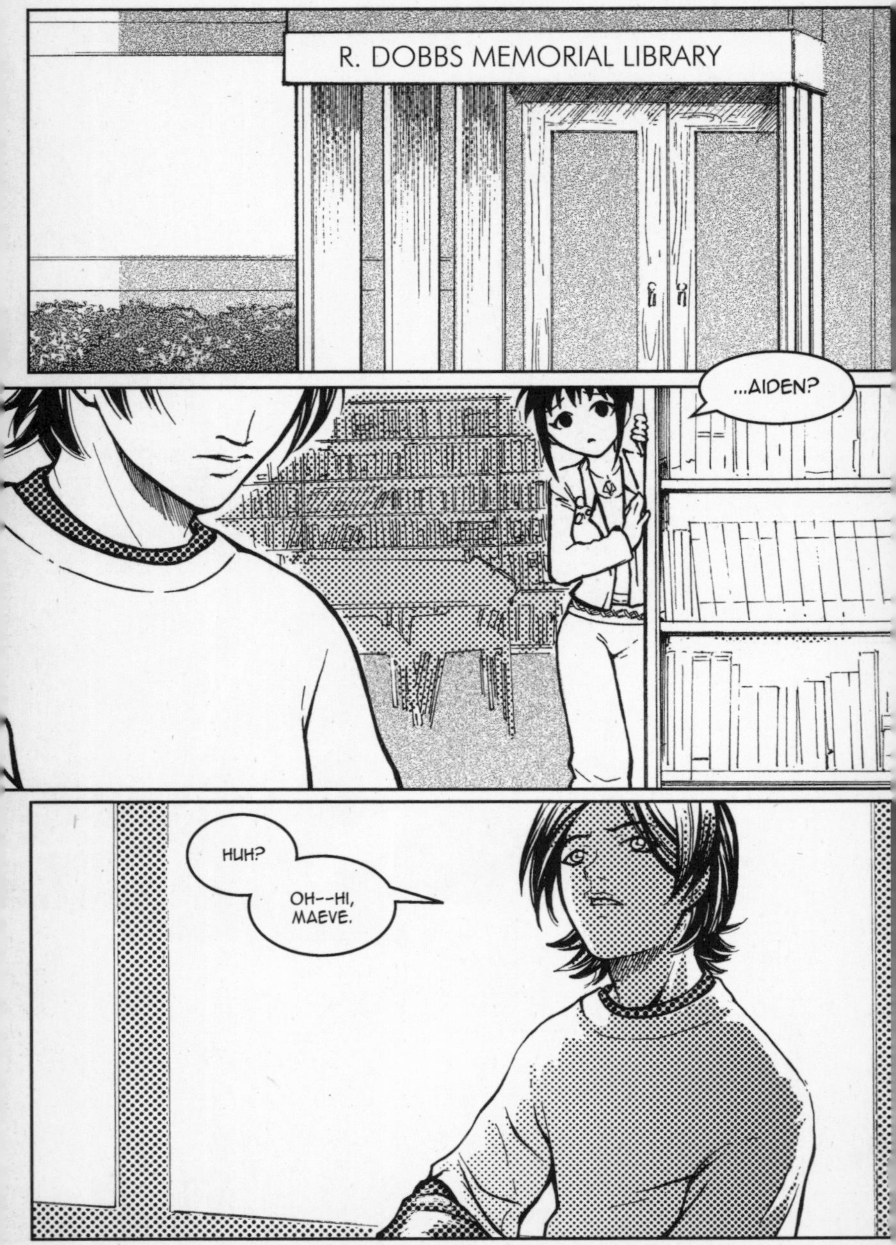
R. DOBBS MEMORIAL LIBRARY
...AIDEN?
HUH?
OH--HI, MAEVE.

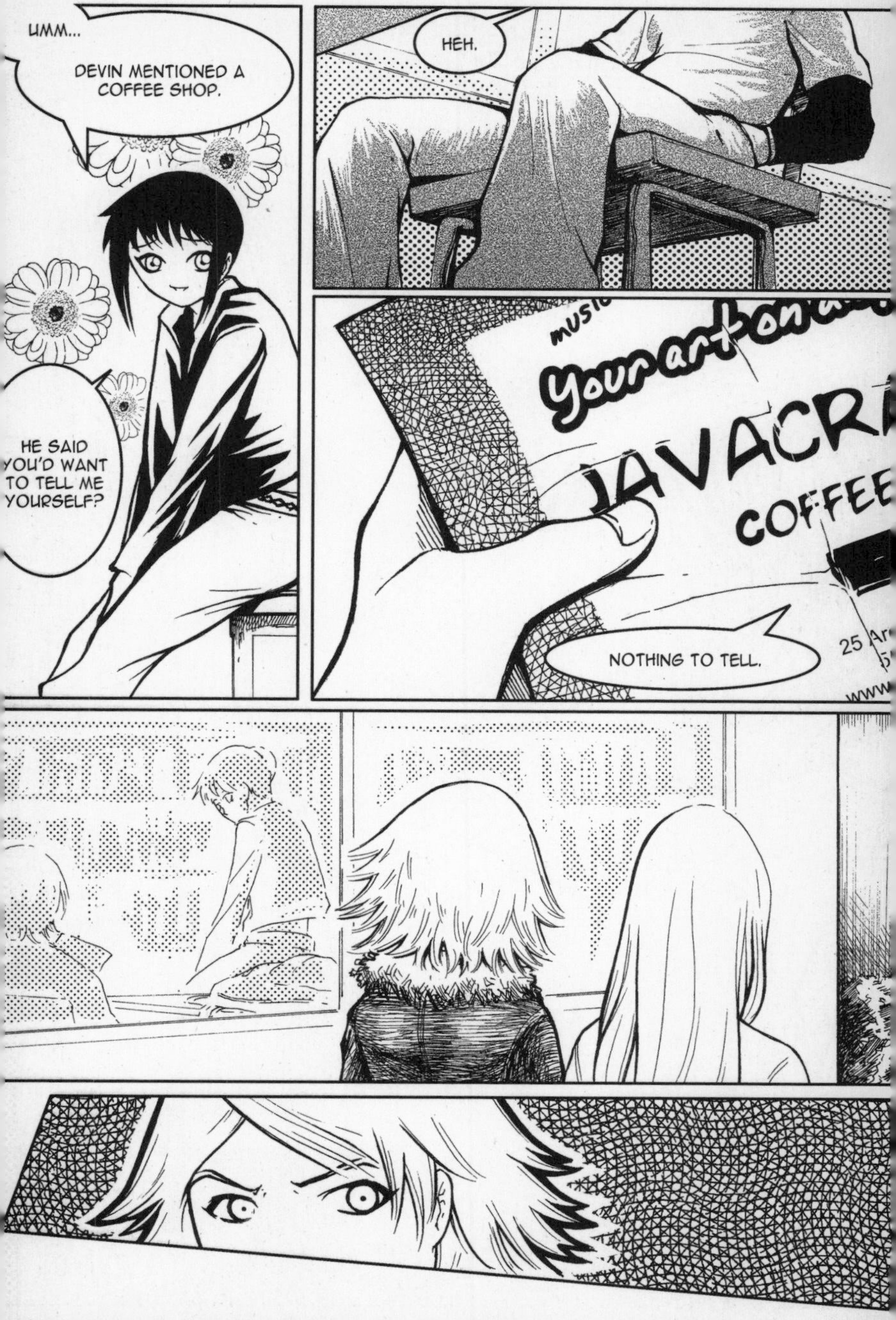
UMM...
DEVIN MENTIONED A COFFEE SHOP.
HE SAID YOU'D WANT TO TELL ME YOURSELF?
HEH.
NOTHING TO TELL.

TO BE HONEST, I DON'T EVEN KNOW IF I WANT TO DO IT. I MEAN...
IT'S ONE THING TO PLAY BY MYSELF BECAUSE I LIKE IT...
BUT PEOPLE BEING THERE MAKES IT... WEIRD.
YOU PLAYED FOR ME.
DID...DID I MAKE IT WEIRD?

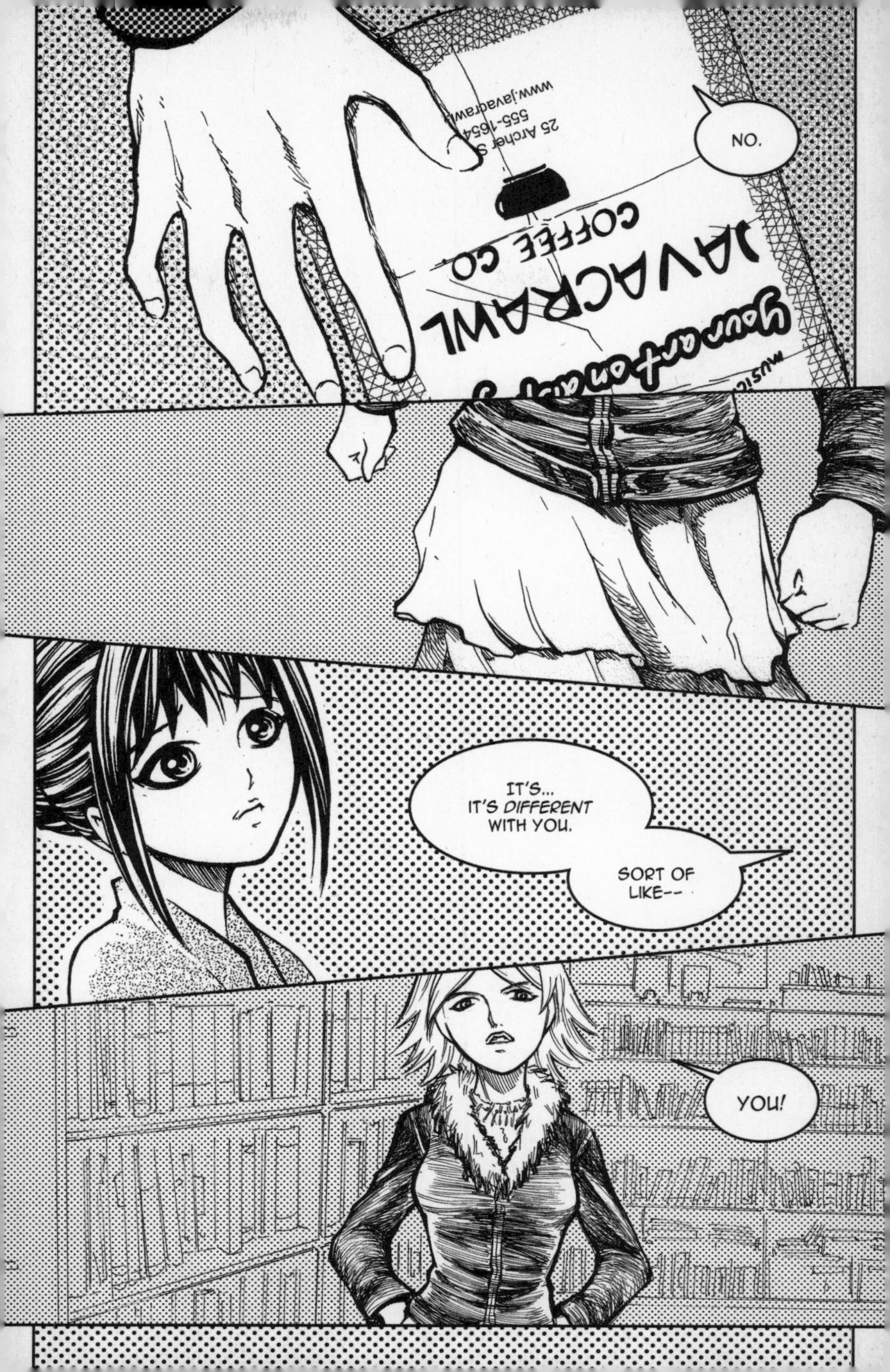
JAVACRAWL
COFFEE CO
NO.
IT'S...
IT'S *DIFFERENT* WITH YOU.
SORT OF LIKE--
YOU!

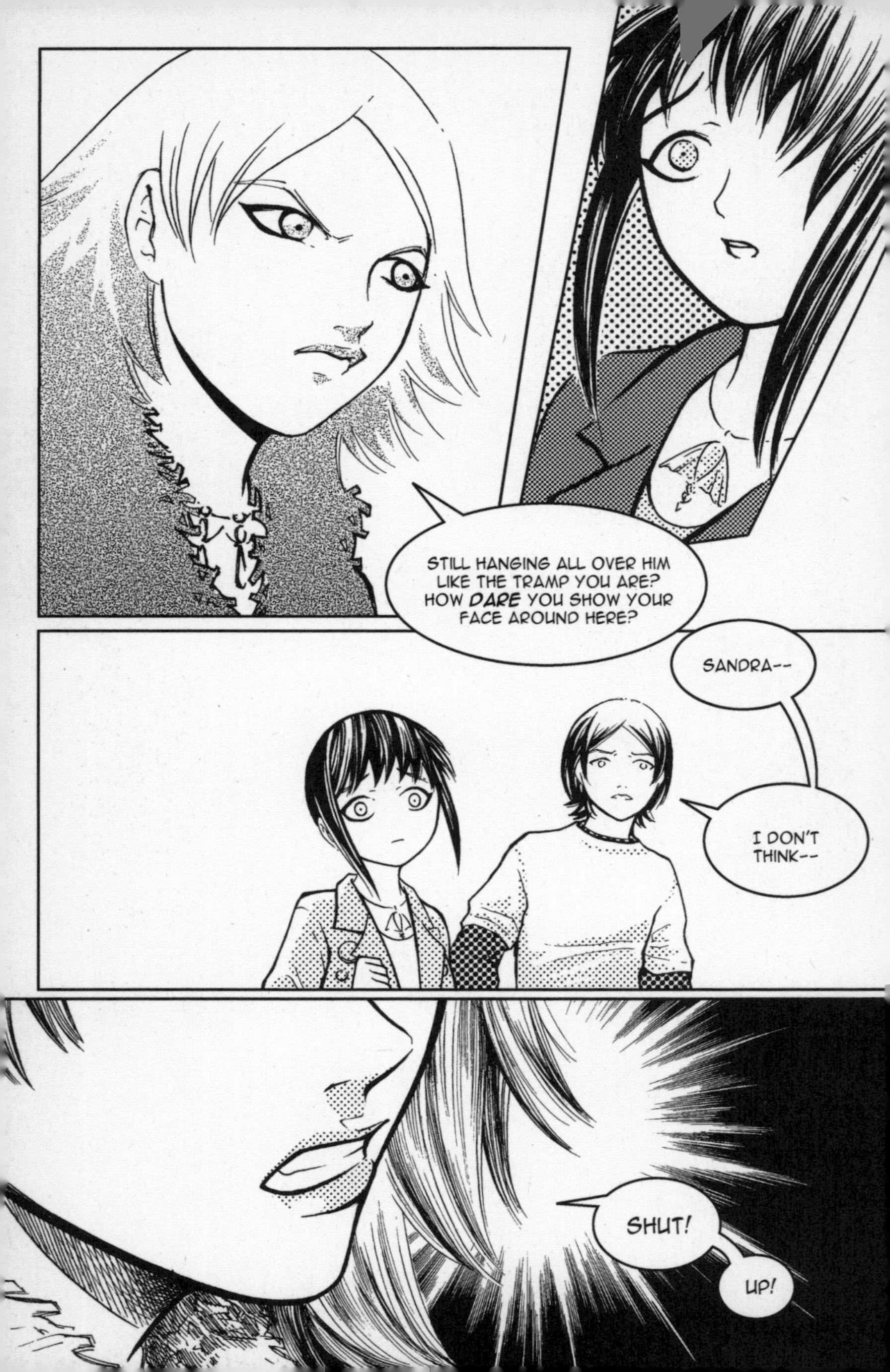
STILL HANGING ALL OVER HIM LIKE THE TRAMP YOU ARE? HOW *DARE* YOU SHOW YOUR FACE AROUND HERE?
SANDRA--
I DON'T THINK--
SHUT!
UP!

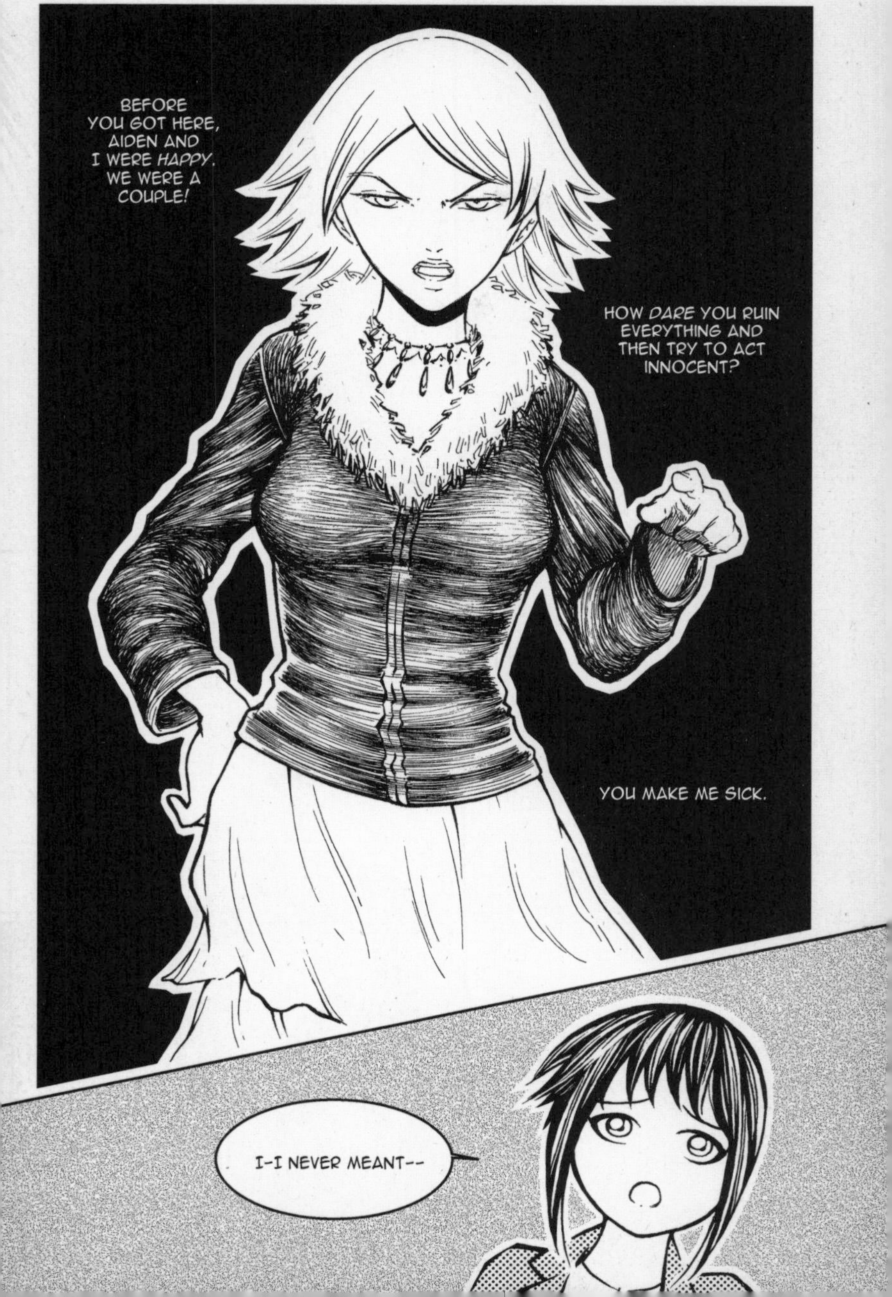
BEFORE YOU GOT HERE, AIDEN AND I WERE *HAPPY*. WE WERE A COUPLE!
HOW *DARE* YOU RUIN EVERYTHING AND THEN TRY TO ACT INNOCENT?
YOU MAKE ME SICK.
I-I NEVER MEANT--

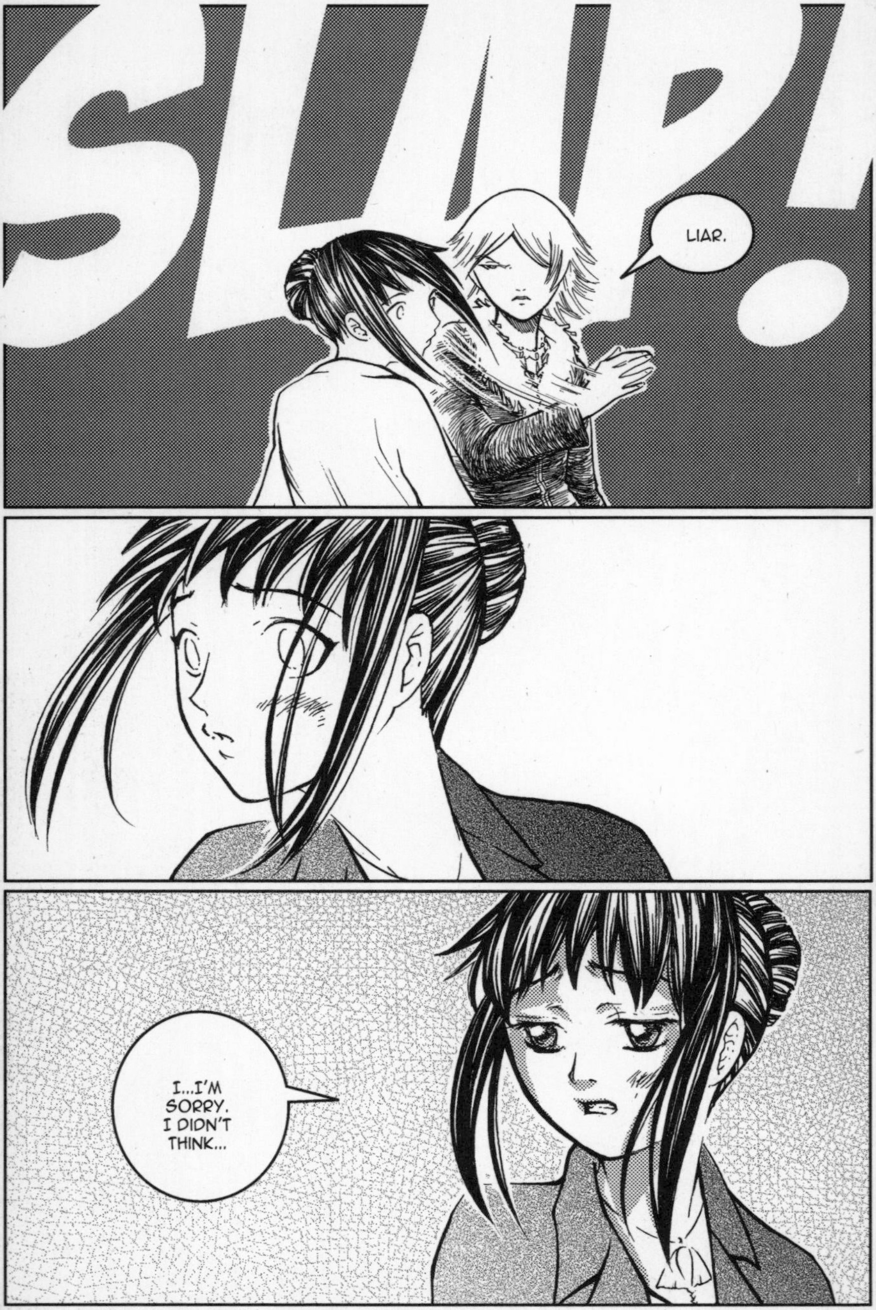
SLAP!
LIAR.
I...I'M SORRY. I DIDN'T THINK...

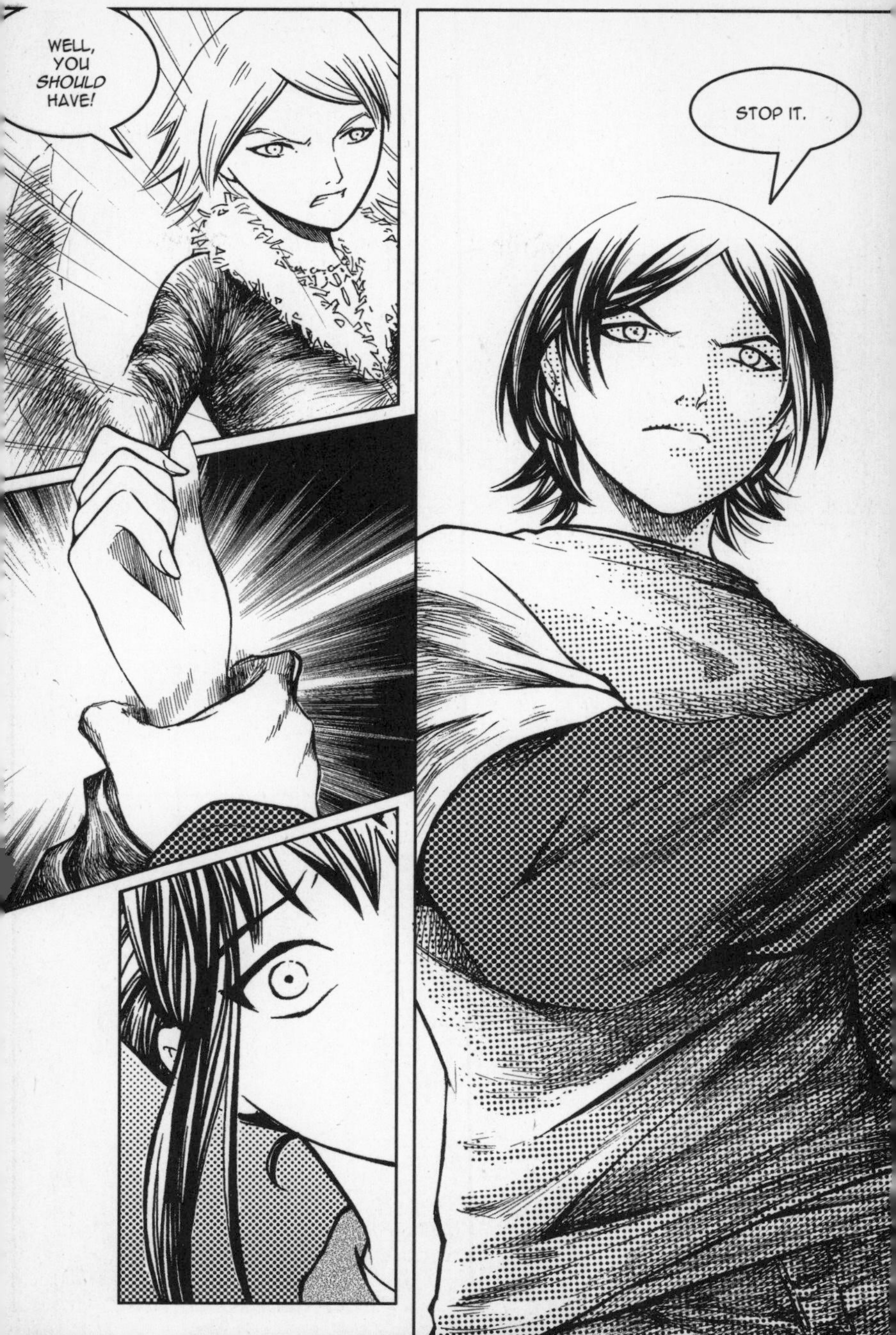
WELL, YOU SHOULD HAVE!
STOP IT.

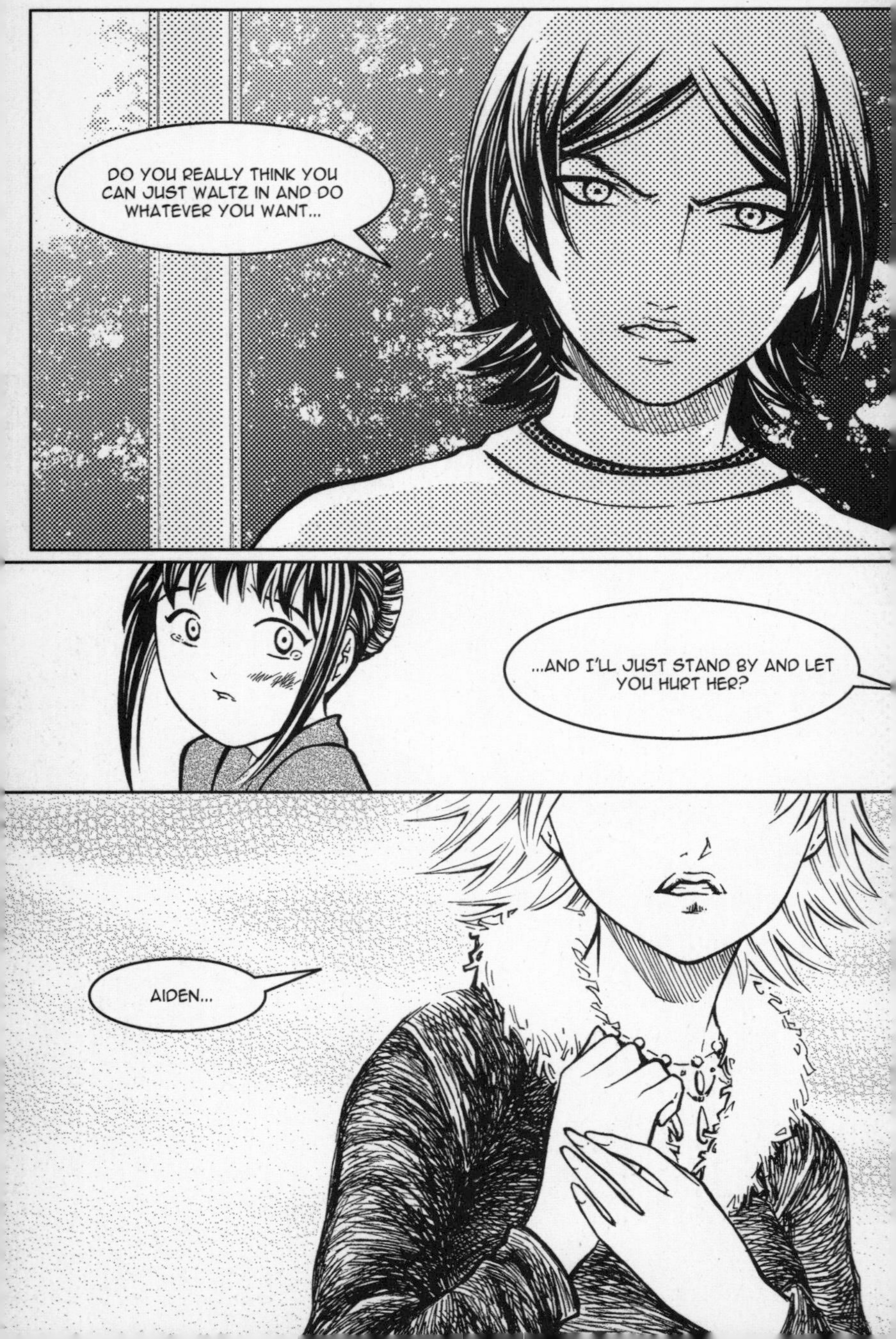
DO YOU REALLY THINK YOU CAN JUST WALTZ IN AND DO WHATEVER YOU WANT...
...AND I'LL JUST STAND BY AND LET YOU HURT HER?
AIDEN...

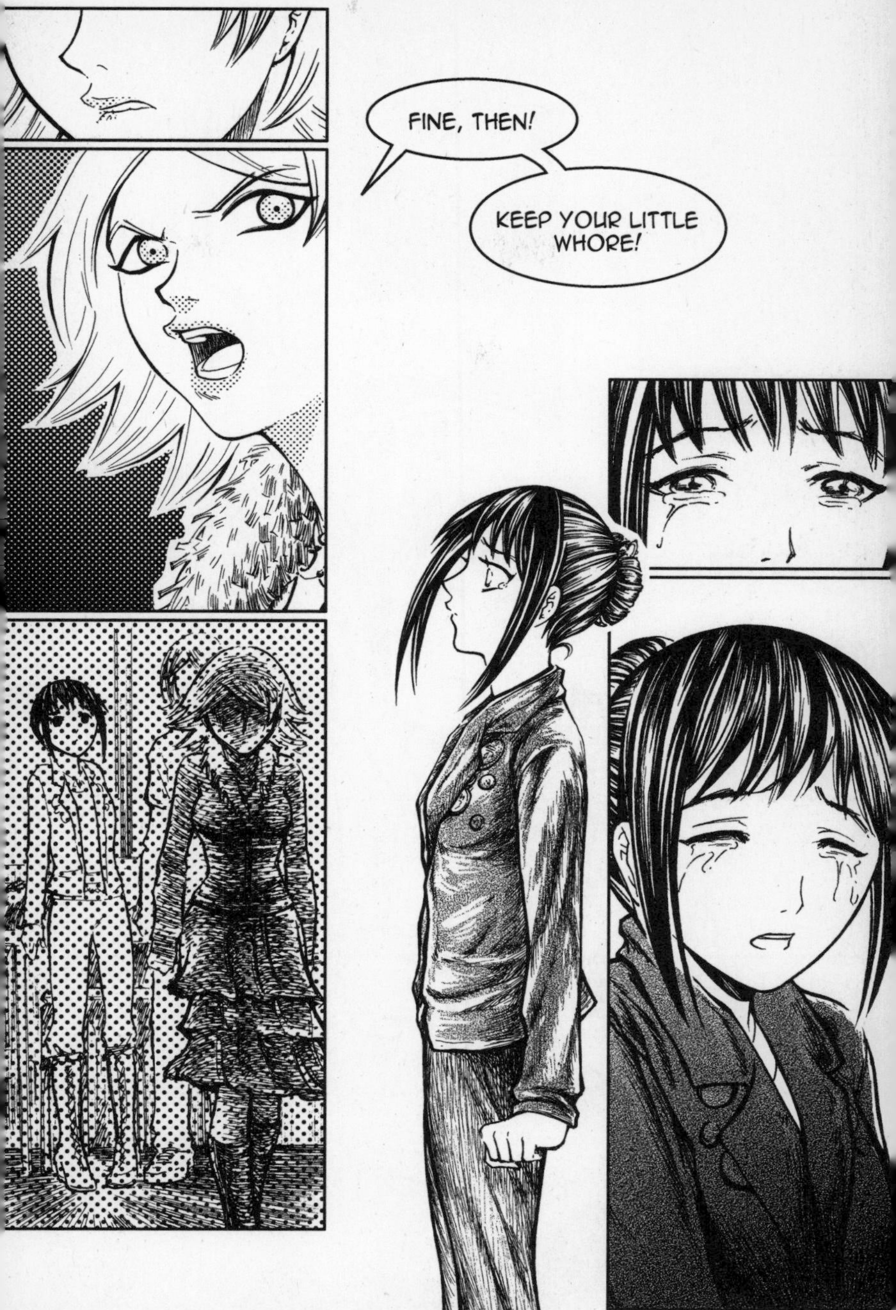
FINE, THEN!
KEEP YOUR LITTLE WHORE!

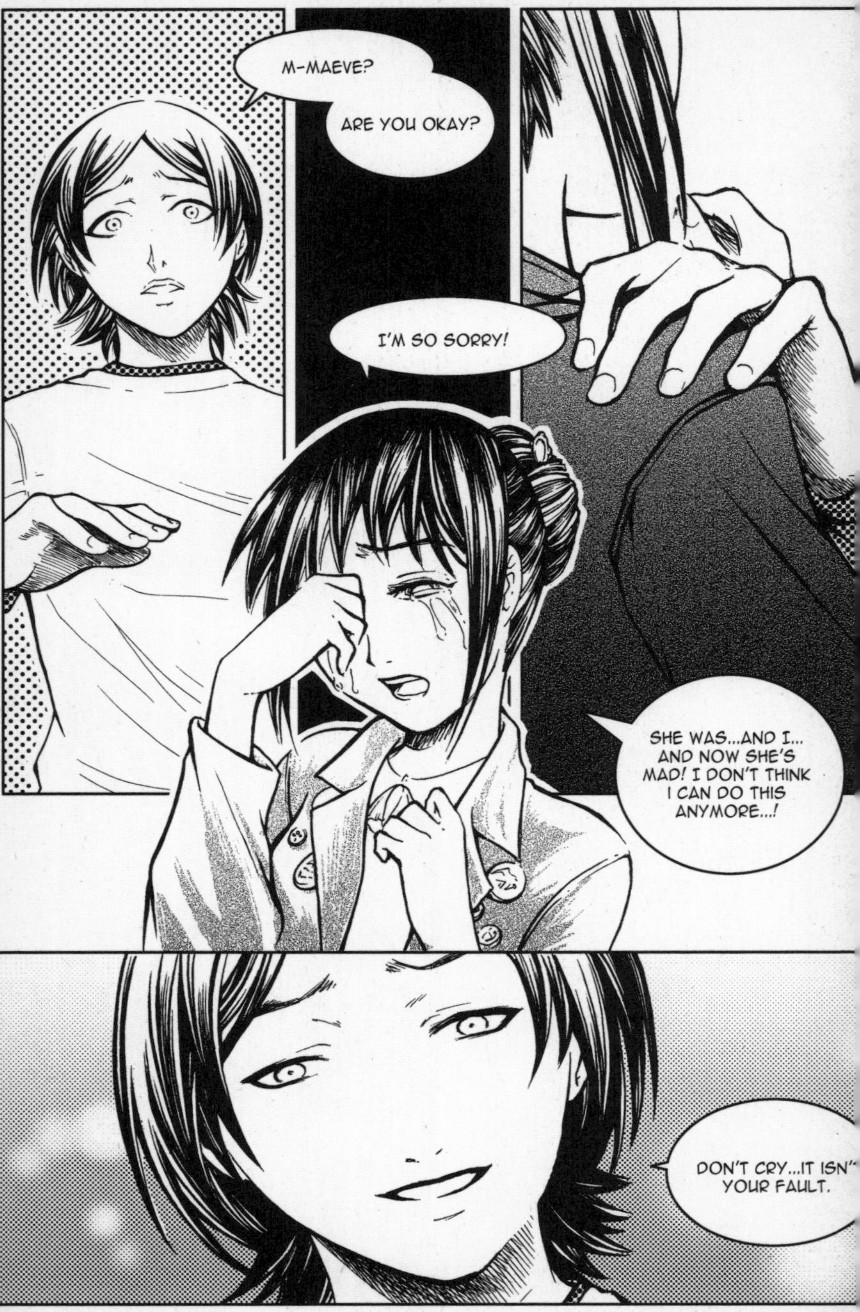
M-MAEVE?
ARE YOU OKAY?
I'M SO SORRY!
SHE WAS...AND I... AND NOW SHE'S MAD! I DON'T THINK I CAN DO THIS ANYMORE...!
DON'T CRY...IT ISN'T YOUR FAULT.

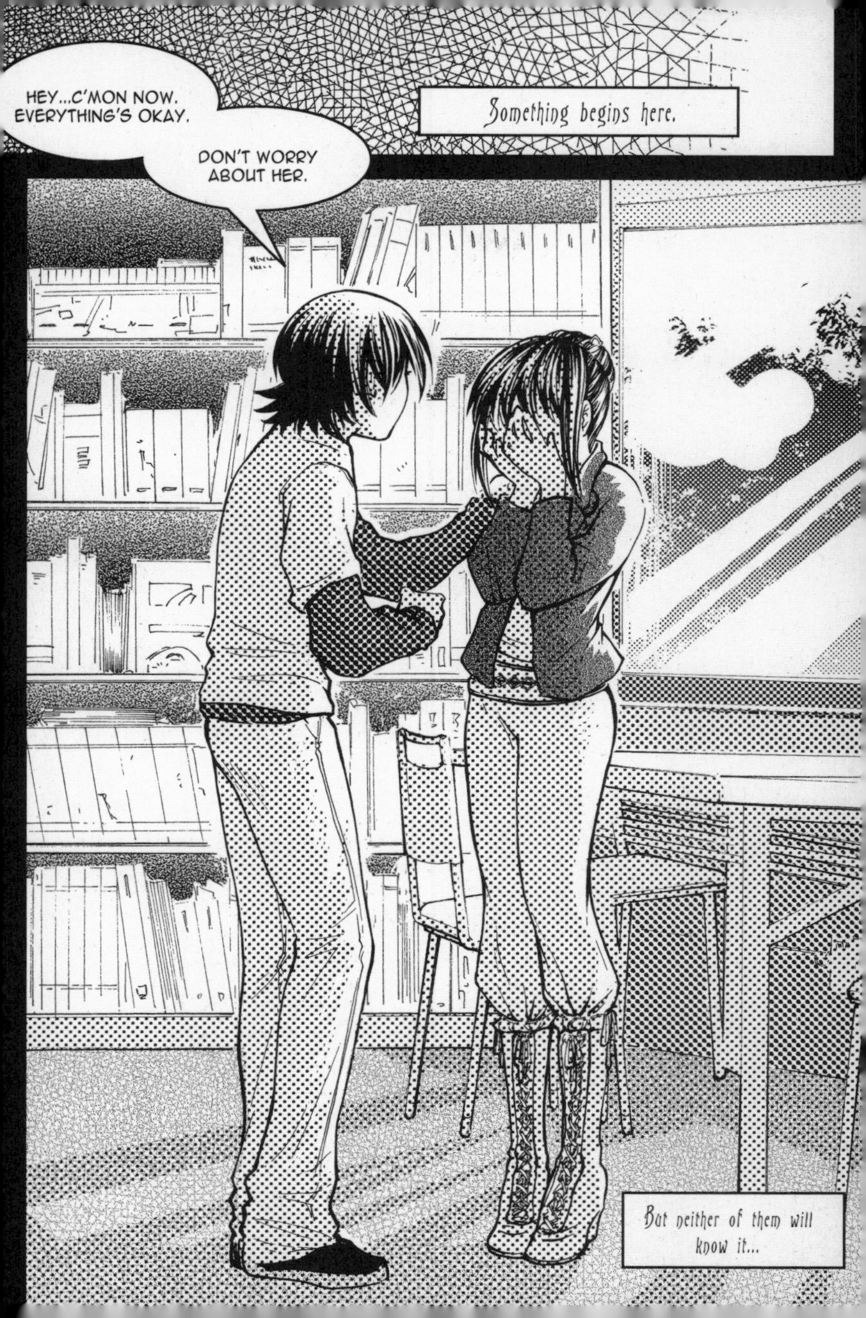
HEY...C'MON NOW. EVERYTHING'S OKAY.
Something begins here.
DON'T WORRY ABOUT HER.
But neither of them will know it...

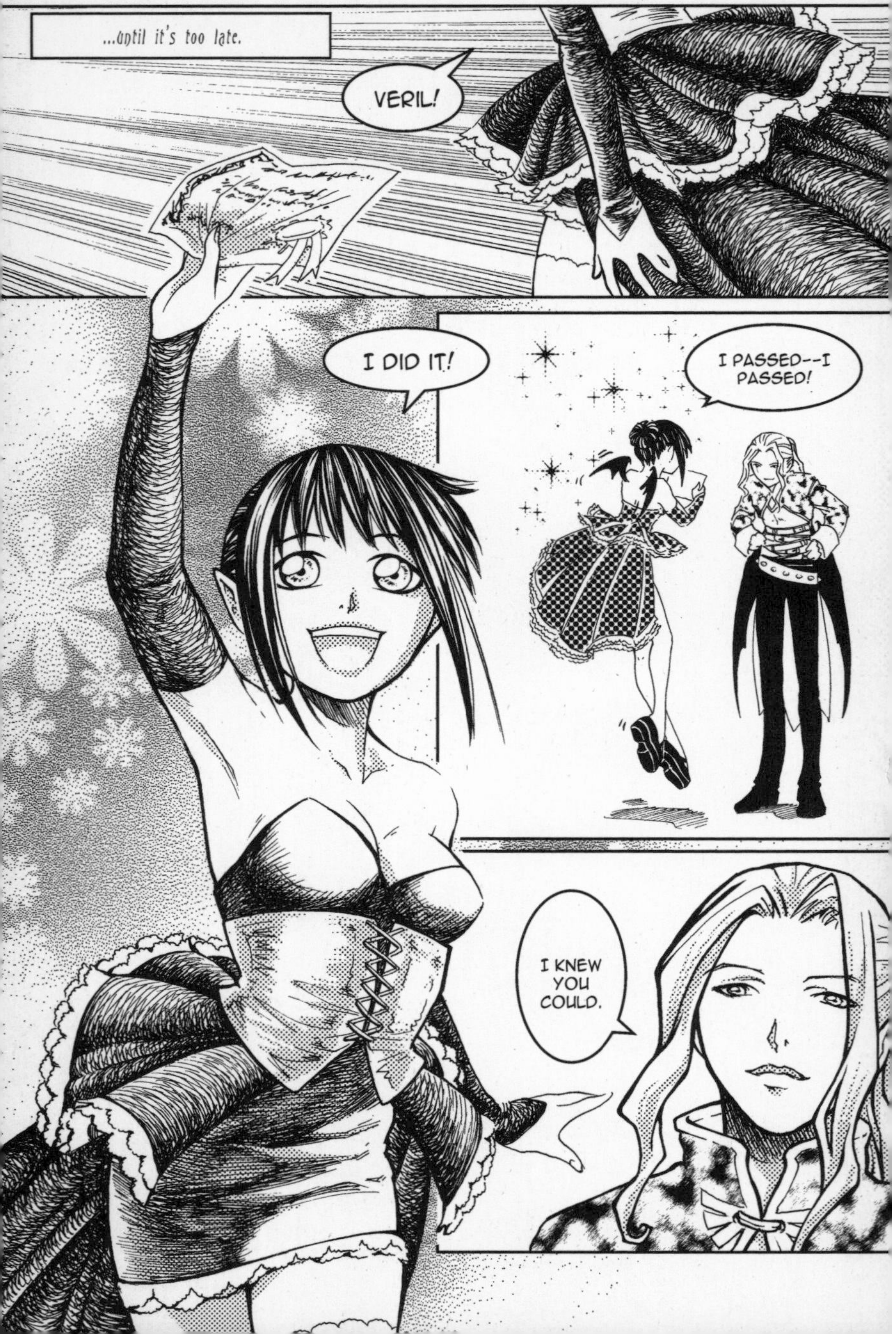
...until it's too late.
VERIL!
I DID IT!
I PASSED--I PASSED!
I KNEW YOU COULD.

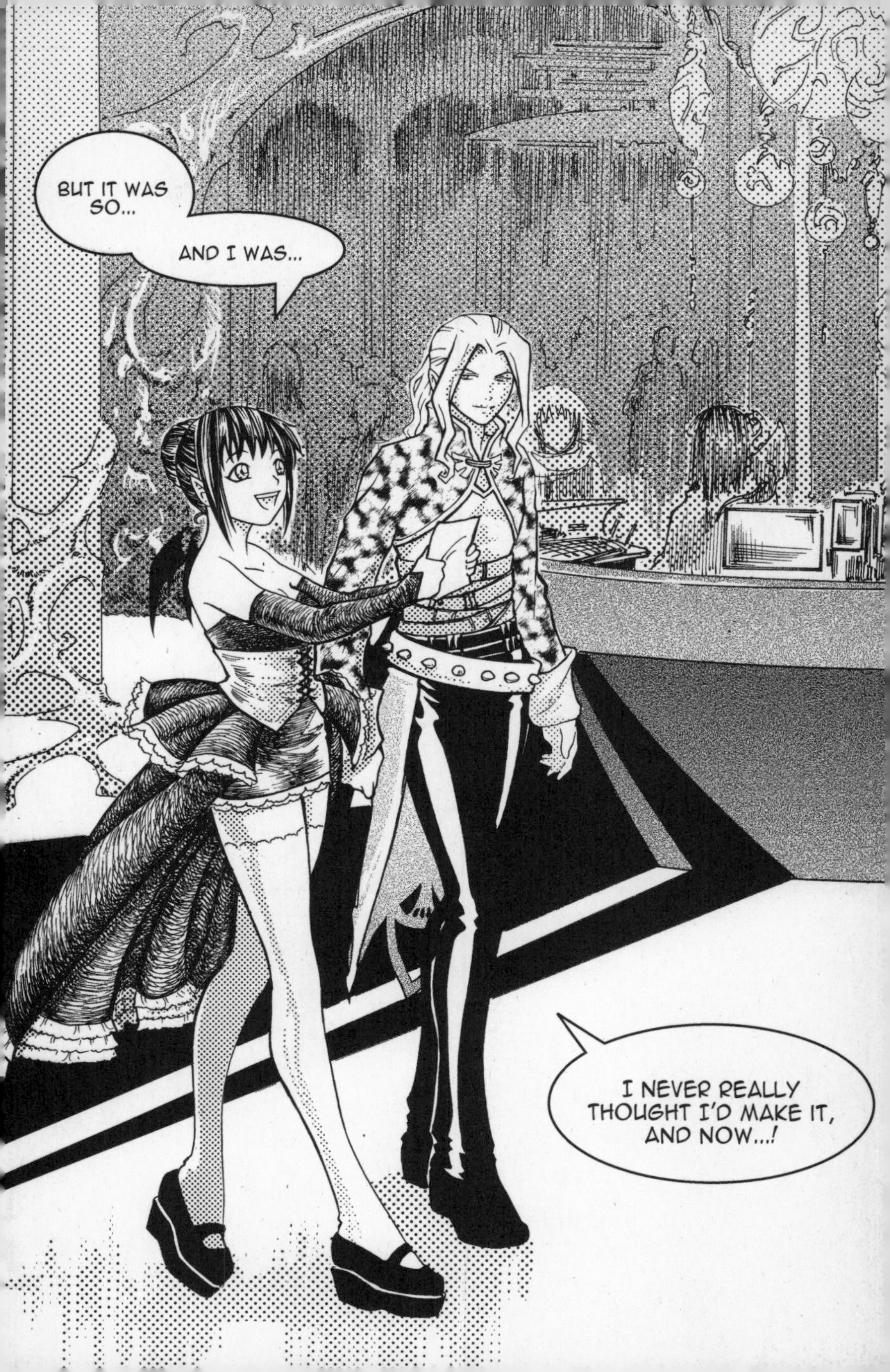
BUT IT WAS SO...
AND I WAS...
I NEVER REALLY THOUGHT I'D MAKE IT, AND NOW...!

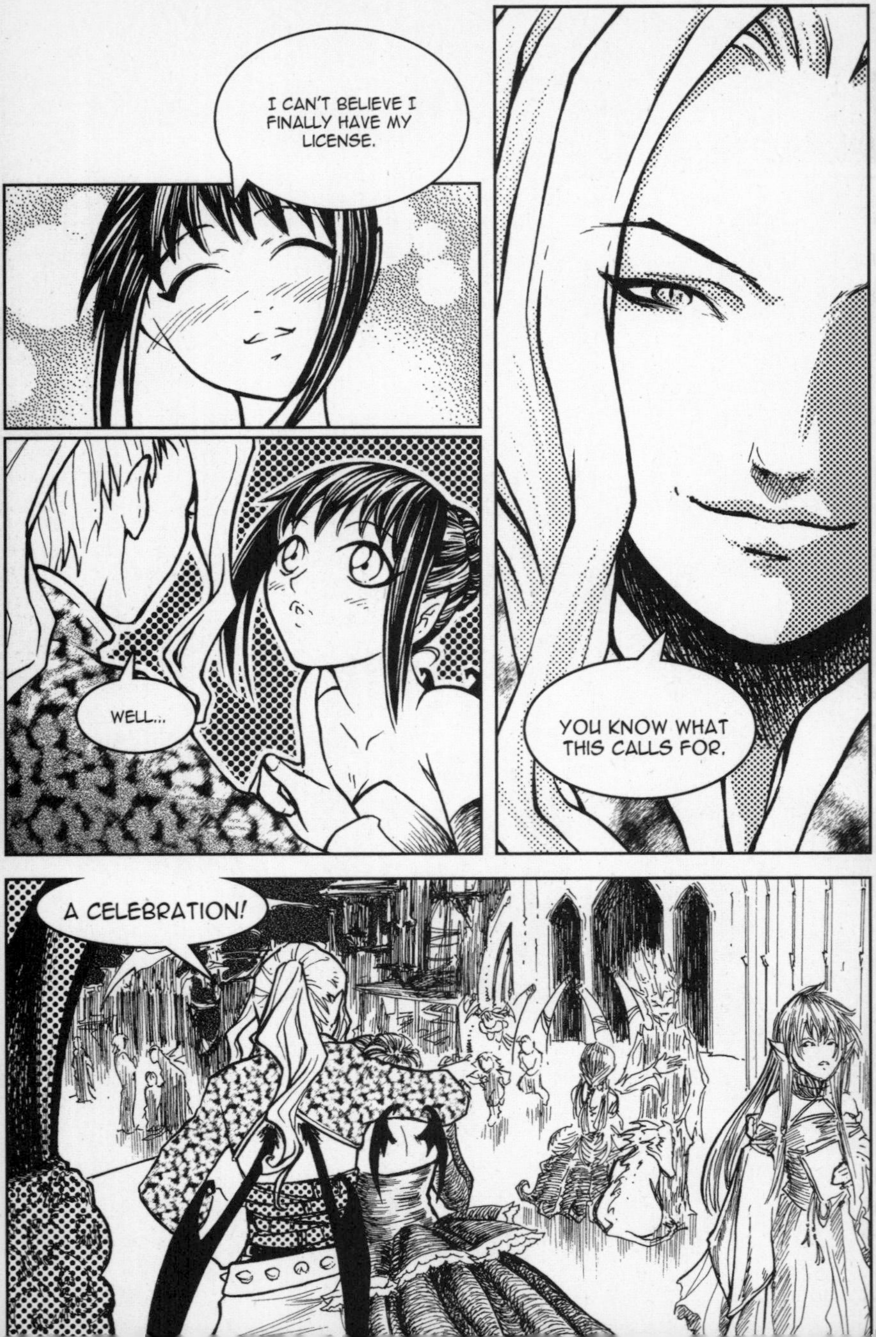
I CAN'T BELIEVE I FINALLY HAVE MY LICENSE.
WELL...
YOU KNOW WHAT THIS CALLS FOR.
A CELEBRATION!

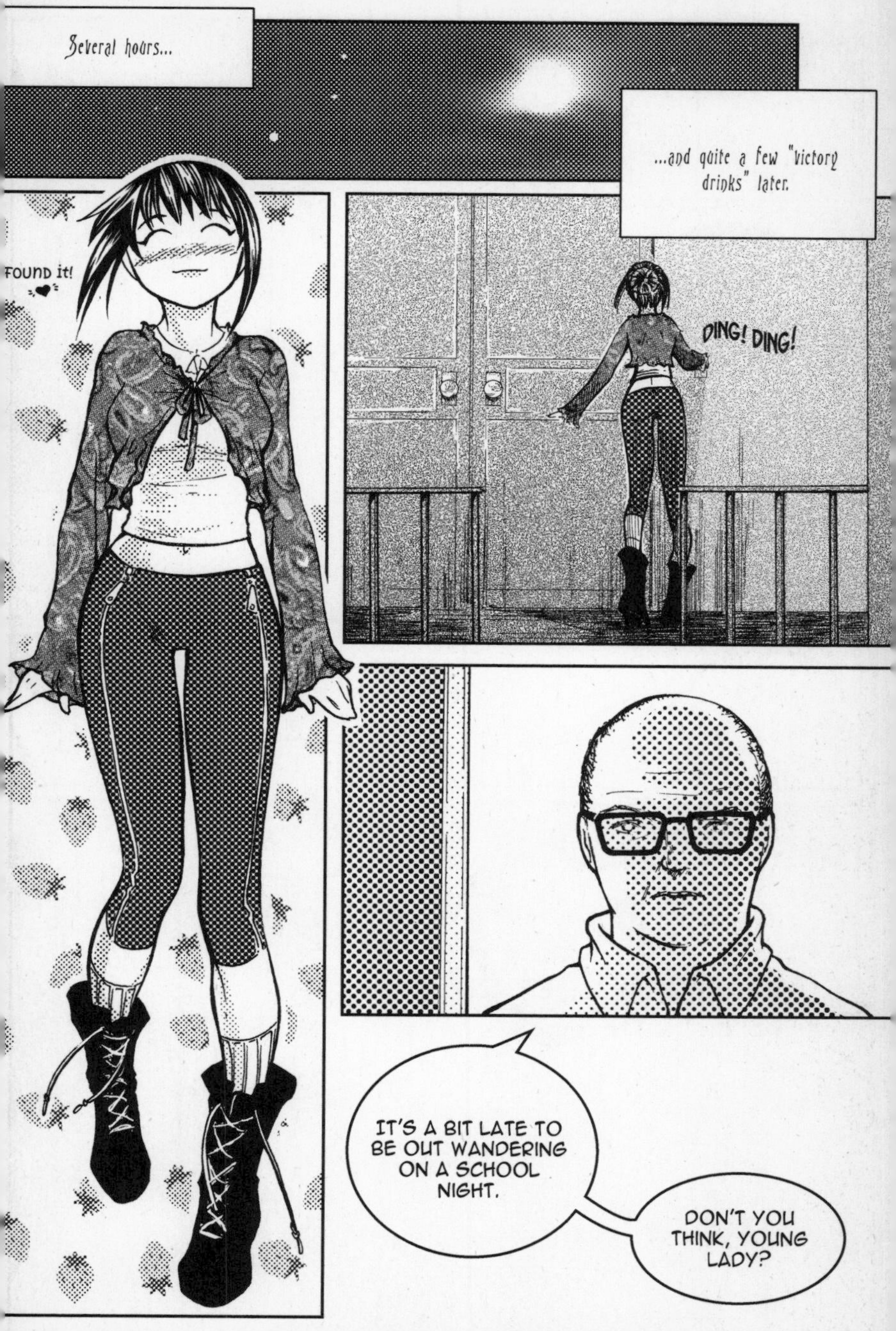
Several hours...
FOUND it!
...and quite a few "victory drinks" later.
DING! DING!
IT'S A BIT LATE TO BE OUT WANDERING ON A SCHOOL NIGHT.
DON'T YOU THINK, YOUNG LADY?

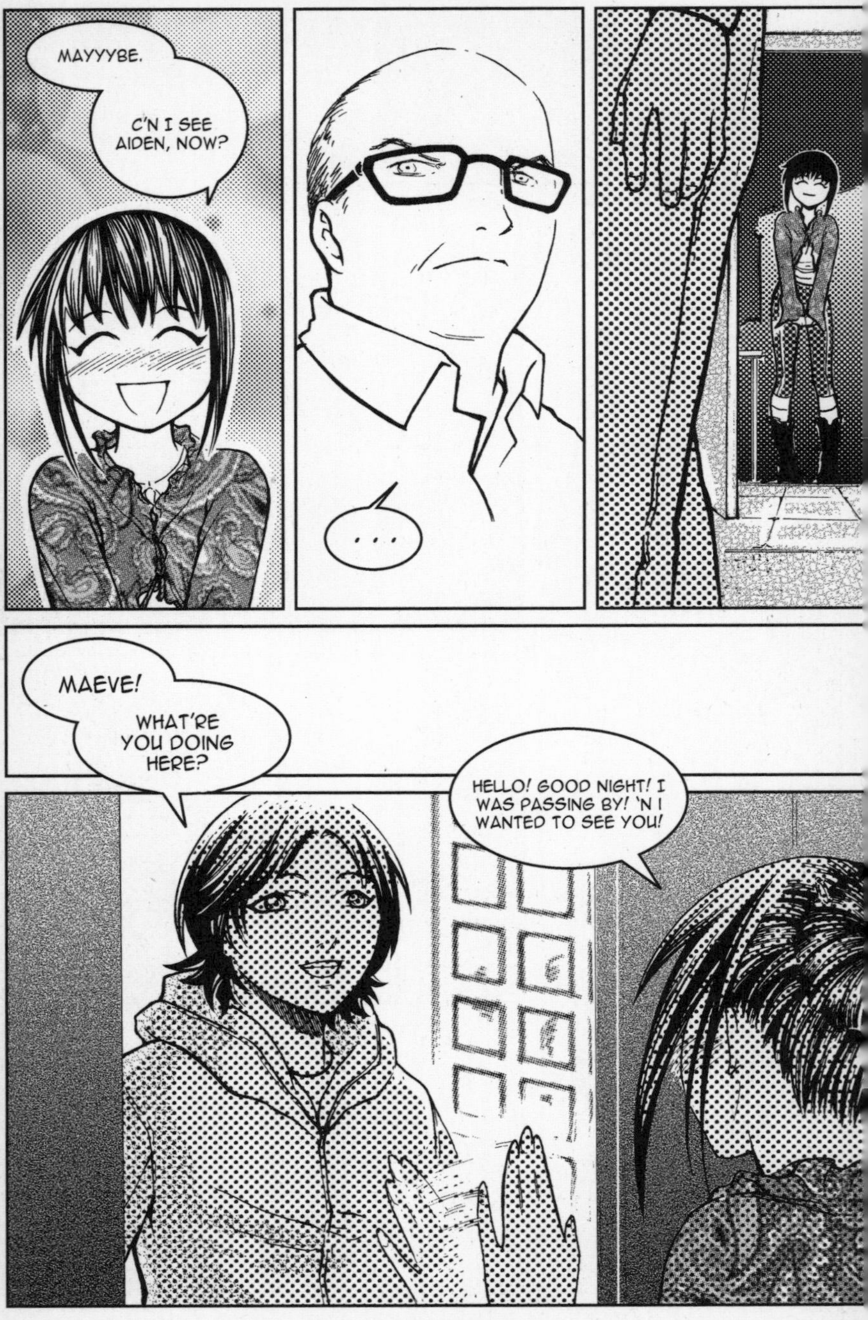
MAYYYBE.
C'N I SEE AIDEN, NOW?
...
MAEVE!
WHAT'RE YOU DOING HERE?
HELLO! GOOD NIGHT! I WAS PASSING BY! 'N I WANTED TO SEE YOU!

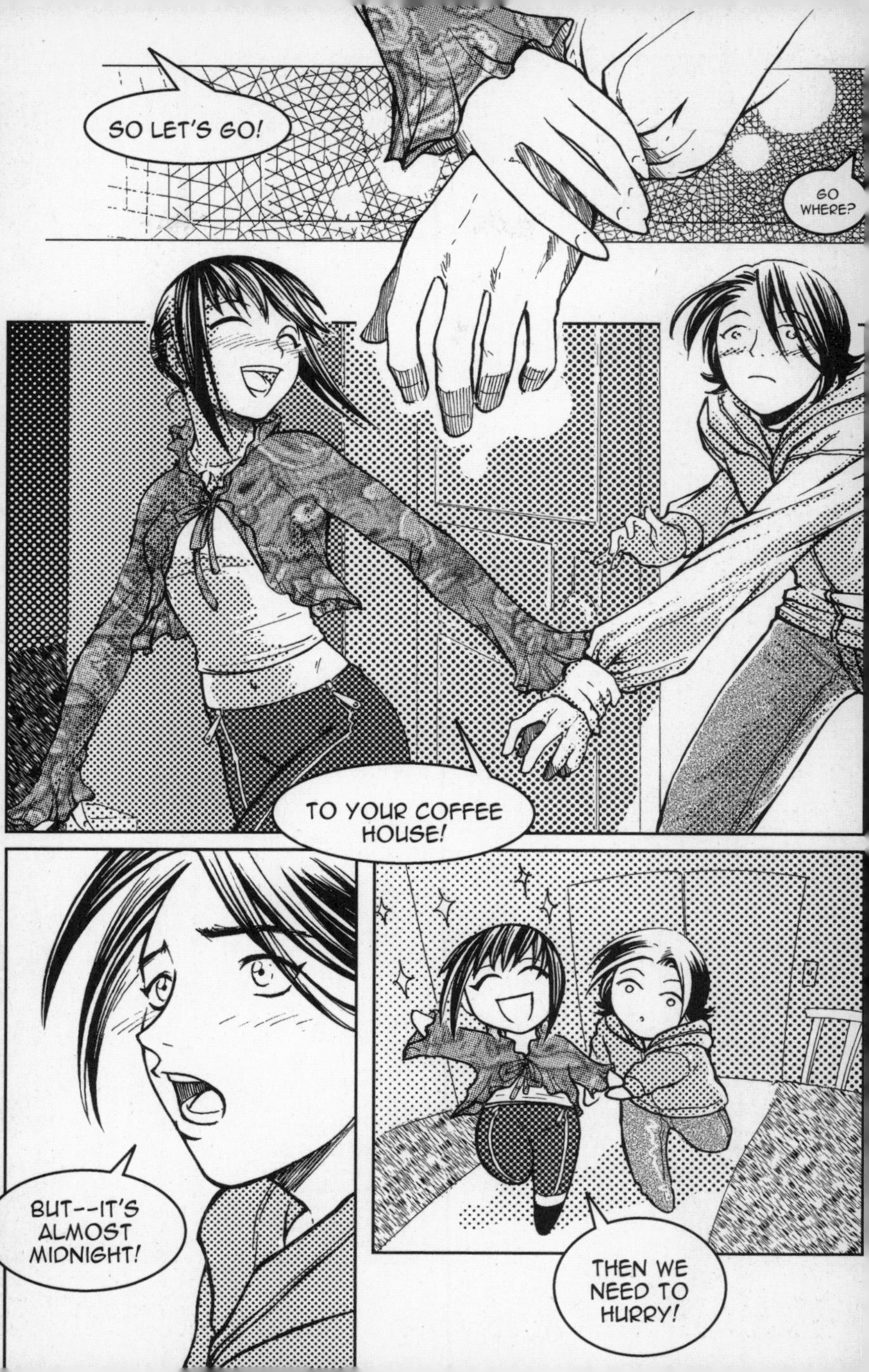
SO LET'S GO!
GO WHERE?
TO YOUR COFFEE HOUSE!
BUT--IT'S ALMOST MIDNIGHT!
THEN WE NEED TO HURRY!

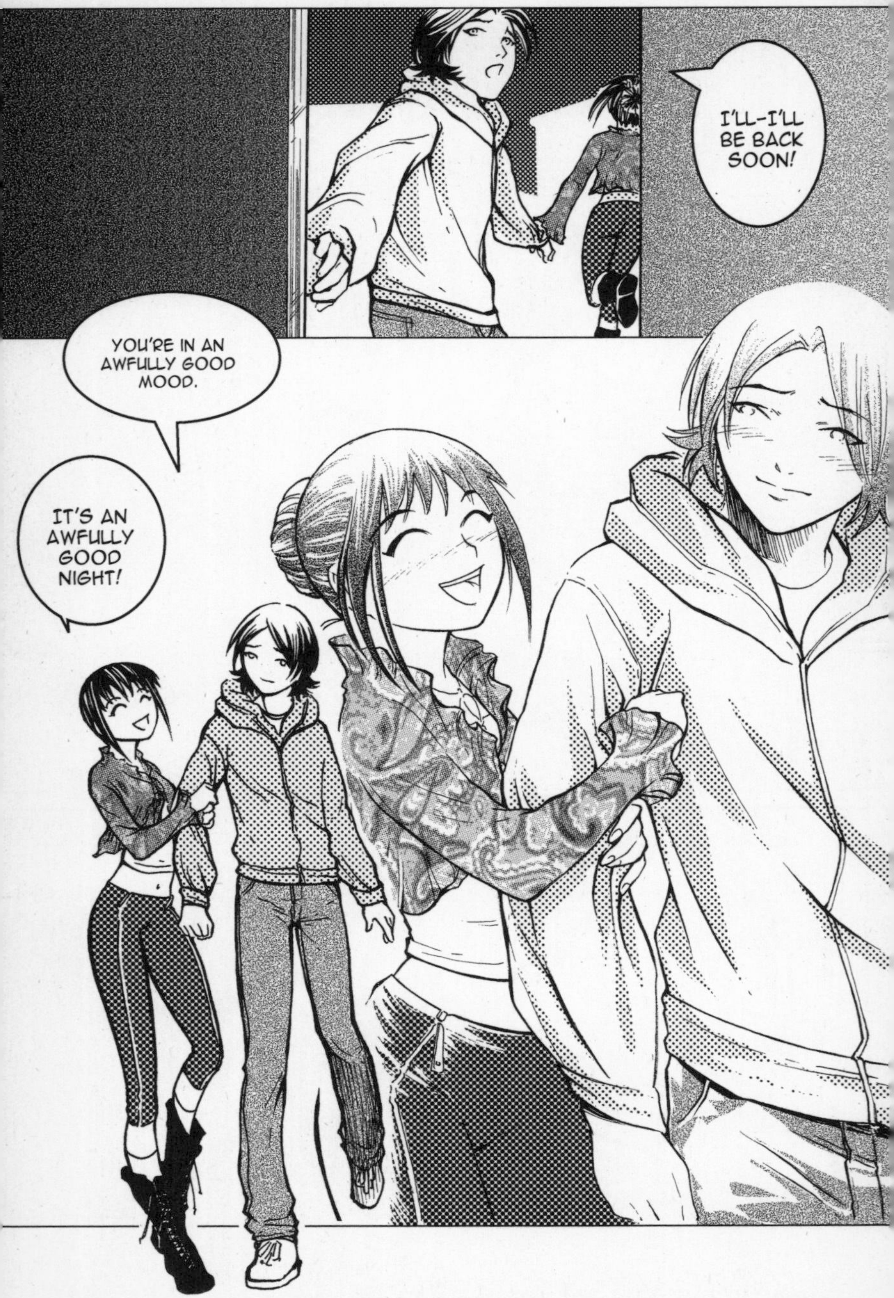
I'LL-I'LL BE BACK SOON!
YOU'RE IN AN AWFULLY GOOD MOOD.
IT'S AN AWFULLY GOOD NIGHT!

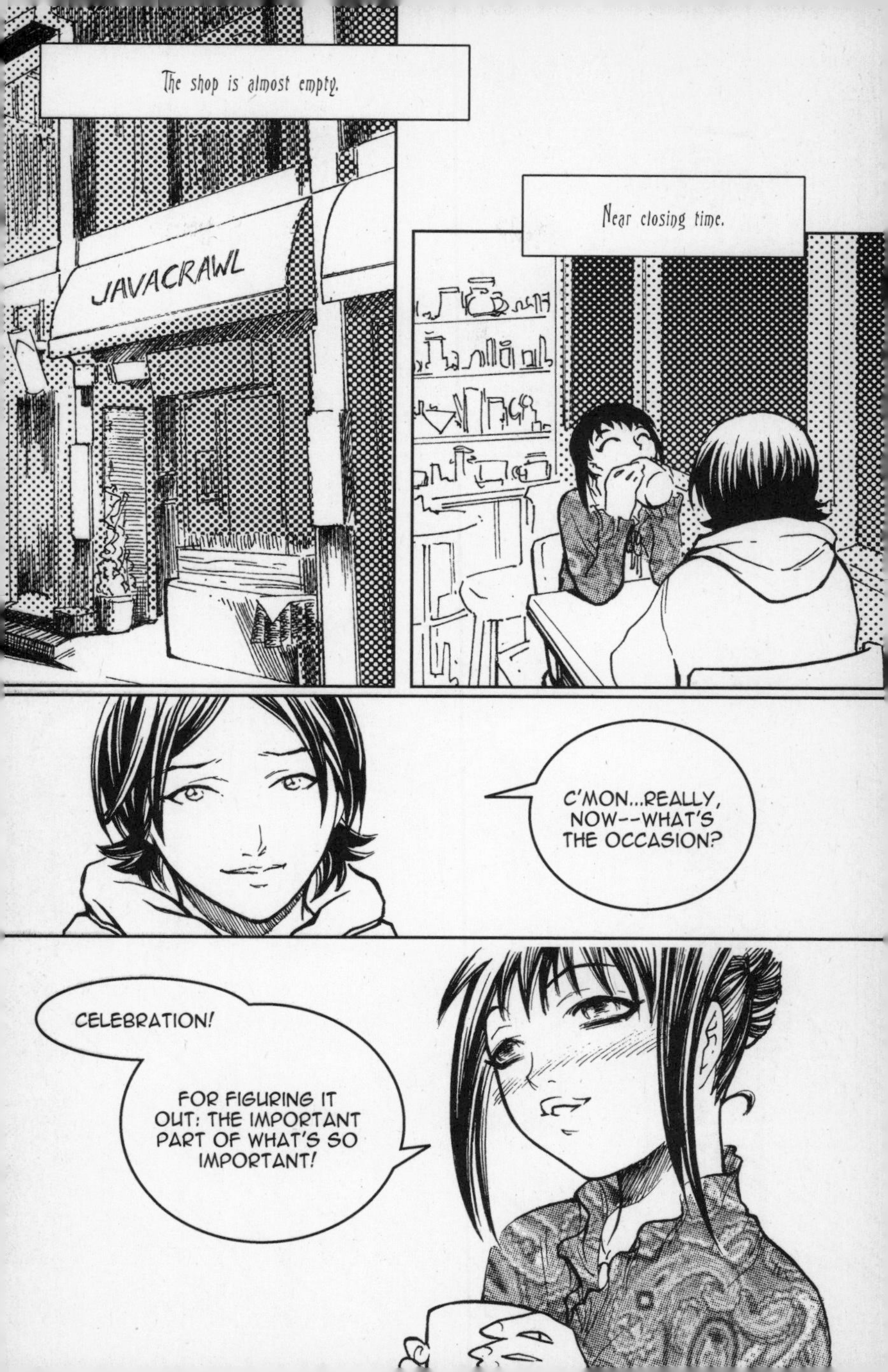
The shop is almost empty.
JAVACRAWL
Near closing time.
C'MON...REALLY, NOW--WHAT'S THE OCCASION?
CELEBRATION!
FOR FIGURING IT OUT: THE IMPORTANT PART OF WHAT'S SO IMPORTANT!

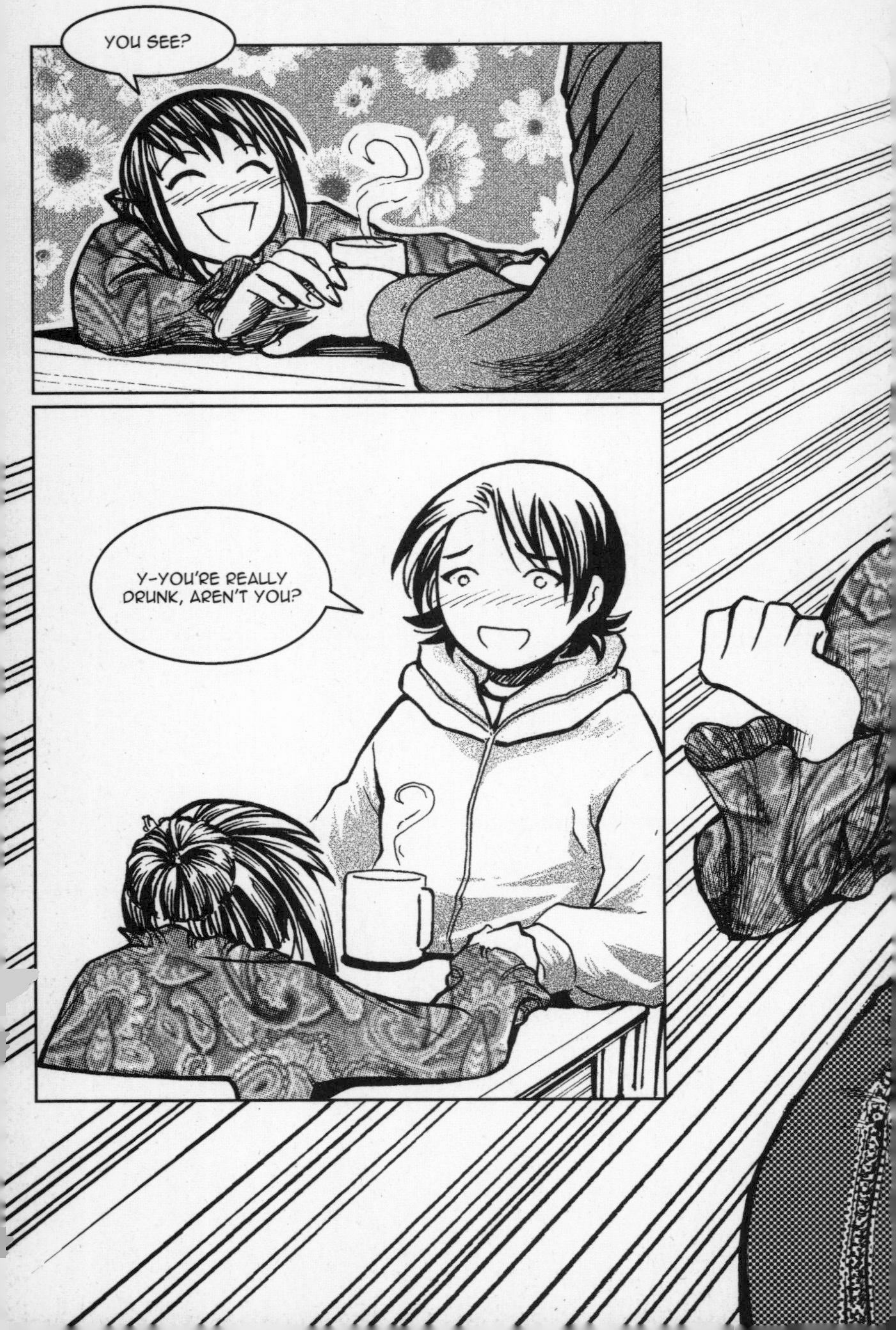
YOU SEE?
Y-YOU'RE REALLY DRUNK, AREN'T YOU?

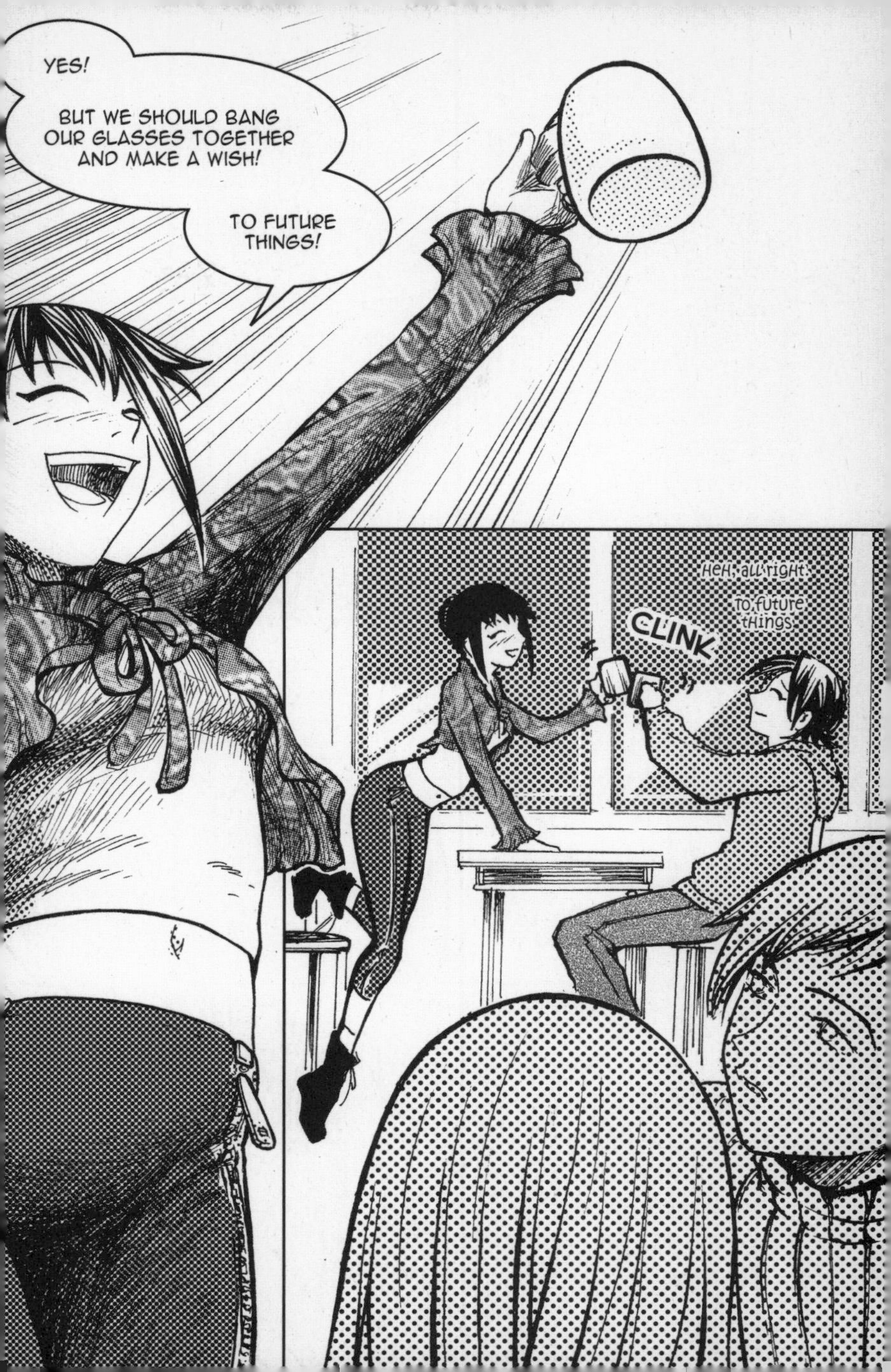
YES!
BUT WE SHOULD BANG OUR GLASSES TOGETHER AND MAKE A WISH!
TO FUTURE THINGS!
HEH, ALL RIGHT.
TO FUTURE THINGS.
CLINK

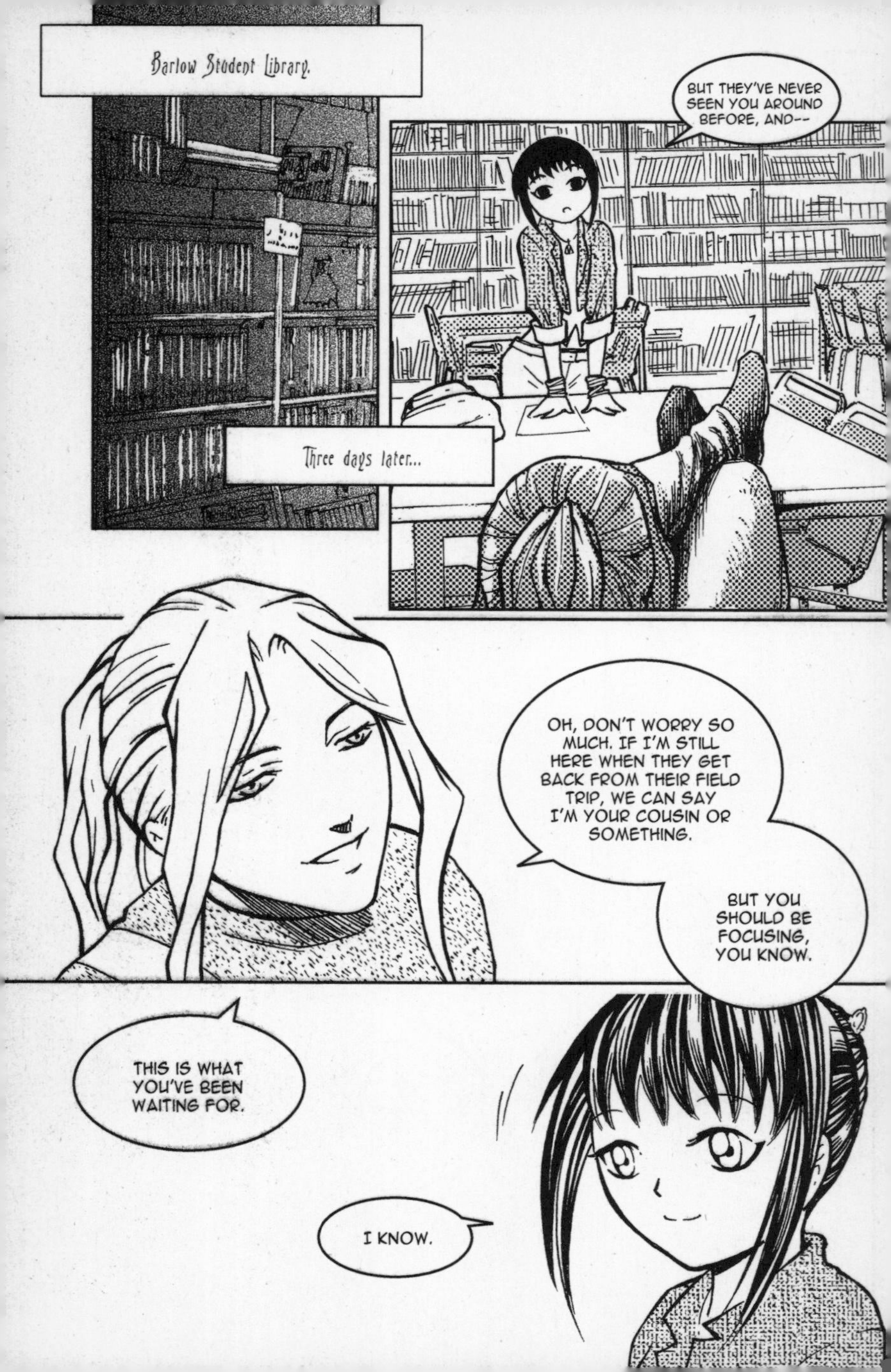
Barlow Student Library.
Three days later...
BUT THEY'VE NEVER SEEN YOU AROUND BEFORE, AND--
OH, DON'T WORRY SO MUCH. IF I'M STILL HERE WHEN THEY GET BACK FROM THEIR FIELD TRIP, WE CAN SAY I'M YOUR COUSIN OR SOMETHING.
BUT YOU SHOULD BE FOCUSING, YOU KNOW.
THIS IS WHAT YOU'VE BEEN WAITING FOR.
I KNOW.

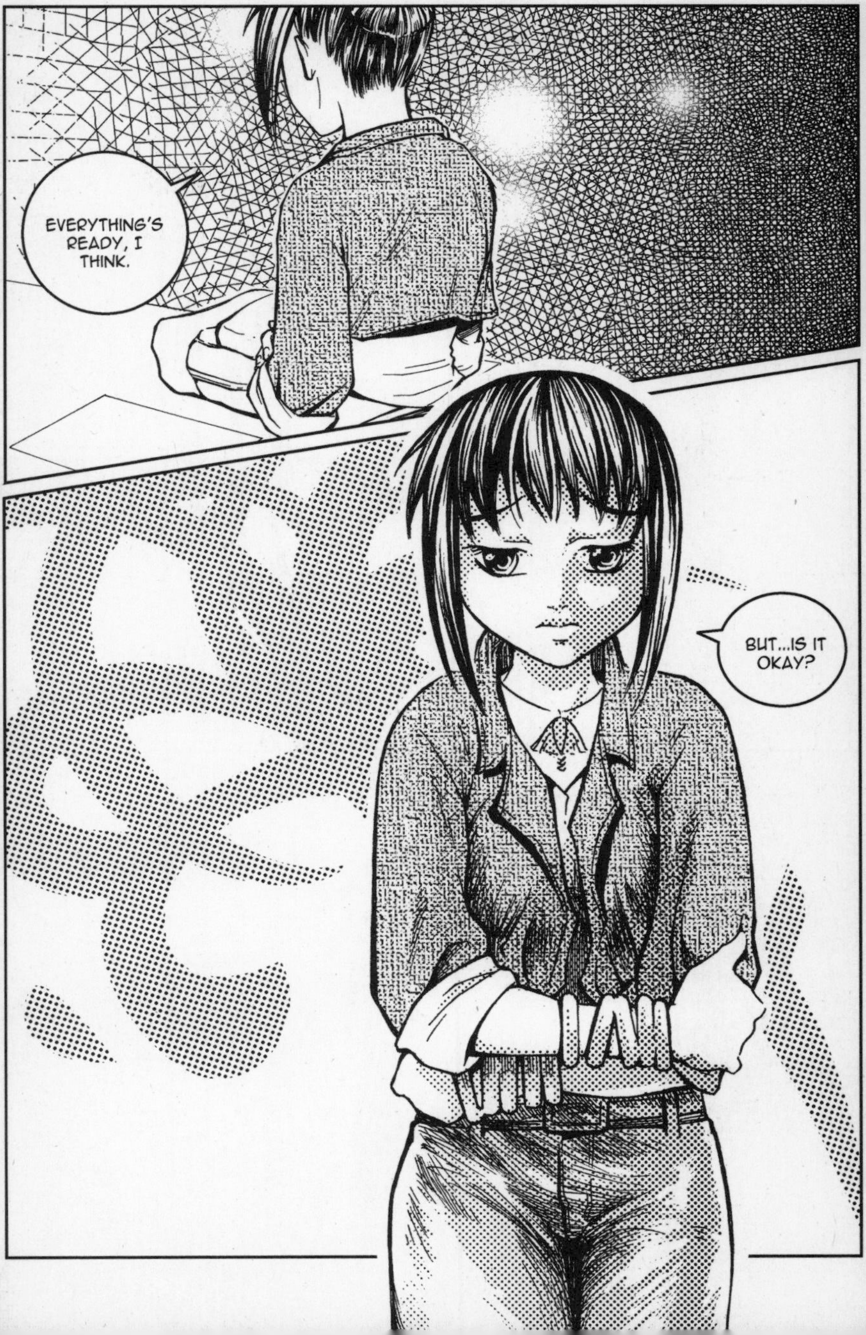
EVERYTHING'S READY, I THINK.
BUT...IS IT OKAY?

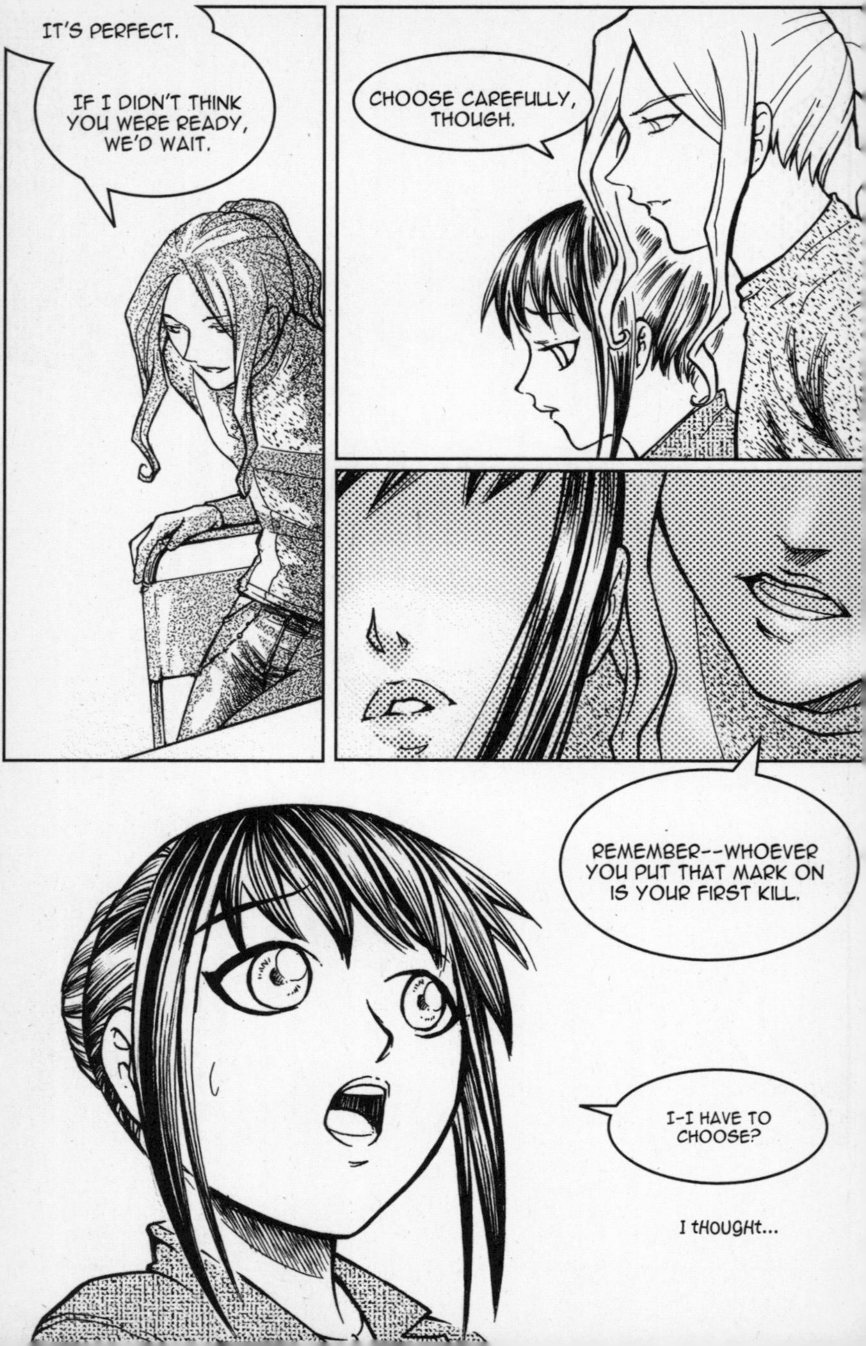
IT'S PERFECT.
IF I DIDN'T THINK YOU WERE READY, WE'D WAIT.
CHOOSE CAREFULLY, THOUGH.
REMEMBER--WHOEVER YOU PUT THAT MARK ON IS YOUR FIRST KILL.
I-I HAVE TO CHOOSE?
I THOUGHT...

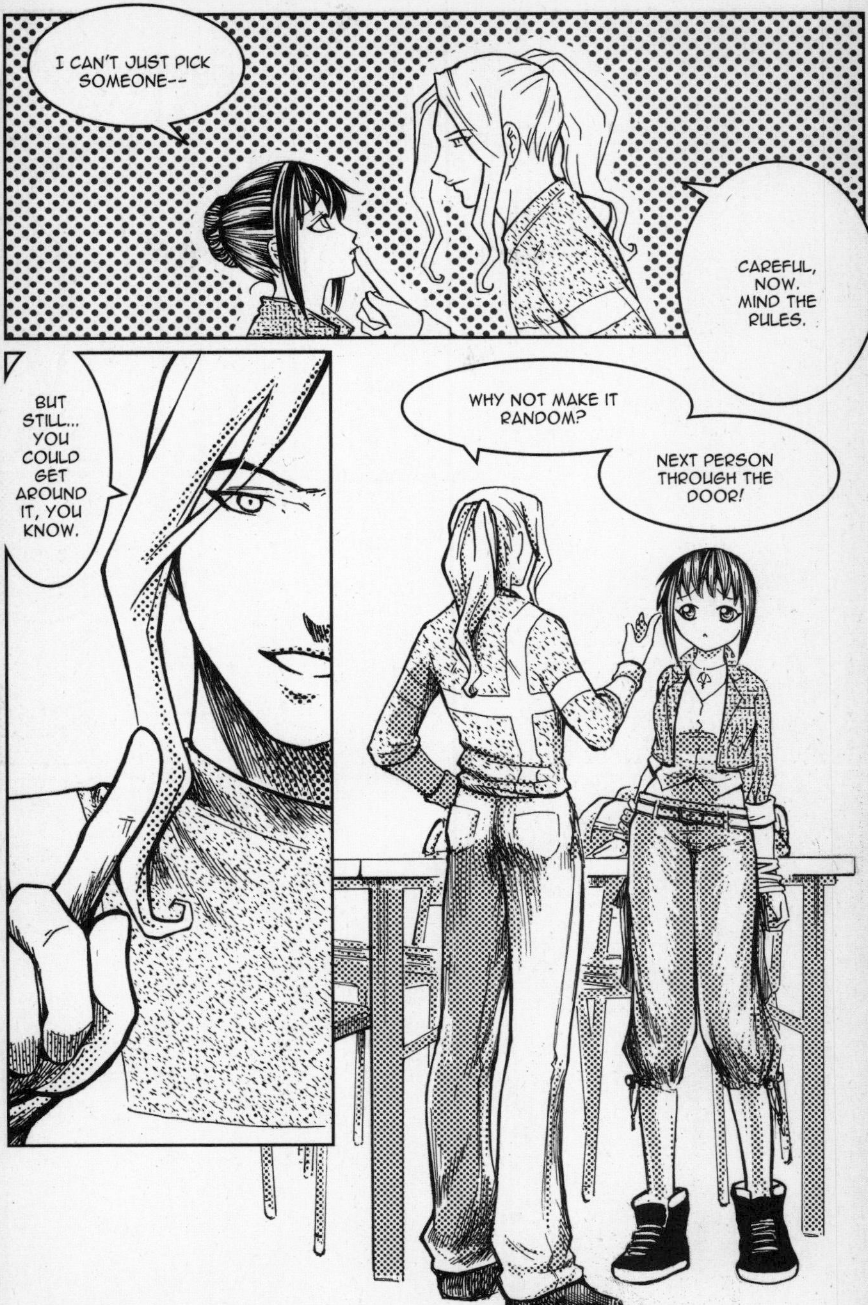
I CAN'T JUST PICK SOMEONE--
CAREFUL, NOW. MIND THE RULES.
BUT STILL... YOU COULD GET AROUND IT, YOU KNOW.
WHY NOT MAKE IT RANDOM?
NEXT PERSON THROUGH THE DOOR!

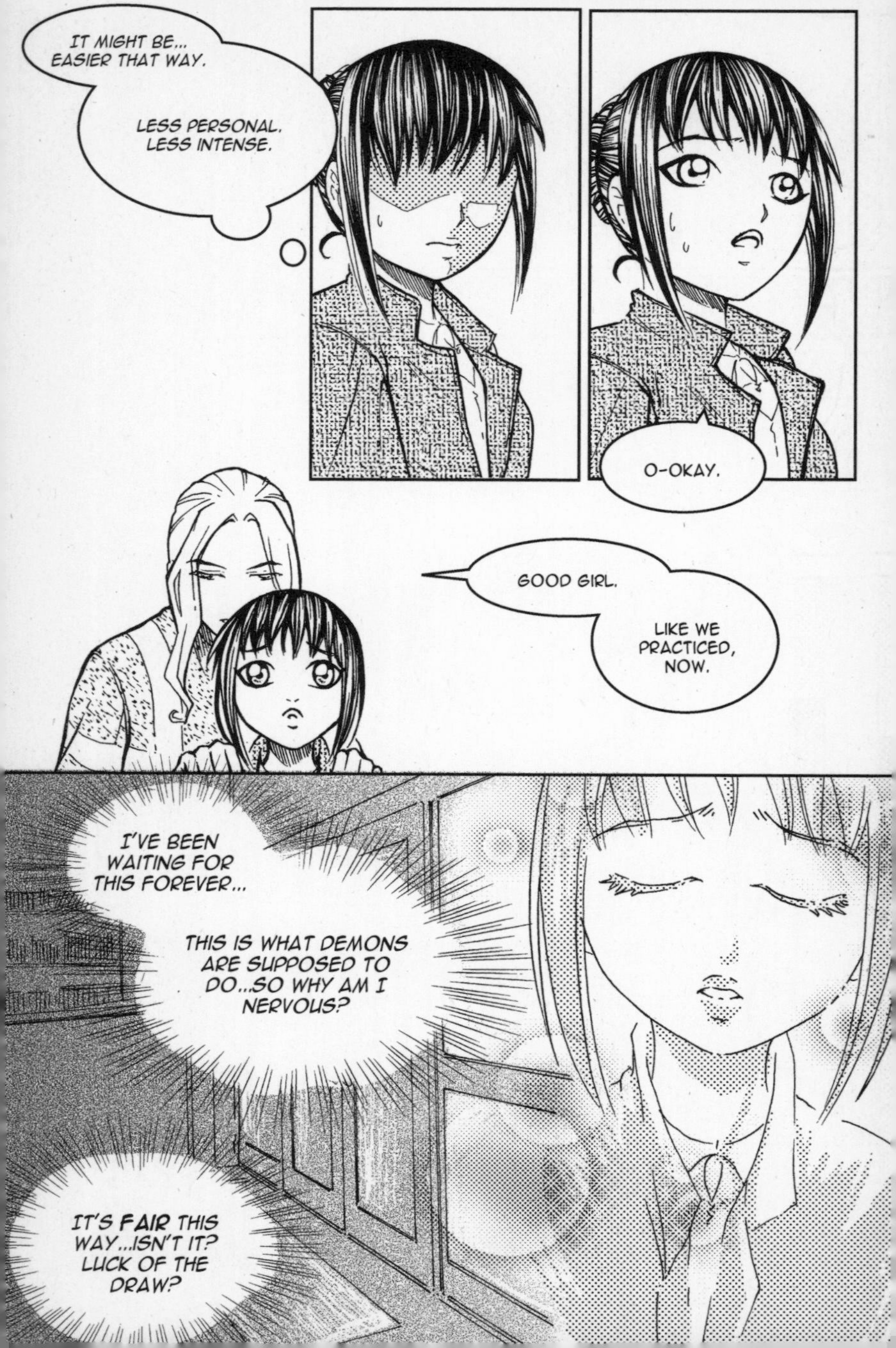
IT MIGHT BE... EASIER THAT WAY.
LESS PERSONAL. LESS INTENSE.
O-OKAY.
GOOD GIRL.
LIKE WE PRACTICED, NOW.
I'VE BEEN WAITING FOR THIS FOREVER...
THIS IS WHAT DEMONS ARE SUPPOSED TO DO...SO WHY AM I NERVOUS?
IT'S FAIR THIS WAY...ISN'T IT? LUCK OF THE DRAW?

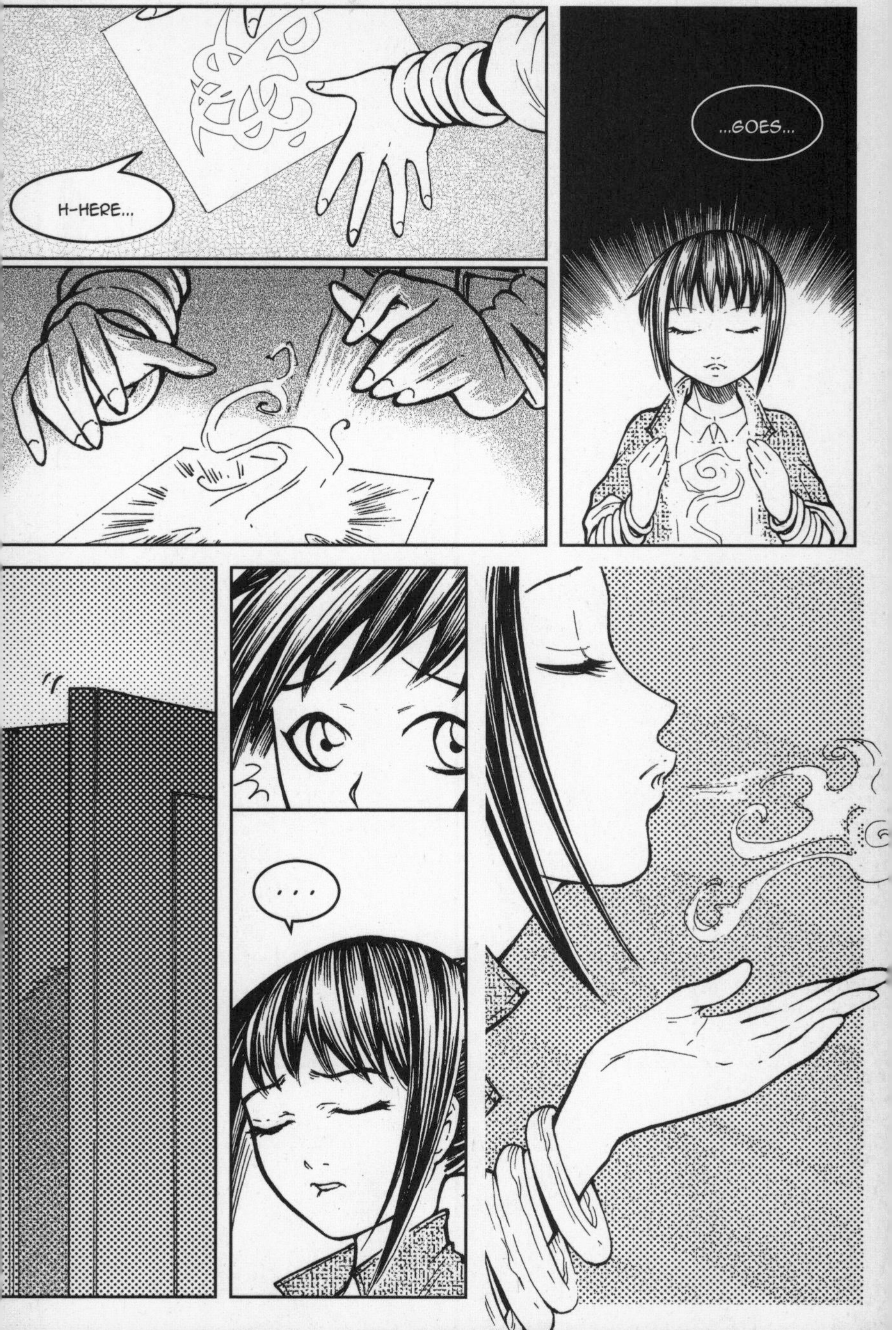
H-HERE...
...GOES...
. . .

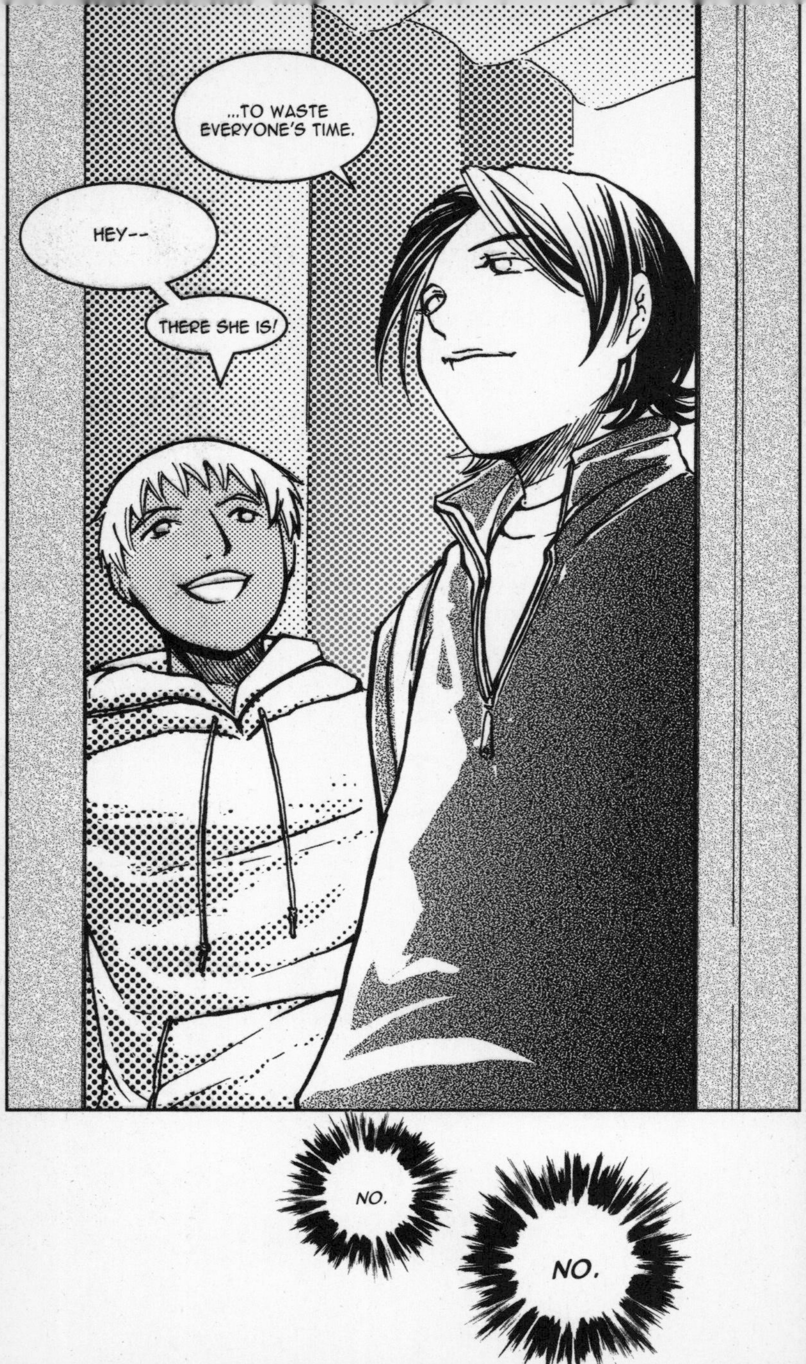
...TO WASTE EVERYONE'S TIME.
HEY--
THERE SHE IS!
NO.
NO.

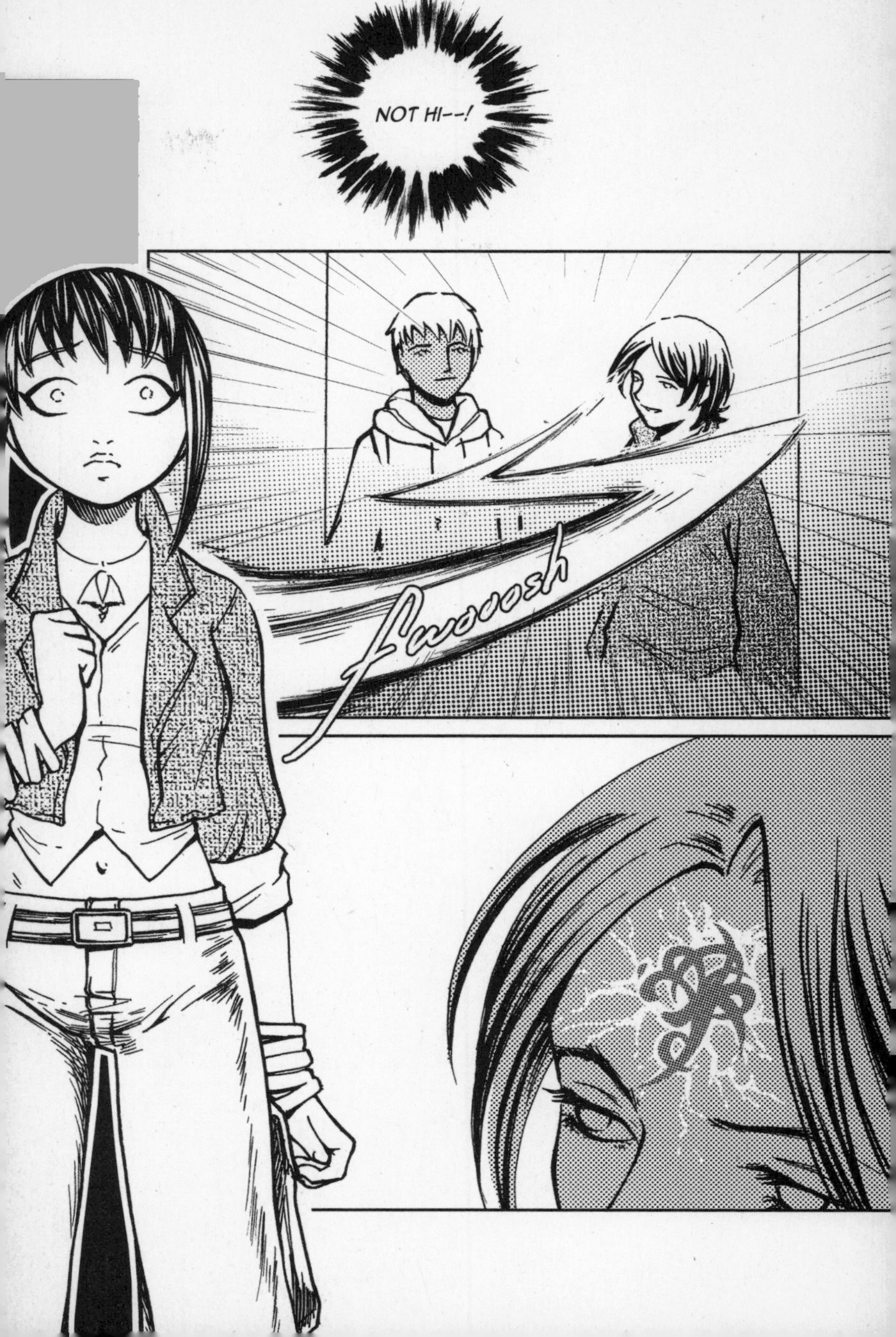
NOT HI--!
fwoooosh

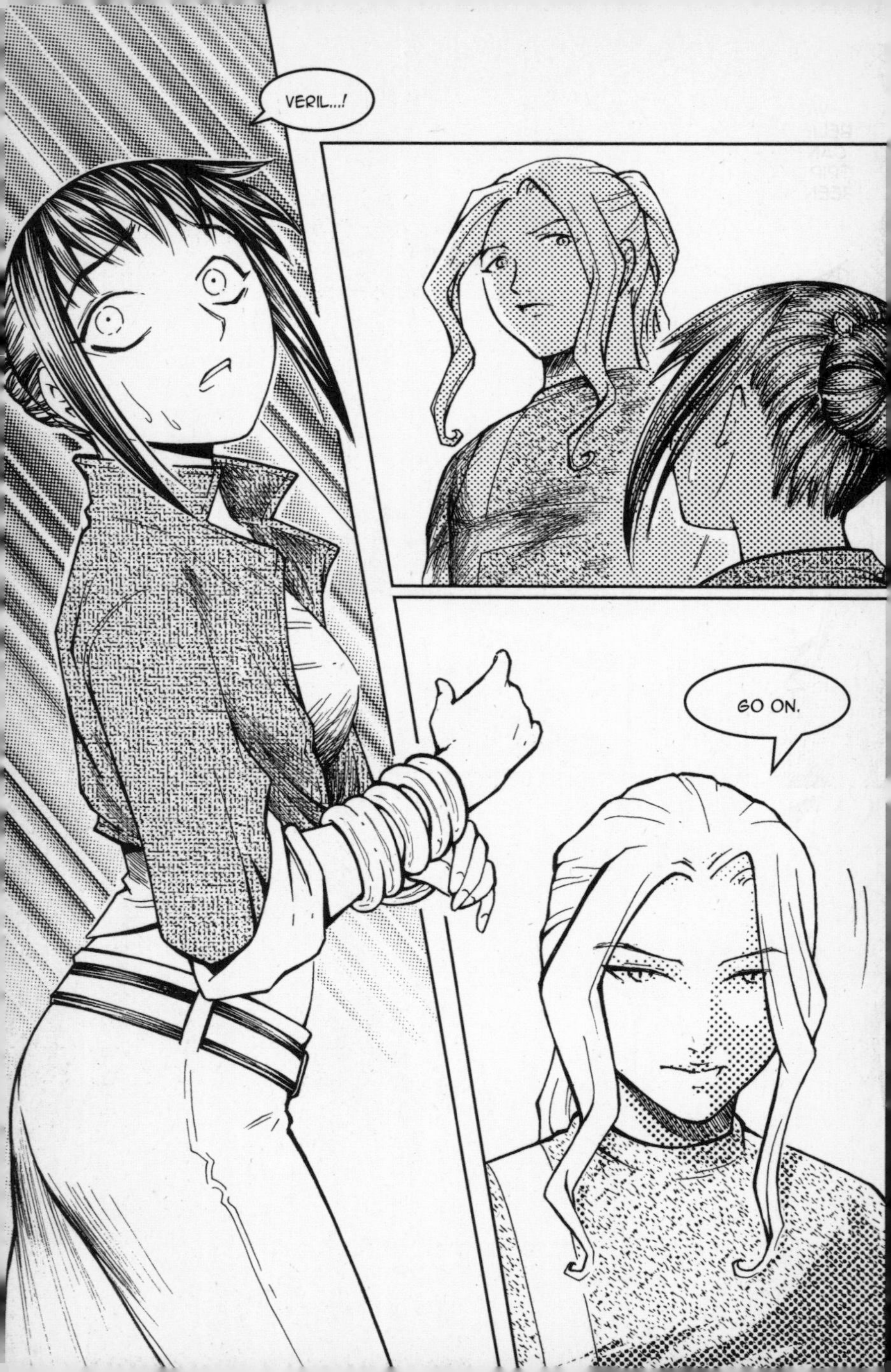
VERIL...!
GO ON.

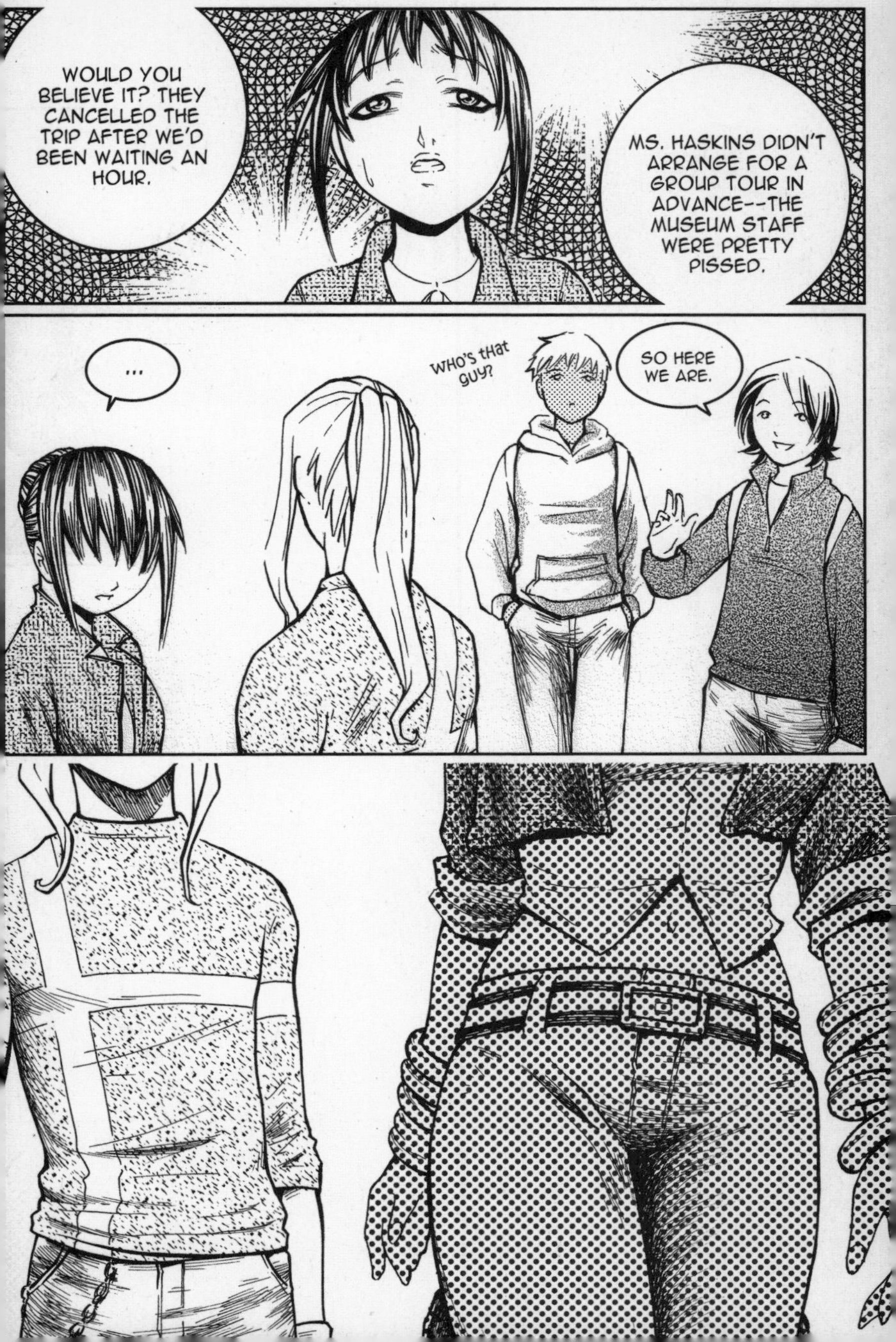
WOULD YOU BELIEVE IT? THEY CANCELLED THE TRIP AFTER WE'D BEEN WAITING AN HOUR.
MS. HASKINS DIDN'T ARRANGE FOR A GROUP TOUR IN ADVANCE--THE MUSEUM STAFF WERE PRETTY PISSED.
...
WHO'S tHat guy?
SO HERE WE ARE.

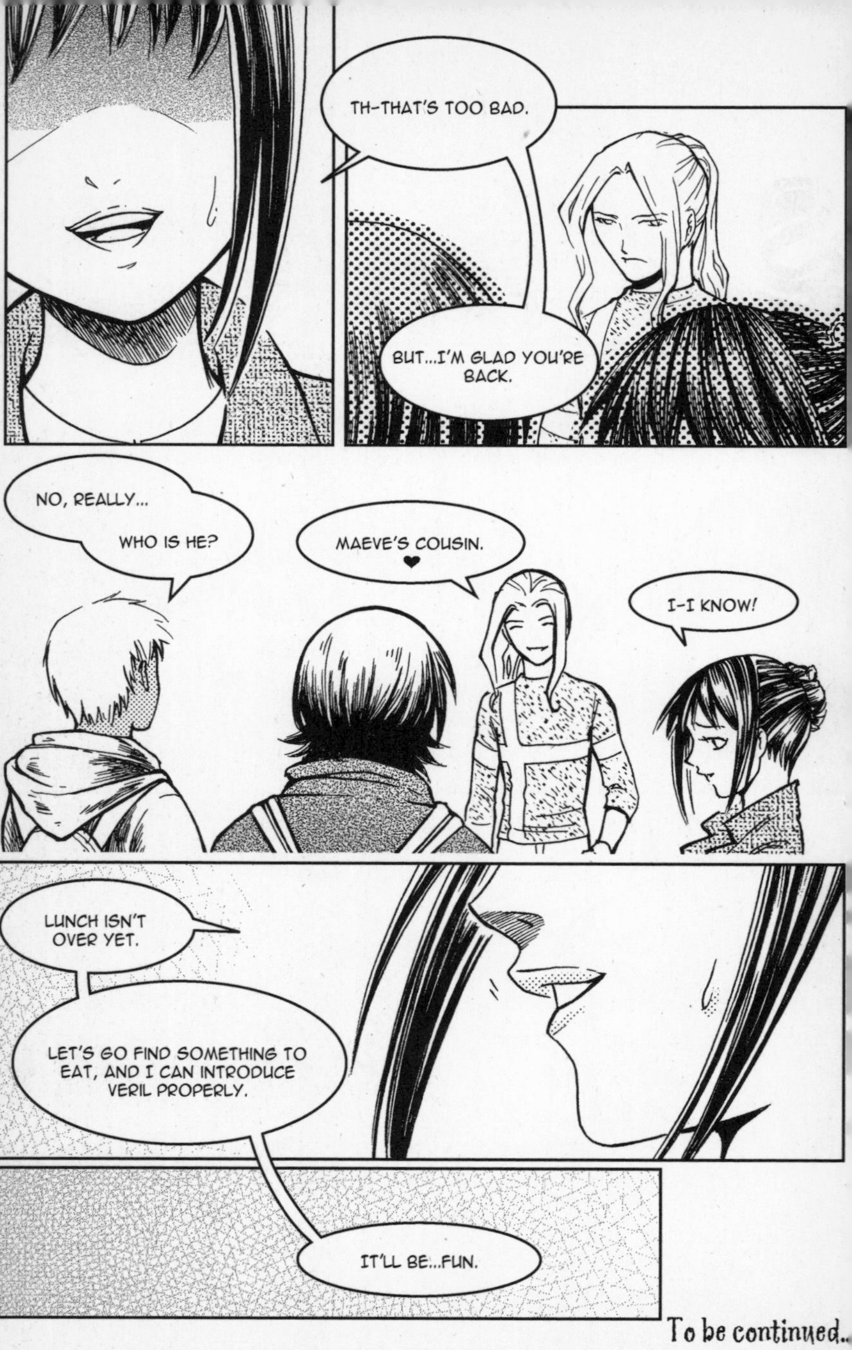
TH-THAT'S TOO BAD.
BUT...I'M GLAD YOU'RE BACK.
NO, REALLY... WHO IS HE?
MAEVE'S COUSIN. ❤
I-I KNOW!
LUNCH ISN'T OVER YET.
LET'S GO FIND SOMETHING TO EAT, AND I CAN INTRODUCE VERIL PROPERLY.
IT'LL BE...FUN.

To be continued..

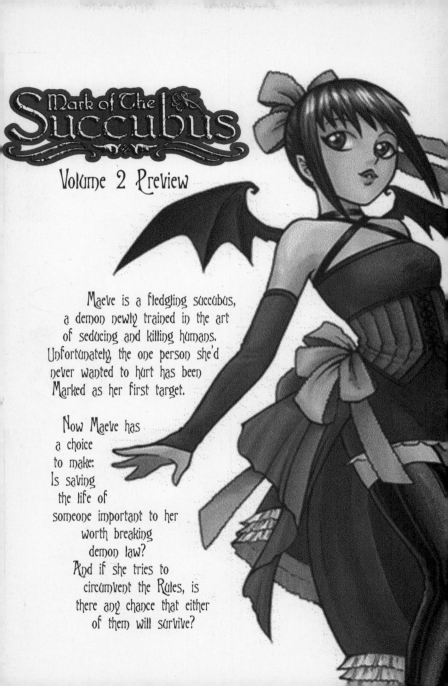

Mark of The Succubus

Volume 2 Preview

Maeve is a fledgling succubus, a demon newly trained in the art of seducing and killing humans. Unfortunately, the one person she'd never wanted to hurt has been Marked as her first target.

Now Maeve has a choice to make: Is saving the life of someone important to her worth breaking demon law? And if she tries to circumvent the Rules, is there any chance that either of them will survive?

Mark of The Succubus

flap
flap
POUNCE

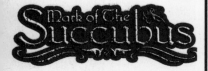

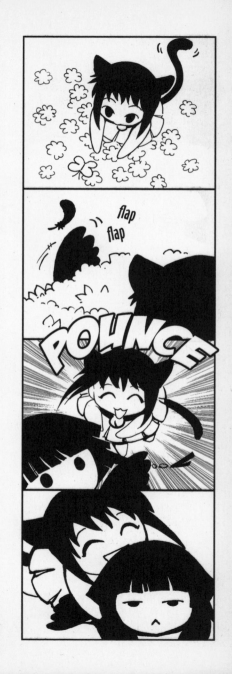

ABDUCT!

Mark of The Succubus

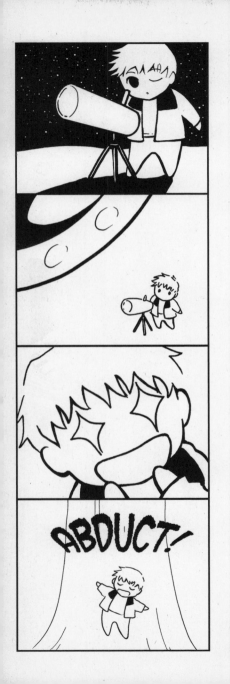

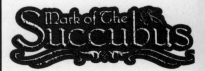

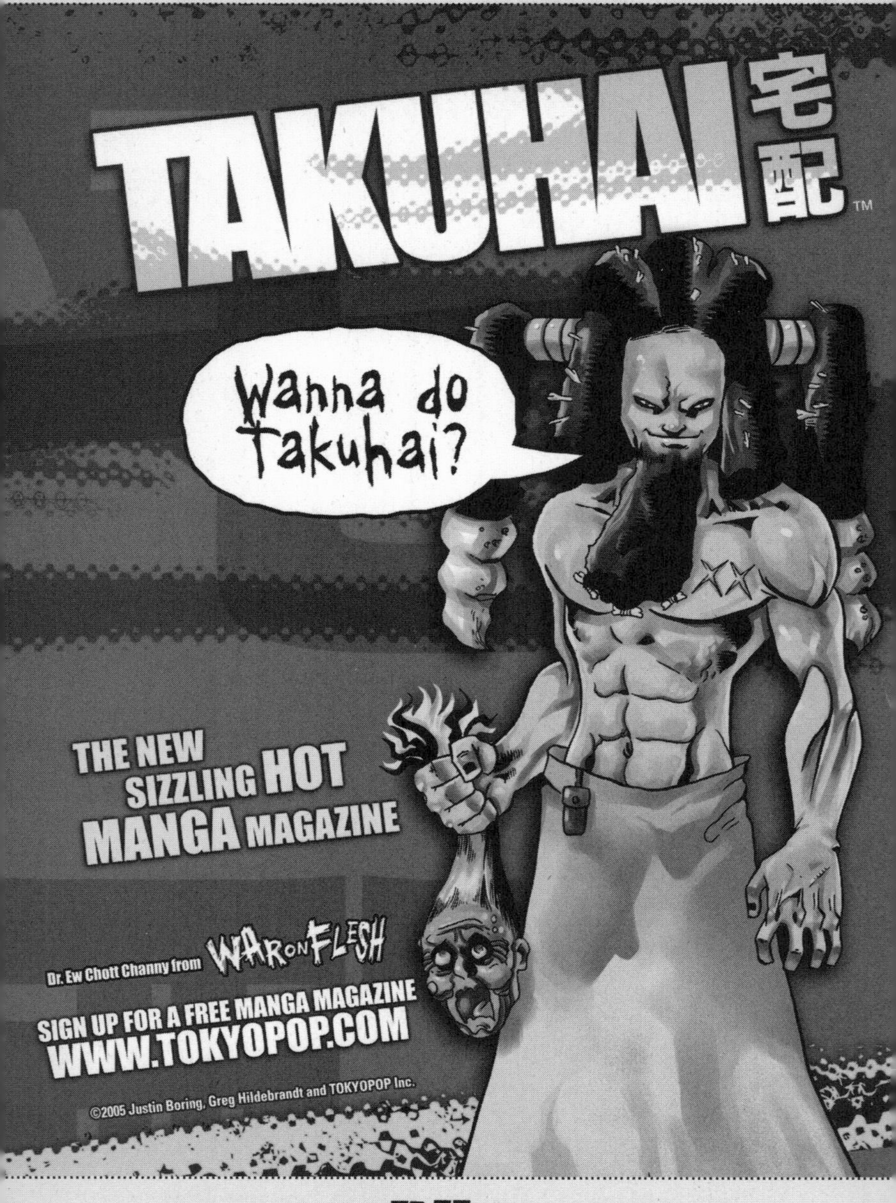
TAKUHAI 宅配 ™
Wanna do Takuhai?
THE NEW SIZZLING HOT MANGA MAGAZINE
Dr. Ew Chott Channy from WAR ON FLESH
SIGN UP FOR A FREE MANGA MAGAZINE
WWW.TOKYOPOP.COM
©2005 Justin Boring, Greg Hildebrandt and TOKYOPOP Inc.

TOKYOPOP SHOP

WWW.TOKYOPOP.COM/SHOP

HOT NEWS!

Check out the TOKYOPOP SHOP!
The world's best collection of manga in English is now available online in one place!

SAMURAI CHAMPLOO

KINGDOM HEARTS

DRAMACON

- LOOK FOR SPECIAL OFFERS
- PRE-ORDER UPCOMING RELEASES
- COMPLETE YOUR COLLECTIONS

A Midnight Opera™

Immortality, Redemption, and Bittersweet Love...

For nearly a millennium, undead creatures have blended into a Europe driven by religious dogma...

Ein DeLaLune is an underground Goth metal sensation on the Paris music scene, tragic and beautiful. He has the edge on other Goth music powerhouses—he's undead, a fact he's kept hidden for centuries. But his newfound fame might just bring out the very phantoms of his past from whom he has been hiding for centuries, including his powerful brother, Leroux. And if the two don't reconcile, the entire undead nation could rise up from the depths of modern society to lay waste to mankind.

MARK OF THE SUCCUBUS

BY ASHLY RAITI & IRENE FLORES

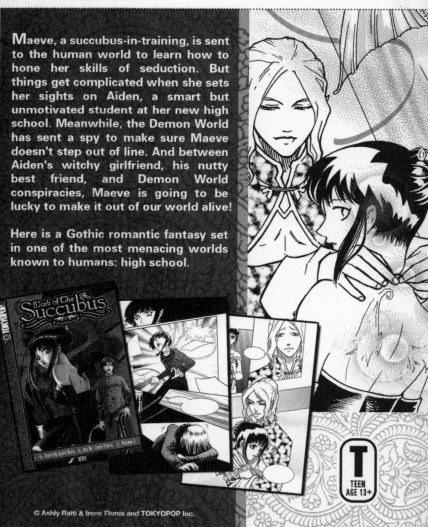

Maeve, a succubus-in-training, is sent to the human world to learn how to hone her skills of seduction. But things get complicated when she sets her sights on Aiden, a smart but unmotivated student at her new high school. Meanwhile, the Demon World has sent a spy to make sure Maeve doesn't step out of line. And between Aiden's witchy girlfriend, his nutty best friend, and Demon World conspiracies, Maeve is going to be lucky to make it out of our world alive!

Here is a Gothic romantic fantasy set in one of the most menacing worlds known to humans: high school.

T TEEN AGE 13+

FOR MORE INFORMATION VISIT: WWW.TOKYOPOP.COM

TOKYOPOP® PRESENTS

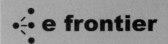

e frontier

MANGA STUDIO™ 3.0

WHAT WILL *YOU* CREATE?

The Best Software For Digital Manga Creation

e frontier's Manga Studio lets you draw, ink, tone and letter your manga in the computer. A library of **1800 digital tones** uses vector technology for moiré-free results. Automated drawing tools speed the process of creating your sequential art. Twelve types of layers keep your work organized and easy to edit. Scan in existing artwork and finish it in the computer, saving time and money on materials. Manga Studio's 1200-dpi resolution ensures professional-quality files that can be saved in several popular formats.

SPECIAL INTRODUCTORY PRICE FOR MANGA STUDIO 3.0 DEBUT: $49.99

For more information or to purchase, visit:
www.e-frontier.com/go/tokyopop

CALL OFF YOUR MONSTERS, ADONETTE.

***VAN VON HUNTER* MANGA CREATED WITH MANGA STUDIO.**

VAN VON HUNTER™

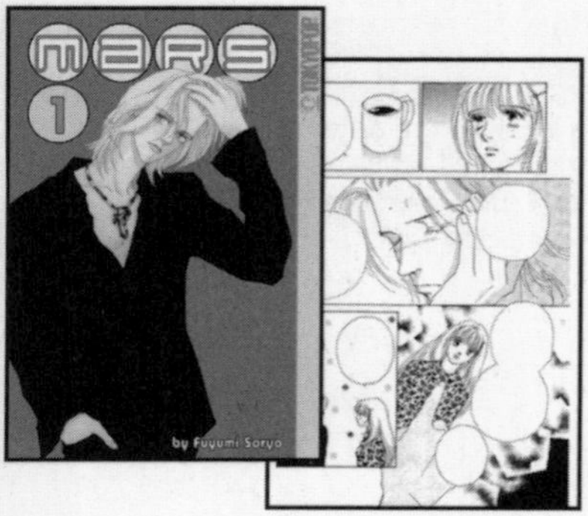
MARS
1
by Fuyumi Soryo

BY FUYUMI SORYO

MARS

I used to do the English adaptation for *MARS* and loved working on it. The art is just amazing—Fuyumi Soryo draws these stunning characters and beautiful backgrounds to boot. I remember this one spread in particular where Rei takes Kira on a ride on his motorcycle past this factory, and it's all lit up like Christmas and the most gorgeous thing you've ever seen—and it's a factory! And the story is a super-juicy soap opera that kept me on the edge of my seat just dying to get the next volume every time I'd finish one.

~Elizabeth Hurchalla, Sr. Editor

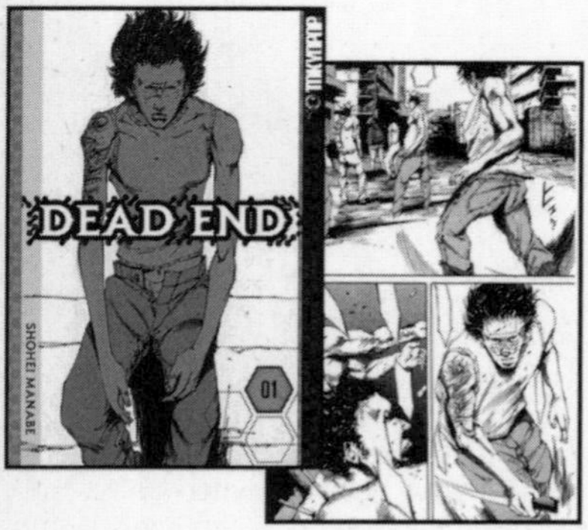
DEAD END
SHOHEI MANABE
01

BY SHOHEI MANABE

DEAD END

Everyone I've met who has read *Dead End* admits to becoming immediately immersed and obsessed with Shohei Manabe's unforgettable manga. If David Lynch, Clive Barker and David Cronenberg had a love child that was forced to create a manga in the bowels of a torture chamber, then *Dead End* would be the fruit of its labor. The unpredictable story follows a grungy young man as he pieces together shattered fragments of his past. Think you know where it's going? Well, think again!

~Troy Lewter, Editor

SHOWCASE

TOKYOPOP MANGA SUPPLEMENT

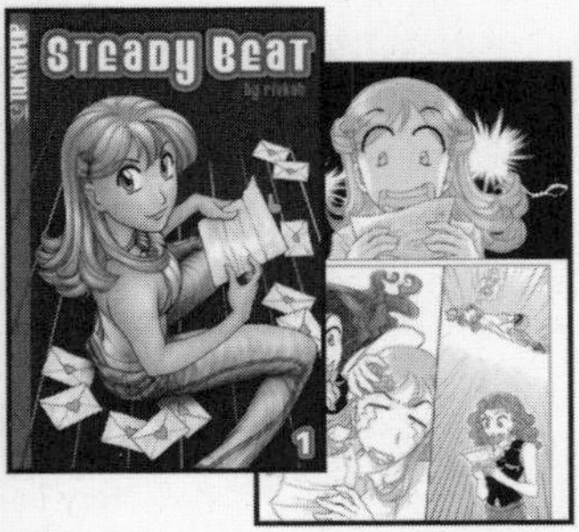
Steady Beat
TOKYOPOP
1

STEADY BEAT

BY RIVKAH

"Love Jessica"... That's what Leah finds on the back of a love letter to her sister. But who is Jessica? When more letters arrive, along with flowers and other gifts, Leah goes undercover to find out her sister's secret. But what she doesn't expect is to discover a love of her own—and in a very surprising place!

Winner of the Manga Academy's Create Your Own Manga competition!

T
TEEN
AGE 13+

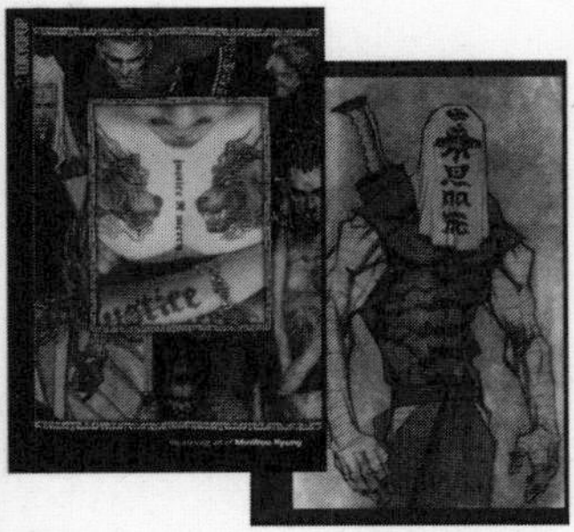
justice

JUSTICE N MERCY

BY MIN-WOO HYUNG

Min-Woo Hyung is one of today's most talented young Korean artists, and this stunning art book shows us why. With special printing techniques and high-quality paper, TOKYOPOP presents never-before-seen artwork based on his popular *Priest* series, as well as images from past and upcoming projects *Doomslave, Hitman* and *Sal.*

A spectacular art book from the creator of *Priest!*

T
TEEN
AGE 13+

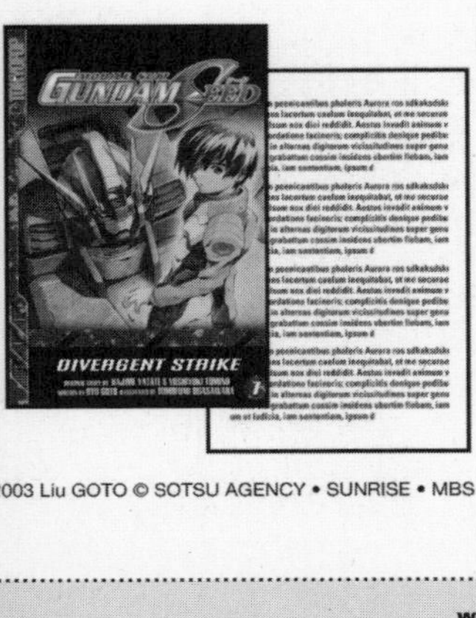
GUNDAM SEED
DIVERGENT STRIKE

MOBILE SUIT GUNDAM SEED NOVEL

ORIGINAL STORY BY HAJIME YATATE AND YOSHIYUKI TOMINO

WRITTEN BY LIU GOTO

A shy young student named Kira Yamato is thrown in the midst of battle when genetically enhanced Coordinators steal five new Earth Force secret weapons. Wanting only to protect his Natural friends, Kira embraces his Coordinator abilities and pilots the mobile suit Strike. The hopes and fears of a new generation clash with the greatest weapons developed by mankind: Gundam!

The novelization of the super-popular television series!

T
TEEN
AGE 13+